BROWN RIVER

A NOVEL

MATTHEW BALLEZA

Copyright © 2019 by Matthew Balleza

All rights reserved.

No part of this book may be reproduced in any form or by any electronic or mechanical means, including information storage and retrieval systems, without written permission from the author, except for the use of brief quotations in a book review.

The more I see of the world, and the more men I meet or books I read or questions I answer, the more I come back with increased conviction to those places where I was born or played...narrowing my circles like a bird going back to a nest.

— G.K. CHESTERTON

For Rosie and nugget

PART I

1

Where we live, storms come on quick and thunder does not flutter: it belts, bellicose, round sounds. The air thickens outside, then there's a hush followed by a sound like an oak cabinet being shoved across a bare floor. Growing up that's what I heard. Our outlook over the creek is hemmed by copses and tall waving bluestem on the near side, and shrouded on the far side by steep cliffs and ingrown arbors and thickets. This coverage prevented us from ever knowing the meditative quality of storms. The slowness of storms which people speak of. Their gradual building, accumulating, generating. How darkness and the smell of asphalt overtake the sky and earth and streets. We never knew it.

For us, the severity of the storm was never its pitch, or its endurance, or the grandeur of its noise and blackness, but its suddenness. Its leonine habit of springing upon us. Never having traveled but always traveled, never having grown to maturity or swollen by degrees. Always arriving in the ripeness of danger, whole hearted, like it were disguised beforehand in the mildness of nature. Encamped, then summoned at a word.

We live on Weems, a marshy, winding creek which

offshoots the Nanticoke River and saunters faithfully into Chesapeake Bay. Weems runs through the town of Skewesbury, where I live and grew up. I have been thinking of this place lately, calling it to mind and recalling what I know of it. Since I was young I have never known the forecast of foul weather to put me off from stepping nearer the machinations of a storm or wanting to watch it orchestrate above. My father said fishing was good when it rained but he said we were strictly forbidden to use the boat during a storm. Its being forbidden made we want to go all the more, and the one time I scorned that law outright, I nearly paid for it in full.

All day I had longed to fish, and by the time I had prepared the little boat and recruited my brother and sister, who came only to appease me, it was raining steadily and my father who noticed the change in weather had taken me aside and said "You know, if it begins..." And I said "Yes, yes, I know." "You come back immediately." he said. "We will, we will." And on we went. My intent was to take us to the other side of the creek and fish for awhile and then return. The mission was not overly ambitious; Weems is a quarter mile from bank to bank, and the other side looks close enough that you could throw a rock and hit it. But it's deceptive. Pushing off, the three of us, James my brother, Adley my sister, and myself, we had barely made it more than halfway when thunder came. It broke above us and immediately the rain fell heavier and heavier. What should we do? they asked. Considering where we were and how long it took to get that far, I said keep going, don't turn back. Are you sure? Yes, it will pass. I hope it will pass. I turned behind to see what I could of our pier and property but could see nothing. The rain was a wall. Storms make my father drowsy, and as I looked back I imagined him sitting in his chair looking out, his eyes shutting and his mouth beginning to snore.

Typically I rallied under this kind of event, but the

elements here were altogether different; we were three instead of one. The boat we were in, a dory, was clumsy and stodgy. The rain was heavier and the wind stood still. On the far side along the shallows were felled trees that jutted from the water. We waited by them as we watched the storm. Nothing changed except that we sank lower in the boat as the water rose around our ankles. We were quiet. We heard the rain washing through the trees behind us, branches snapping. Then the downpour increased again. I steered us to the only safe spot I could see, along that same bank of toppled trees by the cliff. The fishing line which I dropped earlier I abandoned and left in the boat and used an oar to move us on to shore. By then the boat was heavy with rain water, and the three of us pulling together barely dragged it ashore. I fastened the painter line in the stern to a tree limb protruding from the sand.

As we moved forward onto the skimp shore, the first of the lightning flashed before us. We quickly got out and set our feet on the raw tree limbs raised above the splashing. The dory, the one we called 'Sooky' was being yanked against its post and filled like a tub. In it we left a knife, a wood block for bait, the worms, a towel, the rod. Each item floated atop the surface, bumping into the gunwales and cluttering.

It was late afternoon, darkness descending. The wind had not moved. The rain stood above us, unyielding in its intensity. We were marooned and could not see a thing except each other and the boat yanking back and forth. All else was consumed by the curtain of grey. As minutes passed I became terribly afraid of what would happen. I thought of our chances of living or dying. All this because I wanted to fish. I looked aside at James who was standing with his back against the cliff. He was so small and skinny. His eyes were closed and his hands were tucked between his armpits for warmth. I watched as the rain ran down his head, down his legs to the branch he stood upon. He was muttering something to himself. James, are you praying I said. No. Then what are you saying? I'm counting thunder.

Lightning flashed as we were speaking, and thunder boomed right after. He raised his thumb. One second, he said. That means it's close. We went quiet again, the three of us. Adley said nothing. I began counting thunder in my head.

For a time it seemed the rain was the only element in the storm that fell straightforwardly. It pummeled the earth in cold plops. The lightning and thunder fell on all sides of us, dancing at random. One moment it struck the creek in a single, zagged bolt. The next, a chord of three knuckles bleached the treetops to our right. Then it flashed along the creek like a blown bulb, diffusing its light in a white haze.

We continued counting thunder to see if the storm was moving away, but we could not tell. It thronged at random moments and in random places all about us. The cove we stood in precluded us from seeing the movement of anything above us. Shielded by the overhanging trees, we each took James's position, waiting with our backs against the clay as the rain flowed over us. We were cold, wet conduits. Goosebumps covered our bodies. We shivered and rubbed our limbs and waited. There was nothing more to do. And still the sky darkened, and the rain cussed from on high like an angry string of words.

In a desperate appeal I said stay put and I scrabbled up the cliffside through undergrowth and roots and bracken to an opening in the treeline where I crouched at the edge of a flooded farm field. I was at my knees in water, moving slowly along the border, looking for any sign of shelter. A long way off I saw a light, an orange gas light more than half a mile away. As I stood there wondering how long it would take to reach it, I heard the other two scraping behind me. I was about to point at the light in the distance. But the moment they emerged from the treeline, lightning struck the open field beside us. It was not thirty yards from our faces; deafening, and so close we could see the purple imprint where it burned the air. Immediately we fled back down the cliff and put our backs against the wall. The sky darkened and the rain cussed.

We tried to speak, to say anything, to joke as an attempt to keep our minds off the interminable rain and pulsing sky. But all we said was drowned out. I don't know how long we were there; though the experience of standing and waiting for either the storm to pass, or be turned to smoke, was unbearably long. I began to lose my wits. Guilt grew in the pit of my stomach. Impulsively I hopped off my perch and tried to untie the boat from the tree. My brother stopped me and said No, we can't! Not yet. We have to try I said. Just wait he said. So I left the knot and climbed back. Right then another lightening flash bloomed across the creek. I looked to him and nodded thank you. For a while, all we heard was the rain. The steadfast pounding. I lowered my head and slipped into a coma of the sound.

Then, as quick as the word itself, it slowed. It slowed more and more, quicker and quicker, until only a mist was falling and a heavy heat filled the air. Excess water flowed down from the field and trees; a pure, healing sound. All else was silent. More surreal than the clamor of storm was the sudden absence of it. The astonishing clemency of weather. My siblings and I looked at each other and smiled in surprise. We were as cut by quietude as by trumpet.

We did not linger; as soon as it desisted we lunged forward off our steps, putting all six hands on the boat. We tipped it to one side, dumping all the water that filled it to the brim. I unsquared the knot that held it to the tree, then set its bow forward and pushed us off with the blade of an oar. We moved sluggardly and frantic at first, eager to get home. We took off our life vests to row as fast as possible.

My fishing rod, which I had not reeled in since the storm began, leaned off the stern. The styrofoam cup of earthworms floated on a film of rain water at the bottom of the hull. We paddled and paddled, desperately and mightily, throwing our bodies into every stroke. As the rain lifted, we began to see the foggy outlines of our home again, and that spurred us, and we charged faster yet. Soon we were there. There was no greater relief than to run aground over our local patch of marsh and eelgrass, and drag the boat onto solid land.

The sky was still dark, and the storm had not vanished altogether, but we were safe. The thunder was distant and the lightning ended. As an afterthought I took the rod and reeled it in. To my amazement, there was a fish on the other end. I couldn't believe it! A small white perch. It struck me as a peculiar and wonderful sign; to have caught it without trying to, completely unaware, in the middle of a nightmare. Pulling that line up and seeing that creature dancing on the hook held the essence of trip, seemed to justify the splendor of surviving.

But as I brought the rod forward to the house, I became convicted. I felt I owed the fish to my father somehow. The guilt of taking my siblings on that voyage demanded some compensation; even a small bright gesture that could say "I know, I know, I'm sorry, I won't do it again. But look! Look at this!" and maybe that would settle it. So I made up my mind to offer this catch, this miraculous catch. The perch would be an olive branch between us.

I dragged it through the grass to the back door, my pole bending and the fish on the line five feet behind. The trepidation of seeing my father and of coming in from the storm heightened the effect. I was both frightened and jubilant. The other two ran before me and I followed them, eager to show him. He met me just outside the door. He didn't look angry, but his eyes were muddy and his face was fatigued and a look of concern was growing over it. He had one hand visored over his eyes and the other waving me in. He was looking up at the sky and down at me alternately.

"Come, come." he said. "Come in, it's raining. What are you doing out here still?"

It was raining so lightly I couldn't feel it, but I came forth, and when I was close enough he reached out and grabbed me by the wrist. Immediately he felt the coldness of my skin.

"What happened?" he said. "I was sleeping. You're all cold and wet, what's going on? Where did you go?" He looked out past me to see where the boat was, then down at me. "Why are you shaking? he said. "What's that smile for?"

I raised my other arm, holding the pole and said "I caught this, look." He saw the fish and shook his head. I could not read his expression. I could not tell if he was glad or upset. Then he looked up at the sky again.

"Come in, come in. Enough."

I followed him in, toting my rod, but he turned to me and said, "Leave that right there, leave it by the door, don't drag it through here." I stayed where I was and he shut the door behind me- and the fish, the fish that would be my peace offering was still on the line, on the hook, pattering on the step in the light rain. An image I won't ever forget. How electric it felt to stand there shaking, with the rod in my hand, the fish dying on the other side of the glass door, the mark of my father's grip around my wrist. To be back home. The boat grounded. Our small troop having snuck through the eye of lightning and lived to tell it.

2

I'm asked often enough by the people we take out how I got my start in this fishing business that the question is common fare by now, and I have two instinctive responses depending on who's asking and what kind of time we've had on the water. If we were successful I tell them I fell into it, which is a pale, uninvolved response that speaks to many people nonetheless. People understand chance, and people fall into all sorts of things. Half of what I say to that crowd won't matter anyway because I know they're only half listening; the other half of them is counting up the number of fish they caught. Whatever I say will only affirm them of their good fortune, and I don't blame them for that. They have come for the catch and there is glamour in the haul.

Other times, I appeal to the sensational; we'll be heading home full speed, the boat skipping across the water at 30 knots, the wind roughing our hair and I'll gesture to the sky, to the sea. 'Hard to beat this for a day job', I say, as though it were the obvious truth in life. They nod at that. And it is obvious what I mean. You can't unfeel the sea. It gets a hold of you, and in my case it hasn't let go.

None of the people I've taken out has ever asked me about my being a woman in this business, let alone Captain. But I am aware of their skepticism from the very moment they get out of their car by the docks to shake my hand. The skepticism does not last however, because they remember they have read the reviews and know my reputation. You cannot build a name from nothing.

Whatever I say I do not mention money. When I had just started I used to say with a bit of humor in my voice that I got into this business because I found the job where I could make the most money doing the thing I love, which is a great, supercilious, American way of talking. But I think money is all people hear, even if they don't intend, and it soils the conversation. Money has a way of decaying speech. They'd start thinking about how much they paid me to take them out, and that's not the point. The point is that they nearly sank the boat hauling fish.

More than that I try not to impress. Sometimes the people I take out, even when they've caught a good amount, get a look on their face that is the syndrome of thinking of their lives on shore. It's a pensive look that says I'll leave my plain job and plain wife and come back to this spot where I caught plenty and fish forever. Their eyes say that. Their sighs too.

All those answers are skirting, however, and they don't get nearer the truth to what I tell the group that came with me and caught little or nothing. Those that got 'skunked' as they say. You can speak honestly to those people. 'It's a mystery I'm still getting at.' I say, regarding what brought me here. If people understand chance, they understand mystery too. And life, so far as I've lived, seems inextricably woven of both. Only time, and sometimes not even time tells which strand is which.

I don't mean mystery as something inscrutable. No, I

mean it as a concrete reality, something knowable. Yet something you won't ever exhaust the full meaning of. The sea is a mystery too, full of surprises. Any fisherman knows it. It contents itself by humbling you every time you've believed yourself to be self-sufficient, able to rule the waters at will. That is not how it works. The ocean may be generous and she may be stingy, and you must reckon with all her sides.

It all depends on phrasing. To those that caught much I often say 'You fished well today'. A good catch as has something to do with effort obviously, and I want them to feel like they made most of it happen on their own skill. It's not just spin. Part of my job is encourager. But sometimes I catch a look in one of their faces, those who did not catch much; a look of piercing let down that moves me every time I see it. It is an expression you imagine they've retained since childhood. An innocent look, when you've lost something that you wanted. 'It was an unlucky day.' I say, and leave it at that. Many people have something upbeat to respond with, and I appreciate those comments that try to level a loss, to see the best in a situation. Optimism is a hard thing. 'Well' they say. 'Well at least we had fun', something like that, to make amends.

Overall I think a good bit about what I do and where I've been, and I struggle as everyone else to connect the dots. Fishing gives you plenty of time with yourself and others, and much of that, the things you don't know or haven't connected, is bound to surface. We took a farmer out the other week. On the way back he sat closer to the bow and tilted his head over the side of the boat, watching the prow break the oncoming waves. He said 'Reminds me of a plow, furrowing the ground.' When he said that I recalled an old plow that sat in the corner of our outbuilding growing up. My father said all it needed was some love. It needed more than love too, it needed hands to put it to use. Maybe the two are related, but that tool had not split the earth in a generation.

That's what I mean, you learn things about people's experience that somehow touch your own. Luis, my son, helps me on the operation. He's very young, but he's willing and likes being by the water. He's diligent and helpful and lets me do the talking. When he's older I hope he'll learn about making small talk with people. How important it is, that innocent back and forth, the establishment of some common humanity. Many more of my days out here have been lifted from a doldrum or discontent just by opening my mouth with someone else, than by carrying on silently with my thoughts. It will take time.

The docks are located at a boatyard called Margo's, located on the eastern bank of the Nanticoke river, a few miles north of the town of Bivalve. The marina is named after the first owner's wife and we've been here many years. Mornings are my favorite time to be here. There is nothing like the stillness of the water at that time, and the first lights of day; pinkish in the sky and the air cool- the surrounding atmosphere on the river glistening; birthwet and new. Other boats are out, their trolling lines hoisted high. This is rockfish season and charters aim for an early start. Still, the broken fleet of us make only a small whirr of commotion on the great, enveloping quiet. But evenings too I enjoy; boatkeeping has its solitary pleasure, when the gulls and fowl have left, and what remains are the sounds of hose water dripping of the boat, the creak of knots, the clink of clips against sail spars.

Our boat is called Hogsty. It's officially pronounced Hogsty, rhymes with Hog-pie, but most people pronounce it as Hog-stee and that's the name that has stuck and what it's known by around here. Recently someone asked me if Luis would 'take the boat off my hands when it was through,' those were his words, and I can't remember how I answered, but I remember taking offense to the way he put it. Firstly it struck me as too personal, and secondly, it pained me to think I was being perceived around here as passing off a failing rig to my own son. Hogsty's not a looker and never will be, so it's possible that the comment touched upon a simple truth, and that the simple truth hurts. The boat's an old dog, I know that. It pants back to shore. My slipmate JM tries to defend me. He says 'Boat looks don't matter as long as you catch', but I think he pays that compliment too much. Anyhow I'm not thinking that far ahead. By now Luis has seen what it's like owning the boat; I could not idealize it if I tried.

––––––––

When my siblings and I were young, my parents suggested in little off-hand ways the qualities each of us possessed that made us unique, that gave us a special claim in the world. Smarts were James's. He still has that clear, natural intelligence that populates readily with information of all kind. An intelligence made more impressive by his humility. He's not one to simply regale what he knows, it must be courted. Chair-bound as he is nowadays, you get the feeling that when he speaks to you about something of great interest, the chair disappears and he is standing up tall, a set of wings fledged behind him.

The looks belong to my sister, Adley, who resembles my mother more and more the older she gets. She has a serene, beautiful face, with a pair of lips that are composed and firm, yet not cold or austere. Her bright brown eyes express a sort of astonishment, a radiant blankness or dispassion that she has always had. Of all our personalities hers is the most underspoken. It has always seemed to me that her underspokeness commended much of her beauty. She had a particular gift for feigning, dodging, and avoiding a numberless amount of arguments, of withholding herself from many accounts of ugliness. From childhood she has been that way, and as she's grown older, her manners, marked by the same steadfast quietness, have given to her an air of allure and refinement.

The three of us look similar, but I have darker hair and darker eyes than the other two, and unlike my sister I'm more the tomboy; these looks are nothing to turn heads at. Growing up I never received such straightforward compliments as my sister and brother, with their beauty or brains. I was told I had a good memory, rather. That I had a way of remembering things and names and events just as they were. Well, so much for that back then. A fine memory is nothing to flaunt when you're young, when life is skipping by and little seems worthwhile remembering. I would have traded a good memory for an average one, or any other gift for that matter. This is Constance, I hear them saying: the one who could remember.

Yet, one never quite gets over the old nicknames, the old stations in life. Experience takes them up and molds them, ratifies them to new purpose. There is now, more than ever, reason to look over our whereabouts with a candid eye, to see what came of what, and to see it perhaps anew. My circumstances have changed, and the passing of time has restored some faith in my ability to recall and given some inclination to put it to good purpose.

On our flat creek, Weems, which is shallow in most areas, there is a channel where the bottom has been dredged to make way for the passage of boats. If you're swimming you'll know you've found it because you lose the silt bottom and find the cold currents under your soles instead. Hugging close the confines of our banks, listening in, a likewise homage I've tried to pay, so that when he or anyone draws close to the page they can feel the coolness under foot or hear the scraping sound of a terrapin sliding off a warm rock in the creek, such things as liable to overlooking.

3

Always I see him there in front of me, my father laboring against the tide on that hazy coast of Carolina, his ragged cargo shorts rolled to his thigh, surrounded in furls of waves. It is late summer, the time of day when the sea tints dark and the sun, farewelling, pours one last, long libation of brilliance upon the water. The undulant surface is gold and flecking. In the scene the crowds have left, his back faces me. I am six years old or so. I call him over the water but he does not hear me, at least he does not turn to acknowledge that he hears me but goes on trudging slantwise into the voluble wind, brandishing his pole overhead like a bayonet, careful not to soak it because salt corrupts reels- he's warned me before. Again I call in vain, and again the wind steals my voice away on buffets, and I know that even if my voice did reach him he would not hear it. Beyond a certain point I know he does not hear anything but the bell-like voice of his own fishing intuition telling him where to cast, *There,* when to cast, *Now.* His figure folds into sea glare and the waves roll by, I lose him.

Careful, Constance, my mother warns from shore. Around my hips the water breaks, pulls, full of playful danger. I scoop a handful of sand from under my feet and let it slop back, then shake my hands clean in the water. I do it again, then I see him again. The glint of black hair. The pole raised behind, set for casting. He casts, noiseless, but I see the whip of the rod at the end of the motion. I retreat to the firm wet sand on shore where the foam of crashed waves ends, and draw shapes in it: letters. I look up and my father has not moved. He is waiting steady. Minutes pass, then I hear him say something that sounds like a laugh. I look up. The rod bends, he jerks the rod twice, reels, begins back peddling shallower, sticking the butt of the rod into his arm pit. I leave my letters and plunge into the water, jumping the waves in his direction.

"What did you get?" I yell.

Finally he looks to me and there's a smile on his face.

"Constance, I have something for you."

Whatever it is is hidden below the surface of the water, but he seems to know what it is, and when he's close enough to shore he hoists the end of the line up and the fish emerges from the water hanging, a dark one with dark eyes. It flops and jounces on the line. My eyes are fixed on it. My mother claps from her chair. I yell Fish! Fish! and watch as my father lays it on the wet sand where I was sitting, the hook still in its mouth. Cautiously at first I watch it. Then instinctively I reach my hand to touch it, but it jumps and I look up to my father.

"Go ahead. You can touch it."

With the same drawing finger I pet along its slippery side, feeling scales for the first time, feeling tail for the first time. It curls stiff at my touch. It flops again, making the lure jangle. I take my hand away. The gills flare, and I can see inside the redness, the frilled redness. I touch its lips, feeling the tiny gritty set of teeth, the hard slick lips. I notice the pulse of its white belly. My father is crouched with me, his kneecaps lined and sandy.

"Can I touch its eye?"

"You can touch the eye."

I dab it with my forefinger. It's bouncy.

"This is a black sea bass." he says. "See the black on its spine? See the color?"

I nod. I touch it again, and this time all the fins flare boldly, electric and needled.

"You'll catch one soon, huh?" he asks me.

"Yes." I say.

"Hold this for me." he says, handing me the pole while he unhooks the fish. He goes into the water up to his shins and flings the bass into the waves, the black fish catching the sun off its side and shining one last moment before disappearing. I stand with the pole, mesmerized, the shapes under me smudged by then, washed over, whatever letters I was drawing.

4

My full name is Constance Avery Gonzalez. Avery I get from my mother. It's her first name. Constance and Gonzalez I get from my father. They've recounted the story before. My father said one week before I was born they still hadn't settled on a name for me. He wanted Emma. My mother wanted anything but Emma.

"Why don't you like Emma?" he said.

"Because you dated someone named Emma."

"So what? That was long ago."

"I still don't like it."

"Why don't you like it?"

"I just don't. And it's the name of your old girlfriend. That should be enough."

"I don't see why that matters. Our Emma's not going to be that Emma."

"It matters. It matters to me. She's my daughter. Emma's not her name. I don't want that association."

My father says at that point he had reached his limit with her that day. He grabbed his fishing gear and said I'm going fishing, and marched out the front door. I asked her what she said in reply. She said that won't solve it. He drove to a place called Parker's pier, where he'd never fished with any luck before.

"Why'd you go again?" I asked.

"That's a fisherman's mystery. It was less the fishing I went for than the scenery, to get out of the house. But it only takes one good day to turn it around. It could be years of nothing, then you catch and suddenly everything's different, it's your new favorite spot. And that day was different." he says. "They wouldn't stop biting and I couldn't stop pulling them up. Blues, spot. Everything. The miracle, or the irony of the story is that the man fishing beside me caught nothing, even though he used the same bait and cast in the same area. He kept walking over, inspecting what I was doing, trying to find some secret, but there was none. He got upset and I got embarrassed because I didn't know what to say. At one point, as he checked his barren line and watched me take another, what he said was, 'You are constant. Just constant. I can't get it. They don't want my stuff.' and he laughed and left me alone, because that's all there was to do."

When he got home, my mother says he was quiet but had a smirk on his face he couldn't hide. She called him where she was sitting and studied his face.

"Where'd you go?" she asked.

"Fishing, I told you."

"I don't believe you."

"Don't then."

"Tell me the truth."

"I am."

"Is that all? You're smiling, what's it for?"

He paused and said "I think I've got a name."

Then he said my name. She frowned and said Definitely no. He told her the rest of the story from the pier and she shook her head. But the next day she said she liked it actually, and apologized, and said 'but don't try and find any more names that way.'

5

My brother James was born two years after me, prematurely. It was a time of exceptional fear for my parents who thought he wouldn't make it, and though he did, his life since then has never really lost its edge of grief and worry. He resembles neither of my parents closely, though he has my father's dark hair. My mother says he was an incredibly happy baby. He loved to grin eat. But she says I didn't like him right away because he stole her attention from me. Apparently I would take his toys throw them at him, and my mother had to stop me.

In the photo albums from that time, he is mostly with my father, being cradled and adored. My father took a special liking to him because he was the first and only boy of our clan, and the heir of the last name Gonzalez. Those things mattered a lot to my father. In a burst of creativity, my father built a crib for him in the outbuilding; a crib shaped like a little boat. It was one of many gestures and attempts to pass on to this child a meaningful inheritance, a liberal upbringing by the water. On the mantle of the piano there is a picture of the four of us at Christmas; my parents, myself and James; Adley wasn't born yet. I'm holding James in my lap.

During that time my father still worked for an oil company. They had an office in Washington DC. Three days a week he would commute from our home on the Eastern shore, leave very early, and return very late. The other days he was at the house, spending his daytime hours at his desk writing letters, reading, on the phone.

My mother kept the rest of us out. We ran errands with her, visited to the grocery, the bank, the consignment shop. I sat in the back with James. Once she said she looked back and found that I had spit a piece of red licorice out of my mouth and put it in his car seat, where it got all over his legs.

I used to play nanny with James too. I can't recall all the rigors I put him through, but my mother remembers some because she would watch us. She said my nannying was a cross between a boarding school nun and a coach. I liked discipline and drills. I would have James practice being a baby, even though he was not much older than a baby. Apparently I would say 'Pretend to sleep', 'Now pretend to cry', 'Now pretend you're hungry', in quick succession. If I was satisfied by his performance, we would move to another part of the room and I would have him 'cook' whatever it was he pretended he was hungry for. I gave him other chores too, like folding laundry and washing his imaginary work car with imaginary suds—things I saw my parents do. When I was tired of nannying, I would switch the game suddenly and become James's teacher. He had no choice. He would sit obediently on his small plastic chair, watching as I lectured away. Then I would test him on it. That's how it went. He began as my pet, he ended as my pupil.

I asked my mother what James thought of all this, and she said, "You obviously really enjoyed yourself, but he suffered through it."

. . .

Then there came Adley. She was born three years after James, during the middle of a storm. I remember the car ride to the hospital because the rain sounded like it was denting our vehicle. Everyone was quiet but my mother who made a hard sigh now and then. Outside I could see only black streaks and white flicker and hear the whish of cars in other lanes. I was not worried, but the trip felt surreal. I can still feel myself snug against the cushion and smell that unforgettable backseat too; humid and clothy, the moistness of the cabin mixed with the smell of rain and road drifting to us back from a cracked window.

For the first time in many weeks my mother was not smiling or playful, only quietly looking ahead and sighing, and her hair was up when usually it was down.

Small as I was, I saw that there was something both joyful and perilous about birth. It came to me plainly. 'God put a baby in your mother's belly.' my father would say. Later I would touch the big belly, my mother's hand guiding mine over the hard, taught skin. 'Can you feel the baby kick?' Then the tiredness; and later the severe look of pain on her face. Many days later on a dark, rainy night, I don't remember what else happened, she came home with us, this bald little girl, my sister, who I was told to kiss on the forehead.

Early the next morning, the sky was pink and the foregone storm had brought down a windfall of apple tree twigs in the backyard. Some blooms made it all the way to the water. My father and I picked a few of them up. We took them inside and I saw my mother coming around the corner to the kitchen with the baby. Seeing her face smiling again I yelled 'Mommy!' and she put her finger to her lip, for quiet. She bent to my level, and said 'She's sleeping.' I looked at Adley's placid expression, then back to my mother who stood and carried her away, and for the first time in my little life I felt jealousy ripple through me from head to toe.

6

My father fished often when we were young; so often that I do not remember him not fishing, except as he got older and his interest waned. But it has always been there. More than a hobby, it was a labor of love for him, and it became a labor for me too, who was his first reluctant help. My siblings were off the hook from the beginning, but I was my mother's relief I suppose, and she never went fishing much after she had me. Not actively. She would sit by and watch sometimes, but that was it.

"I never liked fishing to begin with. Bores me to death." she says. Sometimes she's right about it being boring, though my father would disagree. For him the boredom was the best part. He could stand on the shore for hours, heels sunk in sand, waiting, and I doubt he'd ever call it boring. Quiet was the word he used if nothing was happening. Anything biting? someone would ask. Quiet, he'd say, For now.

As solitary as he could be, he did not like fishing alone. He desired an extra, even idle set of hands opening his tackle box, organizing weights and hooks, sniffing around putting things in order. I could be occupied at such tasks for half an hour before he'd notice and say 'Constance, have you checked your bait?' I'd check it and it'd be gone and he'd shake his head.

Those trips were the most content I ever saw him. To cast a line to water and wait was how he bargained peace with himself, and we who joined came to know his preferences, his ways, his spots, his tactics; which for a fisherman are the soul of him. What was his soul like? More saltwater than fresh, preferring cut bait to lures, open surf to piers, a boat if possible.

By acquaintance and routine I came to inherit a set of his preferences, and found that fishing grew on me steadily. The more I did it, the more it drew me and I acquired a taste for it. I still helped my father sort the tackle box, but over time I began to sort other things- like why he fished at all. My observance piqued. I watched closely. For any man's passion, anything he loves for itself, that makes him throw off covers and sneak away at 4am, is worth watching and learning from.

I learned that of all spots, shore was his favorite. He had an unmistakable look in his eyes when he fished from shore, not at all piercing. A stern, intent, yet entirely peaceable gaze that drew his eyelids almost all the way close, but not fully. So near to shutting you wondered if he was looking out at anything at all, or if he faced his blindness willingly, restraining his sight so he could read the world more vividly; catch the light more clearly, as if it were a fabric draping off the water. And feel the tremble of the line under the pad of his finger like a shock, a throb.

Whatever else rubbed off in those days may be summed in a story my mother recounts: when I was 6 or 7, one of my friends from grade school, Derek, invited me to his house which had a pond in the backyard, and asked if I wanted to fish. But I said No, 'because that's not real fishing', which is something my father would say. That poor kid. I doubt we stayed friends after that, but my mother heard it from the boy's mom and told my father the story later and he laughed and said 'she's right, though'.

7

Another trip. I was 9 or so. By then we had moved from Texas. Early in the morning when I was still sleeping my father came into my room and sat on my bedside and said 'Get ready. We'll go fishing soon.' My eyes were shut. It was still dark out and I pretended I was sleeping. Then he left and a few minutes later my mother came in, dressed in her pajamas.

"Constance." she said softly. I rolled over, knowing what she would ask. She sat down and began stroking my hair as I lay there feigning sleep.

"Constance, are you awake? Your father wants to go fishing with you today. Come now," she said. "enough, enough." Her voice was firm but she continued stroking my hair until I turned slightly toward her and opened my eyes. She has always been persuasive by her soothingness.

"I know." she said, "It won't be too bad though."

"Yes it will." I said.

She rubbed my back.

"Go with your father, won't you?" she said. "If not for him, than me."

"I don't want to. No one else does." I said.

"Go for him, he wants to be with you, he wants company, the others aren't awake."

"Can't you wake them?" I asked, but the effort was futile. The next thing I knew I was putting on old clothes, yawning, walking my body downstairs to eat something. Before we left I ate toast in the kitchen and she sat behind me at the table, braiding my hair so that it was would stay out of my face while we fished. I took a bite and she would tug. I took another bite and she would tug again. Back and forth. In the meantime my father walked the house filling the car with gear; running through a checklist in his mind. When we were ready, I kissed my mother goodbye, and my father kissed my mother on the cheek.

"Constance is going to catch a big one for you today. Aren't you?" he said, turning to me.

"No." I said.

"Come, don't be like that."

Then we left. I slept some more on the way to the destination and through the morning. The middle of the day was hot. I did not know where we were exactly except that it was some private shore overlooking the Chesapeake Bay. I remember the stones on the beach were large and that they clacked together as we stepped over them surveying a spot to fish. It was windy and a few gulls and starlings danced along the shore. There was no one there but us, and it felt lonesome with the wind blowing as loud as it was, and I wondered how long we would be there. Of course we stayed there for many hours. My father caught two fish and I caught a small rockfish that we threw back.

As the sun fell the wind did too. My father told me were going to fish on a boat tonight, but not to get upset. He said, "We won't be gone the whole night, and I promise we'll catch more than we did this afternoon." Then changing the mood he said, "You see this reflection, the colors even. Grey, gold, pink? It reminds me of the grass field that was behind the house I grew up in, very familiar"

"In Texas?" I asked.

"In Texas, yes, west of Houston. The ranch. My father-your grandfather, owned a ranch and was a rancher by trade. Eduardo was his name, you knew that. Our house was flat and clay colored, with many rooms. It was nice even in summer because the wind kept it cool. My brother and I would find lizards on the ceiling."

His voice was gentle as he spoke. The wind over our beach was whispering and the water was calm, and we were alone, and nothing was biting. We drank Cokes. As he spoke, I listened, and the more I did I began to picture him as he was back then, at my age, what he must have looked like and where he lived.

"We had one pond in our pasture. That was all there was of water, nothing like this." he said, pointing out with his finger.

"But we made the most of it. The cattle never had access to it, so it was mine and my brothers, Antonio, your uncle. The bottom was slimy but we did not care, although our mother did not like us swimming there because she thought we would get bit by a snake. Sometimes she would find our wet footprints on the floor of the house after we returned and come after us. We were barefoot. We could not hide well because the dogs would find us and bark. They were loyal to her. Other times she knew because we would use the bath towels to dry and put them back the wrong way. She could tell."

He reeled his line in a few feet, watching for any movement on the tip of the rod. Then he said,

"I'm sorry you never got to meet her, or your grandfather. It's a pity. It was a good place, very simple. We had two horses. Beautiful, black horses that my father was very protective of. He was always afraid they would get away somehow. Sometimes Antonio and I would sneak into the barn when he was gone and watch them."

He looked aside to me.

"I haven't taken you to see horses yet, have I?"

I shook my head.

"You would like them very much."

Then he reeled again.

"Anything?" he said, looking over.

"No."

"No nibbles?"

"No."

"Be patient."

When the quietness settled again he resumed his revery.

"Your grandmother was like you. Always looking out, looking at things, quite inquisitive. She liked to be outside. The hair too, when she wore it down was black and wavy, a bit wild, very long. It smelled like coconut, I don't know why. There was a product she would comb through her hair, maybe that was the coconut smell. Who knows. And we had a grapefruit tree out back. Antonio and I would climb it, but our father would not let us. He was strict. He would say to my mother, they'll ruin the branches. Do you want to have fruit? They can collect them when they fall. Again though we were sneaky. We stole them from the tree when he was not around and brought them to our mother."

He pulled an old picture from his wallet and handed it to me.

"Be careful with that. Put your rod down. It's fragile."

I took it in my hands, cupping it in my palms.

"This is her, Luisa. Your grandfather too, you can see."

"Eduardo." I said.

"Yes, Eduardo, exactly. You've seen this picture, haven't you?"

"Yes."

He had showed me before. In the picture the two of them are on the porch of their house. My grandmother has hair he described; big, dark, with long, unkempt whisps. Gypsy-like. She's wearing a skirt bunched around her knees and her arm is hung around my grandfather's shoulder. There's a carefreeness in her pose. She has strong features in her face; high cheekbones, thick eyebrows and sharp eyes. Bare feet. My grandfather looks younger than her. He is lighter skinned than she, wearing a crisp collared shirt and his arms rest solidly on his knees.

I handed the picture back to my father.

"You see?" he said. He put it in his wallet then said "Check your line."

I picked up my rod and reeled until the line tightened again.

"The tide can move the line pretty quickly. Always keep the line tight. That way you can feel if anything goes for it."

A few minutes passed, then he turned to me.

"Do you know the difference between waiting and fishing?" he said.

I looked down at my reel, then up at him.

"It's not a riddle." he said. "I'm just asking."

"They're similar." I said.

"What do you mean?"

"They feel the same."

"When?" he said.

"When nothing's biting."

"Would enjoy fishing more if you never had to wait?"

"Yes." I said.

"Why is that?"

"I hate waiting."

He laughed. "Do you?"

"Don't you?" I asked.

"Most times, yes. The waiting is always longer than the catching. But sometimes you have to wait. It wouldn't be the same if you didn't."

"Why?"

"What would we do if we caught all the fish as soon as we started?"

"I'd like that." I said.

He laughed again. "Yeah, I bet I would too. It's never happened, so I can't say. All I know is that there's nothing like it when you catch something after a long while, when you were about to turn in."

He reeled his line a bit, then I reeled mine.

"Can I bring my line in yet?" I said.

"No, keep it in there, give it a minute."

My mind went back to the stories he was telling before, and I asked him,

"You used to speak spanish?"

"I used to." he said. "When my father entered the oil industry we stopped speaking it at home. Well, we did, but we spoke it much less. He did not want us speaking anything about Mexico. It was very strange. He wanted us to speak english only. He wanted his boys especially to know english and he punished us if we could not say something in english and tried to say it in spanish instead. He would not let us eat. It was harder for my mother. She only knew spanish so she could only speak brokenly in english. My father bought a radio and made her listen to it. She hated it. She would curse it under her breath in spanish. He would say things to her in english that she could not reply to, sometimes to spite her, and she would be silent. She did not always have self control. Sometimes she would snap and yell back in spanish, and he would say 'stop! disgraceful' That's when Antonio and I would leave the house and go to the pasture. We did not know what to say. Usually we walked around not saying anything. He's two years younger. We were very similar then, and now, I don't know."

My father grew more exasperated as he spoke and had to cut himself off for having shared more than I think he intended. The empty beach and the empty lines did not help. Perhaps he believed that I was old enough then to care about what he said, or young enough that I would not remember what he spoke, but the words stayed with me. There is, I think, a perceivable innocence in children, a wideawakeness that allows them to hear stories with the full effect of their pathos, to feel deeply if not completely for those they hear about. That's what I felt like standing next to my father, holding my rod, listening. I was struck with sadness. He would have said more, but his line twitched in that moment of pause and I watched as he reeled a small rockfish onto the stony shore.

"Only a baby." he said. He took it by the lip and threw it back.

8

It was dark when we left the scant beach and pulled into the marina. My father took our gear from the car to the docks where we met uncle John, and loaded his motor boat which was waiting by the ramp. The engine was idling thickly in the water already, and the air above it was rich with exhaust. After coming aboard we made off quickly into the night. My father and John stood by the console, steering and pointing. I sat facing backward, holding my seat. We cruised past red and green buoys, gaining speed by each consecutive. Occasionally a big wave lifted us off the water for a second and thumped us back hard. I remember the V shaped wake turning thicker and whiter like a crust as we went.

We passed under a bridge where the sound of passing cars echoed above. On the far side, uncle John, who was wearing a dirty white t-shirt and cargo pants, slowed us, then cut the engine and dropped anchor. Our boat was spotted among the distant light of towns.

My father said 'It's close to 20ft here.'

From the deck I couldn't see over the side rail, so I stood on my knees on the chair and looked over. Beyond the columns of the bridge our boat swayed on the surface like a trinket. The dark water was rippling with glints of bridge and shorelight.

I had no bearings. If I was told it was 200 ft. deep where we were, I would have believed it. The wind was strong and wisps of hair began to unbraid behind me and fly in front of my forehead. We were close to marsh, my uncle said, and the very word unlocked the secret of our whereabouts. Suddenly the exhaust smell dissipated and marsh came through clean and strong. The smell of standing water, vegetation, egginess, of mud and reed and root onions, each smell altered slightly by nightfall.

I stood, finding my balance, joining my father who was sitting tying line, nipping off the excess with his teeth.

"This rod is yours." he said. "There will be big ones here tonight. This is when they come out."

He tugged the line knot tight and handed it to me, hooks dangling.

"You can cut bait, can't you?

"Yes." I said, but truthfully I hadn't done it by myself. I had always watched him.

He pointed with his elbow, "The squid is over there. That's what they'll hit."

On top of a cooler in the stern was a dull steak knife, a block of scrap wood, and a white grocery bag, folded down, with a box of frozen squid inside. It had partially thawed already and the juice ran inky over the bag and block. I pried one loose with the knife and cut it in half, then strips, like I had seen my father do before. I wove a small flappy piece on each of the two hooks, then lowered my rod over the side of the boat and lifted the bail on the reel so the bait sunk straight down. I closed the bail and felt the lead hit the bottom, twenty feet down. Then I waited.

I looked over at my father and uncle, who had lines in the water too. Three of us there, waiting, rocking. No sound among us but the wind- no heat, no chill.

My uncle caught the first one. We turned when he shouted.

"Come on!" he sang. "This is a good one."

He had his tongue out like a boy as he reeled. As we were watching, both mine and my father's rod dipped hard down, clipping the side rail with a chime.

"All three of us now! The party's started!" my father yelled.

Soon enough each of us were in a tousle.

"You got it, Constance?" my father asked, shortly after I started to reel.

"Yeah," I said, but the catch was heavy, too heavy for me. When my father pulled his line in he came over and helped me. Meanwhile the fish he caught was flopping along the deck. He let me reel the last few feet, then raised the rod and swung the fish over the side rail, all 16 inches of gunmetal blue and silver, swishing its tail as it came to deck.

"You caught a blue." he cheered. I had never caught one before.

"I caught one!" I yelled.

"You caught one!"

I was exhilarated. I was bouncing and filled with life. I worked as fast as I could to set my next hooks, and when I dropped it, my hands quivered with anticipation.

After each of our first catches there was no more quiet. One came up after another. I was the slowest, but I pulled some up on my own. Uncle John and my father helped take the fishes off the hook for me. It was astonishing in a way to be pulling fish out of the darkness, without seeing the water at all, like it was some kind of divining.

I said "How can the fish see? How do they know the bait is there, it's so dark?"

No one answered me for a minute.

Then uncle John said,

"They smell it!"

. . .

Then there was a lull. The wind calmed. No one caught anything for minutes, which felt like a long time. I stayed in my spot, looking off into the distance, looking at my father and uncle John. Uncle John was wiping his face with a towel. He looked back at me. "Hanging in there?" he said. I nodded. Then there was a splash not far from the boat. We all turned in its direction, but I alone could not see the water, so I watched my father for his reaction. Another splash, closer this time. Then another, on the other side of the boat.

"Over there." my father said, pointing. "See them?" he was talking to uncle John.

"Oh, yeah, we're in a good spot." my uncle said.

My father came to me and took the fishing pole and readjusted it in my hands so that I held it sturdily. It was a two-piece rod. He joined the top half to the bottom tighter.

"There, hold it well now." he said. I looked up at him.

"Keep a finger on the line, I doubt you'll need it. These guys won't nibble, they'll just strike. You're good on bait?" he asked. I nodded.

"Remember to set the hook if they take it. Just pull up." I motioned what I thought he meant.

"Yes, but don't do it unless you're sure there's a fish. Now keep steady. They'll come to you."

He returned to his spot, opposite uncle John. They exchanged a giddy look.

Then the water began to move. It was audible. First little sounds; whorls and whooshes near the surface. Then splashing; spontaneous first, then more and more intermittently, growing louder. Our heads turned all around. Fish tails were slapping the water; the action rising to the surface, building to a commotion.

"Get your lines ready." uncle John said. When he said that, almost with perfect timing a big fish pounced on my line and my rod snapped down and I began pulling and reeling blind with adrenaline. My father and him hallooed.

"Pull him in!" they yelled.

All I could make out from where I stood was the tip of my rod wavering up and down in the partial light of the sky and the beads of water jumping off the line as I cranked it through the eyelets down to the bail. My father and uncle had caught too and pulled them in. I heard behind me the wet, fleshy, solid plop against the floor. But my arms got tired so I called for my father and he helped me reel the last leg. "He's almost here, almost. Come on." I backed away from the rail and heard the sound of tackle jangling, the fish and bottom weight knocking against the outside of the boat.

"Beautiful." my father said. " A beauty, a real nice one." Without even seeing it I felt proud. He lifted it aboard for me and laid the rigging down on the floor with the others. It was a beauty, the skin shiny and lustrous.

"Your second blue, how bout that?" he said. I crouched and admired it on the deck. Then my father unhooked it, put it in the cooler and we stood, raised our rods, rebaited and dropped our lines again. The commotion had not cooled. It came in bursts. The next line I dropped did not touch the bottom before something struck it and up I yanked, as he told me. It was feeding time, they said. I pulled the next blue in by myself since it was smaller. I showed my father and he gave me a thumbs up. And still I could hear them outside thumping but could not see them.

I have always loved fishing for the paradox of its rewards. How happiness may be found in paucity. One fish waited for all day may exalt a person to their very depth. And a full net taken without fight may be a kind of defeat, a bore. So that night we struggled not with scarcity, but abundance.

There was wonder in that scene. No single element

contained it all, but each suffused it. Could my father or uncle have told the hour of night? When I laid my rod down I paused a moment listening to all the sounds and sensations peeling around us. The rocking of the boat, the marsh beyond, the feeling of animal life contradicting your wrist strength, and finally, to cap it, the starry and dim lit dizziness of where we were. The all in all driftedness. Wonder, if that is the right word, came from everywhere, sponging up memory, leaving no drop to forgetfulness.

I paced to the front and stood beside my father as he reeled.

"I want to see." I said.

"Not now." he insisted. "Wait."

When he had hauled the fish above water he hoisted me by the belly and leaned me over the side so I could see, not only that single fish, but the school of them. I remember the peaks of choppy water made by their movement. I tightened my grip on the oily rail.

Now I saw them. The grey tossing surface, the bulk of them in their frenzy. Dark, sleek, slitherine, the way they mashed and swam together and against each other. They made a clapping sound. My father put me down, but I wanted to see again so I went to the other side and climbed on the steering seat as uncle John shined a flashlight into the water, and the fish came piling on each other, drawn to the light. I kept my hands on the rail and pushed my head slowly forward outside the boat, equally drawn to the light which cut into the water like a razor, splitting the night, rousing the fish. Uncle John turned to my father, whose back was turned, reeling.

"Ed?" he called.

"Yeah?"

"They're right under us."

His voice was secretive, low, and foreboding. He turned

off the light and it was dark again. I came off the chair and stood in the middle of the bow, the steadiest ground.

"Constance," my father said sternly, "Take up your rod again. Put fresh bait on. They're still biting."

I did as he said and lowered my line like before. I waited and waited, this time a good while. Nothing happened. I began to get frustrated, waiting while the water thrashed.

"Nothing's biting it." I said aloud. He didn't reply. I said it again.

"Wait!" he said. "And remember to set the hook. You have to be patient, even now."

I waited, looking up at the sky. The wind was rising, whistling. When I had all but lost my focus on the line, a huge fish took my bait, nearly taking the rod out of my hands too. I yanked up carelessly and I struck my hand against the boat, cutting the top of my knuckle on the rail. I lost the fish. My father was watching, I could see him. Then the fish struck again, and I again I mistimed, making the same yank and cutting my knuckles on the same spot on the rail.

I remember burning with frustration. I began to reel my line defeatedly as if to say 'I'm done, no more fishing for me.' while my father watched. When I pulled the line aboard he flashed the light on it. The hook was stripped clean and bent.

"That was a big one." he said.

I sat down.

"You don't want to fish anymore?" he said.

I shook my head. I pitied myself losing the big one, and I pitied myself more losing it while he watched. I turned away. I did not want to be seen or bothered. In my fatigue I cried myself into a calm and almost fell asleep when I heard the engine begin. My father came and sat by me and put his arm around me, then helped his friend raise the anchor and coil it in a pile at the bow.

The movement of the boat during the ride back helped

soothe my spell of frustration. I closed one eye and kept the other open, watching. I grew sleepier and sleepier except when the boat steered sharply and my father held me firm to my position. Out of the one open eye I could still see the shape of the wake, the white frothy train of broken water behind us. Why I ever did such a thing remains a puzzle, except that by closing one eye I made it a game and captured something of the whole feeling of the trip. I don't know. There was a silliness, an aloofness I had then that I do not possess now. That detail assures me there's a callousness between the instinct of childhood and the instinct of maturity that remains through life, that remembrance alone cannot wholly diminish.

When I think back on that night, and try as I sometimes do to conjure the childlike nostalgia of it, I find it is my senses that have kept the best record. I feel the wind strong at the back of my neck, neither cold nor uncomfortable. Across my lap, my father's arm. The wind in buffets, slowly and steadily picking apart the braid my mother tied, bringing the hair in loose, easy strands in front of my face.

I switch eyes. The smell of night; marshy, muddy, brackish. Salty blue mussels split open, furrowed ground. The engine slowing. Before I know it I'm sitting in the stale van. Sleepier and sleepier. The muffled goodbye of my father and uncle John. My father's footsteps over stones. Stones, the sound of stones that day. His door opening. The windows cracked. The smell of the water again, A bucket in the backseat. My hurt knuckles. Before I sleep my senses mingle with a dream, a linkage; my hands are inky from the bait, the dried squid. In my mind appears the picture from many hours earlier, of Luisa my grandmother with her long, black, brittle hair, sitting on the porch, looking outward.

9

My grandfather Eduardo died when I was three years old. My memory of him does not exist outside of my father's stories, yet I've felt indebted to know more. There are pictures of me as a baby sitting on his lap, but I do not remember it. Through him I have the complexion I do, the thick black hair, the widow's peak. The same year he died our family inherited a huge amount of money from him. Then we moved to the Eastern Shore of Maryland and my mother became pregnant with my sister. The inheritance was my grandfather's oil money, whatever that meant. Money from the oil well he owned the rights to, from working and saving. Who knows. But it was so much that my father didn't need to work if he didn't want to. Apparently the inheritance was a surprise, given how frugally my grandfather lived toward the end of his life. He never told anyone about it. Growing up, my father said their family exchanged grapefruits for presents, like some proof of their poverty. The inheritance threw doubt on that for obvious reasons.

There was a feud between my father and his brother Antonio because my father received substantially more, eighty percent of the inheritance. He says it was because he was the first born, but I know that is not the only reason. The two exchanged long letters arguing the case. When the letters came by mail my father would take them to his study, read them in his rolling chair, then tear them to strips, throw them away, lean forward to his desk and begin writing his reply madly, his forearm forcing pens and pencils and miscellaneous notepads to the ledge of the desk. I knew because he would call me to come in and pick up whatever had fallen. He would dictate the words audibly, sometimes in spanish. It was the only time I heard him speak it in our home. Sometimes he forgot I was in the room with him because I would leave when he got upset and he would say 'Who's that? What do you want?' vacantly, not lifting his head, as if speaking to a ghost. But I never replied.

The last letter he received from Antonio was many years ago. The day he received it his mood changed drastically. Usually he was provoked to anger by the letters. This last one made him sullen. He did not eat, he turned down all attempts at affection, including James, who he pushed out of the way.

"Enough," he kept mumbling, "enough."

Then for a long time, the anger died, fortifying into a decade long silence. My parents outgrew Dallas, and they outgrew their inbred need to be close to their parents. They desired to move far away for a while, to live on their own and raise their family under a different sky. The money freed them to do so. It was hardest for my mother, who was close with her family, and who, unlike my father, had no feud to settle. Whether the move was intended to be permanent or sabbatical I do not know, and do not think they knew either. It was reactionary, I know that much. My father wanted a place offering seclusion without being reclusive. One of his colleagues told him about Assateague Island in Maryland. He described the wild horses, the long remote shorelines, the wind beaten homes, the abundant seaside and soundside waters.

"We had never been." my mother said. "We had seen pictures, that was all." But apparently it was enough. The place, rather the idea of the place began to assume in my father's mind a new stature, a new provenance, and possibility. He bought maps of Chesapeake Bay country, circling towns he wanted to visit. He bought traveling guides to the waterways. His company had an office in Washington DC, which incentivised him further.

A fortnight's trip was planned for our family that began in Dallas and ended in Assateague. We nearly made it to the end before my parents settled on a house to buy. I was five then. It was early Spring. Our family was growing like the earth around it. Pictures of the house from the day it was bought show the apple trees out back heavy with a spate of white bloom, the water shining.

10

My parents still live in the first house we moved to and it is still too big for them. It was too big even when all five of us lived under the same roof. But my father could not have conceived of living in humbler means then, nor could he now, though he hasn't the ambition anymore to manage the whole property by himself. It is much too involved. He has a list of handymen scribbled on a piece of paper hanging on the fridge. Lately there have been painters retouching rooms and kitchen cabinets and banisters; it is mostly unnecessary work, but my father likes the bustle in his home, even if he won't admit it, the open cans of egg shell, the mixing sticks, the step ladders; all of it makes the old place feel productive again, likes its donning a new outfit.

My mother dresses for the day and spends long hours in the sun room patio, which overlooks the creek. She keeps her plants and her wicker furniture there. It is the one room besides the kitchen that is unmistakably hers; white, warm, and floral. Most other rooms have my father's dominant print on them; heavy, oaken, antique, rustic. The two contrasting styles are the testament of a long fought war for the personality of the home; for every furnishing of his there appears a counter-furnishing of hers placed opposite it. For every dark, wooden chest filled with old boat classifieds, there is a white, woven basket filled with tea candles. For every big, brass handled cabinet, there is a vase and set of china placed inside it.

Back and forth they have gone for years; my mother claiming she should get to furnish the house because my father got to pick it. Here again surfaces the long standing disagreement about how the house was chosen. It was during the same Eastern Shore trip they planned from Dallas. Apparently my mother liked a smaller property, and told my father that they should commit to it before someone else buys it, but my father held out. He wanted to be 'on the water', not just near the water.

When they came here to Teal St. for the first time, my mother was silent with hesitation, seeing how much work there was to be done. My father was the opposite; he could not stop saying 'wow', and he is fairly superstitious too. He tells us he went to the pier out back where the water was perfectly calm and said a prayer in his heart asking God if this was the house they should buy. Right then and there he says he heard the croaking call of a blue heron, which flew right in front of him, and which he had taken to mean 'Yes' from above. My mother, whenever she hears that sentimental retelling of his religious moment, frowns with doubt.

"That heron has been here since the beginning. He wanted food, not for you to decide to move your family into this giant ramshackle boat museum."

Then she looks at us and says,

"And it had nothing to do with your father's prayer. I have no doubt God answers prayers, but I believe he would have answered very differently if your father had consulted me and not the heron."

"You never spoke up." he says.

"You never asked."

And there is the standstill, time and time again.

Our home at 84 Teal St. was built and owned previously by a retired Admiral in the Navy who was a widower at the time we moved. He was downsizing and going to live with his two daughters and their families in Norfolk. At the time of purchase the house was not yet twenty years old, but it looked older than that, being filled with obscure tastes and furnishings; the pastimes of an aging, military man. Over the years he had stockpiled a collection of nautical antiques that found their keeping place in all corners of the home; decorative anchors and real anchors, ropes of every braid, stanchions, chooks, shackles, cleats, winches, amateur ship paintings, disused propellers, Navy flags. These objects laid about everywhere in a half witting way, with no eye for balance or proportion or color or overbearance in the room, but in any corner or any ledge that accommodated their physical size. Objects were grouped together often, like the man got tired of placing things and simply let them heap unrestrained.

Additional shelves were built to the walls to handle the collections which grew seemingly without end. Except for a crates worth of his favorite objects, the Admiral left most of the pieces behind and they became for us a strange, dull, chromy inheritance, cluttering the rooms and leaving a strong, polished-brass smell that lingered long after. My mother wanted to throw them out or donate them, but my father believed them to be points of appreciation, things that gave the home its 'character'.

Throughout the process of buying the home, my father developed some inexplicable reverence for the Admiral that he could not fully shed, even after we moved in. It was as if he felt he owed the man a debt. In this case, the debt was a scrupulous and museum-like caretaking of all the Admiral's old belongings; the propellers and boat parts etc. It was pitiful how my father kept things that he did not want, and could not part from them. What remained on the ledges created a boundary to our comfort, and we took over the house with trepidation, as if enlisted to change as little as possible, the very walls and surfaces of the place being not ours yet.

In the front of the house was a tired looking flagpole that used to fly the American flag. But it was torn down in a storm and my father had my sister retrieve it. She left it drying in the sun by the outbuilding and forgot about it. When she found it, it was completely sun bleached and lichen covered. My father had her bring it to him, and he folded it exceptionally neatly and placed it in the basement where it has never been unfolded since. We offered to throw it out, but he will not part with it. Even the suggestion makes him angry. The flagpole flew nothing since. Every few years a brave bird will make a nest at the very top, but soon enough it leaves and abandons its nest. There is no protection up there, and the flag rope clinks endlessly against the pole. It makes the sound of a sail clip in a light wind. That sound I do not mind, but the birds do. It is no place to make a home.

The outside of the house, like the inside, has the appearance of tarnished opulence, of shabby grandeur. It misfits the architecture of the neighboring homes, which are small, brick built ranchers, most of them shaded by oaks and situated on a half acre lots with either gravel or mud driveways. Ours is two storey and manor-like. It has a wide, white stone exterior with twin columns standing before the front door, and an ornamental trim along the roofline. The driveway is a paved roundabout. We are on three acres, two of which are shared between the front of the house and the left side, which wraps around, where the horse pen, outbuilding, and boat rack are. There is one acre in the backyard, where the slope of the land gentles down to the creek. Near the water, the grass muddies to sank bank, and our pier, though sagging in some places, extends eagerly into Weems.

All three acres are generally exposed. The trees we do have grow along the property lines and blend more readily with the neighbor's yard than with our own. But we do have some variety. Pines, ash, dogwood. Willow, oak and maple. Pin and live oaks, and maples line the left side of the property. Most numerous are the pines. These sturdy trees drop the pinecones I gathered when I was young. Black and stunted pines are on the right side of the house. A line of them hedge the overgrowth beyond, where bulrush, bracken, and poverty grass finally turn to marsh a quarter mile in.

Since I was young I imagined the pines as soldiers or guards, the way they stood with their tall, dark-red trunks and blocked the thickets and weeds from charging into the yard. It was like a clash of two dwellings, the domestic fending off the feral.

Speaking of pines, I have always loved pine cones. Like the creek itself those brown prickly ornaments summon this place to my mind. Since I was a girl I picked them. My mother was the first to take me foraging for them. She told me they were good luck. She also said that if there was anyone she could convince to do little outside chores with her, it was me. I must have been gullible, I say. No, she says. For the other two, it would have been a chore. But for you, you enjoyed it. You would keep collecting them even when I had gone in. You wanted to be out, Out! and she motions like she's pushing a window wide open. That is how I got you outside.

I do remember it clearly. Impatiently I would yank the green ones from the tree and carry them in the pouch of my shirt til the shirt was damp and stretched and I stunk of sap with stickiness up to my forearms. They were my first toy; my first ardent fascination with nature. A few pines would drop cones by the water's edge and some of them I would collect, and others, the unshapely ones, unfit for my collection, I threw back to the creek and watched idle away like bobbers. Even now I remember the studded imprints they left in my palm, the odd pleasure of their painful touch and how I brought them so close to my nose to smell the ripeness of the pine.

Piles of them I made around the house, and some I hid in places I could not find again. I loved their gradual drying, their lightening of weight. Their turning from green to every stippled tone of brown: saddle and peat and the color of clay. These hollow keepsakes, all of them slightly different. My mother collected her own cones in a white bag, and I gave her many of mine. Later we put them out in empty flower pots and placed the pots on each step of the stairs on the side of the house. Some mothers leave lights on, mine left pinecones. They're one of the surest signs of home I have.

11

None of the trees on our property cast their branches anywhere near the house, which makes our place the special target of the sun. At times, the absence of shade has been a blessing; we've seen limbs come crashing through our neighbor's roofs during storms, and been spared.

But compared to every other house on the road, our plot is a clearing, which makes summers harsh. The sun burns every living thing nearby and the marsh humidity doubles the effect.

Our grass has been seeded, chemically evaluated, resodded, watered, drowned, fertilized, and so on. Every kind of treatment has been attempted to breathe new life into it, to no avail. The neighbor's yards are soft and green, but ours keeps a yellow, half-dead color. It's stiff as bristles. It was then, and it is now.

Until recently we had a next door neighbor named Mr. Corey. He was an old bohemian man with a fluff of grey hair. He wore paint-smeared trousers that he rolled at the bottom like capris, with big, billowing Hawaiin shirts. He was a quiet, joyful man when he was active. He was always barefoot, dirty with outdoor work, but never filthy. He kept a garden at the edge of his property that extended into ours. That part of our yard was not kept for a long time. It was neglected and it looked it. At some point, we don't know when exactly, he began tending to our little plot as well as his; sticking tomato tresses into our ground, growing flowers, cucumbers, lettuce, all kinds of things.

Adley and I would watch his house through the trees between our two places. When we were young it was the height of our scandal to peer into his house from afar. I always did; it made Adley uncomfortable though because she thought he would catch us. We noticed he hung some of his trousers over his windows as curtains. Now and then we'd see him walking across our property early in the morning to garden. He looked like he was humming to himself or speaking to someone we could not see. There was a woman who lived with him for a while. She looked much much older than he, but it was not his mother and not a relative either because they would kiss on the lips. Eventually we stopped seeing her and he never mentioned it. He went on living his solitary gardening life. Sometimes by surprise he would bring over a beautiful vine of tomatoes and hang them on our door knob for us to find later.

He became less active as he got older. Although he still came out occasionally, he gave is garden less attention and let his yard become overgrown and mangy looking. The tomatoes on the knob became rarer. Some days after we hadn't seen him for a while I would look to his house and notice the progressive disproportion between his land and his house. While one grew the other shrank. His dwelling seemed to cower under the heavy eaves and deep vegetation he could no longer tame. I feared he would be swallowed up eventually by the oaks that loomed over his yard. His trees weren't tall and stately like ours. They were gnarled and twisting, almost elvish. They arched over his home like the rotten fingers of giants.

In any case, it was a pity to see him decline. I felt sad not seeing him swaggering barefoot between our yards anymore. It seemed like he had lost a certain fundamental order to his life. There was no more vitality, or whimsy. He had become an indoor man. And of all the neighbors I knew, Mr. Corey was not meant to be an indoor man.

It stands out to me that I never entered his house through the main entrance. On the few occasions we went to his place, it was only through the side, and even that felt a kind of trespass. Once he had our family over for dinner and made us a meal of vegetables and rice. He gave the girls fancy colored glasses to drink from, and the boys he gave jars. He was barefoot and as enigmatic in his home as he was out of it. He did not make much conversation that dinner. His eyes floated about. He kept asking "You're good? You're good?" and when we said yes, he would say "Oh, I'm so glad. So glad" repeating his phrases like that. He never mentioned the woman we saw with him, and we didn't ask.

For all his barefootedness and trousered curtains and colorful garden, there was an air of uptightness or insecurity about him that we all felt. He smiled often, but very fleetingly. It was a smile that looked like it might suddenly fall apart. Overall, he was very kind to me and my siblings, but our parents did not like us spending too much time near him. They did not trust him so much, and for that we only knew him at a distance.

There was an outbuilding between Corey's house and ours, a left over and underused tenement the Admiral built when he built the house. When we were young my father stored it with ladders, tools, horse equipment, always thinking he would purchase a horse since we lived in horse country. But the closest we ever got was being loaned a scraggly looking pony from a farmer up the road who had no place to put it. The farmer asked because he had seen a pen being built on our property years ago. What he didn't know is that the construction was begun but never finished.

As it turns out, the farmer's asking prompted my father to finish the project. When it was complete, the farmer came by with his scraggly creature, 'Jitters', who was white and tawny colored, and very skittish. The pen received a sliver of shade from the outbuilding, and that's where the horse stood for most of the summer days until sunset. Two weeks later the farmer came back for his horse and the pen remained empty every since. It was never fully disassembled either. Like other additions and renovations around the house it survived in a state of mid repair.

Other features around the house had that quality. There was a wrap-around porch that did not fully wrap around. The unfinished section was turned into a storage space for planting pots, rakes, hoses. In the front of the house were holes placed seven feet apart in the ground for a fence that was never raised. Alongside the outbuilding there was a kayak rack, which never actually held a kayak.

The closer one looked at this place, past the columns and the sheer size of it presence, the more one saw a certain makeshiftness; a tinpot quality that never went away. In a way the house typified the whole Eastern Shore of Maryland: that region beyond the Bay Bridge, glimmering of rich, waterfront land and lost potential. Of vacant, newly-built strip malls and foundering crab shacks along the highway.

12

My father bought a kayak once, second hand. He ordered my mother and me to bring it through the house through the back porch door to the pier to use that day. Adley and James asked to help carry it too, but he thought they might drop it, so he turned them away.

"Why couldn't we bring it around?" we asked.

"I'm aerating the grass on the side, I've put new fertilizer down, I don't want us stepping on it for a few hours."

He went to retrieve a lifevest and paddle from the outbuilding. The kayak was strapped to the car, and when we went to unstrap it, my mother pushed too hard and it slid freely off the roof and hit the driveway and cracked the side. My father didn't hear since he was in the outbuilding. Nonetheless we carried it frantically along, hoping it wasn't as bad as it sounded. We turned it on its side and squeezed it through the main door, but the main hall is narrow and even sideways the kayak scraped along, leaving red dented streaks on the wall. It was getting worse by the minute. I dropped it in the living room.

"Pick it up." she said.

"I can't."

"Pick it up, he's coming."

We heard the back door open.

"Keep coming." he said. "I've got this door opened."

My mother and I looked at each other, a vow of silence. I picked it up barely, carried it ten more feet over the back of a couch and dropped it again, making an ugly fractured sound. As soon as my father heard it he pounced, swift and furious.

"What was that? What the hell happened?"

He looked at me. My mother put her end down and stood in front of me, to defend me.

"What the hell happened?"

He began looking for the damage, and when he found it, his anger filled the room. Silent, swelling anger. I stared at something small and inanimate, the bottom of a leg of a chair, and did not take my eyes off it until his presence had moved from where it was.

"She didn't mean it." my mother pleaded. "It fell accidentally when we were taking it off the roof."

He shook his head. He knelt and felt the crack. I could see him in my periphery. The more he observed it the more it infuriated him. I could hear the breath of his anger.

"So much for that." he said. He looked past us and saw the walls. "Those too? How will that come out?"

"We'll get it out." my mother said.

He licked his thumb and rubbed it along the mark, to test it. It wouldn't come out. The whole time he was wearing a life jacket which made him look childlike and tragic.

"You will?" he said.

"I will."

"Take this." he said.

My mother left me and took the other end of the kayak with him out the back door. He jerked her around the corner and I watched as they went down, stepping over the fertilized grass to the rack- my mother stiff and compliant, and my father with his pale orange life preserver, the gut strap swinging at his legs. They left the kayak in the rack and I took paper towels and hot water and tried desperately to remove the marks, but they didn't come out.

My father left to go somewhere. My mother came inside and said "Stop. Don't worry about it today." All I wanted to do was remove the marks. When she left I tried again. I rubbed the same spot over and over. I spit on the wall and tried that. I tried using the bottom of my shirt. Nothing worked. My mother came back and scolded me again because I could not take my hand off the wall.

"Stop it, Constance. I'm telling you seriously this time. Give it a break. You'll make it worse. You keep doing that you'll take the paint off."

Somehow my father still used the kayak the next day. I remember watching him drag it down the hill to the water, hoping for my own sake that it would still float somehow. Fortunately the crack was above the waterline when he got in. He paddled out a hundred yards from shore then turned around and came back. He flipped the kayak on the sand and laid the paddle and vest overtop, then he left and I don't know where he went. A few hours later the boat was gone. He had put it back on the rack and come in the house to make an announcement.

"I don't want anyone using that kayak. It's damaged and unsafe."

"What will you do with it?" my mother asked.

"I'm not sure yet."

"Well, would we keep it?"

"Just stop asking questions. Please. I spent money on that. A good amount too. Now it's just,"

He paused.

"Just what?"

"A waste." he slurred, and walked away.

13

I have looked back on those early years when I was not yet 12 years old, acknowledging the inseparability of the fond memories from the unkind. There were two worlds at all times occurring under the same roof, and they cohered in a way I have never fully understood, except that both are part of that cruel, exquisite patchwork of experience that makes up family life. The house, the physical house I would suggest too was an embodiment of the varied moods that one felt from one day to the next, passing from one room to the next. Later we learned that the admiral was a submarine commander, and it made so much sense because the corridors and hallways of his house were tight and squeezing. They created the sense that you were aboard the ship, that you must square your shoulders. Yet such narrowness flowed into generous spaces.

The kitchen, like many kitchens, was the heart of the home, the place where the most footsteps flowed from, the room connecting every artery and vessel of the abode, where the sorriest sobs and heartiest laughs were heard. Brown tiles covered the floor. The counters were white granite. Below the cabinets was a long fruit tray and set of clean mugs.

There was a round coffee table with a green glass bar light over it that illuminated the table in a hovel. I never liked eating at that table alone, under the hovel. It made me feel like I was being watched or about to be interrogated.

Sometimes I would take my food to the dining room which was better lit and had more comfortable chairs. The high crowned ceilings in the dining room gave it the atmosphere of a military banquet hall. It was a room for proper hosting, although its the formality was also a deterrent from eating there. It was dark usually, and on the walls were the discolored outlines of picture frames, where portraits of the admiral and his late wife once hung.

The kitchen was connected to a large pantry of almost equal size, though it was a space that was never fully utilized. On the pantry shelves were bulk stores of seasoning, pasta, flour; enough for a year's rations, even hooks for hanging meats, glass cabinets for alcohol, and a secret entrance that opened by two metal doors down to a rock hewn basement, a cool and damp covey with a wine cellar and the smell of moisture and mold. The basement had two window wells; one facing the right side of the house, and the other facing the rear. Neither let much light through because they were always filled with debris; leaves, mulch, duff, mouse nests, and the like. During storms the cellar would leak through the stone cracks and turn rank if someone did not sop the water with buckets or towels. If it flooded we had a wet-dry vacuum for the water, and a dehumidifier. Otherwise the smell would escape though the doors and into the kitchen. It was a lot of work for such an underused hole.

14

My father's housekeeping was animated, as I've said before, by a peculiar and longstanding obligation to the man who built it. For years he played the admiral's unworthy steward, bent on liking what he did not himself like, trying to see the value of the little attic rooms and the cellar and the oversized pantry and the unfinished porch. All of this because he had paid for them, though they were mostly a source of contempt.

The bedrooms were like this too. There were enough rooms for each of us to have our own, including one at the end of the house with only a boxspring and mattress, where my father slept if he was in a bad mood. The extra bedrooms became storage rooms by default, one of them holding old high school gowns and my mother's wedding dress. That closet in that room was my favorite hiding place in the house when I was young. I would crawl under the curtain of dresses, through the cellophane, and sit upright against the wall, with my mother's sewing basket beside. I never shut the door full. I always left a crack, a thin stripe of light before my toes. Sometimes I had to bunch the dresses together to get some breathing room, and I would sit there, waiting to be heard, listening to the sound of footsteps across the floors of the house.

The roominess of the house made it drafty especially in cold seasons, and everywhere but the kitchen, long shadows stretched across bare walls, lavishing the home with feeling of forlornness. Some of that mood was effected by noises and voices. Voices carried and echoed. One felt that words were lost on space, and yet we yelled across rooms, and we yelled across the yard, and we yelled across the creek. Something or someone was always falling apart, or in need of help, so we yelled for it. I would yell looking for a sock, and my mother, deprived of peace, would come to the bottom of the stairs and yell back, "What? What?"

My father was less a part of it. He often withdrew from the urgent household fevers and allowed them to be settled among us. What followed him rather were spells of long brooding, of gloomy discontent. In every crawlspace, under the floorboards, in each wall and hinge we could feel the gloom rubbing off like residue.

I could not always tell where the terms of my father's discontent began or ended, but I could sense it involved money. When we were young, he had very little urgency in his life because money was plenty, and it put a buffer between our family's situation and others. As we grew though, the wealth anchored a certain part of my father's ambition. The longer he relied on the inheritance the more disillusioned he became, the more inert.

It was a both a freedom and a weight. We weren't happier than others, but we also weren't sad or discontent. I remember being in school and hearing about other kid's sick parents and family troubles, and thinking, very naively, 'It's too bad they don't have money, but it's a good thing our family does.'

We had fewer perceivable worries was all, and the absence of worry appealed to my young mind as one of the great gifts life might bestow.

Sadly, though, it meant that we had a very hollow concept of work and challenge. It often meant that work was hobbified, and not actually work. It removed certain consequences. Money kept our hands off manual labor. My father admired craftsmanship from afar, but he did not want to be afflicted by it, or survive by it, nor did he want any of his kids to take up a mean living.

In our family, productivity was not as important as normalcy. Normalcy was a matter of appearances. It was not the midpoint between poverty and riches, but a quality unto itself, a positive status that ensured comfort without drawing attention to itself. Over time the house came under the censure of normalcy. There was a semi-conscious effort to prevent the place from looking too much like an estate. Whatever my parents wanted, it was not ostentation. The outbuilding, the mangy grass on the side, the piles of chopped wood, the lopsided pier- these features fulfilled their role in humbling the appearance, giving it a rustic look.

A place may become rustic by use, but ours became it by disuse, which is sadder. The pen, the unraised fence, the garden, those too- everything that wore away slowly were vestiges of my father's old life; structures he kept because they were nostalgic of South Texas, of simpler days. But we never quite got there.

Our place was confused about what it should be. And it was confused because my father was torn about money. What influence it should have in our upbringing. We suffered his confusion and our own too, though we found common refuge in Weems, our brown creek that flowed undismayed through all confusion.

15

It is easy to paint a picture of my mother and father with too quick a stroke. While it was true that my father could be unreasonably cold, angry, indifferent, demanding, unjust, and plain abusive, he was never so perennially. Often his warmth showed in the interest he took in our intellectual life- in reading, ideas, words, the cultivation of imagination and curiosity. More than anyone he opened our minds to the world.

What I did not mention previously is that the Admiral who left behind antique chocks and stanchions also left behind books; a numberless hoard that flowed from the shelves below to a cramped, half-pint bedroom upstairs where volumes of naval histories and biographies of stone-faced war generals amassed in piles across the ground. All the piles were different heights; some teetering, some tottering, others already fallen and their book covers cracked. A great number of the books were military subjects, but there were others too; Hemingways, Faulkners, Dickens's, Brownings, and Poes filed in the ranks, as well as our own childhood picture books, mystery novels, and adventure stories that found their way into the stacks. The reward of dawlding in that little room was to rummage, to spread the books across the ground, to lift one stack here and replace it there, to build almost inadvertently a barricade of the piles and play beneath them.

My father commandeered that room and it became our library. We called it 'the library' too, though to untrained eyes it was only a hodge podge, fusty and disorganized. We even hushed our voices there. Looking back I don't know why we did, except that perhaps our calling it 'the library' sanctified it as such, and bestowed on it the customary quiet. In any case, quiet or fusty, I reverenced that space. My imagination was baptized among those stacks where I hid for hours, turning the pages of Nancy Drew, or Cabella's wilderness adventure tales, or one of my favorite books, Misty of Chincoteague. Each book passed down the line; from me to James, from James to Adley, and as we got older we weaned off those and went on to the Poes and Dickens and such. We never stopped rummaging and we never stopped reading.

We read often, and we read much, and we read in all weather and mood. We read to pass the time and we read to transfix the time. We read to be at home and we read to flee home, whatever our fancy. One thing my father did forbid was our camping out indefinitely in the library and not leaving. Unless the weather outside was foul, we were turned out eventually, in mid-sentence if it had to be, pulled by the ear and told to go waste time in fresh air. He was serious about that. For as much as he admired books, he never wanted them to dominate our minds to the seclusion of the natural world, especially the creek and river where we lived. He wanted the words we read to be nourished by the realities they referred to, and vice versa. Neither to the exclusion of the other, but both at play in the forming of our thoughts. He wanted the pages and the creek to be like complementing tutors, like two antiphons chiming back and forth.

Something precious and irrevocable grew out of the boredom that came from being turned out of doors, when we went to the water. Weems is an idle creek, and being idle it stays your vision. Keeps it from skirting. Eyes do not dance across Weems anymore than they dance across the moon on a clear night, or an empty vale. They stare, rather; they linger, and find that by lingering on something you begin to know it, to abide it. It opens you to subtleties you did not see before. Whether that was my father's intent for us to glean I'm not sure. But certainly it was good for us, even if I do not know what to call it precisely: being able to sit and look at something for a long time, and be held by it. Yes, that must be good. My father also gave us little learning assignments based on the books we had in the library; memorization tests and pop quizzes about 'who said this?' or 'who said that?'. Occasionally he had me transcribe a poem from one of the anthologies onto a plain piece of paper. It was not punishment, per se, but it was a tedious, obscure task, and I often found myself wondering what its purpose was, or why I was there at that desk, my head bobbing from page to page, my hand scribbling lines of Elizabeth Browning verse, copying not words, not meaning, not anything comprehensible to me, but merely symbols, and going about it as any rushed, obedient scribe would.

But blind and rote obedience has magic to it. The wrist learns something that it teaches the mind. And later when I was older, and when I least expected it, a word like 'fulmination' would come to my thoughts and I could trace it to that task. What a thing. What an odd thing that was. And there were other times when I would be in the library reading, and my father would enter and give me eyes that said 'That's enough', and I would say

"May I just finish this part?" And we would relent and say "You may."

Waiting for me he'd slowly drift in and take a book off the

top of a pile and begin reading it. Thirty minutes later we would still be there; him standing and reading, me sitting and reading- both of us absorbed. Finally he would catch himself, very discreetly shut his book, and turn to me and say,

"Ahem, have you read enough now?" And then we would go.

So there was that clemency he had. Devotion to us. It never left. My mother says that when they were newly married they lived in a small house, very simple, and she remembers the sound of his keys in the door lock, the squeak of the hinge. She said he never came through the main door, always the back. She would hear it and come close to the door and wait until the knob turned. She said she would pretend she was doing something, to make it seem like she wasn't there just waiting for him. But of course she was.

He'd come in and hang his jacket, and underneath it would be flowers, daisies and geraniums, roses, depending on the day. 'He never gave me a small hug or a small kiss- everything was large, even the flowers. They hardly fit in the vase.' she said.

She told this story to us with a convincing air, a showmanship, because she wanted us to know it was indeed our father she was talking about. But I knew she told the truth. I have seen his tenderness.

Years back I asked her if she remembered telling us that story about the sound of the door lock. She said 'Yes, vaguely. It's good that you remember.'

I said "Do you still like that sound?"

She said "Not like I did. And I don't hear it like I did then either. The kitchen's a long way from the door. I can still tell it's him though?

"How?"

"He slams the door now." And she laughed at the thought.

My mother, for all her kindness, is one of the stubbornest women I know. In high school I took her grocery shopping once, just to get out of the house. It was cloudy that day, a bit gloomy, and that's all we seemed to talk about. When we returned, we made it to the front door- she was finding the key and I was holding the bags, and I said 'Once these clouds clear, it'll be a nice day.' She stopped searching, looked me square in the eye and said 'I really don't care, I don't want to talk about weather for the rest of my life.'

She was not mousy either. She never let my father run away with a temper altogether. She would yell or cuss if provoked. More likely she would match his cynicism. But in matters that pertained to us, her children, she was unflinchingly strong. More times than I could recall she made herself a victim of blame on our behalf. She would physically step between my glaring father and us, and confront him- 'Leave them alone' or 'Leave her alone, she didn't do anything. She's just a kid.'

Each of them had their separate faults, many which emerged later in life, under the burden of the passage of time, the changing responsibilities of families, normal worrying over the future. But no setback altered their fundamental tendencies toward kindness and tenderness, nor cast doubt on it.

The two of them met in college through mutual friends who invited them to go dancing. My father tells the story slowly, measuredly, as if he were giving a report of it. I think he prides himself on being able to recount the story so level-headed, because it takes him awhile to get going. He hems and haws to start. Sets the stage. Mentions incidental details. Go on, go on, we say. But it's like he's warming up. Like the story is an effort that requires much of him; a thicket of obligation he has to move carefully through, weighing his words and delivery, showing the proper amount of masculine embarrassment, so that it comes across without any needless enchantment. He wants this courtship to sound plain as day.

"She didn't want to dance, and I didn't want to dance. And so we danced. She was actually good, an excellent dancer, in fact. I followed her most of the night, not the other way around. She would say 'Here, like this and like that. Put your hands here, not there. Not so bouncy.' She would sound out the step counts so that I could hear them."

Whenever he told the story, my mother would lean in from earshot distance, just to listen. She feared if she intruded he would stop his telling. And she likes when he tells.

"And then what?" I ask.

"Then we started dating."

"That's all?"

Humor at his own reticence catches him.

"What else do you want to know?"

"The details."

He pauses. My mother waits to hear what he will say.

"You can ask her for those."

He looks over to her, aware of her listening in. He shoots her a look, a deferral. She shoots back her own look, mild disappointment, as if she'd hoped he'd indulge the request. But he doesn't. He stares off and I turn toward my mother who looks like she's been transported, like she has moved her memory nimbly to that day.

"It was not as straightforward as he says." she begins. "I did want to dance, but not with him."

"Why not?"

"He was too cool. It seemed like he didn't want to make any effort to ask a girl to dance or learn how either."

"Not true." he interjects.

"Is true. That, and he kept looking at other girls even when we were dancing."

"You always say that." he says.

"I've never said that. Even if I did you can't deny it."

He turns in his chair, frowning at her. He's involved now. And she sees this and smiles, because she likes that he is involved now.

"Tell the truth. It's true, right?" she entreats.

He shakes his head, looks at me, frowns- a frown of incredulity, of 'don't believe her'

"I was seeing how the dance was. I was trying to get the steps by watching others. I wasn't watching other girls."

My mother looks at me, rolling her eyes. Despite their disagreement and the vying countenances, there is an invisible jest between them, a play of sorts, created by the way they turn and notice and roll their eyes and retort. There is a candor in their voices they are unaware of. It is a sing song quarrel, lively and sharp, yet too delicate to make any real, deep cuts.

Suddenly this memory leaps to another.

"Did you tell her about the apron? my mother says.

"The apron?"

"Yes, the apron incident."

I sit there, watching them as the banter unfolds. I am somehow mediating this conversation while also being excluded from it.

"Oh. OH, the apron. Yes. That one." He looks at me first, to establish that he is addressing me. "The first time she came over for dinner." Then he continues the story, and looks at my mother to establish the accuracy of his details.

"This is when we had been dating already. I brought her

home once for dinner. My mother lent her a red apron and asked her for help in the kitchen."

"In Spanish." my mother adds, "She asked me for help in Spanish."

"Yes. Which was bad of my mother, because she knew she didn't know Spanish."

"Why'd she do that?" I ask.

"Because she was intimidated to have another woman in her home, let alone a white woman standing in her kitchen, in her domain."

"Anyway," my mother says, taking up the story, "His mother goes to set the table and she leaves me in the kitchen to stir the pot of sauce. I'm stirring, and I feel something move against my waist, slightly, but I don't think it's anything, so I keep stirring and I feel it again, a small movement, very small, but noticeable. The apron I had on that she lent me had a pocket in the front. Well I opened the pocket and looked down and there was a snake inside!"

I look to my father. He nods.

"It's true."

"A snake?"

"Yes, a green garden snake, probably a foot long."

"What did you do?"

"I shrieked first. Then I took that thing off and threw it on the ground, and kicked it away."

"The snake too?"

"Oh yeah, I hate snakes, I was afraid. And guess who comes back, right then, with a priceless look of surprise on her face?"

"Where was he?"

"I don't know. Off with his father and brother. I don't know. I just remember his mother balling up the apron that I kicked, saying something angrily to herself, and taking it outside while I stayed inside mortified. Then she came back in and took the spoon I was using and stirred the sauce herself. And I was still shocked at that point, with no way of saying anything. I felt apologetic too, I don't know why."

Then my father takes over.

"When we came in I said what's going on? And your mother had this stricken look on her face; my mother was still cooking, but I could see something was wrong. I said what's the matter, and she told me there was a snake in her apron. And I look at my mother, who does not acknowledge me for some reason. When my father came in she left the kitchen and went to their bedroom until he went to check on her. I had no idea what was going on. When we asked my mother later what happened, she said a snake was in the apron. We asked how it got there, how could it since the aprons were hanging on the wall, she said it 'climbed, or jumped in' So…"

"So she put the snake there, you think?" I say.

My father, fessing for both him and my mother, says,

"I think she did, we can't say though. She denied it, but, based on the evidence…It's unfortunate it had to start that way."

"How was dinner?" I ask.

My mother laughs deeply, recalling something else.

"Remember what we had?"

He shakes his head.

"Of all meals. Spaghetti! You don't remember?"

"No." he says.

"Of course not."

16

My grandmother Luisa never came to my father's wedding. Neither did Antonio. It was said that she was very sick during that time and that Antonio was care taking, but when I've asked what she was sick with, I'm told 'It's not worth getting into', and my father's whole manner changes and becomes grave. My mother says nothing either. I can tell that there is a solemn understanding between them by the look they exchange.

The question arose because long go I found their wedding album, which is really only three pictures in a box. One picture is of the two of them, one is of the two of them with their wedding party, and one is with both their families. That last picture is the most imbalanced because next to my father is only my grandfather Eduardo, who has the short, military haircut he began to get when he worked in the oil industry. He is a small man in stature, and he appears especially so in the picture. He is wearing a brown suit too big for him, and his face is pale; it has lost the glow of sun and manual labor and has become the face of meetings and nodding and decision making.

There is a stark difference between the picture of him

sitting on the porch with his wife and this one. In this picture his chin has a patch of silver stubble, and it droops with older skin, it does not cling healthfully to the face. There is so little affection in it too- not so much as an arm around his son, no ostensible sign of pride in the moment except a wry smile, a controlled expression. His arms are locked together in front of him. On the other side of the portrait is my mother and her parents and her two brothers; the Pritchards, who still live in Dallas. They are linked and smiling. Grandma Pritchard is an older, shorter version of my mother. She is directly beside my mother in the picture, in a cream colored dress. Next to her is grandpa Pritchard, with his wire-frame glasses, and next to him are the boys, my uncles who are bunched together wearing glossy tuxedos.

Together, the Pritchards are the image of American normalcy, counterbalancing the Gonzalezes, the frumpy, vacant staring other half. This is the picture I come from. These are the bloodlines.

17

There was a common stricture to our lives growing up. It was a place both circumscribed and enlarged by the watchfulness of my father and the worrisomeness of my mother. It was a world disciplined yet liberal, miniature yet vast. We were yoked together in chores, and the hard times were imputed to us all.

When we first moved to Maryland we had three apple trees in the backyard. They stood directly behind the house, partly obstructing the view of the creek, but beautiful nonetheless. In summers they bloomed white, sweet smelling petals, and dropped hefty green crab apples that were tasty and tart.

For a time, my father had a complicated relationship with the trees. Until I was ten, he loved them. He sprayed them with pesticide, laid stones along the base of the trunks and mulched them over. He had us collect the apples and bring them inside to wash and enjoy. 'Here, eat, eat' he would hand us each one, although my mother in private told us not to.

"Are you sure they're good to eat?" she asked him once.

"Yes, of course they are." he said indignantly.

"Perfectly good? How do you know?"

"I asked the admiral when we bought the house."

"Did he eat them?"

"Yes he did."

"How do you know?"

"Why are you so paranoid about the apples?"

He placed one on the counter.

"Constance, grab me a knife." he said.

I gave it to him and he cut it in half and gave my mother one of the halves.

"Here, look. An apple. Try it."

Looking over it hesitantly, she bit the edge with her front teeth, slowly chewing the skin. Her face soured. She went to the trash and spit it out.

"I don't think they're good."

"Why?"

"They're mealy. Feel the outside, it's bumpy."

"And that means?"

The whole family was in the kitchen and he looked from her to the rest of us.

"Where are your apples? Here, take one." he said, handing us each another. We held them, unsure whether to eat or not eat.

"Go on, eat them." he said, taking a big bite from his. He watched us, so we ate them, and they weren't as bad as I thought. When we finished we threw the cores and went swimming.

Later that night we got terribly sick. We all threw up. The three of us came and stood, sickly, at the end of our parent's bed. My mother was furious, but my father said it wasn't the apples.

"They probably swallowed water." he said.

"They didn't all swallow water."

My father was asleep on his side and my mother got up,

took us to the bathroom, had us wash our mouths, and said sharply,

"No more apples- I don't care what he says. No more-"

Even after that though, my father stood by his conviction that is was not the apples that made us sick that night. He continued gathering them from the ground and put them in a fruit bowl in the kitchen. Some weeks he ate them. Other weeks they went brown. He collected some to prove a point, but eventually he too became sick of them, and the next season his attitude toward the trees changed.

First his interest in them waned. He stopped gathering the fruit and did not ask us to either. There is a telephone wire that runs from the corner of the roof, along the back, to a telephone pole on the right side of the house, that squirrels would use to access the trees. From the back patio we could hear them scratching along the roof and see them as they trapezed across the telephone wire, making it bounce and droop. At first, my father had no problem with the squirrels. They were a kind of vindication for our underuse, of letting the apples go to waste.

"At least they like the trees." he would say as he watched them scrabble to the top of the trees and throw down apples indiscriminately. The squirrels, however, took one or two bites and threw the rest to a stinking pile of mush on the ground. That blatant disregard angered my father. Twice he became so livid from the abused trees that he plucked his own apples and threw it at the creatures hiding in the high branches. It became a taunting game. The wily creatures waited till he left, then they returned and threw more down. That would set him off again and he would throw more in the other direction. On and on it went.

His anger wasted away, and eventually he came to despise the trees by association. The other problem was yellowjackets. The large pile of sweet, rotting fruit attracted yellowjackets, who revolved around the trunks all day, and built homes in the ground. We sprayed them with poison, but they were resilient and grew in number. Eventually we just stayed away.

To my father, the apple trees were more than a minor distress. They symbolized some loss and corruption of his dominion. A spoiling he could not easily correct. And my mother, who generally liked the trees, would also make comments about their obstruction which did not help the matter; how the unpruned limbs, which grew wilder and leafier, now blocked the view of the water from the house. I don't think she meant her words to influence my father the way they eventually did. She only wanted them trimmed.

So my father went from loving the apple trees, protecting them, idolizing them, to wanting them done away with. They were fine as they were. But it is amazing how a seed of a suggestion can grow to something unthinkable. My mother knew my father's tendency to brashness, and she retracted her complaints about the trees. Instead she commented on how beautiful they were, the green they brought. Perhaps that was a stance too far in the other direction, because it had no effect on him. It seemed he no longer saw their beauty. I remember windy, fall days when he would come home from work and stand at the back porch watching the upheaval of wind and branches with such a stern look on his face. Like it was never really the trees he was leering at, but something else; a live and rooted grimness, shaking and mocking him for reasons we did not know. He would make many small, disenchanted observations about the trees while he watched.

"Look how they block the light coming through. Don't they?" or,

"They are too private, aren't they? They hide the house, wouldn't you say?"

But these were rhetorical questions, and no amount of arguing in their favor could make him see differently. It upset my mother that he had become so obsessed about them. She said it was because of his money that he had nothing else to worry about, so he fretted about trifles and could not see past it. She tried what she could to ameliorate his obsession. Every other week from late summer into fall, whenever she would rise early to water the plants in the back patio, she would bring with her two white plastic bags; one for collecting good apples, the other for rotten. She threw the rotten ones, and took the other bag, cinched it closed and left it on the kitchen counter next to my father's lunch so he could take it to work. She wanted it to look like someone cared again. Like the trees weren't abandoned.

For a while the tactic seemed to work. He took the bags to work and brought them back with eaten cores. He said less and less about the trees, which was a good sign we thought.

One day he came home late, and the rest of us were at the table eating apple pie. He had an unhappy look on his face. He put his bag down in the empty seat, but did not sit down. He stood over the table. His face was dim outside of the table light. He loosened the tie around his neck, breathed heavily, and leaned forward and put his hands on the back of the chair.

"So, what are you eating?"

My mother spoke up.

"Apple pie. Corey brought it over."

"Corey our neighbor?"

"Yes, Corey our neighbor."

"Why'd he do that?"

She shrugged. "He was being nice. He brought over extra."

My father pulled the sticky plate from the middle of the table and rotated it slightly in front of him. There was a knife in the middle he cut a slice with.

"You want a slice?" my mother said. She got up to get him a plate.

"You didn't think I would want one?" he said.

"What do you mean? I didn't know when you were coming home, that's all. We left some you can see."

She put the slice he cut on the plate. He shook his head and pushed the plate away.

"Come on." she said, "You don't want a slice? There's some for you."

"No." he said.

"Are you sure?"

"I don't want one."

He got up and left the kitchen. When he returned he said to my mother.

"Why couldn't you make it?"

"The pie?" she asked.

"What else would I be talking about? Yes. We have apples. We have more than we know what to do with, just being wasted. Good for nothing."

She turned away from him. "I don't want to get on this again.", then she turned back quickly. "And I don't waste them, so don't accuse me of that. You should know better- I put them in your lunch."

"All I'm saying is that I don't want us getting any more pie from him if we can make them ourselves." he said.

"That makes no sense." she said. "He was just being considerate. You're making it about something it's not."

"Be quiet." he said, moving closer to her as she picked up the plates and forks.

"Stop it." she said, "I'm trying to clean."

"Yeah, I bet." he said. "Clean clean clean. Clean some more. That's all that gets done around here."

She said nothing

"You should make them clean for once." he said, referring to us.

He turned to me.

"Constance, you can make a pie, can't you?"

"No." I said.

He left again, this time to the back patio. He turned on the back lights and watched the trees gloomily in the dark. I heard my mother mumbling to herself. "What's he doing out there?"

When she had loaded the dishes from the sink, she followed him and said "What are you doing, Ed?"

"Leave me alone."

She had a moist dish towel in her left hand.

"Why are you making something out of nothing. What is it? What is your fixation with these trees? They're fine, completely fine. We don't need to make pies from them. Ed? Do you hear me? Are you listening? We're not comparing ourselves to Corey. He can make-"

"I don't want him to bring anything else over." he said, cutting her off.

"Fine. Fine. But we're not going to be bad neighbors. I just don't get what you're after. What are you upset with? I honestly don't know."

"Everything." he said. His voice was low.

"So it's not the trees."

"It is."

"You just said-"

"I know what I said. It's the trees, and a million other things." he said.

"What else? Are things ok at work?"

"Just let me be."

. . .

She left him, and we all quietly dispersed and went to our rooms. I remember the despicable mood of the house, the bleakness of the hallway stairs, the shards of light peeking out of the bottom of doors. The next day was Saturday, and through the morning the mood of the previous evening lingered about the house.

I looked in the kitchen for something to eat and saw the pie tin turned into the trash. My mother found me and my siblings and said we were going shopping with her that morning. It was obvious to us by the way she said it that this errand was a diversion more than anything. My father was up too, dressed in work clothes. Before we left he said,

"James, Constance. I'll need your help later." That was all he said.

We thought he meant the boat. He had recently bought a small dory in need of repair, and asked us before if we would help him, and we had said we would.

The morning errands ran into the afternoon. My mother's wisdom told her to keep us away as long as we reasonably could, so my father had time to himself. When we finally returned I remember hearing a loud, zinging sound as we pulled into the driveway. My mother heard it too and came fast to a stop, getting out before us, and running through the house to see what it was. There was a panic in her face, in her whole manner. She left the front door open and we followed behind, catching the first cries of her cursing.

"Damn it, damn it!" She looked back to us, then back to the place where the noise came from. "Damn it, oh no, damn it." she repeated compulsively. My mother rarely cursed, which made the expletive all the more alarming. By the time we caught up to her we could see what she saw, the middle apple tree tottering, my father squatted at the base, the chainsaw ringing and squealing, sending up a cloud of dust.

The back door was jammed by the work he was doing.

We went back around and watched, with fascination and horror. My mother put her hand over her mouth. He saw us when we came around, and let the chainsaw idle on the ground of pulp. He had a white dust mask over his mouth and leather work gloves. The tree was all over him, covering his forearms.

"Damn it, Ed, what are you doing!"

"Get back." he said, shooing her off.

She stepped closer. The first tree was already down, the trunk severed from the base and attached only by a strip of bark. The wood on the inside was a pale ash color, the branches and blooms were sprawled across the grass, and my father stood there, in the middle of all the fallings and dismemberment, the pale dust spattered on his pant legs and shoes. He started the saw again, but my mother did not move. She kept calling, but the noise of the machinery drowned her out. He cut another chip away, and then the middle tree, 15 ft high, tottered more and expunged a thick, snapping sound from the center of its trunk. It did not fall, but it was close. Again, my mother stepped closer, dangerously close. My father looked at her furiously, pulling his mask down. The saw was idling in his grip.

"James! Pull her away!"

My brother tried to, but she was obstinate and shook him off. My father put the saw down and came and pulled her roughly out of the way. When he took the saw up she started pleading again.

"Edgar! Stop. Stop, don't do it. Oh come on, don't! You love those trees!"

The more she yelled the more her anger and bewilderment became plaintive and sad. The three of us watched all of this unfold and none of us said anything.

"Stop it! You love those trees. Ed! Ed!" she cried, her exasperation turning to tears.

It was true what she said, but if any of those words

reached my father, it did not matter, and it did not show. He raised the saw, deaf in the labor of its scream and cut it through, the great mass bending gravely, surily down with a splintering crash.

Then there was silence; even the saw died. My mother, spent of her energy and unheard, went inside with Adley. I stayed outside with James. Both of us stood at the edge of the branches, waiting for my father's orders. This is what he requested our help with. Now we understood. My father stepped slowly between the felled branches, taking account of the damage. There was only one tree standing of the three, and it was the smallest one, a sapling compared to the other two. Muteness cloaked my father's demeanor, so absorbed he was in his plan. He did not look relieved by what he had done, he did not look upon it with any appearance of accomplishment. It was like putting down an animal, regrettable and sad.

When the saw was laid aside and he had stepped away from what he'd done, we could see he was not himself. He was sluggish; he would take one step, then stop and look around, like he had lost directions. He would take a glove from his back pocket, put it on, then take it off. His face told nothing; sometimes it formed a frown, and other times it formed a smirk. He appeared to be caught between some state of stupefaction and admiration, like his judgement of the whole was still catching up to his physical actions, and the easy, impulsive weightlessness of a moment was settling suddenly, acquiring gravity.

"What can we do?" I asked at last.

He looked up at my question as if seeing me there for the first time. He looked down at the tree, then up at me.

"Grab another pair of branch cutters from the outbuilding and cut the small branches."

James came with me. We went at the task for two hours. It was tedious and slow. Many of the branches were too thin for cutting, so we let them be. My father came behind us, complementing our work with his chainsaw, trimming the smaller limbs. After three hours, the sun was setting and we were tired. James and I left the cutters on the pile of branches. My father took his saw to the outbuilding. Before we left I took three apples from the ground and pitched them as far as I could into the creek. It had been years since I picked them. They were smaller than I recalled, shrunk like piths.

The next day we continued our work with the first tree. We had nearly lopped it down to a single naked trunk. We chopped the branches smaller and smaller, then dragged them away on a tarp to a pile of brush we had made beside the outbuilding. James and I loaded the tarp and heaved the mass of it across the yard, each of us taking a corner. We had to stop often for James, who would lose strength in his grip. At the stumps, we set aside the long heavy branches, which my father later sent through a chipper, and the trunk which he later cut into logs and firewood. For the time being, we loaded them to a wheelbarrow and stacked them next to the same pile of brush beside the outbuilding.

The second tree lay there untouched. For a week we did not work on it. It rained everyday in between, and two days into the rain my father told me to lay tarps over the log pile and the second tree to keep them dry. This time I got Adley to help me. The pile we left uncovered was already soggy and rotting. The leaves were lichen and black-brown colored and they dripped with a kind of desolate drip; the drip of leaning shovels, of rain soured tools, moldering spades. The branches were sturdy though. They retained their strength. I stepped on the pile and put my full weight down, feeling the springy resilience of the thatchwork. Then we went to the other. I remember the cold, mud-sodden ground as we walked across it, and how funereal it felt to lift the blue threadbare tarp over the snagging limbs, like we were covering a corpse.

We were not done yet. The work rambled on. When the chipper came, it was James and I again working together. We stood back and watched more that we helped. We all took a special pleasure feeding wood into the machine and watching the violent gorging of the chipper, the deep bellied squelching, the shaking and cavorting, as it took all things into itself and turned it to the clean, fragrant pyramid of wood chips amassing. It was enjoyable to watch. The ground was tamped with our boot marks going back and forth. We killed the grass there, and we killed the grass where the stumps were. When the second tree was trimmed of its branches, the ground underneath was pale and lifeless.

On the first tree, every branch passed through the chipper unbothered except one. It was a branch with a large knot in the middle that looked like a swollen eye. Back and forth my father shoved it into the grinding teeth, but the machine resisted, it spat it out, and even ceased. Onward he tried. The knot's physical stubbornness spurned him along. Instead of passing it over he invested all his frustration into that one length of wood. Finally he gave up.

"We have to find another way to get rid of this. You and James figure it out. I don't want to cut it now." He went inside for a break. While he did, we lifted the branch which was gnarled up to the knot point, and I said to James "Let's dump it in the water." So we did. We carried it to the shore then rolled it down to the water, and pushed it out. It floated slowly into the creek. We watched it float uneventfully for a few minutes, then we rejoined our father who had started the chipper again and was feeding away.

The second day we put the second tree through. We

added logs from the second tree to the first pile, and it was then, when the space was finally clear of impediments and litter, that we saw the place for what it was. It was barren. The stumps were stark. No more shade. No more rustle. No more blooms. Even years after the sawdust was swept clean of the area, there was an unhappy light cast on that plot with the one rueful tree remaining. I'm not sure why he left the last tree, except that it was the smallest of the three, and perhaps he felt guilt from the other two. But the last tree grew at a slant, thickening in trunk, squatly, with mottled bark. It's sole virtue was that it stood. Who could say what its fruits were like? For it was left untended, bound to the kind of ugliness that comes with the same.

And still the work was not finished. After we chipped the branches, it was weeks before we split the logs. The progress depended on my father, who vacillated between days of intense industriousness and debilitating lethargy. He commuted long hours to work many days during that time, and he came back exhausted. Yet, he looked forward to the weekends when he could leave his suits in the closet and put his hands to work around the house. Usually we worked on Sundays, a day that felt dismal as long as I can remember.

The logs were dry on the Sunday we chopped them. Again, Adley excused herself from helping, so James and I were left with my father. My mother did not mind it that way; she preferred Adley working inside more than James and myself, even if she would not admit it if you asked.

My father found an old tire in the outbuilding and set it down a distance from the wood, and we took turns carrying logs from the stacked area and standing them in the middle of the tire so they did not tip over. Our little assembly line of lifting, setting, chopping was running smoothly until James began dropping the logs before he placed them. It began to irritate my father, whose back was turned to us when he chopped. He would hear the log hit the ground. Again and again it happened.

"Come on James. What's the matter? You can hold it, come on, you're slowing us down."

But it continued. My father put the ax down and watched as James took a log from the pile and made it all the way to the tire and dropped it in. He made it that time, but it looked like it took all his strength. He looked in pain. My father didn't notice.

"See," he said. "it's not that hard. Your sister's been doing it without complaint."

The next log James took he brought all the way to the tire again. But again he looked depleted. As my father was chopping I said to James "Are you ok?" He neither shook his head nor nodded, but kept on with what we were doing.

After my father split the log I brought, he waited as I removed the split pieces. He stood broad legged; the ax head reposing on the ground and his right hand gripped on the upper handle, ready to raise it for the next. However, James dropped his log as soon as he took it in his arms. He tried again, but it lifted only a foot and fell. A third time he dropped it. My father looked at us together, then at James specifically.

"Are you using your arms only? You have to use your legs. You're not using your legs."

James looked down at the ground and I could see his eyes were red. My father could see it too and said,

"That won't help. Now come on, we're all waiting."

"I've got one." I said. I carried mine over and stood it in the tire.

"Wait, take that out." my father said. "Your brother needs to do this."

I spoke up for James.

"He can't." I said.

"He can." my father said. He looked at me, then at his son. "He's just choosing not to." He wiped his face with a rag and ran his fingers through his hair, a move he made when he was impatient.

"Try a smaller one, James." he said.

My brother was frozen. My father went and took a smaller log from the pile and gave it to James and said,

"Try this." but the boy dropped it after a three feet. His arms shook with effort, but they gave. James looked up, helpless, confused by his very weakness.

"Enough of this." my father said. He rolled his sleeve, went to his son, and grabbed the boy's bicep with his hand.

"You want to be strong? he said. "Do you want to be strong?"

"I don't care." James said, with defiance.

My father took his arm off.

"Then you won't be. You won't be strong, and you'll see how that works out for you. And your sister will help me instead. We've got work to do. Constance, let's keep going. But don't go inside, James."

I obeyed my father and brought him logs, and he chopped, and James stood by not moving, not doing anything but looking stiff and provoked, and shamefully weak. I did not know what to do. I pitied him, though at the time I did not understand what was happening. None of us did.

We finished at nightfall, in silence. The wood was split. Sunday sadness waded through the air, the creek, the productive stack of firewood, the resting hilt of the ax, the tire. James did not follow when we left for the house. I looked back and he was still standing there, thin as a scarecrow.

"Get your brother." my father told me.

I went back to get him.

"James-" I whispered, "Come on."

I took his wrist and he came along, like all he needed was a touch and a pull. He went to his room and I went to mine. I came out when dinner was ready and heard my parents speaking about us in the kitchen.

"He couldn't lift anything today." my father said.

"Maybe it's not his fault." my mother said.

"In what way?"

"I don't know. If there's something the matter-"

"The matter? That can't be it because he was lifting fine for a while. He just didn't want to be out there, so he became stubborn. I saw it in his face."

"I doubt that." she said. "He's not a stubborn person, Ed."

"He was today."

There was a pause in their conversation and I came down a few more steps, quiet not to interrupt.

"Constance helped though." he said.

"You made her carry all that?"

"She can carry it. She has strength for the two of them."

He laughed at himself a bit.

"Oh stop." she said.

"What?" he said, in the humored tone.

"Don't ever say that around her."

When dinner was called I slunk back up the stairs to my room and thought about what they said. What my father meant by 'strength for two', why my mother got mad. I was thinking of my brother too. Adley was the only one to come to dinner when it was called. Later I came down, but I ate little because I was still ruminating on what was said, and had no appetite. It took me a long time to finish the meal. I sat at table, opened my mouth and chewed, but my mind was elsewhere, denouncing things like lifting and carrying, and logs and strength.

18

As some reward for our help with the trees, my father gave us permission to use the little boat he'd bought recently, a dory that sat in the outbuilding waiting for someone to take it out. We were told not to take it far and to wear life vests, but beyond that we were free. It was the first time we'd gone boating unsupervised.

The boat was 10 feet long and built of wood. It was sturdy, but not bulky; wider than a canoe and only a bit heavier. My father bought it months before from a neighbor down the street who had it sitting in his garage for a while. When he brought it home we spent an hour pulling handfuls of broken leaves from the stern. The oars were in good condition. So were the benches. It was painted white originally, but the color had faded with age and was more or less speckled grey by the time we acquired it. In the time since we'd bought it my father had taken it out a handful of times. He took it just around our cove to test its integrity before he let any of us use it, and instead of the oars, he used a small 35 horsepower Evinrude engine that clamped to the back. It was a loud little motor you could hear chopping from a long way's off.

It was a day in fall when we decided to take the boat on a maiden voyage. It was chilly outside and some of the leaves were already yellow. A light drizzle spattered across an overcast afternoon. We were stir crazy which prompted us wanting to go out.

"In this?" my father said, looking doubtfully at the sky. "Not the best day. Why not try tomorrow?"

"We won't go far." I said.

He shifted between what he was reading and my request, then he finally said,

"Alright, that's fine. Take James and Adley. You'll need their help bringing the boat down. The jackets and oars are inside. Remember, not far, and keep your vests on." I said thanks, and went to fetch the other two.

The three of us went to the outbuilding and each took a grip of the dory, lifting it hull-up. I took the prow and the others took the back. It wasn't as heavy as we thought. As we got going the rain started coming down harder. Adley suddenly halted, rested her side on the ground and said "I don't know if I want to go."

"Come on." I said, "We won't go far." Reluctantly she took up her side again and we stammered along a few more steps. James dropped his side next, quite suddenly, just like he had the logs. We waited for him to pick it up and rain increased again. The day was reminiscent of the day, later on, when I took them out in the middle of the storm. The harder it rained the more I insisted we should go, but the other two did not share that sentiment. When we were still a ways from shore James dropped his side again and Adley, receiving the brunt of the fall, dropped hers too and said

"James! Why'd you drop it again? That hurt."

"I'm sorry." he said. "I wasn't trying to."

"I don't want to go." she said. She walked off and said, "Another time. Good luck."

James looked at me dolefully as she walked away, and the burden came to us.

"I'm no help here, Constance. Sorry," he said, "I'm going in too."

I was still holding my end. I had not dropped it, and I kept going, gritting my teeth, dragging the dory foot by foot over the slick grass. My head and body were soaked, as were my shoes and shoulders. The rain was cold and uncomfortable. All I could hear was the sound it made across the creek, upon my jacket, upon the gutters, upon the ground. Then I heard the door open from the house and my mother yell

"Constance, come in!"

I waited there; halted, wet, angry, the boat in my grip. Wanting to drop it, but also not wanting to drop it just yet.

"Come in!" she yelled again. Then, upon her words the downpour came. It came with a whoosh; definitive, loud, and obstinate. It came thundering into the grass, stripping my grip away. I finally let go and dropped the boat right there in the middle of the yard. I ran to the side porch and took off my sopping clothes, and wrung my hair at the ends, and stared out vacantly into the cold haze of rain pounding the earth. As I stood in one place, watching the ground steam, I felt my heartbeat slow and a chill move down my spine. The porch door was cracked, and the warmth from inside touched my heels. Gutters flushed overhead; the smell of clay in the yard, and brine from the creek, and the sourness of the wood porch each wafted to my nose.

Nothing moved. Nothing moved at all. Each element in the scene left some eminent impression in my mind; at once dismal and irresistible. The way things caught in a downpour look almost paralyzed, and compact, and sleeping. The outbuilding, the pen, the dragged boat, the mark in the grass made by the dragged boat, all of it swallowed and timeless. And I remember I was happy to stand there. I was not upset looking out, with nothing in my hands.

For weeks the boat remained in the yard where we left it. The longer it remained where it was, the more it became an anomaly, a capsule outside of our perception. It became a fixture of the landscape, and no one was much motivated to move it except the actual landscapers who my father hired, who came once a month to cut the grass. They left the grass high around the boat, perhaps because they did not want their mowers getting that close, but the higher it grew the more it looked abandoned. We started school again, and there was less time to go out. Also, around that time my father bought another boat; a brand new powerboat that made the dory look like an ancient vessel. He kept the new boat on our pier and parked its trailer next to the outbuilding.

The one reason we did not forget about the dory entirely was because it was an eyesore. One day my mother and I decided to move it. It was after school, before my father was home. My mother's hair was tied up in a bandana from working around the house all day, and I knew the dory was on her list because she'd mentioned it days before. My mother's not a big woman, but she's the kind of woman that puts her whole self into a task once she commits to it. When we came to the boat there was a large yellow jacket swerving through the grass around it. When it passed we squatted from the bottom of one side and lifted the boat over onto its hull. It groaned over, and as soon as it was turned we saw more hornets emerging from under one of the benches. We ran off, clearing the space as they swarmed the air around us.

James and Adley came out to watch the commotion and my mother told them to go back, but they did not listen.

"Constance, grab the wasp killer under the kitchen cabinet." she told me, keeping her eyes on the hive. I went and got it and gave it to her. She shook it vigorously and armed it in front of her, finger on the trigger, giving it two test sprays and stealthing her way to the boat.

"I don't see the hive." she said. "They're coming from everywhere."

"I'll find it." James said, coming down.

My mother turned to me.

"Constance, stop him. I'm not trying to play any games right now." She was looking up and down, dodging, ducking. She leaned over the side of the boat and sprayed blindly into the middle bench, filling the air with a plume of poison. She retreated, coughing into the crook of her elbow. Then a hornet stung her on the side of her ribs. She threw the can down and grabbed her side, wincing. James dodged around me, took the can of spray from the ground, and stormed the boat with one outlandish stream of spray, swiping the can this way and that, until it formed a cloud about him and every drop of aerosol was gone. The hornets, you can imagine, were angrier than ever and we weren't even sure we had killed one. Then James was stung. The hornet stung him on the knuckle and he threw the can down like my mother. We retreated farther and farther from the boat. Finally we counted our losses and went inside.

When my father came home, he found us on the couches huddled together, my mother and brother nursing their sore sports, Adley and I keeping them company. Each of them had a big red welt where they had been stung.

"What happened?" he asked.

"They got stung." I said.

"Stung by what? Where?"

"We tried to move the little boat, but there was a hive inside."

"What did you use?"

I pointed to the kitchen counter where the empty can was. He picked it up and put it down.

"That's for wasps and bees. That won't cut it for yellow jackets, especially not the ones I've seen around here. You probably didn't hit the hive either if it was under a bench."

He looked at us pitifully.

"I'll try and take care of it." he said.

Before dinner he walked out, dressed in two pairs of work jeans, two long sleeves, a winter jacket, a hockey helmet with mask, and leather gloves. He was swinging a blue crowbar at his side. We watched from the porch as he got inside the boat in the tall grass and scraped under the bench with the crowbar. The boat was far from the porch, and he was small from a distance, but you could tell he was working hard at it. The boat rocked back and forth. Randomly his arm swung around his face, keeping hornets away. Finally he reached to the bottom of the boat, lifted out a hive the size of a cantaloupe and threw it in the grass, then got out and stomped it with his foot and broke it one more time with the crowbar. When he was done he turned to us, who were standing on the porch, and he held up the mangled hive, victorious, and we clapped and cheered for our exterminator.

We were all in good humor that night at dinner, each one tickled at another's expense. I laughed at my mother and brother holding their stung spots, and at my father who was still dressed in his amateur pesticide getup, with his hair a mess from the helmet, and a childish look of accomplishment on his face. My mother laughed from relief. My father laughed from his own dramatic recounting; how the hornets came this way and that, here and here, and how he warded them off bravely. And Adley was perhaps the most humored of all of us, having watched everything unfold with a calm demeanor, at a perfect remove from the foolishness that was the hallmark of her family.

19

The first trip I made on the hornetless dory was with James. After we had fitted the oars and fastened our life jackets, my father and Adley helped us carry it down to the water's edge and shove us off.

"Watch out for other boats." my father said. "And don't go too far, you've only got oars."

We sat facing them as they pushed us off the dry beach into the water. We drifted for the length of the pier before we got a proper hold of the oars and dipped them to the water and pulled them a few times in unison. Even when we did they were not perfectly in sync, and one of us usually pulled the boat too much to one side and had to readjust. We set our sight on the other side of Weems. There were no other boats in sight. When we reached the middle of the channel we took our shoes off and pressed our feet to the sturdy wood of the hull, getting our legs into the work. Then we moved our feet from the ground to the side of the back bench for extra leverage, and continued zagging our way cumbersomely across. We did not discuss where we would go so much as we pointed and nodded, and pulled. Our sole speaking was the rhythm of the oars.

"Now me." I said.

"Now me." he said.

"Now me."

And so on, until we righted ourselves.

When we reached the other side we saw the opening to a smaller creek, indiscernible expect from proximity. We entered the creek and raised our oars out of the water momentarily, to drift inward. The current, though gentle on the main creek, was barely noticeable there. The farther we went, the easier we glided, moving less and less by effort and more by momentum. The water changed as we pursued it, becoming stiller and blacker. There was a rich glassiness to the surface of the water. It was autumn at the time, and the sky, spotted with wisps of white cloud, was utterly blue, and shone in the reflection of the creek.

There were woods on one side of the creek, marsh on the other. The woods were bare and golden; many leaves had fallen to the ground already. Through the sparsity of foliage, atop a hill where the woods climbed, we saw a clearing in the distance where a field or a farm began. In the same direction we saw chimney smoke rising in a high column, and the building where it came from.

The marsh on the other side of the boat was a thick bank of green and brown grass. We could not see much beyond it. The high, verdant sawgrass was soughing on the breeze. As we passed along, we could see inside the marsh hedges, where there were pools of standing water, shallow trails of root, mud, detritus; little, inaccessible paths winding on and on, as far as the eye could see in some directions. Far in the distance, over the tops of grass, the marsh bordered the woods and formed a cove.

Ahead of us on the wooded bank was a large red maple hanging over the creek, with heavy limbs and a load of leaves still left on its branches, yellow and brown bunches, fiery fingertips dangling delicately over the water. We went toward it. I placed my oar in the water and made the slightest stroke after it, creating a tiny whirlpool that followed in our wake and dispersed gradually into the still water. The water was weightless. We mushed gently into the bank, resting a moment under the arbors of the maple. Looking up we could see into the dappled movement of leaf and branch and trunk; light shapes and shadow strobed brightly over the dark wood and water.

James pulled a few leaves from branches and some from the surface of the water, pinching their stems together in a small bouquet. I scooped silt and mud from the creek bed with my oar and let it plop back. It was black and brown marbled, cold to the touch, smelly like eggs, and mixed with black rotting twigs and branches. I could smell the chimney smoke faintly, like it had wandered from its source and found us there - it gave the scene a sweetness, a coziness I have never forgotten. Past the tree the creek dried up and became marsh and mud, so we turned back. James put his leaves on the foremost bench, raised his oar, and together we rowed out, out of the shade, out of the black, sleepy water, into Weems where the water was ruffled and shining.

The wind was at our backs on our return. Now and then one of us turned our shoulder to gauge our distance, but otherwise we were two oxen to a yoke; our heads steady as we warmed into our strokes. The harmony of pulls, the cluck of the water beneath us, the feet pushing off the back bench, held off the bottom where a cold layer of water had seeped into the old craft.

Between us was the pleasure of our going. A smile surfaced us as we glanced at one another in our effort. The boat carried the tonic of competition and cooperation equally, as if the return was a race too, a harmonized race, with each of us depending on the other to keep straight. We broke in the last 20 yards, our composed exertion melting into perfect laughter. We spun our way onto shore, dizzy with relief, arms singing. Glad to be back.

20

We propped the boat temporarily against the side of the unused kayak rack. When the weather got colder we moved it inside the outbuilding, clearing space so that it would fit against the back wall once we brought it through the side door. The outbuilding, which my father dubbed 'the den' was a cross between a shack and a barn. It had the size and character of a barn, including an upper attic, unused horse stalls and unevenly joined wooden walls that let in light and creaked at the slightest weight set against it. When the wind came through or logs were stacked against it, it sounded as if the foundation might give- but in all its years, in so many weathers- it stood.

Its being underused gave it the additional feeling of a shack. It was disorganized and the air was close. At times it was a rank smelling place, and other times it smelled sweet, of rope, and pounded dirt and feathers. It also smelled of dried gas, engine degreaser, and mildew. What you smelled depended on the day. For a long time it was unlit and we cleared space by daylight, although the windows were filthy and covered in a thick grime that barred the sun from flowing generously in. It was a dank, dim place otherwise;

the only shelter for the dory. If the boat stayed outside it would have rotted through and become useless.

There were two big doors in the front of the outbuilding, but they had been shut and chained for a long time. We only ever used the side door, which did not close fully, but was kept shut by kicking the bottom edge until it wedged firmly into the ground. Just inside the door was a blackened welcome mat, which instead of preventing the trail of dust inside seemed to spread it. At the entrance were piles of tools, empty pails, hammers, pliers, shears, stooks, bundles of drop cloth, and cratefuls of spray chemicals- all of which covered the ground in no discernable order. Only my father could find what he was looking for, but he himself rarely went in there, and I believe the disarray kept him out too.

I tried to move the boat into the outbuilding with James one afternoon when my father was still at work. The day was beautiful and warm, the warmest of the fall. Leaves had blown into the yard and we crunched through them to the outbuilding. Adley came and helped when James got tired. We turned the boat on its side and tried to slide it along the ground through the doorway, but it would not fit, it was too tight. We tried forcing it, and we got it halfway through only, and each time we pushed it, we could feel the stress in the joints. It sounded like either the boat or the building would break, so the only option left was to try the main doors.

I went inside and asked my mother for the key to the chain shackling the big doors- a small brown copper key that fit right away when I tried it. I uncoiled the chain and threw it on the ground behind me, and took both door handles and yanked backward. The doors gave just a few feet then jammed under the ground. James and Adley came and tried with me. I put my hands at the bottom of the door, James above mine, and Adley above his. I counted "One, two, three."

and we pulled with all our strength, but got nowhere. The jam was too much; the other twin door was the same.

"Get me that trowel inside, James." I said. He got it for me and I began to carve away the ground under the doors so that we could pull them further. My siblings found their own misfit tools and joined the effort. James scraped up the earth with a crowbar, and Adley found a hatchet. For nearly an hour we loosened dirt, chipping away at the mound keeping our boat interred, and finally we drove the doors far enough back that we could carry the boat through. For the first time we saw the noonday light illuminating the dormant space. A creature of some kind- James thought a feral cat, sprang from the back and fled out of an unseen hole in the building.

By the time we had opened the doors, we were exhausted and almost forgot to lift the boat to the back. We cleared a path through the rubbled tools and laid it down, putting all the equipment inside. I was impressed by our effort, impressed that we had opened those doors without my father. When we were done, James and Adley left and I stayed inside exploring the space and neatening the piles of dirty zip lock bags filled with screws, ratchet heads, washers. You could never tell what was in what because the bags were cloudy and unmarked. But also I savored the feat of opening the big doors, and that led me from task to another. I anticipated my father's reaction when he came home. I wanted him to see the transformation.

Pretty soon I brought a short stack of wood inside and laid it on a bed of old bleach-blue tarp. What did we do with so much tarp? There were shreds of it everywhere, patches of it covering everything. I dropped the maul and ax beside the wood and rested. It made me glad to put things in order, even in a small way. They were the kinds of tasks that pull you in, that insist you finish them all the way. My mother came to check on things, observing the little project of restoration I had begun.

"Looks good. Don't get carried away though." she said.

My last task were the windows, which needed to be opened and dusted. I found a rag and bucket, and carried it to the side of the main house and filled it with freezing water from the squeaky ground faucet. My spirits were high and the weight of the cold water in my grip was like the assurance of a job well done, a kind of hope, the ablution of a rancor and weariness in our property and place, not exclusively material in its form, but expressly so, seen in the things that decayed and needed attention; the smeared windows, the dissolution and dankness of the outbuilding.

Unfortunately some of my zeal was eclipsed by a mistake I made cleaning the first window. I unfastened the hinge holding it down, but it would not budge. It was rigid and rickety. As I pulled it made a tense splintery sound. Suddenly it gave. The bottom edge of the window detached from its encrustment and shot up, hitting the top of the frame hard and causing four out of the six glass panes to pop out and shatter on the floor. I started sweeping the large shards about my feet into a pile with my sneaker. Just then my father came in. I looked up, red with guilt.

"What's going on?" he said, looking around.

I saw him backlit against the light of day, his outline shadowed between the two big doors, a briefcase in his hand. I suddenly felt embarrassed for the whole attempt to improve the space.

"I was cleaning, but I broke the window."

He came closer, seeing where I had moved things. He also saw the glass at my feet. With a broom nearby he swept around me and said "Stay still." Putting the broom aside he grabbed the window and tested it, sliding it up and down.

"It was jammed." I said.

"It's no problem." he said, which was a relief to hear.

He looked around again.

"Who helped you?" he asked, emptying glass to a

trash can.

"The other two." I said.

"The boat didn't fit through the side?"

"We couldn't get it when we tried."

He walked to the entrance where the baggies were placed on the ground, and riffled through them.

"Grab me a piece of tarp." he said. "From over there." pointing without looking. I went in search of a good piece and found a silver, lightly used one outside by the woodstacks.

Outside, through the giant, brooding doors and cavernous space I noticed how even with the doors opened, the building retained some darkness to it. In the yard a flock of blackbirds descended and began pecking the ground, flurrying up and down. I remember standing there with the tarp tucked under my arm watching them when my father called again. He had four nails dangling between his fingers like cigarettes. In his other hand was a box cutter.

He wore a pair of orange-leather wingtips that began to dust around the heel. He asked me for a stool to stand on, which I got as well. Before he climbed it, he unwrapped the tarp and cut the proportions of the window. Then, putting the nails in the front pocket of his dress shirt, he tossed the boxcutter on the ground, took a hammer and told me to keep my hands on the stool, to steady it. Still it was precarious; his feet filled the width of the stool.

Thock, thock, thock.

I watched his wingtips as he hammered away, the way the leather shifted and poked as he kept his balance. He dismounted and hammered the final two nails so that the silver tarp was taught over the open window.

The temporary fix became the permanent solution. Afterwards I never went to the outbuilding without seeing the patched window and thinking back on the time when I tried to put the place in order and it fell at my feet.

21

It was early November of my junior year of high school when we heard the news about James. One Friday after lunch, before I took my seat in English class, my teacher approached me and said,

"Your mother will be here in 20 minutes. You're going home early today."

"Do you know what for?"

She shrugged.

"She came by earlier and said she was in for a meeting at the health center."

I returned to my seat, speculating what she meant, but I had no idea. At 20 minutes I packed my bag and left. My mother was standing outside the door. She looked me over, brushed my hair to the side in a half concerned, rough sort of way.

"What's going on?" I said.

"Come on." she said, not answering me to my face, but walking quickly down the hall, her purse jostling at her side. It alarmed me, the whole thing; the secrecy, and her manner. She was dressed well that day, her hair done, her face made up with lipstick on.

"What's going on?" I asked again, trying to keep up with her. Outside the health center she looked back at me and said,

"Just come in."

I sat in the chairs by reception and heard her at the desk say my brother's full name. Her tone was very business-like. She was anxious I could tell, everything about her said it. As the receptionist prepared something, my mother left the counter, adjusting her skirt higher on her waist, and brought her purse and placed it beside me in my chair.

"Hold this." she said, in the same business-like tone. Then she returned to the desk, signed a few papers, and joined where I was sitting. She kept her hands between her thighs, and every minute adjusted her shirt or scratched the middle of her scalp with her finger.

The door to the main hall opened, and Mrs. Finely, one of the two nurses who worked at the school, was there waiting with my brother. She was an old woman with short, white hair and a gentle smile. We were sitting right by. My mother rose and followed them. Midway through the doorframe she looked back at me and said,

"Just stay put Constance."

After a half hour they came out, my mother's arm around my brother's shoulder. I rose and gave my mother her purse and she took it from me without a word, neither rudely or kindly, just quickly, like she was thinking ahead already, a new preoccupation in her mind. She held James's backpack as we left, slinging it over her shoulder, and moving into the hall. In the hallway James reached for his bag but she shook him off.

"I can carry my bag." he said.

"Not now, James." she said. "Let me carry it for you."

. . .

I was so confused. I looked aside at James, inquiring what all this meant. He shook his head, like he himself were confused, or like he didn't want to explain it out loud. In the car my mother put both bags on the floor of the passenger seat. James and I sat in the back. We picked up Adley from middle school on the way home. When my mother went to get her I took the moment to ask James what the matter was.

"Nothing." he muttered. By the sad way he said it I could tell it was not nothing.

He turned away from me. I looked him over to see if there was anything in his appearance that gave me a clue.

"Why were you in the health center?" I asked. "Did you do something? Did something happen?" He sighed frustratingly, either toward my questioning or the episode itself. I never saw him frustrated like that. Usually he was so mild mannered and sweet.

"James, what happened?" I prodded some more.

He turned around but did not answer me to my face. He kept his eyes on the floor of the car, and said,

"I was in weight training and couldn't lift."

"What do you mean?" I said. The weight was too heavy?"

He frowned.

"I don't know." he said. "Not really. The weights slid off and fell as I was putting them on, and Mr. Allen came and supervised me. It kept happening even though I was trying not to drop them. He gave me smaller weights, but-"

My mother and sister joined us and he cut off his story. He unbuckled and scooted next to me. Adley sat next to him on the other side. Her cheeks were red and her hair was in a braid. She looked distraught like the rest of us. My mother put Adley's bag up front with the others, and away we went in haste toward home, for reasons I did not know.

James's story was as murky as my mother's behavior. Adley and I sat at our separate windows upset and unconfided in. I almost felt guilty for what I did not know.

Through the rearview mirror I saw my mother checking on James every two minutes; her eyes would float into the mirror and land on him, and then away. James got sleepy on the way back and I knew that sleepiness overtook him whenever he dreaded something. It was not uncommon. He would doze during the middle of a family argument. He would start yawning and yawning, like his body was shutting down. Then his eyes would flutter and his mouth become idle.

Alternately, when my mother became anxious she put on a stern, hyperproductive persona. She got things done, she walked fast, she made lists, she put things in order. Anything to avoid the one glaring disorder, whatever it might be.

At a stop light she took a pad of paper from her purse, bit off the cap of a pen and began making a list, stabilizing the pad against the top of the steering wheel. As James began to fall asleep, his head nodded against my shoulder, but I was upset then, and shrugged it off and said,

"Get off, get off." So James in his half dozed state dragged his head to the other side and tried it on Adley's, but she did the same thing, "Get off James, get off." He bobbled back to me and I said "James," nudging him to stir him.

My mother said "Constance!" and looked at me provokingly in the rearview mirror.

"Let him keep his head there." she said through her teeth.

"Why?" I said.

"Because he's your brother. Let that be enough. He's tired, can't you understand?"

Her anger emerged plain as day. I felt it was not directed at me or at anyone in particular, but at the circumstance itself, and maybe herself. Then it was quiet for a while as James slept.

"It's probably nothing." my mother said aloud to herself. "Hopefully it's nothing."

"What happened?" Adley asked. My mother lowered her

voice. She looked back at us in the mirror, then at James, who was nodding away.

"He couldn't lift in weight training today. His teacher sent him to the health center because he dept dropping the weights. Light weights, really light weights they said." The thought of it, as she verbalized it, aroused another panic and she sighed heavily through her nose. Then she continued,

"I don't know what it could be. It could be he just got nervous, or isn't developing like he should, or needs to change his diet. I don't know. I don't know…"

She kept muttering some form of 'I don't know' under her breath, caught in the verbal treadmill of it. Adley had no response to this or any of it. My mother reached back blindly and gave Adley's leg a squeeze, an affectionate gesture. My sister was like a life-sized doll; sitting upright, awake, but completely unresponsive. Her eyes were staring out the window, lost in an impervious daydream.

I looked off too. It was a long drive to school, made longer by the day's events and the threat of the unknown. My mother's voice came on and off until we reached home; speaking, but not necessarily to us; speaking to speak, to shape her thoughts, as if that offered some improvement over the stiff quietness that consumed the car. As we turned down Teal St., our house visible in the distance, she said,

"Constance, Adley, you haven't noticed anything, have you? About your brother?

"No." Adley said.

"And you, Constance?"

I waited, unsure of what to share. There were things I had noticed before, some even years before, but I did not know what to say, or how, or if it mattered. Sensing my trepidation, she said,

"You can say, whatever it is, it's ok."

Before I spoke, James suddenly awoke, ground his hand to a fist and and began pounding the backseat cushion furiously. His eyes were open and his teeth gnashed. He moaned angrily,

"Ughhhh!"

"James!" my mother exclaimed, shocked and disturbed by his fit.

Three more times he pounded the seat and looked at her.

"There's nothing wrong with me! Stop talking about me."

"James…"

Pound, pound, pound.

"Stop saying there's something wrong with me! Get me out of here." he said. He unbuckled and tried reaching over Adley's lap to open the door while the car was still in motion.

"James!" my mother cried. She reached her arm back and I pushed it way. "Hold him!" The car swerved dangerously to the side, nearly knocking down our mailbox. Adley shrieked and began crying. She held the door closed and I pulled James back to his seat.

"Let go of me!" he yelled, "I don't want to be touched!"

But he finally relented and sat forward, tears standing in his eyes, anger swelling over every inch of him.

"We never said there was anything wrong with you." my mother said.

"I heard you the whole time. I wasn't sleeping."

My mother did not melt into compassion. Her sternness became sterner. She jammed the car in park and snatched her purse off the floor, her seat buckle smacking the window as she stormed away. We all got out of the car and went straight inside. James came out last, remorseful as ever I saw him. He ripped his bag haplessly out of the car and threw it in the doorway then went off by himself, where he could not be found.

22

Days of treading over-cautiously around James's situation cast a pallor over the home. Instead of talking, yelling, arguing, everyone retreated into their own unnatural privacy, emerging only briefly for meals. The days were short. Darkness fell at 5 and filled the evenings with itinerant waiting. Waiting for what? For sleep, for dinner, for some news about my brother's condition?

I'm not sure what my father suspected about the change in mood, if anything. A haze hung over him too, which was entirely his own, and independent of James. A scrim of distractions; work; house projects searching for boat parts; making calls. He had a legal pad he kept in his office that he used for planning everything from home repairs to our futures. I had seen once a list of our names written with a colon next to them, and an objective or word. Mine said 'Constance: career?' and my mother's said 'Mom: car registration, check oil, air, tires' That is how his mind roved, and why sometimes he said very little- his thoughts were churning disquietly inside. That week there was a letter addressed to him that came from Texas, and I wondered if it was from his brother because if it was, it was bound to cast him into a ponderous mood.

The agitation reached the dinner table inadvertently. Three times that week, by mistake, I spilled my glass of water at dinner. The first time was purely accidental; Adley bumped my glass. The second time I moved my placemat and the glass tipped. But the third time, even to me, the spilling had a portentous feeling to it. It was the clumsiest of the spills too, like my hand was rigged or mastered by some dark luck. The water slid out perfectly and fled to all corners of the table. My father looked at me incisively as he stepped off from the table and stopped the water with his paper towel.

"What's going on?" he said, looking at me but then scanning the others too, ending with James, who looked dour and distraught.

"Sorry." I said "It was an accident."

"It's not the first time it's happened this week. Is anything the matter?"

My mother disarmed the agitation by wiping down the table. When she was done we sat down and resume eating. My father, unfinished with the earlier question said to me,

"Constance, is everything ok?"

He looked suspicious, and my mother interjected sharply, "Edgar, quit it."

"Please," he said, cutting to her, "don't instruct me."

My mother's lips pursed. She tilted her chin back and breathed through her nostrils. She stood at the other end of the table and offered more food to anyone, moving plate by plate with spatula and pan. No one took anymore except herself, which was the more surprising because she rarely took seconds. This was a diversion though, and I reasoned to myself that she needed some movement, a prop to prevent her from the full divestment of the James news. She ate fastidiously and the rest of us sat there waiting for her to finish.

My father, setting his hands on the arms of his chair leaned back and interlocked his fingers in his lap, twiddling his thumbs, and looked around at us again until his eyes settled once more on James. There was a sneer on his lips.

"So," he said to his son, "are you going to help me move that trailer up besides the outbuilding? It's been sitting by the pier too long, and it's been rained on, and probably rusted by now. I haven't checked."

He looked away as he thought of it. Then he brought his eyes back to rest on his son.

"Yeah, I can help." James said.

My mother spoke up.

"They all can." she said. "Make it easier for you two."

My father looked up at her, dubious of her suggestion.

"He's my son, Avery. Thank you." he said.

"And?" she said.

"And we can handle it on our own."

"I'm just saying."

"Saying what?"

"Why not have the other two help also? You'll finish faster."

"How'd you get so insistent on this? Of all things. Half the time you don't say anything, the other half all you do is say what you want. Plus, I don't know about that, more hands are not always better." he said. He threw his napkin on the plate in front of him.

My mother shot her eyes at him directly.

"I'm not going to fight you on this one, Ed. You're being difficult, can't you see? I only want to help."

"And I thank you for that. But for this it'll only be James and I. I'll recruit the other two to help me clean the window wells, or bring in firewood, something. There's lots to do."

She thrust her fork down on the table, making a sharp metallic noise.

"No."

23

Before I went to bed that night, my mother approached me furtively and whispered in my ear,

"I don't want him bringing that trailer in. I can help you if you want. It's not that heavy is it?"

"I don't think so."

"Can you take Adley out on the little boat tomorrow? I have an appointment with the Doctor to see James in the afternoon, and when I come back I can help."

I said I would. The next day we followed the plan. Every hour felt marked with secrecy.

Adley and my father knew the least. My father rarely saw us in the mornings, since he was out before us. And Adley, by virtue of being the youngest always caught onto things late, whether jokes or scolds, secrets or known plans. She did not grovel for attention the way some youngest siblings do. My mother often commented how reasonable she was when she was being punished or corrected, because she never complained or whined. She just accepted it. Sometimes her very docility got her off the hook, being too appeasing to be punished.

She had no qualms helping me rig the boat though.

Everything was set to a single color that day: brown, and so many variations thereof. From the pale brown reed grass pushed low as we carried the boat through it. To the large wet stones quarried from the side of the house, that formed a rude receding wall between shore and yard; those blackish-brown and green-algaed, slippery loafs of rock. And the shore itself, which was no wider than a car's length. Our little landing where the creek lapped; with the cold, lumpy sand, gritted with roots and twigs and cone seeds.

When the boat was set, we pushed off onto Weems, and every stroke we took the brown palette unfurled before us. It was effusive, like the countenance of a face turning from shadow to light. The sun was faint behind a dense wall of clouds, and the light was meager. Yet the meagerness disclosed the pied colors, the spare and muted tones that were easily missed under brightness.

It was not often that Adley and I did anything together. But that day we coaxed our way down Weems, that brown, glistening alley of a creek. Our creek. We did not speak much, but then again, we did not need to, for we were *held* in muteness, afloat of it even- like it were some vital essence of the creek itself.

What was it about two oars making way on an empty creek that rewarded silence? The gravamen silence of nature, which is fervent and living? I have only ever approached an answer by being *in* it, and even after many years of boating, with motors and without, it remains elusive, if not imminent.

But I don't mean serenity, and I hardly mean beauty. This was a scene eschewing symmetries and bright colors and lushness and green.

We bore toward black creek on the other side, where I had gone with James before. In the cold steam of our movement the smell of the place arose again, a familiar smell. Woods, dead leaf, coldness. The rime of the river, algae, smoke. There was no distinct a creek smell or land smell; but like sounds, they bled into each other. They commingled.

We went leisurely and discursive, with no sudden commitments, except to make it to the other side eventually. As we rowed Adley would sometimes stop midstroke and wade her hand gently through the ice cold water, letting it comb through her fingers, then wipe it dry against her leg, and keep rowing. Soon we reached the peninsular bank where the entrance of the little creek, hidden as before, appeared to us at last, and we paddled through.

It was different this time around. Even the blackness of Black creek had lessened since last I was there. Though it was as still as I remembered, the water had brindled in color, and now I drew from its shallow bottom the cloudy plumes of bronze silt, and a fresh layer of dark yellow leaves that swept off the bank into the water. Our oars hung limp over the water as we drifted, and we used them to pry from our path large, half submerged branches that had fallen recently, jungling the way. The smaller ones we pulled with our hands and tossed aside. These were freezing and slimy and gangly-black, still holding the stems of dead leaves. They were quite beautiful I thought. Like the beauty of a swamp, of something wholly undisturbed. They made a soft gushing sound when we threw them back, like crab traps. Adley and I both did this and I think we got the same satisfaction out of it.

I hardly recognized the maple tree from before; the one that had spread a colored canopy over the water. The leaves on the tree were stripped, and the branches, bare as they were, were fine as a willows.

As we got closer to it, I heard the sound of leaves munching across the bank and looked up into the passing eyes of a man who looked close to my father's age, wearing a flap eared winter hat. The man's front lip glistened with a runny nose. He rubbed his face on the inside of his sleeve. In his right hand was a tall coil of chicken wire, in his left hand was a pair of wire cutters. We went slow enough to watch him. and when he saw us, he put his coil on the ground and came down a few steps to speak a word.

"You shouldn't be back here." he said, pointing with his cutters. "From here, along this back, all the way back, is mine."

"We're not coming on land." I said.

"That's fine." he said. "I'm just letting you know. There's not much back here but marsh thataway." He took up his wire. "I'm puttin up a fence as you can see." He started unrolling it, wiping his nose, trapping his foot on it from rolling back. "That's all." he said, his voice firm, like it needed no more explaining. We waited and watched as he cut a piece of wire, then took up the rest of the coil, walked ten steps up the hill, kicked the ground clean of extra leaves, and then thrust the cut piece of wire down into it and stomped it in hard so that it stood up. Then he wiggled it in further for sturdiness. Our boat was in the middle of the creek floating. The man went around his property until we lost sight of him behind the trees. We knew he was the owner of the land above, with the field and the smoking chimney, and whatever else was up there. Someone shouted for him from high up and he shouted back, the calls echoing down the bluff, through the woods and creek.

Up the hillside we could see more of his property, the barn facing the woods, and the field, which at that distance was pale colored and shorn of crops. Behind the barn, smoke drifted up, tall columns of it, thick and billowing at the base, dispersing as it rose into the overcast. The back of the barn, the side facing us, had nothing remarkable about its features except for a single window high up in the garrets that was opened, and another on the opposite side which was shut- and when seen together, looked like a face frozen in a wink.

The open window, unlit from the inside was an eerie black eye looking out over the hill, scouring for trespassers down below.

After our exchange with the man we turned around and rowed for home. I felt we were being watched and that made me uneasy. Despite the brevity of our exchange, the image of the man's sharp wire cutters in his hands made a troubled impression in my mind. He had never introduced himself or asked for our names either.

"What'd you think of that man?" I asked Adley on our return.

"He didn't seem friendly. Sounds like he doesn't want anyone back there."

"It's not his creek though."

"He seemed to think it was."

"Yeah, who knows."

We took a break from that subject and rowed on.

Then, out of the blue, Adley said, "Brown river, brown river." with a lilt in her voice

She looked at me, smiling. "Brown river, brown river." she sang again.

"What's that from?" I asked.

"Nothing." she said, again smiling.

"It's a song." I asked.

"I just made it up. I mumble a lot of things."

"But isn't it creek though? Shouldn't it be 'Brown creek, brown creek', since this is a creek?"

"It is?" she said.

"Yes." I said, "Weems creek, that's what it's called."

"That's funny." she said. "I've always thought of it as a river. I like it that way too. River sounds better."

"Then river it is."

"Brown river, brown river, you make me wanna shiver!" she said cheekily.

"Brown river, brown river, you make me wanna...

"Wanna what? Come on!"

"I don't know! You make me wanna...row!" I shot.

"Brown river, brown river, you make me wanna sew. Haha!" We flitted back and forth like that. We were rowing and working up a sweat. We took off our life jackets and left them at the bottom of the hull.

'Brown river, brown river'. That phrase shone in my mind ever since. In more ways than she knew, Adley was right, profoundly right. It *was* a river. Weems was a river. Our river. If not by name, then by every look of it, by every trip we took upon it, by our knowledge of the way thunder struck across it. I think of it nowadays under her title, the perfect name mentioned in a mumble.

There was not a hint of passion in the sky that evening, as the day drew to a close. The most it became was a pale pink, but even that seemed only to heighten the brownness of the world; the mud and the woods, the pines, the marsh, The slanted pier, the outbuilding, the dead grass. The two solemn stumps where apples trees once stood. And the brown river.

24

Adley and me tied the boat to the pier and managed to pull each other onto dry ground, without dipping our feet in the freezing water. I unlooped the rope and led the dory shoreward, walking beside it on the pier. Then we both pulled it ashore, resting frequently, and managed to carry it back to the outbuilding. We brought the trailer in too, which was quite a feat for a couple of young girls. Adley pushed from the axle and I held the hitch latch, an awkward hold, but it worked and we wheeled it next to the outbuilding. My mother's car was parked in front of the house. We came inside and she was sitting in the kitchen by herself, looking forlorn.

"What happened?" I said. She looked up at us then down at her hands again, and shook her head.

"It's a long road." she said. "They believe he's got Becker's."

"What's that?" I said.

"It's a disease. Becker's muscular dystrophy. An autoimmune disease; it means you get weaker and weaker as you get older, much more so than other people."

"What does it mean for him though?" I replied.

"It means he's not going to be able to do a lot of things we thought he was. And he thought he was."

Her voice broke as she said it. She looked up at us standing there, her gaze moving back and forth between our faces. There was a napkin between her thumb and fingers which she stroked unconsciously; crumpling and smoothing, crumpling and smoothing.

"He's upstairs. He knows as little as I do. But he's upset obviously. Go up and tell him it's ok. Comfort him. I still have to tell your father. Go up." she said.

We entered his room with a small knock, Adley behind me. James was lying on his bed facing the wall, with his shoes still on.

"James," I said, but he didn't move. His finger drew over the white wall lazily. We came and stood over him. Adley, who was not usually physically affectionate, put her hand on his shoulder. He turned his neck back and saw us, and turned back.

"James, it's going to be ok." I said.

"James, it's ok." Adley said.

We waited a minute in silence, but he did not respond. So we left him and went downstairs where our mother had started dinner. That's when we heard my father's car.

"Great." my mother said.

The first thing he said when he came in and saw us all assembled there, stolid and quiet, was

"Where's James?"

"He's tired." my mother said.

"He doesn't want to eat?" My father dropped his bag at the door. "That's unlike him. Also, who moved the trailer?

"Adley and I did. We went out earlier."

"Just you two? James didn't go?" he asked. "You should've taken him. He could've helped you bring that thing in. That's what I was planning to do with him."

My father walked to the bay windows and closed the curtains. The house darkened. The kitchen was the only lit room on the main floor, but even it became dim. And I felt all of us slipping deeper into the prevailing mood; becoming thoughtful and sober, none of us talkative, each disquieted by something we would not mention.

My father was hungry that night. At dinner we took turns passing all the food to his end of the table, where it stayed, and he looked up, half astonished that none of us wanted more to eat. It was only near the end of dinner that he noticed James wasn't with us.

"So he's not feeling well? he asked around, seeing if any of us knew anything.

"I'll check on him." my mother said. "You two clear the table."

My father sat there for a while, glazed in his eyes with fatigue and a full stomach while the table was cleared. Then he stood and went upstairs, the steps creaking slowly. I felt some great loyalty to my mother in that moment, as I seldom did during that season when I was 17 years old. Almost a protectiveness. I felt loyal to her down to the very way she would wipe a counter with a rag, folding it in squares and wringing it dry, cupping her hand underneath the counter to catch the crumbs, and laying it out over the edge of sink when she finished. Trivia like that, which before then mattered so little to me, I wanted to do her way. Anything to soothe her burden.

We heard the door to my brother's bedroom open and the sound of distant conversation. Then the door closed again for privacy. I could only imagine how it went. Soon it was clear. My father came downstairs in an undershirt and work pants and sneakers. He looked at us severely as soon as he saw that we were there listening up. He grabbed his keys and his coat, and left out the back door, pulling the door behind him hastily. It didn't shut all the way, and what I remember last of all was his hand reaching from the dark and pulling the knob definitively shut, with a clap.

25

When he left he went nowhere I'm sure. He needed the car alone. Driving is syntonic for him. It puts him at ease to have the wheel between his hands and the pedal obedient to his foot. He went to the pier if had to bet on it. There's a small fisherman's pier 20 minutes from where we live that makes an easy loop with our neighborhood. It's just down river on the Nanticoke. It's a short pier but a good catching pier because of how close it lies to the mouth of the river. You can see the Bay opening from where it stands. It's a popular place during the fishing and crabbing months, then it's completely deserted after that. At all hours, peopled or unpeopled, the pier promulges a marine, fish grime smell. Cut bait is literally stained and smeared into the wood and pilings, and it gets into clothes like smoke.

I don't know where he went that night. Maybe he went there. I would have.

For all of the fear that filled the house because of it, there was very little we actually knew about Becker's condition: what the treatment was, how costly, how much was involved. These were not even questions we asked. Maybe my parents did. But in reality, it was the knowledge of his sickness that brought us low. It loomed over us. We walked and went about our days as usual, yet hemmed in by the unknown spectre.

That winter my father put his motorboat up at Margo's boatyard, downriver, instead of winterizing it on his own. He had used the new craft only a handful of times that season, and I went with him to drop it off.

The boatyard was tucked into a cove off the main river. It was a chiming place, full of the sound of sail masts and birds and the beep of forklifts lifting and transporting vessels. The same forklift placed my father's boat 20 ft into the air in an oversize shelf with other smaller motor boats.

Later my mother came to pick us up and take us home, but before we left the three of us got an appetizer at the restaurant on premise. It was a nice restaurant with tinted windows overlooking the cove and boats. My mother said to me,

"You should work here this summer."

"Maybe I will." I said.

When our waitress came by, my mother asked her about applications, and she came back with one and said to send it in whenever. She said they could always use more help in the summers. I folded it and put it in my pocket. Then we left.

On our way home my father finally broke the long silence and asked my mother,

"What's the news on James?"

She let out a heavy sigh.

"What?" he said, reacting to it.

She shook her head.

"Nothing." she said.

"Is there news?"

"Nothing you don't know."

"Have you looked into physical therapy?"

"I asked his doctor. She's looking into it."

"Who's his doctor?"

"Dr. Lippin."

"Have I met her?"

"I don't think so."

"Is she ok?"

"What do you mean? She's his doctor, she's fine."

"Why do you have to raise your voice, I wasn't arguing."

"I know your tone though."

"What tone?"

"Like you're suspicious."

"I'm not suspicious, but I want to make sure he gets the right care."

"You don't think I want that too?"

"No, but sometimes you're not insistent enough. These doctors don't always know what's best. He's our son."

"I know he's our son."

My father looked away and my mother looked back at me, exasperated, hoping I would change the subject.

I said, "Adley and I took the dory across the creek."

There was silence. Then he said,

"Where to?"

"The other side."

"Is there anything over there but marsh?"

"There's another small creek where the water is really dark. We've gone back there a couple times. The last time we went there was a man who was putting up a fence near the bank and said it was his property."

He turned around to me.

"Who is it?"

"I don't know him. He was putting up fence and said we shouldn't be back there."

My father shook his head.

"No. He can't tell you to do that, unless it's his property."

"We were just on the creek."

"Then he has no right to say that. He shouldn't be talking to you like that, regardless- you're just a girl."

"I'm old enough to talk to him." I said.

"That's not my point." he said.

"He shouldn't be speaking to you that way. Was he rude?"

"He wasn't nice." I said.

"Come with me tomorrow. We'll go over there and see if he's still making a fuss."

The next day, instead of rowing we used the engine. I helped my father lift the boat down to the pier. James was ordered to trolley the small outboard engine behind us. My father kept an eye on him and he did fine. Then my father helped James lift it off the trolley and attach it to the transom.

James stayed ashore as we motored across. It took us five minutes and we were there. I pointed where it was. As we came to the entrance of the creek, he killed the engine and lifted the prop out of the water and we drifted slowly inward. The fence still stood, but now there were 'no trespassing' signs posted along the bank that said 'Notice: this is private property. Severe action will be taken against violators.'

Before we reached the overhang tree, there was movement in the leaves ahead and we looked up and saw the man I described descending the wooded slope following a skinny mut of a dog whose hair looked shaken with dust and who started barking at us incessantly. The dog came right up to the waterline, barking madly, looking back at its owner then back at us, barking more and more. It's gums and teeth were purple at the edges, and its eyes were bulging from the noise it made.

"Yip. Yip!" the man said, coming toward. "Yip on!" he said to the dog, until it ceased. Our boat was wading in the shallows when the man came down. He held a rifle in his arm. When he came beside his companion, he tossed the gun to the ground, crouched to the dog's level and took both his hands and clamped them around the dog's jaw and whispered something in its ear, which made it growl. The dog's eyes were still fixed on us. Then the man stood up and nudged the dog in the ribs with his boot "Away! Now!" He picked up his rifle and said,

"Sorry about her. She's unwelcome to newcomers."

"No problem." my father said. "We were just exploring the creek."

"Uh huh." the man said. "Which ways?"

"Just here and out that way. We live across Weems on the other side." pointing with his thumb backward."

"Uh huh." the man repeated. He walked forward a step into the mud and put the barrel of his gun into it and looked down the alley of the small creek to its opening, where we came from.

"Well, this is all mine." he said, motioning with his hand behind him. "And some there too, on your other side, the marsh."

"You're keeping watch over your marsh are you?" my father said in jest.

The man nodded to the ground.

"I take care of what's mine." he said "I'll say that much."

"We'll stay clear of your land, you can count on that, but we intend to use this creek, if you don't mind."

"Uh huh. It's your prerogative. It's not much to see though." he said.

After taking a lap, the dog returned, barking the same as before.

"Hey." he said to the dog. "Hey! You hear me? Yip!" he said, the creature looking up at him, riled but obedient. The man put the barrel into its shoulder and pushed it on and it left. When the man looked back at us my father said,

"We've been here a while, so we're familiar with these waters."

"How long you say?"

"14 years. Living on Teal St, across the way. I'm Ed Gonzalez. This is Constance."

As he was speaking, a boy and girl about my age ran down from the ridge and followed up beside the man.

"Well, we're the Siggins. Been here 8 years. This is Tate, and Beverly." The two made no gesture when they were acknowledged. "I'm John. My wife's somewhere up there." I recognized the kids from school, but didn't know them well. They were dressed in work clothes.

"Speaking of which. We got a farm up top we need to get back to, and a sick hog that needs something before it dies. See you round." He nodded and left. Tate and Beverly nodded too and followed him. The dog lingered and began barking again, and John Siggins told his son,

"Grab her. She's pissing me off." The boy grabbed her roughly by the collar and dragged her up the way.

26

In school I began to notice the Siggins kids more than before, but still I did not know them well. Beverly was my grade and Tate was James'. James knew Tate because they tried out for the football team together and neither of them made it. The more I observed them the more I saw that there were like us in some ways. They were not of the popular bunch, but they were not uninteresting or dumb either. I felt that their homelife was more telling of who they were, and that their presence in class was marginal, that school was a sideshow only, that it was requisite and sufficing.

We attended Wachapreague high school, a regional high school, which for all its size and impressive facilities, having been well funded by the state to be one of the top performing high schools on the Eastern shore, was always underpopulated with students, who came from far stretches of the area to go here. I remember the cafeteria was sparkling clean and all grades eating together occupied only half of it. It had everything, it was just waiting for people. There was an air of loneliness to the campus, indicative of the land it sat on; the football field was constructed next to a field of chalk and crabgrass, which led farther into a marsh and then one of the nameless Nanticoke creeks eventually. But there was no limit as far the eye saw, no boundary separating the school from its environment. Egrets, ibis, even ospreys were spotted regularly around the school and circling above the athletic fields. The expansiveness of the land, the omnipresence of the marsh, and the wide swaths of chalk deposits and stone made the school feel an unnatural place by contrast; like it was just out there, isolated from home and town.

Beginning in high school and onward, I felt that there were two sets of people who lived on the Eastern Shore of Maryland. Those who lived as if under a curse, who were there because they were stuck there, who wanted nothing more than to leave at the first chance they get. And those who had found a surprising contentment with the little it had to offer, most of which surrounded the water. The rivers and creeks, stretches of marsh and eelgrass and shallow sounds. And of course the boating.

I did not know what I was. Some mix of the two. I know that the place was not as disagreeable as it was to some of my classmates, even some of my teachers. Most of those who taught at school were townies who did not even like the town. For reasons I surmised was their own malcontent, they seemed so often bent on pushing us out into the wider world.

Perspective was their word. We were told we needed perspective, and the Wachapreague zip codes would not give it. There was common disdain for anything provincial. The prospect of sticking around was considered restrictive, small minded. Truth be told, I had no overwhelming desire to run away. My imagination may have been less inspired than others; it did not glow with the ambient lights of big cities. Perhaps that was my fault. I did not know what to say to people, so mostly I kept my mouth shut. The more I admitted such thoughts to classmates and counselors, the more it was held over me like the banner of ill fortune.

If I went to college it was going to be at Salisbury University, just down the road. Junior year my guidance counselor said disappointedly,

"So that's the *only* school you're applying to?"

"Yes." I said.

"And that's because?" she said, as if I were hiding a secret motive.

"I'd want to go there."

She took a piece of lined paper and wrote down the names of five more schools and pushed it across her desk for me to read.

"These are all local schools, if that's what you're concerned about. I'd like you to look into them. Do you have any sense of what you might want to study?"

I shook my head.

"That's alright for now. But think about it. Business, education, law, there's lots of options. Think about what you're good at.

She took her paper back and drew three precise tick marks below the name of the schools in dark blue ink. She had impeccable penmanship, I remember that. And I remember receiving an impression of her in that office, between the spotlessness of her desk, and her thin reading glasses at the end of her nose, and the way she tilted her head over the paper, and her quick cursive spelling, and the general scent of classroom and hand sanitizer. All if it representing my future and higher education, the promise of a degree, and beyond that who knew?

But I did not like it. I complied and said the right words, but deep down, I did not like it, not any of it. I took the paper, folded it in my pocket and laid it on my nightstand that evening. I don't know if I ever opened it again.

One day in the same office, I sat down next to Beverly

Siggins. We were in the waiting room. I recognized her but I didn't know if she recognized me.

I sat for a moment, then said.

"Hi, are you Mr. Siggins daughter?"

She turned to me.

"Yes, I'm Beverly." She shook my hand strongly. She had a nice smile and a big set of teeth. She was dressed in jeans and a t-shirt.

"I'm Constance." I said. "My father and I traveled up the creek behind your house."

"I remember." she said.

"What are you here for?" I asked.

"To change a class, and talk about my plans. I'm looking into the vocational school, or the military."

"Doing what?" I asked.

"I don't know specifically, but I want to go and see. I think I'll end up back on our farm someday."

"You do?"

"Uh huh." she said, like her father. "I don't mind it. Most days it's fine. I like it a lot more than school. And you? What are you here for?"

"College application for Salisbury."

"Salisbury? I might apply there too."

When her name was called she stood up, shook my hand again and said, "You should come by the creek. Anytime. My Dad thinks he's a hardass, but he's not. He doesn't care, long as you're with me or Tate. We can show you around."

"Thanks." I said. "I will."

27

It was December of that year when I first went over. The days were short and bleak, but snow had not fallen yet and the cold that came from the air was the kind that seeped into clothes and shoes. I seldom used the dory during that time, and I forgot to go to Black creek to see if Beverly was there. The more that time passed, the more I was disinclined to go, and I assumed she had only said what she said in passing, as a courtesy for living so close, but not because she meant it. However, two weeks before Christmas she stopped me in the hallway and said,

"I thought you were coming over?"

I said, "When?"

"Whenever you can. We're usually there. Our sow just had a litter. There's a hundred little pigs now, total."

"This afternoon I can come." I said. "I could bring my brother James."

"Yes, you should. Bring him along. I'm free, so is Tate. Have you met my brother?"

"No, I don't think." I said.

"You'll meet him. He's my younger brother. Anyway,

come over around 4. We'll be back there waiting for you." So just like that the offer was back.

We had to haul the boat from the outbuilding. It was frigid to the touch from being so long in the cold, and heavier too because of it. We finally got it to the water. The water was icy and brown, placid, reflecting the grey-white sky and the black trees. We fit the oars in place and pushed off across the empty, slushed creek. I had two jackets on, and a winter hat. So did James. It was not long reaching the other side; the wind was minimal and the water parted smoothly. There were no other boats out to worry about. When we arrived, Beverly was there, standing by the big, overhanging maple, with a stick in her hand, swatting at the leafy ground. Her brother was there behind her. We flung our painter rope to shore and she picked it up and Tate came down and helped her pull us in, and make us fast to the trunk of the tree.

"Hi Beverly, this is James."

"Hi James, I'm Bev, and this is Tate.", pointing at him sidelong with her stick, and then turning and leading us up the slope. Tate seemed the quieter of the two. Quiet, but imposing. He was tall and sturdy, with short brown hair, flushed cheeks, and a pair of work gloves sticking out of his back pocket. He and his sister wore the same pair of work boots. The four of us climbed the slope, on one side of which was the chicken fence, and on the other the creek. It was with a kind of awe or trepidation that we followed them up, this pair that we only recently met, who led us up the previously forbidden slope to their home. The dog nor the father was in sight. At the top of the ridge we looked down from where we came upon a nice overlook. Through the woods, over Weems, we could see our house on Teal St., small from that distance, and a lean stack of smoke where my mother had started a fire in the fireplace.

I hadn't told her where we went. To the left of the big

white barn was the field where the Siggins grew soybeans. The field ran to a ridge in the distance also overlooking the creek. In the summers that bluff flowing down from the top of the field ridge was overtaken by blooms of ragweed and bluestem and bulrush, and shrunk back as the year progressed, revealing the raw clay and mud and ash root surface. We boated by there frequently. At the time, the field was furrowed, but that was all. Nothing was growing. The ground around the perimeter of the barn was cold, stiff, muddy. We entered the barn through a back door and each of us took turns kicking our shoes against a wood post then scraping them off with Bev's stick, which she handed backward as we entered.

We came suddenly into the presence of dozens of piglets, the smell and noise and scuffling rushing on to us in a pen when we entered, and the sow laying on its side in the corner, panting. James and I were shy with the pigs, but Tate and Bev showed how comfortable they were around the animals; lifting them, pushing them away with their feet, knocking the little creature's hind legs from under them and they ran about. After 20 minutes, Bev said to Tate,

"Tate, you show him the punching bag. Constance, you wanna come inside?"

I said sure and the two groups went their ways. James followed Tate out back again. I followed Bev through the front of the barn where there was all sorts of mowers, trimmers, appliances, and tools, disorganized and scattered on the ground. Above us were two canoes and a punt laid across the upper beams of the rafters.

"You go boating?" I asked.

"We do when it's warmer out."

After that we went inside. The house was small and very close to the barn. There was hardly a driveway. It was more so a general area of ground driven over, compacted, worn down by many vehicles, and machinery, connecting the house and the barn and field, and whatever else there was on the property. We entered through the kitchen and took off our shoes. Their house smelled so different than our house; like old carpet and over scented candles. Someone was back in the bedroom and someone else was watching tv in the other room. I saw legs stretched out on a chair and socks.

"What're you doing?" the voice said, and I recognized it as Mr. Siggins. Bev brought me in and we stood in the doorway, me behind her. The rough dog was beside him resting with its head on his paws on the ground.

"I invited over Constance and James."

He looked up at us, then back at the tv.

"I remember." he said. "Good then. Get what you need."

"We will." she said.

It was interesting to see that man in his home, with his legs propped in the chair and wool socks on his feet, and the dog, which only a few days prior was set on chewing us to pieces, now tame and docile beside him. The domestic image of John Siggins softened the version I had formed of him from our previous encounters; those times of interrogation and rifle bearing, with his unkempt appearance, against the background of the dark, shorn woods, and the fence, and the incensed dog whose name was Jip.

Everywhere we went, Bev picked something up and wielded it, or made a motion with it, or used it to poke something else. Inside she found cardboard piping from leftover wrapping paper, and when we returned outside again she dropped the pipe and picked up her old stick and brought it with us, swiping and slashing and brandishing to her own delight. Who would have ever seen this side of her at school? At school she did nothing of the sort. When it was dark already I told her we needed to get back, James and I.

"You've made it back in the dark before, haven't you?" she asked.

"No, not really." I said.

She had a smile on her face and she took her stick and bounced it in her palm, a few seconds, thinking about it.

"You'll be fine." she said. "I hope you'll be fine. I've got a flashlight you can borrow. It's real bright. And it's not that far anyway from here to your place."

When she went to find the flashlight I went to find James. I heard them on the other side of the barn. It sounded like they were fighting, the grunting and huffing of it, but it was only a punching bag they fought with, which dangled by a rusty chain on a makeshift hook jutting out of the wall. It was a makeshift bag that did not swing freely, but clung close to the wall and thudded against it, and depending on the punches, or the anger behind it, shook that part of the barn when it made contact.

Both boys looked up at me, exhausted, their heads steaming, their cuffs rolled, and four extra pair of gloves on the mud ground. James was punching when I came, and Tate was holding the bag high, by the chain. He was watching him closely. Then he looked up at me.

"He's getting pretty good." he said, "He's got stamina for days, we're just working on the power. My turn." he said, and he took one big punch to the middle of the bag, and it sounded heavy, much heavier than the ones James was throwing.

"Like that." he said. He touched James with the glove. "He'll get there."

"We have to go." I said.

Bev came from behind, and turned the flashlight on and led us down the hill to the boat, which was still there, slowly lapping against the bank. There was no moon, just the flashlight and the ashblue remains of day, and the ambient skuds of light skittering across the brown surface of the water. Tate held the prow of the boat while we got in. Then Bev handed me the flashlight and untethered our line from the tree and we drifted back a few feet while we got our positions set up and came to a still. They watched us until we got out of Black creek, then they turned and walked back home. From every angle the water shone with the same midnight blue, mysterious and noiseless, and frightening how cold it was. The thought of keeling over in the dark…

James sat forward, holding the light, and told me which way to row.

"Little more to the left."

We went slowly, and the distance seemed drawn out with every stroke. The only other lights we saw were from the houses surrounding the area; cozy interior lights, which in that blue coldness looked orange and warm as flame. At last we saw our own. It was the one house with a bright outdoor light on, apparently for us.

"They're gonna be pissed." James said. I made no reply. The flashlight began to fade, but by then my eyes had adjusted to the dark, and I began to flag in my rowing.

"You want help?" he said.

"Sure."

He put the flashlight on the floor and carefully found his seat next to me, so that we were hip to hip, facing backwards to the house, but close. As he was taking the oar from me he pulled it too abruptly, and it came out of its crutch and fell overboard. Instinctively he rose to grab it from the water, but I yanked him by the shirt tail back to the bench, as the boat rocked dangerously, and held him there and said,

"You want to drown us both tonight?"

He looked off, not at me, but upset with the knowledge of what he had just done, and what he had attempted to do after.

"Sit still." I said, "And don't move an inch. Slide up there."

He moved to the front and sat forward looking, scorned and scolded in all his manner, his head low and unwavering.

"I'm sorry." he said.

I sat at the crossbeam bench and traded strokes freestyle

with the lone, unhitched oar. Only looking backward on the moment as I recall it now, do I remember specifically how I looked backward from the bench as the lost oar dawdled adrift on the cold, black surface of the creek that night, with the one given flashlight subsumed in the pale blue darkness, and my brother without strength, who sat strengthless and still before me.

How many times have I reckoned the image of that scene so near and ubiquitous to all my memories of Weems and growing up, how it took on the pattern of my life thereafter, cornerstoning itself, and bestowing both a curse and blessing. That our home shore never failed to fill me with equal dread and satisfaction to reach, or that the single, unhitched oar overshadowed and steered me wherever I went. I see parts of only now.

We hobbled back, touching the shallows at last, a great, safe, secure feeling. We dragged the boat well onto shore and left it where it was, with the life preservers, oar and flashlight inside. Inside the family was gathered around the fireplace. My father was building it, feeding it with extra logs. My mother was there, and Adley, who was dressed in a throw, came over and looked at us. My mother, taking one of my hands, said,

"You're freezing! Where'd you go?"

"Black creek." I said. "To see the Siggins kids."

"Who?" she said.

"They go to school with us."

She turned to James.

"Are you ok?"

"I'm fine."

My father spoke up.

"No more boating in the dark."

He turned, facing us. There was a wad of newspaper twisted in his hands.

"Did you think of that? You're asking for a disaster. You've got no lights on that little thing."

"We had a light." I said.

"I sure didn't see it. We were watching from the back windows."

"It died when we got close."

"That's my point." he said. "What would you have done if you or he had fallen over in the dark?"

My mother, who was still warming my hand, said to my father,

"Let's not think about that now."

He turned back to the fire and blew at it.

"When will they think about it then?" he said.

For a few seconds there was no sound except for the fire sputtering and snapping. My father pushed it with a poker. Then he threw another log in and the whole fireplace coughed out sparks and he said,

"When it's too late I suppose," answering his own question.

We went to bed by turns that night. First my mother, then Adley. James and I sat by the flame, warming, recovering from the cold. Then James went up, then I. My father stood over the fire as I left him alone. He looked pensive and uneasy. When I left he was prodding the coals with the poker, keeping it going, like he would be up all night.

28

That winter I became fast friends with Bev. We began talking more in school and I came over to her house frequently. Bev's father warmed to me the more I came over. I tried to be of help too. Bev and I would clean the pig pens, the chicken coop, brush the horses, organize the greenhouse. I learned that these were her assigned chores, but she was not bashful about asking me to do them with her.

"You want to see how to clean the pen?" she would say to me.

And I would think to myself, "No."

But the thing I liked about Bev was that she was bold. She didn't care about my response; she was going to show me anyway. Before long we were neck-deep in a chore and her father would find us and say,

"Now what do we have here?"

Bev would turn around, and her face would be red.

"We're cleaning the pen." she'd say.

"I see that. Who's idea was this?"

"Ours."

"I bet so. It's some kind of fun you're having with your

friend, huh Beverly? Looks like someone's recruited some extra help."

"I'm showing her how." Bev would say.

"Oh, are you?" he'd laugh. "Well I guess that's how it goes."

Then the dog would come up and started sniffing around.

"Now Jip," her father would say, "what do you think of the fun these two are having?"

Eventually the dog would run off and her father would smile from the humor in this situation.

"He don't care. Not even Jip wants a part of this. As long as Constance doesn't mind it, I'm fine. You two do whatever you want – but don't go pulling her into your chores, you hear me Beverly?"

"I'm not. She doesn't mind it, do you Constance?"

"Yeah," I'd say, sort of embarrassed to be caught between them.

"Ok, then I won't be holding you up. Constance, you can stop whenever you want. Do what you please. Just help yourself. Don't let this one boss you around."

Over time I got used to going over there and doing some chore or another. I was not upset at that either. I enjoyed working. I enjoyed it more than talking sometimes. I've never been accomplished at talking to other people. I have no art for keeping a conversation going round and round just for the sake of it. Bev was like that too, which is why we got along. We could space our talking out by working on things, on odd jobs often.

One of those odd jobs was when Bev's father suspected rats were making nests under the hood of his tractor and chewing the wires. It was winter, and he thought they were making nests. I told him once how we set traps for squirrels at our house, to keep them off our trees. He was amused by that, and the next time I came over he asked Bev and I to set a few traps beneath the tractor to try my method. He handed us five brand new traps and we smeared peanut butter on them and set them under the green rusted hood. I remember moving our hands slowly away from the loaded brass spring and peeking under the hood later to see if they had snapped.

Another time we set out strips of duct tape in the basement for 'spickets'; the spider-crickets with the striped, translucent legs. Those are the crickets that jump *on* you when you get near them, not away from you. How we ever discovered that technique for catching them, I'm not sure, but it was effective, and it was strangely satisfying to go down there and smell the rank basement air and see how many we had caught. We would count our separate strips and compare. It was a competition.

I remember Tate from those days too. Sometimes Tate joined us for these games, other times he was sullen and reclusive, and he became more that way over time. He stayed in the basement lifting weights. Eventually he moved his bedroom down there and the basement began to smell like his den; a mix of body odor and the smell of galvanized rubber from the weights.

On top of that he struggled in school and was no shoe-in for his father's farm. He hated the farm work, and I know it discouraged his father to come downstairs and find his able-bodied son burning his youthful strength on dead weight. When we had finished a task, Bev and I would go down to the basement and sit on bean bag chairs and drink cold plastic bottles of water. One day we were there while Tate was lifting, when Bev's father came down looking for a tool. On his way up, he stopped and looked at Tate, who was bench pressing and didn't see him.

"I could sure use some of that strength out there, you know."

Tate did not see him or hear him. He had his headphones on and we could hear the loud music from the corner of the room where we sat. Bev's father looked up to us, smiled, shook his head, then looked back at his son who was still oblivious. He waved his hand in Tate's direction, snapped his fingers. Tate put the bar on the rack. Finally he looked up, breathing heavily, and took one ear of his headphones off.

"What?" he said. His voice was overloud from the music. "I'm lifting."

"I can see." his father said. "I said I could use some of your strength out there." He pointed upstairs with his tool.

"What do you need?"

"Any help I can get."

"I'm lifting right now."

"How about later?"

"Maybe, I'm meeting a friend later."

His father nodded and set his eyes on the stairs.

"Well, don't trouble yourself. Go back to your lift. I think I still got two pairs of hands that haven't abandoned me yet. Is that right girls?"

He looked at us and grinned, but it was a sad grin. Tate put his headphones on and got back to his lifting. As his father squeaked softly up the stairs, all we heard was the sound of Tate's headphones blaring and the metallic clunk-clunk of the bar, the weight of it rattling the floor, and his hard breathing. Bev looked at me and shook her head.

"He's lying," she said.

"Who is?"

"Tate is, about a friend coming over."

"How do you know?"

"I just know, I'm his sister. My father knows too. He's not stupid."

And she was right. Later that day when the work was done outside their father came in and found Tate in his room.

"I thought you were going out." he said.

"No."
"You had a friend coming, didn't you?"
"They couldn't come."
"Alright then."

29

It took only a handful of occasions of me coming over to Bev's house or her coming over to ours to solidify our friendship, but soon she was one of my closest companions. I wondered why I had not known her sooner.

But one experience we had together I remember as one of the worst memories of high school.

It happened after the winter formal dance that same year. I went with Bev and her friend Sarah. I did not know Sarah because she went to a different high school, but she struck me as obnoxious from the start. She carried a flask in her clutch and she would hand it off to Bev and say things to her privately, but she ignored me, and for long portions of the night I felt like Bev was divided between us. After the dance a group met in the Wachapreague parking lot in the freezing cold and made after party plans, and it was settled that anyone who could make it should meet at Shane's island, a scrubby, unpopulated island just off the Nanticoke, accessible only by boat. I said the dory wasn't an option to take, but Bev said we could take their punt, which had a small engine. They asked if I would captain and I said I wasn't sure it was a good idea, but they pushed and pushed until I relented.

It was late already when we drove back to Bev's, changed into some of her sweats, and snuck down to the shore by Black creek, where the punt was floating already.

"My dad took it out earlier." Bev said. "It's still got gas."

So we piled in, started the engine, and left for Shanes. The island was not as far as I thought, but still, the conditions were ugly and they made the trip treacherous to say the least. The wind was freezing, and the water, should anything have happened, would have induced hypothermia in minutes. When we arrived on the island we parked the boat beside four others that were dragged onto the sand and anchored to large stones or branches or anything immobile.

There was a bonfire and voices in the distance.

I knew Shanes from having passed it before, and never liked it or had any desire to go there. It was the reputed dive island of the Nanticoke; a hook-up haunt where high schoolers with boats tramped up the cliffs to small clearings where they drink and smoke. During broad daylight the island looks more like a jut of land covered in trash. It's completely overgrown with sandbar willow, weeds, and thick brown draping vines. It gives off the strong vegetative smell of tangleweed and brush and marijuana. The two beaches have orange muck sand and eroding cliffside, where dead tree roots and fossilized shell sediment fall to the ground and mix with piles of human litter.

That night we went to the bonfire and got separated; me from Bev, and Bev from Sarah. We all sat next to other people and drank liberally. They passed around blunts and plastic handles of rum. When the fire got low, one of the guys took the rest of the rum and poured it on the fire and threw the bottle into the flame. They howled and laughed.

It was loud and raucous for a time, even fun. The bonfire

bellowed and the moon rose in the sky, clean and bright. I kept my eyes on Bev though, who sat on the other side of the fire and who was my one friend in that gathering. I had only a washy concept of time, except that at one point, someone who sat beside me got a hacking cough and could not stop, so I moved away. Then slowly the bonfire began to dwindle again, and I got up and left to check on our boat, to get it ready to leave. Bev was still sitting. At the shore I saw a boat heading out and two people, in shadow, getting on. One was a guy, the other was a girl. As I came closer, I thought the girl looked like Sarah, but I couldn't tell since they were far enough away and it was dark.

"Sarah," I called. "Is that you? Sarah?"

As I walked toward them I called again,

"Sarah?"

What I remember is that the second time I called she heard me and said,

"Oh shit - go, go!" to her companion, the one whose boat it was, who was steering away. Some guy. I could hear her laugh and when I had made it to the shore I saw in the faint light that she was shirtless and her skin was white as the moon. They motored off into the dark with a loud, whining engine that sounded like a weed wacker. She looked back briefly to see who called her, then turned forward, with both hands cupping her breasts.

She left some of her clothes on the shore; a green lace pair of panties and a white bra, which made me wonder what I interrupted when I came down. Not that it mattered. I picked up the clothes. Nearby I found a white grocery bag snagged under a branch of driftwood. I shook the sand off the bag and put the clothes in and tied it in a bundle. I gave the bundle to Bev and Bev gave it to Sarah days later. Apparently when Sarah opened it she said "Oh good, I thought it was going to be something else." I don't know what she meant by that, but it was the last I heard of Sarah, and probably the sleaziest package I ever sent.

That night, after Sarah left, I had to get Beverly and take her home. She was in a sleepy, drunken state and could not understand that Sarah was gone. I told her what happened, what I saw, but none of it got through.

"But why, Constance, but why did she?" she kept moaning and blubbering. I kept telling her "I don't know." like I was explaining it to a little child. But that grew tiresome.

When we arrived at Black creek, I helped her off the boat, took her wrist, then walked her up the moonlit hill to the house. We made our beds in her room. I slept on the ground in a red sleeping bag, and she slept on her bed. The moon was so bright she had to lower her blinds to make it dark enough. Even then the wind blew the blinds up and down at the bottom of the window, because she couldn't shut it all the way. It was cold. I put my hands between my legs. I could see the moon from the floor. The two of us smelled like beer and camp smoke. I closed my eyes and thought what a deplorable and unforgettable night it had been. My ears and hands froze. One girl fled half naked with a stranger. One girl mewled in a drunken sadness. The last girl drove the boat over an ice creek and curled on the carpet in her friend's room.

"We smell sick." I said.

"I smell sick and I feel like hell," she said.

"Are you drunk?" I said.

"Yes." she said. "And tired. But more drunk. My head's spinning. Is yours? Are you drunk?" she said.

"No, just tired." I yawned.

"You can fall asleep if you want. I can't go to sleep right now."

I didn't say anything. I shut my eyes and began to sleep. Then she said,

"Constance."

"Huh?"

"Constance." she whispered.

I heard her turn on her side to look at me and get my attention.

"Yeah?"

"You ever thought of who you want to marry?"

"You're asking me right now?"

"Yeah.

"Why?"

"I don't know. But have you ever thought of it?"

"Not really," I said.

"How come?"

"I don't know. I just haven't. Have you?"

"Yeah."

"Who?"

"I want to marry a guy in the military."

"Why?" I said.

"They got character, and they're handsome. They work hard too."

"Which branch? Army or Navy?"

"Any of 'em."

Then she sighed and we got quiet.

"Ok, you can sleep now." she said.

I shut my eyes again and she said,

"Constance, my head still spins."

"You need something?" I said.

"I don't think. I guess I'll try and sleep it off. Sorry," she said, "You can sleep now."

The room got quiet again, but every few minutes I heard her toss from side to side, and sighing. I couldn't fall asleep either, so gently I got up from my sleeping bag and she saw me and said, "Where are you going?"

"I'll be back," I said.

I went to the kitchen and poured Bev a glass of tap water and brought it back.

"Where'd you go?"

"Here," I said. "You should drink this, but careful." I had

filled it close to the brim and some of the water spilled on my hand as I lifted it to her.

"What is it?"

"Just water. Try and drink some. It might help the spinning. Here sit up."

I put a pillow behind her back as she leaned forward holding the cup with two hands. Her hands trembled some and she took big gulps.

"Try and sip it." I said.

I laid back down on the floor and shut my eyes.

"Ok, thank you." she said.

"You're welcome. Good night."

"Night."

As I faded toward sleep I remember the sound of her trying to sip it quietly for my sake, the sound of the blinds clipping softly again the window. The moon from the ground. I heard her put the glass down on the lampstand beside her bed when she was done, and there was no more tossing and sighing after that.

30

The same winter my father put the motor boat up at the boatyard, he sold it for a loss and decided to keep his eyes open for a boat he would actually get good use out of; something, in his words, 'more manageable'. He worked late those days. I saw him only briefly in the evenings at dinner and on the couch downstairs before he went up to bed, flipping through catalogues.

He took further interest in James too. He showed him an outward affection that he had never shown him before; shaking his hand, patting him on the back, obliging himself to his son in obvious ways. I don't know how James took it entirely, but by his expression, I don't believe the gestures were received as they were intended. There was a stilted air to them, a conspicuousness, even a subtle condescension that came through, that belied the warmth and outgoingness.

One night at dinner, my mother sat beside my father at the corner of the table, keeping a low conversation about my brother's doctor's appointments, while the rest of us ate. We all heard him. He was turned toward my mother, and he said, under his breath,

"All's well with, you know?" and made a motion with his wrist, suggestively.

"With what?"

"Never mind." he said. He took a few bites of food and cleared his throat.

"With James."

James heard his name and looked up.

"I can hear you." he said.

"It's nothing." my father said.

"Then why are you whispering my name?"

"I'm asking your mother something."

The conversation continued in that manner, the private words occasionally audible and provoking. It was not a big table either, so we knew what was going on.

I don't doubt that during that season of diagnoses James felt himself to be the subject of much concern and obsession, especially among his family, and that it disturbed his self image for a long time afterward. As time would prove, he would always either be avoiding his fate or rebelling against it, trying to maintain some posture of normalcy within himself. And there was so much he submerged and hid from us, from Adley and myself, even though we tried not to treat him differently than before.

That evening James stood up from the table early, put his dish in the sink, and took his coat and went outside through the side door, the door we rarely used because it never locked well. Adley and I joined him on the side porch where he stood, his cold quick breaths visible on the air, deeply frustrated. His winter hat was pulled over his brow.

"James" I said, "Come here." and I took him down the soft snowed stairs to the yard. The yard was speckled with mud and snow. The night was serene and very dark beyond the water. There was a dirty soccer ball against the house left from weeks before. I took it and kicked it toward him. He kicked it back, the ball making a soft puff as it sailed along the ground and made a whirr of flakes as it spun forward. Adley joined us and we formed a triangle in the dark, kicking the ball to each other.

We spent a half hour chasing and tripping and falling, triggering the outdoor lights. In the middle of booting the ball, Adley began her little song again,

"Brown river, brown river…" she began. "You remember Constance?"

"Why do you guys sing that?" James said. "It's so dumb."

"Black river, black river." I sang.

"That's not it Constance." Adley said. "You can't copy and get it wrong."

"Your turn James!" I said.

The two of us looked at him. He picked up the ball.

"No." he said.

"You have to." Adley said.

"No," he said.

"We'll make you."

He turned away, and we rushed toward him, hugging him and tackling him to the ground; me piled on James and Adley piled on me, our coats puffy, and the ground, even with all of us on it, was solid and pleasant, reminiscent of childhood. I began tickling James in his ribs and he began to squirm. From under the pile he yelled, "Ok! Ok!"

We released him slightly and he turned over, smiling and laughing. "This is so dumb." He laid on his back with his eyes shut, and shouted up to the sky "Brown rivah! brown rivah!", the richest, freest cry of any of us that night. By the time he opened his eyes we were dashing for the door already, laughs strewn behind us.

"Come on! Get in here!"

31

We were spoiled that Christmas. On Christmas morning we made our way downstairs into the living room, each to our assigned piece of furniture where a stack of presents with our names on them, waited for us. I sat in the middle of the couch. James on the ground against the big cushion seat, and Adley and my mother sat together on the loveseat opposite James. My father stood and watched, passing around a tray of breakfast biscuits.

When my mother gave the word, we tore into our first gifts, then went around, taking turns- youngest to oldest- opening our pile until everything but the biggest gift was left. That year I got a new set of fishing rods and reels, and a small plow anchor for the dory. Adley opened a hutch with a water feeder and pellets inside, and my father came into the room shortly after, holding a bunny, which she had wanted for a long time. It was dove grey with white feet; she named it Dilly and barely put it down that week. It went everywhere with her.

"James," my mother said. "Your gift is in the other room." We followed him into the dining room where there was an upright Yamaha piano with a bow on top and a bench tucked underneath.

"This is for me?" he said.

"You had been saying you wanted to learn." my father said.

"I have? I don't remember. I would like to learn though." His face looked confused but also excited.

He sat down and we gathered behind him, all of us admiring how new and glossy it was, the key cover rising off its hinges, the bright green color of felt between the keys, the shiny gold lettering 'Yamaha' written across the front. The bench was fancy too; it was leather padded, with upholstered studs and a scroll on the side that adjusted the height. Before he had played a single note, my brother looked behind at us and at the keys again and laughed a little bit.

"I don't know how to play." he said. "I don't want you all watching me."

"Try something." my father said.

James puts his hands over the keys very softly, tentatively, like he was being careful not to wake the thing, and pressed down, one finger after another, a simple scale.

"I scheduled you some lessons." my father said. As James played he looked up at my father and back at the keys, then folded down the cover.

"Thanks." he said. "This will be great."

"You're going to be great." my father said, and he put his hand on James's shoulder.

"Thanks."

We returned to the living room after that short performance. Adley put Dilly in the hutch, I connected my fishing poles and spun the reels for fun, checking how smooth they were.

"One last thing I got for your mother." my father announced to us all. He led us out the kitchen door where there was a new white Mercedes sedan sitting in the driveway. When she saw it, my mother put one hand over her mouth.

"Ed! What did you do?" she cried.

"I hope you like it."

"Are you kidding me?"

"It's a good one." he said. "You needed something else."

"I don't know about that, but thank you. Thank you!" she said, giving him a hug. "We'll give it a spin later."

When we came inside, my father said,

"I spoiled myself a bit too," and he showed us a picture of the boat he bought.

"It's sitting at the yard right now. It's got a fly bridge, trolling lines, beautiful cabin, diving platform, all the whistles. Constance, you'll have to bring your new fishing gear along."

The rest of the day we each occupied separate corners of the house, finding amusement in our presents. I organized a tackle box and later brought my new gear to the outbuilding. Adley took her bunny to her room and watched it hop around her piles of clothes. James sat back down at the piano and tinkered. There were two books on top of the piano; a blue book and a red book, neither of which he opened that day.

You could hear the piano from every room. Though the sound was enjoyable for a while, after many hours the plunking became tedious and tiresome to hear. My mother sat at the kitchen table reading the manual to her car. She didn't want to go out because it was too cold. In the afternoon she called my grandmother and grandfather in Texas and put us each on the phone to wish Merry Christmas.

. . .

My father went through the boat catalogues again, which were piled on his office desk. He circled parts he wanted, thinking how he would customize his new craft. And I got bored eventually of looking at the things I got, of picking them up and putting them down. Each of us was subdued by the end of that Christmas day, contented just enough by what we got. Even James got bored of making chaos and not music.

32

The spoiling of Christmas ended on the very calendar date and was succeeded by a protracted month of melancholia that silently and steadily reverberated throughout the whole house. We were marooned in the house in January since it was so cold out, and since there was nothing to do. My father returned to work after the holiday and resumed many long days at the office.

Every week he threatened to be done with work altogether, but that sentiment did not get along well with my mother.

"I hate it when you say that." she said.

"It's true, Avery, I've got enough money put away and you know that. I shouldn't have to keep up this schedule. They can find other managers."

"Yes, but you would go crazy around here."

"We wouldn't have to stay here." he said.

"What do you mean?"

"We could travel. You want to travel, don't you?"

"Not while the kids are in school."

Conversations like that marked the nights, and I did not sympathize with one view or the other. It was part of the bickering of marriage. The kids returned to school and we kept our life on Teal St. separate from everything else. Our upbringing was contrarian on the grounds that our homelife bore little resemblance to those of our peers. For one, we had few friends. We had the Siggins across the creek and whoever we saw at school. Yet we were the only family on the street for a long time.

The second issue was that we had money. Unambiguously so. But there was a certain embarrassment to our wealth. We were told never to mention it, and never to act like it made us different from others or privileged us. But despite all that, it did. It isolated us. And I feared money; for it was mysterious and powerful and never mentioned except in secrecy. I thought back on the stories I was told about my father's father, and contemplated how he must have been when he gave my father his inheritance. He was dying when he gave it, and though I was not there, it exists in my imagination.

I see a velvet drawstring purse opening and an old man's fingers reaching inside to sift heavy gold bullions. I hear the sound of coins rubbing together.

The grounds at home in January were the most desolate of the year. The face of the house held the same colorless pallor of the sky, and the creek alternated between brown and grey. The yard froze and refroze, becoming matted with mud, and except for a few short evergreens and pines, the trees were bare.

Thus all the muted terrain, the persistent flavor of bleakness covered the start of the new year. It was a pervasive, chastening phenomenon, how life moved in accord with weather, how it was shaped by the mood of the creek. It was that way as long as we lived there. We sheltered ourselves. We hunkered down while steam rose off the creek.

Despite the bleakness, my mother wanted the home to be open, to be hospitable, to welcome new faces, and it was in winter that she resolved to alter things by increment. She changed the bulbs in the lamps. She bought plants and set them in the pantry and watered and tended them. If sun came, it poured in through the window in the pantry in a beam, like pure luck. Many times I recall seeing her there at three or four in the afternoon, warm in the sun with a pitcher, going back and forth among her little pots, happy to look after something. They gave her a routine joy. And seeing her raised my spirits too.

We took down the Christmas tree late in the month, unscrewed the base and dumped the pine water, then spent hours with her and Adley taking off ornaments and putting them back carefully in their separate boxes. When it was clean I lifted the tree by the middle while my mother and sister scooched along the ground keeping the skirt around it as the needles dropped. We got it to the side porch and they shook the skirt over the side rail while I dragged it by a bottom branch down the steps and across the yard to the brush pile, next to Corey's house.

Things like that we did. Housekeeping. It kept us busy and more importantly, sane. A physical therapist came twice a week to work with James for an hour, giving him leg exercises, stretches, and encouragement to stay active, which we were told would slow the effects of his disease. My father also hired him a piano teacher who came once a week on Monday nights.

Mrs. Feinstein was a dark curly-haired Jewish woman in her forties. She intimidated James because she never smiled. Music was discipline to her. Not fun. My father would watch the lessons. Sometimes he would get home just as they were beginning and stand by, still dressed in his suit and winter coat, and not unbutton until the lesson was over.

. . .

Toward all of these programs, my brother was appeasing. He withstood the attention and got along as best he could. Adley was the most social of us, and she spent increasing time away. She was no homebody; she wanted to be out, away from the remoteness and quiet of where we lived, with others, at malls, with boys, eventually out of this area altogether. It was a time of withdrawal. When she was at home she spoke little, ate little, fought little. She was hardly present. She was becoming more self sufficient. She stayed in her room and played with her pet until my father asked where she was. He was often aloof, but he had a preternatural sense for missing persons. Then he would knock on her door to coerce or command her to come downstairs.

Once that winter he asked me to go up and ask her to come down.

"She won't want to." I said. "She won't listen to me."

"You don't know that." he said.

"Yes I do."

"Go anyway."

So I went, knocked, and asked if she wanted to come down. She said no. I went and told my father. He got up and when he came downstairs he was carrying the bunny's hutch; a big cage with a tray of food inside, a blankie, all its belongings jostling against the side as he lugged it down, watching his step.

My mother was upset.

"Now what is that for?" she said.

'Don't worry." he said.

She rose to follow him, and Adley stood at the top of the stairs, cold and staring.

"Adley." I called up. "Where's Dilly?"

She shook her head.

"Come on." I said. "What's going on?"

"Ask him, I don't know, I didn't do anything." Then she

turned and went back to her room. I followed my father to the pantry, then down to the cellar and where he placed the hutch against the wall. My mother called down.

"Edgar." she said.

"Don't call me that." he said. He bent over, adjusting things inside the cage.

"It's your name."

"Just don't call me that. What? What do you want?"

"What are you doing with the hutch?"

He turned from his squatting position and looked at us; first at me, then at my mother. He pointed his finger up, insinuating upstairs.

"I never see her. She spends every moment with her animal in her room and never comes out. There's something wrong with that."

"There's nothing wrong with her." my mother said.

"I'm not saying there is, but it's getting to be too much."

"And this will solve it, what you're doing? Putting her cage down here."

"The bunny will be fine. She can come down here to see it. She can bring it upstairs for all I care; she just needs to spend more time outside."

He went upstairs to Adley, and we followed, more for her sake than his. James sat at the piano bench, watching this transpire. He stopped playing.

"Where's the bunny?" my father said.

Adley sat on her bed with her arms crossed. Her nose was flared the same way my mother's became when she was more furious than words. I hadn't seen her like that, so provoked and quiet. He went to her and grabbed her by the arm.

"Where's the bunny?" he said, staring at her face.

She looked up at my mother and I, who were standing in

the doorway. She looked at us shamefully, like we had abandoned her to this moment, to his intrusion.

"Ed, give her space." my mother said. "The bunny's fine. She knows where to put it now."

"It's not fine. She's being rebellious."

"She hasn't done anything!" my mother yelled.

My father looked back at her, annoyed by her resistance. Finally, when the room was still and waiting, there was a noise in the closet, a movement. My father left the bed and opened the sliding closet doors, listening for it. Again the sound came. It came from the back of the closet. Adley stood up, terrified and silent. My father went to his knees and pulled out a pile of clothes and opened a shoe box and found the bunny inside. He took it out of the room and went downstairs, without another comment. My mother went to Adley and brought her back to the bed to sit, to restrain her and soothe her somehow.

I was in the middle of it all, trapped, not sure which way to go or look. My mother was stroking Adleys arms saying,

"I'm sorry, I'm so sorry, don't worry, ok? You didn't do anything wrong."

But my sister showed no affect. Eventually I went down and sat next to James at the piano. I heard the footsteps of my father creaking down the cellar. I told James what happened.

"Why?" he said.

"I'm not sure. He's upset with Adley for always being upstairs."

James put his left hand at the end of the keys and walked his fingers down the whole keyboard, playing each white key. He made it all the way to the other end, reaching over me, and when he hit the last note he looked up and smiled. Then he took his hands off, put them on his thighs and the two of us sat there, thoughtful, upset, slightly amused, slightly relieved by this piano that neither of us could play, that stood like a wall between us and trouble.

The house repaired in twos; Adley and my mother were upstairs, myself and James were at the piano, and my father and the bunny were in the cellar. Over the next hour the intensity desisted and my father brought the bunny back and apologized. He left the hutch where it was. My mother came down, and later the three of us kids went outside into the cold, strong wind to get some air and be alone. We each went our own way. James went to the pier, Adley sat on the steps, I walked along the street. In front of our house was a yellow dead-end sign strangled at the base by thick vines, and behind the sign was brush as far as I could see.

I walked past three houses on the street; Corey's, the Rayburns, and the people after that whose names I forgot. I remember looking at the sign that said Teal St. long enough for it to begin to look and sound strange to me. Teal St. It seemed odd that such a name would be assigned to this place. As I walked back the name traveled through my thoughts. The yard, the shore, the pier, the creek; all of it was brown. Even as my hand pushed the brass knob open into that familiar place, I thought,

'Here we are. Teal street. Teal. Teal. Teal. Teal. Teal street. 1328 Teal St.'

33

In cold months, the house had a smell of dryness to it that came from upright radiators clustered in each bedroom. Sometimes the radiators would wick the moisture in the air so thoroughly that I would wake in the night with a bloody nose and have to keep my head tilted on the pillow with a tissue plugging it. Other rooms in the house got cold because many of the windows were old and poorly insulated. Consequently each room was either overheated or underheated, so there was a frequent migration of bodies from one place to the next in search of proper warmth.

The dryness and coldness coincided with general restlessness too. Life bore on slowly for each of us at that time. Like Weems itself, our family life seemed to stall at certain moments from its regular ebb. Nothing fresh flowed; reticence, boredom, and uneventfulness became the pattern of our conversations. Routine discourses of weather and meals and schedules; the feeling that our lives, though connected, were largely separate, touching one another's only lightly, and therefore vaguely.

The physical seclusion and short days did not help. We were cooped, and whether consciously or not, we searched for intimacy on our own terms. My sister had the pet. Dilly remained in the cellar, evidently happy, well fed, and well visited. Adley would rush down the stairs past my mother, past anyone who might detain her and hold the bunny in the cold dimness of the cellar, smoothing its ears behind its head like she did. James had his activities too. Through piano and physical therapy, he had a regular watch over his life which prevented him from becoming overly and perhaps dangerously concerned about his circumstances. They were stabilizing for him. And for that reason they were good.

As for myself I had time, and nothing compelling me to rush. I had the promise of the turning of the year; the return of fishing and boating and being outside. I wanted to fish and boat seriously; more than I had before. I wanted to work at the boatyard if I could, to see where life took me. These were my plans. I did not sit in my room and dream. If I had dreams then, they were small on the scale of human ambitions, and I wouldn't have called them dreams because the things I wanted were in reach. I could taste them. I went to the outbuilding once a day just to look around. I would stand by the boat, the rods, the crab traps, to rearrange the gear and prep it for the next chance to go out, with no extensive purpose than to look and putter, to be consoled by the simplicity of those things.

I knew my parents looked after me with a certain concern about my priorities, my diminishing interest and performance in school, and what I would choose in the way of further education, work, livelihood. Because at that point I was unspoken about it, and I remained so long afterward. Yet I was not their sole concern. Becker's concerned them, and Adley's withdrawal concerned them. So did their extended families.

All of our issues put together, all of our extenuating unknowns gave them common ground. It formed a grave intimacy between them, but an intimacy nonetheless.

. . .

The squalid cold ended at the start of March and ushered in the season of Lent, a remnant of my father's cultural Catholicism. The start of it every year around February coincided with my father's feeling conflicted about money. It became manifest by the way his whole disposition changed in such short time. He would alternate between lavishing us at Christmas and stripping the household bare at Lent. He would halt what he deemed 'all unnecessary expenses', which included paper towels, pantry snacks, and the use of the dishwasher.

The process of elimination was not systematic, but spontaneous and conspicuous. Whatever caught his eye and appeared in that moment to be too much. Fruit on the counter could do it. My mother bought bananas out of habit, but there were some that went bad each week because we ate fewer, fearing if we ate them all my father would notice and take offence and tighten his grip on household provisions. But wasted food was no good either. So it was a game, a tiptoe. The bananas sat on the counter and blackened, and though we wanted them we left them. By the end of the week the spoiled bunch appeared like tribute before the watchful patriarch- none of us knowing whether the rotten things appeased or angered him, and none with courage to throw them until they stunk outright.

It was unreasonable of course, and ironic that he kept catalogues of boat parts lying in every room, but there was nothing to decry without it only deepening his conviction that our family lacked resolve and resilience and thrift, which could only be learned from having less. Lent was not about about faith. It was about thrift.

"I had very little growing up." he would say at dinner. "For meals we would have rice, beans, small meat, small bread. Only small."

He would show us how small, pinching his fingers together. His voice altered too, sounding more hispanic, more accented.

"We have too much here, I think." He would look around the table at the portions on our plates, judging them. This idea consumed him; though it was a conversation he kept with himself, unless my mother reproached him. Usually she kept her peace, but now and again she spoke up.

One evening he came down to the kitchen from upstairs holding a dress in a plastic hanger. The dress still had tags on it. My mother was at the sink.

"What's this?" he said, holding it up for inspection.

"A present."

"From who?"

"My mom."

"Your mom?"

"Yes."

"You're going to wear it?"

"I haven't tried it on yet."

"Why haven't you?"

She turned the faucet off and wrung the dish towel over the sink.

"Can you please stop with the questions? I'm going to try it on, I just took it out today."

"When did you get it?

She stepped forward to take it, but he swung it away from her reach.

"For Christmas, Edgar! For Christmas."

She turned around and put the faucet back on. He hung the dress on the back of the table chair and sat down, looking at her at the sink.

"Avery?" he said, his voice softer. "I'm trying to take

account of what we have and what we spend. It's not about your dress, it's not."

She turned the faucet louder in the sink.

"Are you listening?" he said.

"I'm trying to finish up, Ed."

"It's not about the dress, I was saying. My family did not have much growing up. My mother had-"

"Ok!" she said, "Ok, I get it. But I'm tired of this. It's been every night that you take fault with something. Can't you give it a break. You're restless, don't you see."

The sink was still running.

"And stop saying, or suggesting you were poor-" she continued. "You weren't. You always say that, like it excuses you from something."

"We were." he said. "You wouldn't know that."

"I wouldn't? I married you. I met your family."

"Yeah?" he said. "And my father passed away for goodness sake."

"And? And then what?" she said, like she had jammed him with the question. "The money, you mean? she said.

He was looking off when she spoke to him, but when she ended her speech he turned back.

"Will you turn that off?"

She snapped off the faucet, dried her hands and took the dress upstairs and put it in her closet. I never saw her wear it.

My father's observation of Lent extended to us too. It was the one liturgical season he observed piously for reasons I never fully knew. Partly it was his family's tradition. But more so I believe, there was something in the penitential spirit of the season that appealed to him; the fasting and sobriety, or the reminder of poverty, which answered some malaise in him that all the year preceding had remained unchecked, undisciplined, or was ignored, or aggravated by acquiring more things and having ample money sitting around.

It produced that incorrigible look of discontent on his face, that sense deep down when he looked on us and on his wife, that we were a family stranded, unmoored, dawdling; if not materially, then spiritually. For all we had we were lacking. But it was something he could not proclaim without also practicing. He demanded that consistency of himself.

At church on Ash Wednesday we sat in a pew, tallest to shortest, dressed in dark attire, timorous, each of us walking the same reverent steps up the aisle to receive ash on our foreheads. My mother received the one clean, distinguishable cross on her forehead. The rest of ours were smudges. Afterwards, we weren't allowed to take the ash off that day. James tried to take his off on the car ride back, but my father caught his hand, and said "No, leave it." We slept in our smudges that night.

Over the next weeks, as Spring came slinking toward our corner of Weems creek, the prodigality of cold, damp days was shortened blissfully by a spree of unusually blue and warm ones. We made what we could of it. Yet even in that warm turn my father's penance persisted like a steady rain, stolid and judicious, falling and falling, til each under that roof was sodden alike.

For James it was the piano that took the penance. His lessons with the Jewish woman were cut in number, and the gap was filled with my father's supervision, who supervised by looming over the upright with his elbow leaning on the corner, as James squeaked on the seat and set his hands on the keys. My brother began by playing scales, all the ones he had learned. He played them regular and choppy, striking the right notes mostly, except for one scale, F sharp, which he messed up whenever my father watched. I knew exactly how it sounded, because the more he played it, the more he fumbled it, and the harder he strained to play it right the more flagrant it came off. At which point my father would respond, "Aghh". The scale became something of an omen, something I dreaded hearing even from afar; repeatable, tragic, and for whatever reason, irremediable.

It was a tightrope of performance my brother walked upon. He wanted to play fluidly and freely, but he could only do so when he was alone. My father's audience impaired him; it produced in him an escalating diffidence. Whatever he performed under his father's watch he lost confidence in.

Sometimes I came and listened too, to aleve my father's presence. When James played mistakes my father would breathe heavily through his nose so that his dissatisfaction could be heard.

"Ok. Again." he would say. And like clockwork James would make the same mistake. If it continued, my father would change positions and tell my brother to scoot over, and sit down next to him. He would take the music book, the red one, and breaking open the spine to any song a random, wag his finger to the title of the piece.

"This one." he'd say, tapping the title twice. "This one. Can you play this one?"

"I haven't learned that one yet."

"But you can play it though, yes? Do you know the notes?"

James would always attempt it. But it was a circus act. He would stumble through the first few notes then get stuck, or creep along, playing one bad note to every two. If it went on, my father would stop, take the book and flip back to an earlier song. Ironically, it was always the same song he flipped back to, 'The Carousel' which in the book contained a small sketch of a carousel above the title. James knew that song and could play it. Two or three times he would play it for my father who sat there, listening carefully, waiting to pounce. Bless James. He was always willing. It's a repetitive song, and it still clanks brightly in my memory.

When my father was satisfied he would stand again and hover behind his son.

"Play another one, you can choose."

So he would, and more mistakes could come hammering out of the instrument, and the breathing, and all of it all over again.

"You need to go back to the scales."

My brother would sit there still sometimes, staring blankly at the keys or the book, hoping my father would relent his attention and go elsewhere. James was so unhappy. So unfree. He was nearly a sophomore in high school then, not a kid anymore.

My mother interrupted one time when my father was there watching James play.

She said, "How can he play with you breathing down his neck?"

He faced her and said, "If he can't play with his own father watching, how will he learn to play for anyone?"

"Edgar, give him space."

"He can have all the space he wants. Practice is what he needs. And stop calling me that I've told you."

She left, fed up. And he stayed, hovering over the kid.

My mother used my father's full name sparingly, but purposefully, at times like that when he was simply wrong and obtuse, and needed correction, when only his name was enough for him to argue with.

For a week in March it rained heavily each day in the morning and afternoon, and in between showers everything dripped and soaked with cold, sour rainwater. The cellar flooded at the end of the week. Days of pent up wetness seeped through the gaps and pores of the home's foundation unnoticeably until my mother saw the film of standing water on the cellar floor as she looked down from the pantry entrance. She called each of us to take buckets, pots and pails in loads upstairs and dump it in the yard. It was three inches deep across the cellar floor. A broom and dustpan floated atop, as did the hutch, which had drifted into the near corner of the room, up against the wall. My mother saw it as she came down.

"The bunny!" she yelled, "the bunny!"

"Ed!" she called, and he came down shortly.

"Give me something to reach it. I don't have shoes. Quick quick, he's in there soaked."

I found an umbrella in the kitchen and handed it to my father, who handed it to my mother, who used the hook of its handle to drag the floating cage within reach. Then she pulled it up, the water falling out on the stairs, and dragged it up until my father took it from her halfway on the stairs and carried it, bumping over the steps, shaking everything inside, including the creature.

"Be careful." she said.

The three of us, James, Adley and myself gathered at the door and back stepped to see what was going on. Adley had a frightened look on her face. She followed my father out the pantry door into the yard, reaching around him to the cage, but he fended her off.

"It's mine!" she said.

"Just wait! Stop!" he yelled, looking at her directly, and she stopped defiantly as he walked on a few paces more then set the hutch upright. My mother called James and I from inside and we proceeded down to the cellar in our boots and filled two buckets with water.

"He can't take that." she said to me, referring to James with the bucket.

"I can too." he said. "Go, Constance, I've got it."

"No!" she said. "No! Put it down."

He put it down. He was visibly upset.

"Take this one." she said, and she handed him a tall pot.

"Constance, go on. Come back for the other bucket."

We struggled up the stairs with our separate loads. I lifted mine step by step, my hands fitted tight against the hard plastic handle. The water was sloshing at the rim. I carried it between my legs at the top, and out the door. In fatigue I nearly spilled it right outside the door. James was about to do the same when my father reproached him.

"James! No. Out there," he pointed. "Farther, farther, where Constance put hers, unless you want it all to go back to the same place."

So James carried it out and dumped it in a puddle near where I dumped mine.

Adley was crying, I could hear. Not dramatically, but sobbing without end. She was still wearing pajamas and she was stiff as a board standing there while my father reached in to grab the bunny. The creature scrabbled back and forth, evading him. Before long my mother called us back.

"Constance! James! Come on, where are you?"

We went back in and took the bucket and pot she had brought already to the top of the stairs.

"Take these." she said.

We took them, but we were still watching what was going on outside.

"When you're done with those, come back. Who's crying out there?"

Neither of us answered. She followed us out, standing by the door.

"Is it ok?" she asked my father. "What's happening?"

"Fine," he said. "If I can get him. He tried to bite me."

James and I emptied our pot and pail far away from the house and walked slowly back, watching the spectacle unfold on the muddy lawn. My father finally caught the pet, and a sick smile came across his mouth, like he had trapped a rodent, a pest.

"Ah ha." he said.

Adley's stopped crying and stepped forward to do something, but again, my father put his hand out to fend her off.

"Uh! uh!" he said, to keep her from coming closer.

He had the creature by the fur, by the skin of its neck, and it kicked madly in his grip; except for his head and ears, his whole body was dark from dampness, from floating in the cellar water. He raised it slightly.

"It smells." he said, then lowered it.

I could see the creature's eyes and sense its tiny desperation. Then my father raised it again in front of him, intrigued by it, proud that he had caught it, but it twisted in his hand and kicked more, its long nails swiping across his forearm and he dropped it. It fell to the ground with a thud. He cussed. He held his arm, pinching the place where it cut him and looked down at the ground below, where the creature sat motionless and small between his feet. Taking a step away he nodded to Adley and said,

"Take it away."

She scooped it in her hands and put it in its hutch and my father watched as she took it away, her thin arms straining to carry it across the wet grass. She placed the cage by the back door. My father went back inside and we followed behind him carrying our containers which we held the whole time. Down and up the soggy steps we went carrying loads of rain, hauling it far enough from the house as we were told, then pouring it out with all the sound and satisfying release of emptying a big, heavy liquid. All that weight gone to feathers.

One after another the consecutive spillings formed pools and puddles, and eventually gulches.

The last half inch of water was the hardest to gather, and we took turns sweeping small skeins of it tediously into our pails and buckets with the dustpan, until we did all we could. My father opened the window wells below which were hard shut and when they opened, it was like the world itself came in, the cool fresh air, the murmurs of wind. My mother took towels from upstairs, bath towels and dish towels, and brought them down, and we fell to sopping and drying the floor as much as possible. We wrung the remains into the containers until the towels were saturated through, and the cold floor glistened. The final load James and I took out and dumped at the end of one of the footpaths we had muddled and mushed by our going. The yard was spattered.

In my periphery I saw Adley. She was by herself by the door, crouched to the cage, where she had moved it. Her hair was down, straight, covering her face. Her hand was softly latched to the front of the cage. Her feet were firm in the ground. She did not move, she did not talk. James called her name as we passed by but she did not answer except with a shift of her head, her eyes watching the ground we passed on, not us, just the ground.

I felt I owed her something in that moment, without knowing what exactly. A nod? A word? Some pittance of sympathy? But whatever I could have given, or should have given, I did not give. I simply walked past her. I went inside, wanting to be finished.

We were spent, all of us. From morning to afternoon the sky marbled inconsistently. Clouds then cloudless. Grey then blue. A whorl of temperaments. As the day waned I watched the sky from inside. My brother played the piano. My father went through his catalogues. My mother continued putting things in order. I think it was her way of keeping out.

The towels were a heavy mess. Before dinner I took an

armful to the side porch and stomped them of excess water. I hung them on the green clothesline that stretched between two trees by the outbuilding. We hardly ever used that line. The towels were so heavy they sagged almost to the mud. Nor did they dry. My mother took the others and put them through the washer, then the dryer. For a time it was the only sound in the house, the tumble and beep of the machine. I brought the hanging towels in eventually. What a waste; I think they got heavier.

To pass the time I sat on the dryer and read Misty of Chincoteague, a story about the wild horses of Chincoteague on the Eastern Shore. It was an old favorite of mine; a book I read for comfort, to leave where I was and go somewhere else. I heard the fireplace door shut in the living room, and from my place in the pantry I watched as sunlight swam through the nearby window all the way into the kitchen where my mother was.

It was warm on the dryer with the book. I've never forgotten the pleasure of that seat, nor the aimlessness of those weekend hours that were so entwined with our family life, when we were past feuding and had settled to some cure. I felt that enmity could melt if given space like that, or been prevented from the start. But one always followed the other. The flooding and the mopping. The sobbing and the silence. The anger of the house and the kindness; kindness which came later, propitiating, like the tide easing off the bank.

After dinner, with daylight remaining, I went outdoors along the side of the house where we worked earlier. By then the cage was moved and left an outline in the mud. Adley and my brother were gone. It was only me. The air was stiller and warmer and more humid than before, which heightened the smell of soggy ground. A front was coming. At the edge of our property, close to shore, the pines, short and squat stood glistening dark. Above the horizon, a band of slate-black storm clouds, strict as a ruler's edge, shrank under the burden of the upper sky, a pale pink brink, luminous and mild. The sky was cut like ribbon. The colors shone in the ground. Water stood in the ruts of our boot prints reflecting shards of sky, and bugs skittered over the surface.

In the finale of the evening, before I left, two tiny bats descended and danced over the area where watched them, delighting me with their circles and cries. When they left, I came in.

Unfortunately, the bunny got a red eye later that week that never got better. It must have been from the episode. The cage was replaced to the basement, but even Adley did not go down as often to see it anymore. The single red eye gave it a wounded, cursed appearance that made it look fearful to touch. Whenever I saw it, I saw my father's trifling with the poor thing, his ungentleness toward it.

It died not long after, not to anyone's surprise. We found the bunny lying on his side, emaciated. His food and his water were full, untouched. My mother spoke that day in a hush. She was not a sentimental person, but she felt for Adley. She went to Adley's room and told her what happened, and through the walls I heard my sister crying.

My father, impatient of the bunny's death, swept the creature in a dustpan and told us to follow him outside. We went to the outbuilding and he ordered James to dig a hole for it, close to the pile of shrubbery and wet logs. James did so, and my father dropped the bunny in and put the dirt over it. None of us cried. Not even Adley. She was finished crying. Adley was the first to leave with my mother, then James. I stayed behind until my father stamped the ground. Then that was that. He turned to me and said,

"We need to get tarps to put over these piles. This wood will do us no good if it's wet."

. . .

So that was my penance. The tarps my father gave me were black, not blue or silver like the old ones were. They were Lenten tarps. I was told to cover the logs with one, the brush pile with another, and a third was to be draped over the bench at the end of the pier which stored life jackets. I tarped the bench first. When I opened it the inside fumed of mildew and there was thick green mold crawling over each jacket. That had happened before and we had to throw them out. I covered the logs and brush last. I weighted the sides of the piles down with cinder blocks from the outbuilding.

Everywhere I looked was some portion of covering or shrouding. The yard was dark with dead grass, and the stumps in back, which every year wore away a little more, looked like festering knuckles above the ground.

PART II

34

Contrary to all sullen observance, my mother found ways of liberating herself from the limitless influence of thrift. Small things kept her cheerful. She lit candles in the morning and in the afternoon when we returned to school. Vanilla, cinnamon, sugar cookies; she favored the baked goods and confectionery variety. She took up her old habit of collecting pine cones and putting them in flower pots on the side steps. She also bought a discrete bird feeder and fixed it to the one apple tree, hoping no one would notice. But of course it was the first thing my father mentioned when he got home.

"What's that?" he said. "Did I put that there?"

Fortunately he thought little of it, and it remained there for the time being waiting for guests.

Come spring the water on Weems clarified, whereas all winter it was clouded with sediment, leaves and mud. Our one apple tree budded, and all that was brown before was sprung into a lush form of lightness. The back creeks and the Nanticoke lightened in color from a dismal ore-brown to a warm chestnut. Sparrows, egrets, ibis', returned and began trooping along the soggy banks, sticking their beaks into the thrush for ghost shrimp and eel and crab larvae. The ospreys returned too, refurbishing their nests above the channel markers.

And the grass, unsung of all living things, which all winter wore away bald and pale, by increments began to green, softening the step and wearing thick again. The pilings on the pier began to fuzz with algae and lichen. Each small testament of change was a lift to the spirit and the home. All that was there was new again.

Whether I knew so or not in the moment, that specific spring marked a shift in my place at home, and carried me farther toward the way of life I've been at ever since.

It was pure enjoyment and liberty that came of it. The boat was out again and I had it under my reigns. I drove it into new paths, going up and down a near endless network of creeks along the Nanticoke and Weems, and all the minor creeks too: Danner, Sigspoole, Troody, Fins, Black Creek (the one we named), and how many others which had no name at all-

progressing slowly toward the mouth of the Bay. The Bay was the limit. We lived 7 miles from the mouth, which does not sound far, but even that was a long distance in the dory, with its one lung motor. I knew not to push it. It was not a boat designed to fare alongside headboats and yachts; it was hardly a craft meant to be maneuvering the midways of the Nanticoke. It was meant for sleuthing, for gripping shorelines and wading still waters and gunkholing the shallow banks of marsh. And I respected what it was capable of.

Rarely I journeyed alone. I brought Beverly with me, sometimes James too. I had them hold the fishing poles and crab traps we brought. We got dirty looks all the time from men passing us on their streamliners; condescending, humored looks. They didn't nod at us like they did for the other boats; they just stared, or smirked, or shook their heads. Maybe they didn't approve of girls piloting boats, or maybe we looked like fools outfitted on that dory. I couldn't read minds to say. But they lacked seamanship and courtesy. All they wanted was for us to get out of their way.

In the stern of the boat I kept a notebook, and as we traversed the creeks and river, I drew rude maps and wrote down the creeks that had names, and those that didn't. Many didn't, and that was part of the enjoyment of the expeditions, naming the hitherto nameless, imparting to each a title, a code to be remembered by, even if just by us. Some afternoons before embarking, I turned the pages from the previous day and saw what little legibility came through. Perhaps they were better read under the conditions they were written in, the pitching and rolling of the river, the windyness. There is a visible mutation in the letters on the page from when they were written on land, neat and square and concise, to when I sat on the back bench and whittled something, and they lost all their squareness, their meticulousness, and took on instead a loopy, unruled penmanship that clambered over the page with scribbles of waterways we passed, landmarks leading into other creeks, etc. I did not consult the maps I drew afterwards, but they helped commit them to my mind.

Some days I made fast at Beverly's, marched the hill to the barn and helped her feed the pigs. Her family was busy because of their farm, and I didn't mind helping out when I could. More often it felt good to put myself to use. Other days I joined my father at the boatyard. I submitted my application for a waitress position, but for weeks I heard nothing. I would sit in the stern of the boat with my father. At the time, there was no official name written across the transom of that boat, but he dubbed it informally, 'the tub', because it was a big white boat, good for relaxing, and it sat there at the docks not moving, like a tub.

The docks were a very good place to unwind, especially for my father. They were hidden, quiet, all but unpeopled during the week. Plus, the trinkets and rigging of the boat were an endless hobby for him, as they are more most boat enthusiasts. He enjoyed all the arcana of boat parts, thinking about them, making plans to replace this piece or that. Such diversions were good for him. The boat floating in its slip gentled the side of him we saw at home; the coiled, calculating side. It quelled his meanness, it pacified his passion.

By casual rabble, mostly listening and acknowledging, watching him show me around and point things out, I came to know the boat's anatomy, and all their intricacies lodged their way into my mind. I retained whatever he showed me because he showed me everything twice and more. Choke valves, seacocks, draft and waterline, gudgeons and pintle. If the boat didn't have something, he would lean over the side and point to a boat that did. It pleased him to locate something he was speaking about. When he found it he would say,

"Ah, that! Just like that" and make its shape or likeness with his hand.

Now and again his family stories would surface, and I came to enjoy hearing about them again after so long, especially the ones I had not heard before. I liked these stories, firstly, because they sounded so different from our Eastern Shore life. And secondly, I saw that he was at ease when he told them. Perhaps even most fully himself. And I liked seeing him that way.

What he shared about his family was spoken in vignettes, and bequeathed over time.

Sitting on deck on day, he told me how he once rescued Antonio from drowning in the pond behind their house. He saved his brother by three strands of hair. How did that happen? I asked. He said he was inside and heard a splash and went to see what it was. There was a bubbling in the deep part of the pond, so he reached his hand in blindly and pulled up his brother by three strands of hair. I never forgot the detail of only three strands because it sounded miraculous, and maybe that was the real story. And if so, it was almost a tragic story. But to my father it was just funny. Certain stories I remember not because they were good, but because of how he told them. It was like that.

He told me about 'chaclas', the house shoes his mother wore, the sound of their flapping on the tile floor. He remembers how she would come after him and his brother when they brought their bare feet through the house, leaving footprints from the pasture and pond. They could hear the flapping in pursuit. From two steps they would hear only one, and they knew one of the shoes was in her hand for smacking.

He said when he and his brother were punished for talking back they cleaned the tack room, a wood built shack next to the stable where horse equipment was stored. It smelled of leather and horse feed; a sweet smell he said he misses. The walls had no windows, and they were imperfectly joined, which let splinters of sun onto the floor and into the quiet air. He remembered the motes of dust and the glitter from the mud ground. Mice scurried and the breeze blew the smell of pasture inside. Equipment hung on nails in the wall, and there was always something falling apart in the tack room. 'You knew it without looking.'

Before their family left south Texas for Dallas, their house was invaded by cicadas; loud, green, bullet-sized bugs they rarely saw in all their time on the ranch. Each day the cicada's rasping rang through the grasses like an uninterrupted siren, overtaking the bellow of frogs and the chirp of crickets. And at night it continued. My grandmother thought they were a sign of bad luck because they were pestilent and seemed to die quickly. My grandfather thought it was a sign of good luck because they were leaving the bugs behind, which meant better things ahead.

Slowly the cicadas went away or died. Not long before the family left for good, the incessant squawking had simmered to a single bug sputtering on its back on the white cement walkway in front of the house. As it seized, my father said Antonio pinched it by its cellophane wing and it silenced for a second, then it seized all the more, raving and squawking. When he dropped it, it flayed and flipped to its back, unable to fly. Then he crunched it with his heel.

One last memory he told me. He said once, at dusk, after a warm rain he saw a drop of gold, or an earring hanging to the bark of one of the small pecan trees on the side of the house. The sun, hitting it just right, made the shape glow indistinctly from afar, but the closer he got to inspect it, he saw that it was a cicada shell; an outgrown husk, amber colored, its hollow hooked claws clinging perfectly to the bark, but when he went to touch it, he took his hand away at the last moment and let it be. He looked it up and down, profiling it from all angles, observing how the old likeness was changed by dusk light, transmogrified into something unlikely; a drop of honey, a shrill thing possessed of beauty.

It confounded me that he remembered moments like that with such pristine detail, with accuracy and sensibility, but if I asked him to describe a person he knew all his life, like his brother or mother, he was suddenly short of words, mute of specificity.

For a long time I never heard about what happened to his family after they moved to Dallas. The history is split in two testaments. The first half of life, the ranch half, which is rich in my imagination, so full of color and ambience. And the second, the indistinct passage of time in Dallas, the coming of age of my father and his family in their new locale, which was so fraught with generalities and so lacking in vividity.

It is like the memory of that period went missing, like it were severed from the first half, like my father heaved it away in chunks. As a result, I had the impression all my life that my father's ranch memory, those pristine, unadulterated years were the ones he wanted us to glean from, to remember, to make our own. They were not just memories; they were an inheritance. He was dogged about it.

"Don't forget that, ok?" he'd say. "I mean it. One day you'll want to know where you came from."

But also you could hear the wistfulness. Like he hoped we would have something to say if we were asked about his family. Maybe one of those memories would spring to mind and we would tell how our father ran through the pasture barefoot or saved his brother from drowning by three strands of hair.

As he grew older those memories returned to him even more. He ached to go back there; not only to the place, but to the time. When he was close to the water those thoughts came.

35

A month later I got the call saying I was hired as a waitress. I started a week later, and before long I was quick stepping around tables, recommending the crab dip to sailors, and rolling silverware in napkins. I was thankful for the job. It gave me a lease from home, put money in my pocket, and kept me honest. Moreso it kept me to a schedule. The job balanced my recreational hours so that I was not solely burning fuel in my free time, but earning some keep. There is dignity in every first job I suppose, of simply being useful. That's what Mel's was. Mel's was the name of the restaurant back then. It was a comfortable, unfancy place serving all the people who came to the boatyard, the rich and the poor, the regulars and the one timers. It was small back then, half the size it is now, with tall windows overlooking the harbor, and a cool, dim interior. People had to squint to read the menu. The tables along the windows were my favorite to serve. I liked looking out over the docks seeing what was happening, who was coming and who was going (or being towed in). The masts swaying against the sky, the busy crane lifting and setting down. All the clamour and movement of it. It was a home away from home.

I was good at being a waitress. Although after awhile the early enthusiasm wore off and many days I found myself working by autopilot; taking orders, bussing food, checking in, smiling. It was not bad, but it could be tiresome, and even the charm of the water view subsided over time. When I started I worked two days a week. By summer I was working full time, and on the weekends I drove the boat with Beverly to the boatyard, and she would drop me off, and come back later.

On calm waters the trip was only 30 minutes away, and we made it so many times the route became neighborly and pleasant. Bev couldn't come every time. Summer was a busy season on the farm and I didn't grudge her that. That was her job. It was work she often enjoyed in the moment, but complained about later. But more importantly, we had solidarity, a happy kinship forged from our separate places on Weems, a mutual interest in the river, Bay, shoals, sounds, marsh, and an unhassled outlook toward life as it came toward us.

Occasionally it arose in our conversations what the future held. What we would do, where we would go. Whether by some reflex or by some fear of having nothing to say, one of us would say 'We're applying to Salisbury right?', the local university. Many of our graduating class was going there, and the others were going far far away. As the time drew closer to make a decision, our tone changed. There was a seriousness in our asking, a summons, like we ought to prick ourselves to reality now and again.

"I'm going to apply." one of us would say.

"I'm going to as well." the other would reply.

It was like a secret bargain we decided on. That we would follow each other wherever. It was a bargain full of the ultimatum of youth.

36

My final year of high school had less of the bittersweet sentiment that was shared among my classmates. It had little of the excitement of passing through a great moment of one's life, and more of finishing to finish, to get on with the next. I don't say that as some subtle form of self-congratulations. There have been times when I have looked upon those years and felt bereft. Like I missed something valuable, that I removed too far and too quickly for my own good.

In the fall I quit my job at the restaurant and took another job at the boatyard, in the parts supply shop. When I applied I mentioned I worked at the restaurant and that my father's boat was docked there, and that I was interested in boats in general. The shop manager, Mr. Bruce, a long time member of the boatyard, looked at me warily when I said those things. He was a white haired man in his sixties, who looked like all the others who came into the shop. I don't know if he had employed a high schooler before, let alone a girl, but I think I impressed him with my broad, cursory knowledge of boating and boat parts. It was more than he assumed I had, I guess.

I worked in the afternoons when class let out. Mr. Bruce

would be there, waiting on the stool at the register, arms folded, his white hair tucked under a red ball cap, the weather channel playing on a small screen in the corner of the shop. Behind him was a wall of rope. Ropes of all kind. It was the most memorable part of the shop by far. A feast for the eyes. Coiled ropes and loose ropes. Spools of it in bright green, white, braided, unbraided, whipped, seized; winch ropes and jib ropes, cleat ropes and mooring lines, and thin, multipurpose strings for anything you could think of. I never saw such variety in one place. When I came in Mr. Bruce would totter on his stool and lift his eyes.

"Oh, you're here." he'd say.

Always with a hint of surprise. Like I had roused him from a midday nap. He would stand and clean the counter of parts, restoring order. Then he would find me something to do. And the next day he would be there again, just like that; just sitting on his stool, encamped in ropes.

When the store got busy, which was not often, Mr. Bruce would yank the spools of rope behind the register so hastily that they piled on the floor and became a tripping hazard. Then, if there was a lull in customers, he would step away from the register and forget to rewind them. He would simply leave the rope on the ground. Why did he do that? My theory is that it made him anxious seeing how quickly the store came undone when things got busy. Mr. Bruce was not a busy man. He did not like commotion, even sales commotion. He preferred to spend leisurely time with shoppers, to talk with them, ask them about their boat. Anyhow, when the ropes jumbled, I would trade places and wind them back until the wall was neat again. I knew it mattered to him, and when he came around he would say,

"Aww, no you didn't have to clean up my mess. That's my mess I left. You shouldn't have to."

"I don't mind." I'd say. And off he'd go, humming.

He was a man who took child-like interest in the parts he

sold. He knew every gadget, plug, and goo on his shelves, and he remained fascinated by them no matter how many were sold or not sold. He took laps around the store, unconsciously picking things up, reading their labels, carrying them around, then leaving them somewhere else and forgetting about it. Like a bibliophile enamored by the feel of books, and comforted by their presence, so Mr. Bruce was with his marine inventory. On most days he would make small hoards of things at the register, sweep them aside when he was ringing someone up, then take them out again for a second study. But they never made it back to their original spot. Fortunate for us, we both knew about this habit of his; he liked to take things out, I liked to put things back. And so we kept ourselves afloat on dead days, by creating errands, then fulfilling them ourselves. The two of us going back and forth. We were busier than we needed to be, but it kept our spirits up, and amused us greatly.

All love of boating begins with love of water and love of boats. But very close behind it are the comestibles of the trade, the trinketware of boats. Clips and ties, tillers and anchors, shrouds, backstays, spreaders, and all those neat details which work by continual fascination to feed the love until that love has mutated into something less than it once was, and become an obsession. Hobby-love can be so. The further the interest goes, the more involved it gets.

I enjoyed the little boat differently, for though I did not own it (it was my father's), I belonged to it, and it to me. One thing I respected about my father is that he never lorded the little boat over me as *his* property. He never made me feel I owed him anything for using it. It was pure generosity. In fact, it was like he passed it to me without saying so, when he saw my connection to it. I tethered it, broke it, and drove it. I flipped its hull and tarped it in the winter. Mine were the legs that wore the white paint down to the wood where I sat each time. Only by many uses and many misuses did I understand this.

The more I worked in the shop the more it was clear to me that the bond between boat and boatsman either throve or corrupted, but never simply idled. Idleness was the death of ownership, and I saw yachts pass from life to death, one owner to the next, unsavored at each pass- a decade old and only 20 trips under its belt. One can become enamored by the parts and forget the boating. That happened to my father to some extent. Many men take boating as a hobby and find, earlier or later, that the hobby has broken them rather than restored them. That it stripped them of their self assuredness and feasted on their savings and livelihood too. Those who made it had discipline. They were plodders in their work. Slow, but consistent. Daily and calloused. Knowledgeable about what they could and could not do. Only in the honest attempt to put something back together does one taste the magnitude of the work. No smart checklist will tell you what that means, or what it includes. New boaters would come into the shop with a long list and state very deliberately 'I just need this and this'. Mr. Bruce would ring them up and one week later that same person would be back with a bag of returns and an embarrassed look on their face. The first of many concessions. After three months of returns, exchanges, deliberations, unfinished undertakings, miniscule victories, minor progress, there was another look on their faces. The charm had left. Yes, it would be a long road.

The didactic of the shop was good for that reason; the hem and haw of troubleshoot, suggestion, try, retry, even the idle chit-chat between myself and Mr. Bruce imparted useful information at times that people overheard. People would divulge their repair plans, launch dates, confessions and blunders; always with that upspeak at the end of whatever it was they were saying, as if it were really a question they were putting forth to Mr. Bruce, and not a statement. He would chime in if someone was contemplating something egregious, like applying brightwork without thoroughly sanding the hull, or asking about depth finders when the engine was still in repair. But often he kept quiet. He was the best kind of bystander; savvy, yet never pushy as a salesman. He dissuaded people from buying what they didn't need. He had that genuineness about him; he had been in their shoes. He was content to watch what happened, for he knew that there was nothing so valuable as lived competence- to allow someone to learn by their own trial, to be schooled by setback. One way or another the long lists people came with would be cut in half. Then quarter sheets, then the backs of envelopes. A few things at a time.

So that is how the shop kept its face; by being the tangible expression and personality of its manager, who greeted all newcomers with the question:

"What are you driving?", and from there he had his kindling.

In 6 months I began to understand the interrelatedness of the boatyard, the boaters, and the shop. I saw the dependencies of men upon this place, the braided strands of weather-talk and shop-talk, the 'stop ins', which were a necessary bulwark, a refuge from obsession and solitariness. Over time I felt Mr. Bruce begin to trust me and take favor in me. When I first started he held his cards close to his chest. He offered no commentary on the many people who came and went. He stocked the shelves humming softly to himself. We did not speak much then. We were like two librarians, conversing only with customers, and privately.

He began to warm though. I asked him questions about boats, gear, navigation- never too many all at once, but scattered throughout the shift. He was kind enough not to turn a question down, and it was that slow process of coaxing and listening that drew him out. Eventually he began to offer his commentary free of charge, and I think he began to view me more as a friend than as a storehand. From my end, none of it was a ploy to earn his good graces. I actually enjoyed boats and being around them. I wanted to be around them for a long time. He asked me what kind of boat I like, and I told him about the dory and how often I took it out.

"More than most men here use theirs." he said. "And a whole lot cheaper to repair. You know, when someone has sunk so much time and energy into a boat, there is high expectation to have a big experience and a great time. That's the people who come in here. You never know it upfront, because when you buy a boat all you can think about is getting the thing seaworthy. But even when you've taken 5 trips, 10 trips, 20 trips- and that's a lot- you still wonder what you paid for. Because that has its limits too, and the cruising isn't always commensurate with the love affair you had when you bought the thing. You realize you could of had as much fun for far cheaper. I've been there though. That's how I can say."

He would speak like that sometimes; not in a monologue, and not directly at me. Like sort of a pep talk, made from a train of thoughts that came to him as he went about the shop, restocking, or ringing the register, stepping around piles of rope. He ended most of his comments with some sting upon himself, a check against his pride. And as I came to know him, it was this natural humility I respected more than anything else.

37

There were other times when indecent, ugly, human drama alighted on our little post. It was not uncommon for boat owners to use their boat to shirk other responsibilities in life. But there was one man whose story I recall clearly. His name was Pat, a lawyer in his forties. He was new to boating and had purchased a huge 40 ft. sailboat. He was passionate, full of research, and knew nothing of boating. There hung over him an air of achievement, of fast learning, the kind of self appraisal that believed he would not be a beginner sailor for very long, and that his ascendancy to expert would be a straightforward and uninterrupted operation, no less straightforward than applying himself willfully to law textbooks and court opinions.

For weeks he frequented the shop every two days. He was neither outspoken nor reticent, and it was during those brief, purposeful bursts of appearance in our shop that Mr. Bruce and myself reconnoitered the man and learned such basic details about his life. He never came with a list. There was always one thing he wanted, and only one thing. He would find it, compare the closest alternatives, and bring it to the register, every purchase researched, weighed, decided on swiftly, and onto the next thing, like he went through life ticking off assignments, setting up cases and winning them.

At the register, Mr. Bruce would scan the item that was being purchased, and Pat would say,

"I'm cleaning the props today." or "They say this is the best rust resistant paint on the market." There was never a question in the statement, because he was a man in perpetual agreement with himself. And he never spoke in a tone that implied he was speaking with someone, but simply that he was speaking. Loud and convincing. It was those sort of men that Mr. Bruce resisted overspeaking to. Actually, he hardly spoke out at all when they came around.

One day Pat came in and bought a length of winch rope for the jib. As Mr. Bruce rang it up, he picked it up and said,

"What will you do with the extra?"

Pat, surprised at the comment, said, "What extra?"

"Is this for the jib?"

"It is."

"I imagine you'll have more length than you need." Mr. Bruce said.

Pat looked at it, dubious at the claim.

"I doubt it, but I'll just take it." he said. "By now I've spent my quota and more."

He shook his head, took the bag, and turned to leave. As he did Mr. Bruce said,

"Long as the wife doesn't mind."

The comment was meant to be light hearted, but Pat stopped at the door and turned around. His face was changed. He pointed a finger at Mr. Bruce and said,

"You can keep comments like that to yourself unless you want to be sued." Then he left.

When he was gone I looked up at Mr. Bruce who glanced at his watch and said to me,

"I think I struck something I wasn't trying to. It's not yet 11 am. That's the earliest I've had him in here too."

. . .

Unfortunately that was not the end. Later that afternoon a well dressed woman came into the shop, talking on her phone, walking about. I was at the register. When she ended her call she came to the front and asked if I had seen or knew a Mr. Morris. I said the name was unfamiliar. She went back to her phone and every now and then she put the phone down and looked out the window. Mr. Bruce, who was in the back, came to the front and I told him what was going on. As we were speaking, the woman raised her voice and said,

"I know he comes here. I know it because I take care of the finances, and that's how I found this place. He hasn't been home in two days. I called his office this morning and they said he wasn't there yet, which has me worried all the more." Her voice was frantic. She kept looking outside.

"Who, exactly are you speaking of?" Mr. Bruce said. "I'm sorry, I must have missed something."

"My husband. He's been gone. I haven't heard from him. Morris. Patrick Morris."

"Oh, Pat!" he said looking at me, then back at her. "We know him. He was in here recently."

"What?" she said. She became more visibly upset with this piece of information than the rest, like it confirmed something she feared. She lowered her head and put her hand on a stack of aerosol cans at the end of an aisle. When she collected herself, she came forward and asked Mr. Bruce where he was. He told her where Pat's boat slip was located. She nodded her head once, said thank you, and then left the shop in a fury, shambling in the direction of that boat without grace, like one defeated.

38

It was a sympathetic moment for Mr. Bruce and I. He sighed out loud and drifted from the register to the front of the shop, where he watched the woman go her way. He turned to me and said,

"That's the unfortunate side of things. We don't see half of it. But I promise you this: every regular who comes in here has got something like that. Maybe not the wife up in arms, but something like it. Boats are a jealous hobby."

He shook his hand around in his pocket.

"They're beautiful from afar, but up close you see another side. The conflict."

He drifted back to the register.

"Anyway," he said. "I only know that from my own mistakes."

Someone came in then and the reflection ended and we got back to work.

After that Mr. Bruce continued to entrust me with more stories like Pat Morris's. The sensitive, offhand, profane, asides, rumors, and degradations he had come to know. The half of it we don't see, as he put it. He mentioned affairs, bankruptcy, suicides, sinkings- all surrounding this boatyard, this shop. One day I asked him about sinkings and he said unflinchingly and unbitterly,

"My wife sank a small sailboat I owned long ago."

"She sank it?" I said.

"Well, she let it sink. It was on its way out, though it could have been salvaged. But that's a long time ago now."

"That's terrible." I said.

"I didn't say I didn't deserve it." he said. But he said no more after that, and I sense he did not want to be cornered by a high school girl on his past sins. So we let that story be.

The more he told, the more his stories reflected who he was. There was no caprice in him, nothing flashy. His tales never devolved into empty gossip, nor invoked the ill opinion of another person; even those he did not get along with. He had a firm belief in the goodness of men, and a firm understanding of their weaknesses. Whatever he told preserved the symmetry between the hardship and the loveliness of seafaring.

"He's in a damned mess." he said of one patron. "But when he's done with that mess, he'll have a glory on his hands." And he smiled at the thought.

Simply by being around Mr. Bruce, I joined in the dialogue of this place; a dialogue between its fortunes and its misfortunes, its grit and its delinquency, its members and its exiles. He rambled and I listened, and I became a vessel for his thoughts. Later those thoughts came back.

I must clarify something. Not all boats are consuming or treacherous. Many people get along in canoes, kayaks, punts, rafts, lightweight cruisers, pontoons, yachts, cigar boats, and know nothing but enjoyment. But *where* we were affected what we saw. This was a boatyard. A boatyard is a purgatory; a place beset by repairs, by attenuated hopes, by abandonment. One had only to walk the yard once to see that for every boat inching toward Bay, there were two more inching toward the grave, and some already there. The people who came to the shop were the kind who took a sacrifice willingly, and often unwittingly. They were stubborn, project men. Those who stuck around came because of a long and loveless obligation to a boat that was both their salvation and their test. They knew the poverties of time, motivation, contentment. They walked through the shop doors wearing the filth of their project on their fronts of their pants. They were up summer nights not sipping pinot noir in the stern under the stars, basking in the company of good friends, but lumbering midway out of an engine cavity, the noxious smell of black head gasket sealant fumigating around their face, their hands humid and wrinkly under latex gloves, a mask around their face; these folks, who were all but hidden from the sympathies and comforts of the world. These were the men we knew, and this was the place they worked.

The flags of ambition flew differently for each, but there was hardship throughout, mingling perpetually with the idylls of boating. They came with purpose. They came with the hope of launching something in the water. You could see it at the center of their eyes; a longing, humbled by discouragement and hard work and unfinished work, but nonetheless there; that desire to be seabound; waterborne; skipping at full knots; free.

Sailing was Mr. Bruce's freedom. It was his first love, and he was intent that I go sometime.

"Have you ever sailed?" he asked me.

"No, not yet."

"Ahh," he said. He was sitting on the stool at the register, smiling out the window.

"I'm surprised I haven't asked already." he said. "One day you'll get to. This shop can wear on you, even me, and I've been here how many years? We mostly see things that aren't right in here. It is a repair shop after all. Still, one day you'll go sailing. Feel the big wind behind you. One day of heeling on a fine wind will fix all that."

He loved that word, heeling. Heeling is the way a sailboat cants on its side when it's tacking, harnessing the wind. All of Mr. Bruce's good nature seemed to repose in that word; whenever he said it he would angle his hand just the same as if it were a model boat slicing through the water. Because he knew I hadn't sailed before he mentioned heeling with a kind of sumptuous secrecy- like once I had sunk my teeth into it, I would know, but only until then.

I spent many hours at that shop, and many months. Early on I thought Mr. Bruce pitied me; that he thought I had better things to do. But the longer I remained, the more I came to believe he shared his wisdom as a generosity, a taken interest in the welfare of the place, and me especially. He did not know much about my life beyond the yard, but he knew I had enthusiasm, a desire to learn, which was more important to him than broad, half-hearted interest.

To others he could be stern,

"You're not going to want that." or,

"You're going to want two more of those." I can hear him saying, moving them along.

But to me he was proverbial and kind.

"A beginner will come in and get such and such, but someone who's been at it long enough knows to do such and such." Little nods like that. I have many good memories of that shop and my time working there. More that I could dredge if I needed to. But before I parted ways with the shop, there was a man who came in I couldn't forget, and whose story is worth telling.

His name was Lane McMurphy, and he was elderly man of 70 or so. We had spoken on the phone a few times and it took me awhile to understand that his name was Lane. I always thought he was referring to an address of something. He always called about the same thing- a custom bronze fitting for an antique compass he was going to install on his boat. It was a boat he had been rebuilding for 18 years. Neither Mr. Bruce nor myself had ever seen the boat before, because Lane kept it off yard, but he would call us since he had contact with other boat yards, suppliers, and part sellers.

The part he was looking for was very rare. It was made by a small Nordic shipmaker who was no longer in business, and the part itself had been out of manufacture for 100 years.

He referred to it as 'That little piece.'

"Any word on that little piece?" he'd say.

All I could respond was "We'll keep an eye out for it." And always he ended the call by saying

"Thank you, I really do thank you. I've been working on this boat for 18 years going on, and this is the last piece I need, the very last piece."

Mr. Bruce said Lane had been calling him for at least three years about that 'damned whatever he needs', and he felt it was some joke life had played on the old repairman.

"No one searches for a single piece that long. What will he do with it, if heaven forbid he finds it?" Mr. Bruce said to me. "He's older than I am, and when you get old, you think about a few things, and those few things are all you think about."

I said "If he finds it, he can move on finally."

"Maybe so. But that is a big IF."

My heart went out to the man though. On slow days I put ads in boating classifieds across the east coast, for the sake of it.

One day we finally got a call from a man who spoke broken English, who said he had the part. I put the phone down and told Mr. Bruce. We were both stunned. I took the address down and details. Later I called Lane and told him that we found it. He was speechless on the other end. I could hear no crackle or breath on the line. It was as though he put the phone down on his thigh for a moment and caught his breath. When he spoke again, his voice was choppy, nervous-like.

"You can have him ship it to the shop?" he asked.

"We could, but you don't want to speak to him directly?" I said.

"If it's in the shop, I can verify better. I would prefer that. I do thank you though, I really do. I've been looking for this little piece for a long time. And I've been on this boat working for 18 or some years. This is the last thing."

So we arranged it. Lane sent a blank check for $600, and the man who answered the ad, good on his word, shipped it in a brown cardboard box, with my name written on the top in black marker, misspelled 'Constas'. Inside was the brass fixture, the piece Lane McMurphy had been looking for for 18 years.

We called and told him it arrived. He said you can go ahead and open it, so we did. Mr. Bruce and I lifted out the bronze spherical stand. It was extremely heavy and about the size of a toolbox. The top casement, where the compass sat, looked like an eyelid, a bronze eyelid.

Lane came later that day. I had never seen him in person before, but he was a small man, and looked older than what I imagined him to be. For some reason, I also imagined him as a wealthy man, someone capable of waiting around for years for something like this, but he did not let on that way. At least his appearance did not. He wore a wrinkled plaid shirt and jeans, and dirty white sneakers. He was shy coming in, as he held onto a box of his own, containing the compass.

The stand was in front of the register, and his eyes fixed on it as soon as he entered. He approached it slowly, apprehensively almost, and then looked up at us. His face was like a child's.

"I can't believe it." he said. "I'm Lane by the way." He shook my hand.

"We found it." I said. I'm not sure he heard me, though, so engrossed was he in the part, observing it from all angles.

Mr. Bruce said,

"Well, make sure it fits."

Lane took his compass from the box and approached the bronze casing. Then he put it in. It was a perfect fit. He stepped back and looked at the complete set.

"That's as good as it gets." Mr. Bruce said. "You found it. You want us to put it back in the box for you to transport?"

Suddenly the old man looked up. He backed off from the piece and put his hands on his hips. His mouth frowned. He glanced at Mr. Bruce, then out the main store window. Then he walked forward, then back; vacillating.

"Oh, no, well..." he said.

Mr. Bruce and I looked at each other. We didn't understand.

"Is it the right one?" I asked.

The old man took the compass from the casement and put it away, back in its own box.

"Yes." he said finally. "It is the right one, the one I've been looking for."

"Are you sure?"

"I couldn't be more sure."

The old man whose face five minute ago was exuberant, now looked crestfallen and confused.

"Is there something wrong, Lane?" Mr. Bruce said.

"No, I can't say that there is. This is it alright, the last piece in the whole puzzle." He went up to it again and ran his finger along the cold metallic edge, looking it up and down.

"Will you take it then?" Mr. Bruce said, pushing the matter.

He said, "Would you mind keeping it here this week. I'd like to think about it."

"You paid for it already, didn't you?"

"Yes I know that. I just want to think a bit more."

His manner now was timid and unsure. He was imperceptibly moving backward toward the door, holding his compass.

"Could you hold onto it till next week?"

I looked at Mr. Bruce, deferring to him.

"Lane, I wish we could, but we need to know in three days if you'll have this. You've been calling here for years about this instrument and now we've found it, and brought it here, and it is the piece you've been looking for. I can't understand what's the matter." There was disapproval in his tone.

"No more than that, though. Three days. Please call."

The man nodded. Mr. Bruce went to the back of the store and Lane left and I remained alone with the bronze compass stand. I was not sure what was going on. I covered the piece in the box and slid it behind the counter.

Mr. Bruce was quiet the rest of the day. He was perturbed I could see because he was rarely ever like that. He kept glaring at the box when he passed it. He made small comments under his breath, not kind words.

"If he doesn't call back in two days, you go ahead and call him." Then he shook his head, already imagining what that exchange would look like.

Two days later I called twice and no one answered. Then he called and his voice was stuttery and distant, like he were simultaneously speaking to me and looking off somewhere, half attentive.

"We need to know if you'll take the stand."

"I know you do." he said.

There was a pause.

"I've been thinking about it." he said, "I think I'm going to go with another option. I'm really sorry. I've just been thinking- I might not need that piece right at this moment. It's good to know it's out there though."

Mr. Bruce was in the door frame of the office, listening to me as I took the call. He could hear the conversation clearly. He had a sad but knowing smile on his face, and he shook his head at the ground. It was not an expression of anger or disappointment but pity.

He motioned for me to hang up.

"I understand, Mr. McMurphy. If you'll send us a check for the shipping, we'll send it back to the seller."

I hung up. Mr. Bruce said,

"You may not understand, but I do. Do you know why he won't buy it?"

"No I don't. It makes no sense to me."

"The search would be over." he said. "The end of the game. Think of it; the man's poured out the last two decades of his life into that boat, and more money than you can imagine. It's cost him blood, sweat, and tears, but he reaches the point where the boat is the only thing in his life worth living for. He wouldn't know his life without it."

He held up his hand to caution his own speech.

"I'm not going to presume more than I need to about his situation, but I've seen it before is all. Too many times. I wish I could say he was the only one with that problem, but he's not."

He looked at me.

"What would he do after he had it? Tinker around another ten years? Start another boat?"

I shrugged. He shook his head.

"Not at his age. Take it on the water?" He laughed and I did too at that statement. "He's past water at this point."

The store was empty at that time of day. Mr. Bruce walked to the front, looked out on the boatyard awhile, then came back.

"That's the tragedy of this place, if you will. You can get so caught up with the boat, you miss the sea. You forget there's any purpose to your repairs besides adding something else to it, or selling it for a profit when you're ready to be rid of it. Or otherwise you keep it pristine and never let it touch the salt and waves."

He removed his hat and stroked his hair and put it back on.

"If you stick with it, don't let that be you, Constance. Stay close to shore. Get out there."

Then, swift as his first thought, the kindness came back to his face, and I saw relief come over him; mildness, his face lightening of the heavy thought, and he replaced his musing with an easy smile the rest of the afternoon.

For all I knew, those were parting words, and I never forgot them because they were spoken from the heart by an old sailor who loved the water, and who had become a dear, unlikely friend.

Many weeks later during spring, I told him my plans to leave. He said,

"It'll be sad to see you go, but you've been a great help here, and if I can help you in any way, just let me know." I told him I would.

On my last day he shook my hand and gave me a partially closed box and said,

"This is a small gift. I hope it serves you well."

I opened it before him and found a depth-finder inside, one of the newer models the shop sold.

"It should work just fine on your little boat." he said.

"It's great." I said. "Thank you!"

"Now you've got no excuses not to fish."

I said "If I find any decent spots you haven't already heard about, I'll let you know."

He said, "There's always some."

He waved me goodbye and I drove home knowing I would miss that place for a long time. I didn't know when I'd be back. When I got home I showed my father the depth finder and he said,

"You must have done a good job working there. He's a good man, Mr. Bruce. I've known him since I've been there. You'll make good use of that."

And I did. The next day I took James and Bev out around the bend of Weems toward the neck of the Nanticoke, in the little boat. The tiny engine was singing. James sat on the back bench with me, holding the depth-finder between his hands, calling out depths every few minutes. Bev, our navigator, pointed where we went. We made it as far as the channel at the mouth of the Bay, big boats passing us port and starboard. There, where the tall trees vanished and the big waters opened, the current was strong, and the wind was whipping wildly and roughing the waters, and was against us. We were tossing on the pitch. We could feel every lath of wood under us. I slowed the engine so that we more or less drifted with the current as it pushed us back, as we rolled over the oncoming waves.

Beyond us, the Bay, the water leapt; the confluent inflowing and outflowing waters were avid and tumultuous. The thick, portly sound of horns on the air. Yachts yielding and advancing. Waves, salutes. Ospreys circling their nest.

Beyond the threshold of the channel Chesapeake Bay widened, and over that wideness boats dotted the distance like seams along a thread. The sun was golden across the ruffled surface. It was wonderful and dangerous all at once. I remember the plunking sound of the bow bouncing off the rolling waves and falling back.

I had never taken the boat that far, and I had the intuition not to take us any farther that day. To be there at the door, looking in, was enough. James said,

"Look here." and he held the device up for me to see a dozen or more fish below us.

"We have to come back." I said.

"It's the channel, that's why." Bev said. "The water's deeper and the current's strong, which fish like."

After that I swung us around and ran us back along the shoreline where we came from. The wind was with us, and the water, as we chased it into narrower courses, smoothed and darkened. We gained speed on the trip back, cruising along the wood banks and dense marsh. Bev kept an elbow in front of her face to block the sprays; James left one hand off the side of the boat, palm up; and I held us to our course- the throttle in my grip rattling through my arm, its noise clamorous and crisp. I followed Bev's pointed finger which held our bearing. When we neared Black creek I slowed us to a rumble, dropped Bev off, then went back home with James. The sound of quiet as we drifted in was sweet. My lifejacket was loose from the ride, so was James's.

We pulled the boat aground, clipped it to the trailer, and retired to the house, beaten from our trip. The house smelled like summer- humid and musty, the accumulated heat of day lengthening the smell of the walls, the wicker furniture. The kitchen window was open and the wind blew through carrying the smell of grass and flora. No one else was downstairs but us. A pot of water was on the stove on low heat. I sat on the couch and James sat at the piano bench, shifting lethargically into his scales and the routine songs he played. My mother came down and checked her pot on the stove.

Why my mind recalls such incidents and details, so many years removed, is part of the *mystery* I mentioned before. The longer I've bided the memory of transitions in my life, and noted and felt along the grains of those early days, the more I've seen that the meaningful moments, the ones that stuck with me, were the oblique ones, the passionless scenes where nothing was waving to be remembered.

Those were times on Teal St. when our home bestowed a solitude that I came to appreciate only when I was separated from it. It happened that when I was least under the yoke of those walls that I missed it most, and wished to return to the quietness, the shade and languor of spring come summer, when my dory rested permanently on the bank, and idleness reigned, and there was dark water on the creek, and the sound of a pot coming to a boil.

39

Whatever fond memories were made that summer came and went as regularly as the tide and were eventually superseded by what came next in my journey: college.

I went to Salisbury University that fall. So did Bev. I said we did not think that much about going. And that's the way it was up until we loaded our cars and went. The fall snuck up on us. We went more by the suggestion of our families, than by any enticement of our own. And from the very get go we struggled to get on. Bev was a poor student, and I was an uninterested one. The university was less than an hour away so early on we came home many weekends. I wanted to be by the water, away from campus, and Bev still had chores waiting for her on the farm. I don't think she hated that work, I think she began appreciating it more after weeks at college.

So many of our classmates went to Salisbury, it was an extension of high school in a way, just in a different environment, and with a few new faces. On weekends when we drove back from home, we would talk, wondering how long we would last, and what we would do if we didn't stay. Bev said she could work on the farm as long as she needed, but that she wouldn't want to do that forever. I said I could take up work at the boatyard again. We never questioned what our parents would think of these plans, but we made them regardless. Our father's were paying thousands of dollars for us to go and make something of ourselves, and here we were scheming to take up blue collar jobs instead.

In the beginning there was an unspoken vow between us to keep those plans secret, and to keep our distance from the school. Whatever we determined about our place at Salisbury, we determined that we were at least misfits and that we would stay misfits together. If I could go back and change something about that time, any of those rides we took home, I would have said to Bev, "Beverly, thank you for being my friend, I'm glad I've got you. You know I'd do anything for you, right?" But I never said anything like it. We never mentioned our friendship.

The first semester we lived annexed on the top floor of a crumby sorority house, all the tenants of whom were members of the women's soccer team, except us. We had no problems with them; they were not rude, but they were numerous, and loud, and athletic, and insular. For a while we never mixed.

One weekend I came home by myself and Bev stayed at school. The cellar had flooded again and Adley was gone for awhile like she usually was, but the rest of us were there, and we cleaned most of the afternoon. Adley came home with Tate, Bev's brother. I guess they were a thing, I had no idea. They came down the stairs where I was finishing drying the floor with my father. She came down first, linking hands with him behind her. They descended just to look apparently. They whispered to each other. In the corner of the cellar was a tin bucket filled with flood water, and a dead mouse was floating belly up in it. We found it on the floor and placed it there. When Adley and Tate saw it they laughed.

"Constance," Adley said. I looked up.

She was pointing to the mouse. "That's your boyfriend." Tate laughed. I made a heartless laugh in response, then she and Tate went off, laughing openly when they reached upstairs.

It was only a brief exchange, but the splinter it left stayed with me long after, and in a strange way set in motion the events that followed close behind it. It was the first time I sensed a genuine change in Adley's personality. Something unbecoming. The new sarcasm in her voice. She never spoke that way before. She was an avoider and recluse all those years growing up. She hid from people not because she didn't care for them, but because she cared too much. She was oversensitive. Now there was an ill humor in her, a dark tone that made her coarse and unnerving.

However little she intended by them, I heard her words as a shame upon me, a sister's curse. The whole way back to school they goaded me; my mind kept producing the image of the mouse belly up, and that high sneer of a laugh,

"That's your boyfriend."

"That's your boyfriend."

Returning to school was no better either. I arrived to find Bev sitting with our housemates, who we hardly knew, and a group of guys I didn't know at all. They said hi to me when I walked in. Bev asked if I wanted to join, but I said no and went up to our room and unpacked my bags, and heard them carrying on below. I wanted to leave.

No single moment spurred me to leave school when I did, but many odd moments accentuated the motion, and those two memories both from the same day were among the most lasting and effectual.

But there were others. Others that showed how Bev and I's friendship changed over time. Although we lived together, our relationship was interrupted by the *experience* of college; the new faces, the classes, the schedule, the autonomy- and we approached the change differently. I remained reticent about college throughout. I viewed it as necessary detainment. But Bev began to see it as liberation. As weeks and months passed it was clear she wanted to 'become someone new', and that she would be given that opportunity. So while I kept my distance, she threw herself headlong into the experience. She wanted to uproot the old self, shrug off her farmer's daughter upbringing. She wanted to party more and lose herself. And that's what she did. She earned a reputation as a heavy drinker whenever there were parties at the house. It impressed the guys that she could shotgun a beer as fast as they could. They would crowd around her yelling and shouting until she finished. That became her trick, her buy-in, her way of getting noticed.

The guys who came over were from the soccer team, and they came to party with the women's soccer team. Somehow Bev and I joined in too. It wasn't hard for Bev, because she had no problem being a spectacle. Truthfully, she aimed to be a spectacle. She wanted to be pegged as the wild girl who could get drunk on command. She was never like that in high school, so it bothered me to see her becoming that among strangers. I felt more like an outsider than Bev did because I had no spectacle to employ. At parties I followed Bev around like a lost child, standing by while she took shots or drank from wine bags. The boys would cheer her. The girls would laugh and snicker in a group. And I was simply there; a shadow keeping watch of my friend.

Most days I felt lonely. I felt a dim dissatisfaction in everything I did. An ache to go away. Bev had her moments too, but they were so abrupt and terrible I doubt they came from loneliness only. Nor did they occur only when she was drunk. One night I was sleeping when I woke to the sound of guzzling liquid and a scraping plate. It came from Bev's room. Her room was essentially a large closet inside my own. I got up from my bed and knocked twice on her door. The door was lit on the inside, but there was no response. I put my hand on the knob and pulled back and she said,

"Stop Constance. Go back to bed."

"What is that?" I said. "Are you eating?"

"Go back."

She grabbed the knob on the other end, to prevent my opening. Then she took her hand away. I pulled the door further open and she looked up at me. Her face was frowning and distraught, like I had caught her in the act. She was sitting on the side of the bed with a cookie tray in her lap. On the tray were brown morsels of fried food. There were three corn dogs eaten to the sticks, and one with the dog intact, where she had only eaten the batter. She glared at the tray and chewed whatever was in her mouth. Then she swallowed, lifted a jug of orange soda from the floor, and took three big draughts. When she was done, she put the jug between her legs, burped, and screwed the cap on. Her back was slumped forward. Her hair was lank and greasy. She continued staring at the tray. Either she stopped noticing me, or didn't care anymore. I picked up a urinous smell in the room mixed with the smell of fried food. She burped again, blew out a sigh, and looked up to me. Her eyes were red and glazy.

"You can go now." she said.

"What's wrong?" I said.

She pursed her lips in anger and beat her fist once hard onto the tray. Scraps fell across the floor. She put the tray beside her and grabbed the edge of the mattress with both hands. Tears began rolling down her cheeks.

"What is it?" I said. "What's wrong?"

"Go away, just go away."

"What's wrong?"

"Go away. I'm not drunk. Go." she growled.

"I never said you were. I just heard you, that's all. What happened?"

"I'm going to sleep," she said. "Get the light."

As she stretched onto her mattress, I noticed the back of her legs were streaked with mud, and her socks soaking wet. I said nothing. She laid back. Her eyes were wide open. Her lips were pursed. I took the empty tray from her bed and the soda bottle from the floor. I turned the light off. Then I closed the door. I went to the kitchen and scraped the food off the tray. The tray was bent, so I bent it back into shape. I put it under the oven, drained the soda in the sink, and looked up at the clock. It was three in the morning. By the time I got back to bed I could hear her snoring.

Later that week Bev apologized for how she acted. I forgave her, but that did not amend things entirely. There were still things she kept from me, and one night in particular she hurt me in a way I never forgot. It was during another party at our house. She was playing the jest as usual. A ring of people formed around her and watched as she chugged beer from an orange plastic cone – the ones used for soccer drills. I was standing behind her, outside the ring. As she tipped the cone bottoms up, she gagged from the excess liquid, coughed hard, and spewed most of it onto the ground before her. The ring of onlookers stepped off. Reeling from the drink, she staggered backward and saw me standing there behind her. Her eyes rolled up and she said,

"Why are you just standing there watching me?" She stood, took her hands off her knees, and pushed me on the shoulder "You don't need to be my mom!"

Then she wiped her mouth and turned back to the ring of people who cheered louder now. One of the soccer guys filled her orange cone with more beer, and I left to go upstairs feeling scorned and unwelcome. From the railing I saw her hold the cone up high and yell "To Moms!". The people around her went wild. Upstairs, their voices poured through the walls. I did not go back down. I stayed in my room and made no sound.

The night did not end there though. I could not sleep from the noise, so I laid on my bed alone for an hour, staring at the ceiling. Soon I heard footsteps, doors opening and closing – the sound of people making plans. Outside the window I heard people yelling in the street. People were leaving. When the house was quiet I heard a pair of footsteps coming up the stairs. Bev entered our room and saw me lying there wide awake.

"Oh, you're still here?" she said.

"Where'd you think I'd be?"

"Nowhere." she said. "I just hadn't seen you. I forgot you were around."

She walked in past my bed and sat in the wooden desk chair facing the window to the street below.

"What are you doing?" I said.

"I'm not sure. I might go out again."

"With who?"

"All of them. A big group went out."

"Where are they going?"

"I don't know. One of the guy's houses. I can follow the noise if I need to, it's not far."

I turned and looked at her. She was looking out the window onto the dark street. There was a breeze flowing through the window and I could smell it from where I lay. It smelled of salty sea air, and marijuana. Bev was wearing a maroon Salisbury t-shirt, a baggy pair of jeans, and sneakers; the same sort of outfit she wore all through high school.

"You're going?" I asked.

"I think."

"They invited you?" I said.

"Not really," she said. "But they didn't say I couldn't come."

She rose and drew her face close to the screen, like she saw something below.

"I think I hear one of them down there," she said. "I'm going to go."

Before she left, she opened the door to her room, took two big gulps from another orange soda bottle on the floor, and put it back. Then she stuffed her leather wallet in her front pocket and walked out without so much as a goodbye. When she left I was the last one remaining in that giant sorority house. It was an empty house. I felt jealous, alone, bitter to my core. I tried to sleep, but I could not. I turned the light off and shut the door all the way, but nothing helped. An hour passed and still I was awake. Three hours passed the same. I had been lying there the whole time, watching the clock, which made it feel like an eternity. I turned the clock away so I could not see it. Eventually I began to hear girls coming in, walking up the stairs, whispering to one another, closing their doors and going to sleep. Many come back, but not Bev.

Then I fell asleep. When I woke again it was in the middle of the night. All I could hear was a noise of muffled pain coming from somewhere close, somewhere in my room. A sound like a wounded animal. Suddenly a cold hand grabbed my arm in the dark. I jumped and yelled, and turning on my side, I saw that it was Bev's hand reaching up from the ground.

"Oh my god! What the hell!?"

"Constance, Constance," she winced.

"Bev?" I said. "What's going on?"

"I'm hurt." she said. "It's bad."

"Oh my god, what happened?"

"Call," she moaned, "Call!"

I rose immediately and turned on the light. She was sprawled to the ground, her eyes shut, her teeth bared. She reeked of alcohol, of piss beer. With an elbow she shielded her eyes from the light while her other hand tapped lightly against the thigh of her leg. Then her mouth fell open and she began moaning over and over.

"What happened?" I said. I was scared to see her that way, writhing and barely speaking.

"Call ambulance," she moaned. "I broke something. Call!"

"What happened?"

"I fell."

"Where?"

"The hill."

The hill was a steep slope close to the fraternity houses. I called the campus police and tried to explain the situation. I could not tell them much, but I told them enough for them to send an ambulance. As we waited for their arrival I sat down on the floor beside Bev and tried to calm her down.

"Here." I said. "Try and sit up a bit." I took a pillow from my bed and laid it in my lap. I carefully propped her head on my lap and cradled her neck and began pushing the stray hairs off her forehead and the edge of her mouth. Loose blades of grass clung to her temple from where she must have fallen. Her nostril was crusted with dried blood, and the color in her face was pale. She began sobbing as I held her – her whole body shook. It was the first I saw her cry. She would cry into a calm, then her body would tense and she would well with anger. She would growl and grit her teeth. She would try to sit up on her own, try to stretch out her hand to the wounded leg, but it was too painful and she would fall back to the pillow, go limp, and sob again.

"It's ok." I said, holding her back. "They'll be here. Tell me what happened."

She covered her eyes with the back of her hand.

"They pushed me from the top." she said. Her voice was low and rusty.

"Who did?"

She reached out again for her leg, but I fended it off.

"Let it be." I said. "Who did that, Bev?"

"The guys."

"What guys?"

"From the house."

"Which house?"

She began to sob more, and tried to turn away, but I wouldn't let her.

"Which house? Who?"

"I don't know." she said.

"Did you know their names?"

She shook her head. We were quiet for a few moments. Then she muttered something.

"What did you say?"

"Moose."

"Moose?"

She nodded.

"They kept calling me that. Moose. The Moose. And giving me drinks. More moose, more moose, they said."

"Where?"

"The hill."

"They made you drink?"

She nodded.

"Then what?" I said.

Her lips began to quiver and she covered her eyes again. She shook her head.

"I don't know," she cried. "They pushed me down."

"When was that?"

"Hours ago."

I took a tissue from the nightstand and wiped her face and nose. I could not feel my legs any longer; they were dead from her lying on them.

"How did you get back here?" I said.

"I limped."

"All the way?"

She nodded.

"Did you know something was broken?" I said.

"I don't know."

"You made it up here?"

"I crawled up," she said, "so you could help me."

The longer she lay, the more the pain spread across her face and turned to silence. For a while she stopped speaking to me, and I was just with her. I was exhausted waiting with her. I could not tell the time within three hours, and were it not for the pain she was in, I don't know how I would have helped her. I felt pity but anger also. I tasted bad blood from earlier, but that night it was rinsed away by desperation. Bev had dragged her broken body to my bedside and dropped her neck in my hands. When we heard the EMT's arrive outside, she said to me,

"Get me my belt. In my closet. Brown one."

I stood slowly and replaced her head on the pillow. I went to her room and found her brown leather belt dangling from a hook on the door and brought it to her. She took the belt, folded it in half and stuck it between her teeth. I stayed nearby while the EMTs assessed her injury. They were two young and inexperienced guys, and every hesitating attempt they made to reposition her limb or move her, she lifted her head, spit the belt out and jeered,

"You idiot –you don't know what the hell you're doing!"

She ended up fitting the leg brace half by herself. When they were ready to leave, Bev looked up at me,

"You don't need to come. I'll be fine." she said.

But I came anyway. By the time she was x-rayed and given the news her leg was broken, it was five in the morning. We took a cab back to school and I handed her the belt she gave me to hold hours earlier. I called her father and told him what happened, and when I handed Bev the phone, I heard him yelling at her through it.

After that night she subdued some. For a time she withdrew from the parties, but she quickly became depressed by her injury. She plunged herself into a season of seclusion and self-hatred. I availed myself to her however I could. I helped her move, get meals, drive to class; not only because she needed these things, but because I hoped they might revive our friendship in some way. But they did not mend us. The injury was a buffer more than a bridge. It pained me she never told the story about what happened on the hill, about 'Moose' and the guys who threw her down. She never spoke about it. More than that, we never spoke openly about anything, least of all how we felt. I was estranged from her, though I saw her more than anyone.

She would tell others how dearly she wanted to go out again, and 'get her life back' when she finally could. That was what ruled her mind. It was all she spoke of, and she spoke about it with such tireless conviction I wondered if it was all a sham. Here was my friend who was everyday growing apart from me, little by little, and I did not know why, and could not stop it. Here she was biding her time, waiting to be taken into the other fold. And how happy she seemed to all but me. I was the one who saw the other things. I was the one who knew about the belt between her teeth. I was the one she flung her sadness on.

For months, off and on, I called my father and explained my situation. I told him I didn't want to stay. During the holiday break, I came home and we sat down on the two wicker chairs by the big windows and I told him again.

"And what will you do?" he said. "You have to do something, you can't just be here."

I said "I don't know what." That was all I could summon at the time. When I returned to campus the restlessness persisted. So after a year I left for good.

40

I draw a veil over the rest of college. I harbored no enduring regrets about my time there; in some ways my departure clarified the importance of setting off in another direction. But also, it was short lived and rather uneventful. I moved back home, promising my father I would enroll in a community college and work part time. It was the best I could propose, and I believe my decision was no surprise for him or my mother, but it hit them like defeat. Here I was, a young person, misplaced in the world, with few friends, and a blurred path ahead. I was biding my time. What was worse was that I hadn't even told Bev I was leaving, or had left.

That was the most insincere part of the whole circumstance. She must have come back from school break astonished to find half the living space evacuated with no explanation.

She called me, shocked and confused, and I said, with a feint, that a financial issue came up. She was silent on the other end, like she didn't believe me for a second. She knew our family. She knew it wasn't money. I didn't say much more than that. I said I was figuring things out and that she should call when she's back, but I didn't hear from her after that. Not for a long time. It was betrayal on my part; ignorant betrayal. What had been my one dependable friendship in the world was lost, and I sincerely thought no one was to blame. A cleavage was created and we drifted our own way like that, further and further apart.

It was a year since I spoke with Mr. Bruce, but he was the first person I thought of to help me find something. I called him at the shop, and instead of inviting me back to work with him, he said,

"That's so funny. I had you on my mind. There's a fellow who's been coming into the shop asking about hired hands for the deep sea charter he's starting. He needs skippers. I mentioned your name actually, even though I figured you were gone. But that's some luck! If you're interested, and he's still in need."

"You talked to him recently?" I asked.

"Yes, he was in the store just the other day. I should add; he's not an amusing man, and I can't say if the job's right for you, or if you'd want it, but you would learn a lot by being out there, at least meeting him."

I said "I'd be willing to meet him. What's his name?"

"Paul Travis. It's a nice boat too, 40 footer, with the works. He plans to charter on the Atlantic.

I said that's fine for me. Looking back, I don't know what I was saying, because in two minutes talking, my mind was already full with the possibility of an opportunity I knew nothing about. I had been one or two months at home by then, and that's enough time to be spinning your wheels. So, I lunged at it, whatever it was.

"Tell him I'll meet him this week. I've got nothing going on."

"I'll tell him then. Good luck, and stop by if you come around. You know where to find me."

Mr. Bruce made the connection the same day and the next day Captain Paul called me and asked me to come to the boatyard for an introduction. I could tell nothing about the man except that he was busy. I could hear him carrying on another conversation at the same time; his voice would return to the receiver and he would apologize, but we found a time, and I came in the same afternoon, on the lookout for a 40 foot troller called "Cast Off" from Providence, Rhode Island. It was not hard to find. It had a custom flag hanging from the flybridge, with the same design as the name across the transom, the black stencil of a marlin jumping from the water, the universal symbol of sport fishing.

When I arrived at back, the tinted cabin door opened and out stepped Captain Travis, a tall middle aged man wearing polarized sunglasses.

"Constance?" he said.

"Yes."

"Come on aboard."

He pulled me onto deck and invited me into the air conditioned cabin. Inside, every seat was leather and everywhere I placed my hand was a shiny metallic trim or polished oak finish. Deeper in the cabin was a mechanic working on a lighting fixture. We sat down and Capt. Travis took off his sunglasses and put them in his lap, and took a sip from a glass tumbler sitting beside him. He offered me something from the bar, but I said I was alright for now. He began by saying,

"As you can see, she's almost done. We've got a few more little things to finish, a few electrical things, a few cosmetic, like the lighting, that's what he's working on in the back. Otherwise, we're in ship shape. My operation is going to be based out of Virginia Beach. That's about, oh, two hours from here, oceanside. We would be in for full day, part week, even multi-week charters. No party boat shit if I can help it." he laughed at that remark.

"Not for how much I put into this. We need to crank it for everything it's got. But she's pretty, isn't she?" He looked around, admiring, but also inspecting everything around him. His glass hung loose between his fingers and he took small sips from it. He pointed to the trolling chair in the stern of the boat, the central feature, a throne of a chair with straps, clips, gears, foot bracing.

"That thing was custom built. I won't even tell you how much it cost, it's disgusting. But I have seen it pull in a 500 lb bluefin like it was nothing. You can actually attach the reel to the gear system, and it will do the heavy lifting for you. You hook it, that thing will do the rest."

He took another sip, then looked at me.

"Have you seen- " he was about to stand up and show me something else, but he caught himself, sat back down and changed his question,

"Actually," he said. "Bruce sent you this way. Where are you from?"

I told him where.

"Skewesbury? Am I saying it right?" he said.

"It's pronounced Skucebury, actually. It rhymes with spruce."

He shook his head unknowingly.

"And you've worked on boats?"

"Some," I said. "Smaller ones. Not like this."

He smiled, taking that as a compliment. His eyes floated about in admiration again.

"I've got a small motorboat, and my father has a boat here at the yard that he doesn't take out much."

That comment made him laugh.

He said, "Most people have a boat they don't take out much. A shame, really- not to mention a waste of capital. These things are number one for killing equity if you don't put them to use."

He sighed and took another sip. He checked his watch. I

looked around as well. Behind me was a glass case with pictures of him holding up all kinds of trophy fish. In each picture he had the same magnificent smile, the same glasses, the same haircut- only the fish were different.

"Those are from years and years ago." he said. I turned around and there we was, the same man, Capt. Travis, unaged, unchanged.

"Come with me." he said. He put his drink down and we went out the doors and climbed up the ladder to the second floor, the canopy, where he gave me a seat and showed me the configuration of gps machines, squawk box, radars, fish finders, weather alerts, every mode of high tech communication, and a drink holder on the console, to boot.

"My favorite part-" he said.

By then I had the growing discomfort of being on a foreign boat with an older man I did not know, concerning a job I could not precisely envision, in a meeting which was more of a show and tell than a conversation. I had said next to nothing.

"The view from up here," he began, "Imagine the sea is all there is when you're up here, looking out, we've got four of the best trolling lines money can buy up here too."

When we was satisfied with the canopy we climbed down. Everywhere we went on the ship he looked over the sides and stern and bow, inspecting his investment and saying some things quietly to himself, like he were going through a mental checklist. When we were on the main deck, he turned around to me with his arms folded, and said,

"One of my main priorities is keeping this boat clean, free of the gunk that builds up day after day, not to mention the fishing gear. I want an operation where our crew cares about sanitation, because the people that charter with us will expect the best. You've been to those highway gas stations. The bathrooms with piss everywhere. You'll never go back there will you?"

I nodded. "Same thing. I want them to be able to fish for two hours, then come inside for a drink, then go fish for two more- on and on, you see? So they can get their money's worth. They're going to want the thrill of the ocean combined with all the comforts of home, and a couple luxuries that only we can add. That's what'll make us different from the dozen party boats you see in the ads, the ones you gloss over without a second thought."

The way he spoke was like he was carrying on a proposal with himself, and I was an onlooker. He spoke with the persuasiveness of someone who was convicted by every word he said. I respected that much about this man, Captain Paul Travis. He was serious about his work. He believed in it. He stood by his words. Finally he said to me,

"I trust you can join me if you're up for it. The man in the shop said many good things about you, and I know he knows his stuff. We'll be docked, I told you where, in Virginia Beach, which is one more thing to consider. If you join it's two hours away and I doubt you'll want to commute."

Just then his phone rang inside the cabin, so he began to wrap up,

"Three weeks, Virginia Beach, deckhand. No party boat shit. Think about it." He shook my hand and returned to the tinted cabin to take the call.

Before I left the yard that day I stopped over at the shop. Mr. Bruce was at the front counter on the stool. He was transferring washers from one container to another. He looked up and smiled, leaving his task when he saw me come in. He shook my hand and gave it an extra shake at the end, which was as affectionate as he could be.

"I see you spent some time with Travis." he said.

"I did."

"The man's got quite the rig. When is he embarking?"

"Three weeks."

"Doesn't give you much time."

"No." I said.

"What do you have to say on the matter? Did he sell you?"

"I'm inclined to go for the hell of it. He talked more about the boat than the position, but it would mean working on the Atlantic though."

"Those are different waters." he said. "Bigger, much bigger."

"I know." I said. "I got the impression he's not a small catch kind of man either."

"Certainly not."

"I'd be a boathand if I joined. He's got a real thing for cleanliness. I didn't get a chance to tell him I've only operated my small boat.

Mr. Bruce said "I don't think that matters to him. He just wants to get going. Besides, you've been around the water. Albeit, not the big seas, but you can get used to that.

Before I said anything else he said, "Heck, you should do it. Take it seriously and give it a go. I wouldn't push you for the sake of it. You'll learn from it. If it's so bad, this shop will be here when you return. So will the Bay. Then you can come back with stories."

Customers started coming in. I said "Thanks for everything." I shook his hand once more and drove off in a haze of excitement and disbelief, amazed that suddenly my life had some real decision before it that would require leaving for good, getting into something I could not anticipate by a mile.

41

That night and scattered throughout the next week I referenced the opportunity to my parents, who were mostly unclear about the position rather than antagonistic toward it.

"Tell me again how you heard about this?"

"Through Mr. Bruce, the manager of the parts shop."

To my mother, these sorts of comments did not go over well; they were just names and nouns, which is why she remained undecided until I left. My father, however, knew more, though he was no more supportive of my going than she.

"And you'll be living on the ocean? he said.

"Not on the ocean, but close to. The boat will be docked not far from Chincoteague."

"Whereabouts exactly?"

"I don't know." I said.

"You should probably find that out. Do you have to find housing? Do you know there's business down there?"

"The captain says so."

"What's the boat?"

"The name?"

"No, not the name, the boat itself, what kind is it, how large?"

I told him all I knew of it.

"It's a big one then?"

"Yes."

"And how far off coast does he want to go?"

"I'm not sure."

He looked across at my mother and nodded to himself.

"I'm not sure what to say." he said.

After a some time considering quietly, he said, "And you're not interested in anything around here? Other jobs? Whatever happened to your classes?"

"I can take them later." I said.

"Your friend is still at school?"

"Bev?"

"Your friend. Come on, there's not many people I can be thinking of."

"Ed." my mother said, halting his sarcasm.

"Yes, Bev is still there."

"You don't want to go back?"

"I already told you, I don't want to go back for now."

At that point, his questioning began to disturb me. It began to expose thoughts I already considered and put out of my mind. It revived them and thoughts came rolling back with a resurgence of doubt.

"Constance-"

"Yes-"

"This isn't a hobby then? Because you can always do this as a hobby. We won't discourage you from that. See, I have a boat. You have the small boat and the fishing gear. That isn't enough? Things become very different when they become a job."

His words, his presence, the way his elbows leaned at the

edge of the table and his hands, at certain sympathetic inflections of his speech, came apart from one another and motioned in the air as if he were toying with something invisible. I resisted these gestures, but they affected me, and I could offer no quick rebuttal or deflection to what he said, nothing sufficient. I only said,

"I at least want to try, that's all, to go and see what it's like."

My mother, who was present for all of this exchange, listened on and never inserted her opinion. Maybe because she, more than anyone, understood both our sides.

Reluctantly though, in no more than a slight nod, my father accepted that I would go. My mother deferred to my father on this. My father had doubt. She had grief; grief at seeing her eldest daughter set forth on an unmarked, and perhaps perilous trail. Though she laid no impediments before me.

It was a time of dispersing for the whole family. Each of us were compassed by separate concerns. My mother took James as her sole charge because his legs got worse and understood they would worsen as long as he lived. Certainly that news threw a shadow over the home, but my mother, who was a full time caretaker by then could only have expected it. James was resigned to his legs and resentful he could do nothing to repay the help he received. He was unsure what the future held for him, what work he could do, where he would go. As I went my own way I could offer him no answers, except that I'd be back to see him when I could. By the time I left, he spent most of his days sitting and walked only short distances.

Shortly after, he was put in a wheelchair. He was not yet finished with high school even.

I saw Adley in passing before I left, but that was it. There was no goodbye; I relied on my parents and James to convey the news that I was going. My father, whose disposition changed frequently, was stuck in a malaise at the time. A despondency fell over him. There was a bagginess in his eyes. He tended to shift aimlessly through the house and stay in on weekends, though he loved being out, and needed it. There were times when I saw my father walking the grounds of our house, no longer paceful and quick as he had been years before, but sluggish, listing almost, from place to place, paving an old man's route through grass and gully, glancing at the facade of the outbuilding, complaining how it began to lean gradually, but without a practical desire for fixing it anymore, only as a witness to its decay.

I cannot claim to know the cost of my going, or the cost of my staying. I will say this: I did not imagine I would be much missed, and the very day I left seemed to confirm it in my mind. My luggage was in the car, and I said "I'm leaving now." My mother came to the car with James. My brother was in his chair and my mother stood behind him with her hands on his shoulders. They gave me hugs and said bye. James said "Have fun!"

My father stood in the doorframe of the house and waved, yet he never stepped down. As I drove away his eyes followed me through the kitchen window, and just like that I was gone, home behind me.

42

I left for Virginia Beach, where the boat was docked and began my work with Capt. Travis the same week. He had hired two others beside me, another deckhand named Wills, and a man about the same age as the Captain, named Jeremy, who had the nickname 'Chief', because he was the chief navigator on the boat.

We were all new to each other; Capt. Travis and the boat were our only common link, and we each arrived initially suspicious of the others and of the work we'd be doing. Maybe that was less true for Chief, who seemed to know the business some, but it was certainly true for Wills and I who were similar in our introversion and eager to make good impressions.

Wills was a tall, brown haired boy, the same age as me. He had long, strandy arms, and a gaunt face, and wore baggy canvas shorts. He was from Plymouth, MA. I asked what brought him down to this area, and he said, very straight, "This job did."

He asked me where I was from and I told him, and he said,

"The smelly river?"

"Smelly? I said. "What river? What does it smell like?"

"I'm not sure. Nothing good. I've been along the Bay and all I can remember is the smell."

As candidly as I could I replied, "Not that I know of."

That was one of those first exchanges that irked me. Many of our early conversations, side conversations and crew talk were like that; each of us sizing the others up, none of us speaking naturally and freely, but each of us, especially the supporting staff: Chief, Wills, and myself, guarding our behavior closely, believing we had somehow more claim to the boat and work than the others did. I don't know if the others felt that; I know I did.

It was fortunate that our first few days cleaning and prepping the rig on the dock were supplemented afterwards with days of booked charter trips. Capt. Travis had booked nearly three months of trips by then, which he posted to a schedule in a small, bare-bones office by the docks. The office had nothing in it but a landline phone, a computer, piles of scrap paper with names and phone numbers, sunscreen bottles, and a half dozen extra pair of sunglasses. A big closet, basically.

We were docked at the Virginia Beach fisherman's wharf - a rank cove bordered by waterfront seafood houses. Beyond that were gloomy insurance buildings and beach shack apartments scattered about. Only much closer to downtown Virginia Beach were the hotels and motels and tattoo parlors and beaches that brought people to town.

The one highway, route 16, was the main road connecting the wharf to the main town and from all places along the road one could see the coast, illimitable and beautiful, but lonely during the times of year when there was no tourists. I remember that highway because so many times I travelled up and down peering out the side to see glimpses of the surf slashing through the buildings and trees and I thought how vast and desertlike that ocean looked when it was motionless and the hotels became ghostly and lit their neon vacancy signs. It was like there were no ocean at all but a great illusion; plains of slate colored stone that stretched off to the horizon. What if there was no sea behind the buildings? Who would live there? Those thoughts came back to me from time to time. They were not the kind of thoughts you settle and get on with; they were boomerangs, always coming back.

43

I rented a studio apartment 20 minutes away from the wharf, past the main part of town, in a house owned by a naval officer and his family, the Teagues. There were other tenants in other units who I never formally met, but whose cars I recognized in the driveway and whose voices carried through the walls of the house when I came home at night.

It was a snug space, but not much of a home. I never took the time to furnish it properly. It had a bed and kitchen and dresser, but otherwise remained undecorated. Its vacant corners, its long white walls and dustless trimmings gave it an air of temporariness. It lacked personal touch, warmth. I had only two or three mismatch dishes which I rarely ate from. But the rent was cheap, and apart from the commuter train which ran behind the house, it was quiet, a place to prop my sea legs and rest.

The wharf was my first home. Before I arrived I imagined the wharf would be like the boatyard at home, but it was not like that at all. The wharf was the docking quarters of run-down fishing vessels and nothing more; dredgers, party boats, a few deep sea charters, each of them rust streaked, overused, and tattooed across the rear with faded family names: Elkings, Wilmore, Clarice III, and so forth, the black and gold lettering now smeared away and retaining only a vestige of its original charm. It was odd to think of them as anything but workhorses that had looked that way since time immemorial. That was my initial glimpse of the wharf, the squalor and insipidness of its vessels, the long sufferance of its regulars.

It became clear to me by contrast that sailors and fishermen, sharing an equal affection for their vessels, are very different about their boatkeeping. Sailors are concerned with cleanliness, fishermen with utility. The wharf stunk of utility; of fish, crab, and oyster refuse littered by the rigs that came slumming back to dock each day. The smell of the day's catch filled the air at all times. It was soiled into the very planks and pilings: brine and filth, saltwater, exhaust, gull, pidgeon, and other fowl droppings- each odor woven into a singular smell of the place and mixing with the nearby whiff of seafood, deep fried hush puppies, crab cakes. On days it repulsed me, and other days I learned not to mind it. I was there so often I would forget about it until some tourist family would visit and a little girl would pinch her nose as she went about.

I had the visual impression that everything at the wharf was sinking, slowly foundering, gradually dilapidating before my eyes; not only the dozens of items that were literally sunk in those foul waters, like old crab traps, and used ropes, barnacle scrapers, fractured pier covers, and tires used as bumper guards, but even those things which floated effused sinking. The whole place sagged. Everywhere you looked were pier boards that were plied and shallowed into a permanent depression, some almost touching the surface of the water. Other boards drooped, the catwalks cankered, the lamp posts leaned. The light posts were spotted and muffled with cobwebs. Hose faucets and electrical outlet stalks were bent, and most of the signs above the stalls carrying the name of the captain and services of the boat, hung askew.

All in all the wharf lacked a certain structural rectitude. It was a place left to rot, but also a spectacle. Because out of that rotting hole came the freshest fish in town.

Early morning boats would leave and return by midafternoon. By evening, most of the boats were back, and by nightfall all of the boats were in and the cluttered lights turned on and the smell of the restaurants wafted over the wharf. You could hear the sound of hoses and bilges excreting water. Whenever we returned from the ocean there were people waiting for us: tourists, locals, and restaurant kitchen staff in black aprons on their smoke break, loitering around the docks, kicking shells, waiting for us to arrive, curious to see what we caught or didn't. It was local fanfare, the revealing of the catch; it was a delight to the children and a delight to the adult as well. The birds saw us from the inlet- gulls and pigeons, magpies, squawking and quibbling next to the crowd, ready for whatever bits and scraps were thrown their way.

At dock, Capt. Travis would unlatch the ice coolers and lay the catch across the stern of the boat, and all the eyes would look down, oohing and ahhing. Some of the other captains would unload their catch in trash bins and haul it onto the pier deck and lay the big fish down and let the children crouch closeby. Tuna, mahi, grouper, red drum, blues, cobia, stripers, kingfish, shark. We caught all of these on the Atlantic and none of them except blues and stripers had I caught before. It was as novel to me as it was to the onlooking children, but I suppressed my fascination in the presence of Capt. Travis and Wills and Chief. I wanted to earn my stripes, to be a good boathand and not some green-thumbed, fawning one. The first trips out I hid my enthusiasm from the crew and adopted their seriousness, the tough, seaward glare as the appropriate expression for our work.

But I had never been to sea like that before. I had never seen the coastline shrink so faintly to my rear, or been the hand waving backward. Children would wave to us from the beach, and I have never forgotten those little waves. I had never seen the water change so dramatically under my feet as it did when we moved from slip to ocean- to watch how the rank, oily brown turned blue- so vibrantly blue, dark, and silvery. The farther we went the more the water became alive to me; the tall, hulking waves, as though it respired, swelling, every breath and undulation of its surface taken like a drawn breath. The wind was boisterous and sonorous.

On Weems the wind blew laterally, nipping, causing chop and agitation. Here it buffeted. Here the waves were muscular, gorged, sculpted, and caving. They moved as though there were coiled springs beneath the surface giving them their motion.

The initial impressiveness of 40 feet of power boat dwindled with each nautical mile we took offshore. How small you become under that much ocean. We were a gnat skittering across the hide of a lion, and the farther back I looked upon the heaving openness, the more surreal it felt to have no landmark to acknowledge, no port town or creek to name by memory, no near bank to hug for refuge.

For the first time in my boating life I did not know where we went, and I had no say in the matter. We had our separate places on the boat. Chief steered us, Capt. Travis conversed with whoever the client was that day, Wills and I kept to our own, prepping what we could around the boat, but generally just waiting to stop and drop anchor. Our vantage was from the stern. We sat on opposite sides of the cabin doors on long coolers filled with ice. Wills sat with his arms folded and his eyes shut. I would look over at him, wondering if he really slept with that much commotion and sound, because his head would bob in front of his chest, but then he would revive in less than five seconds, open his eyes, look around, then going nodding back.

We listened for the slowing of the engine, which was our signal that we were going to bottom fish for a time. By then I would have sliced a tray of bait, squid, and peelers, and mackerel. Wills rigged the line and hooks. Depending on the day we drifted or anchored. There were four to six rods in the water at all times- Travis was the only one beside the client who dropped a line in, and he would pass it off to the client if it had a fish on it.

In the middle of all the action was the chair, the chair Capt. Travis showed me that first day. It became so common to look at that I never thought of it. And I never realized how seldom it was used for its real purpose. Maybe once a week someone stepped afoot and leaned back, less because the size of the fish demanded it, or the strength of the angler required it, and more because Capt. Travis was fundamentally a showman who cared as much about the hype and theatrics of fishing as he did the quality and quantity of the catch itself.

He could swoon any man to the chair. I suppose it was not that difficult. Most men made some remark about it when they stepped aboard. Travis would downplay its importance at the dock.

"We'll see. But I doubt we'll use it." he'd say. "We haven't used it in a long time; it's collecting dust by now."

As the day progressed, he began to play it up again,

dangling the possibility in front of the client. When the catching was good, he would thump the seat cover and say,

"Might have to saddle this thing up, at the rate you're going."

Wills and I would look at each other and roll our eyes. When Travis finally invited his client to mount the chair it was with prestige that the man embraced the occasion. There was often a bit of bashfulness involved.

"Are you sure?" the guy would say. "I don't have to."

"Absolutely, step up, step up. This is one we don't want to lose, and we don't want this chair getting rusty." Capt. Travis would say.

That is how he bargained. Then he led the man up. It was like lifting a princess to her carriage.

44

A man vying with a fighting fish on the open sea is at rigorous odds with nature and with himself. He wears on his face the primeval thrill of his undertaking- the sudden sweat, glee flummoxed with strain, intensity mingled with whatever grit he summons by perseverance; boyishness returns to him in a thousand ways. In smiles and swearing, in grimaces and locked teeth. In outbursts.

It is a test he has begun, a rite of pluck and hardihood; a battle taken down to this bones and knuckles, for it is congenital. The chair braces with his energy. Crank by crank he goes it, spurred on by crew, by slander, ribaldry, pussy-talk, mockery, he goes it. It is like hunting, touching some aboriginal nerve in him to prove his dominion, to win. The sea, veiling her prize until the last fathom finally gives way- a thrash of tail upon the surface, the rod doubled over in a fitful arch; first the crew overlooking the rail sees the fish and names it for the man- a birth of sorts, a victory. A last crank of the reel. After its fury, the catch rises. The kingfish rises from the deep, long and slender and limp, like it were raised by helium.

Then it is gaffed aboard, and the angler, wearied yet

empowered from the bout, stands over the fish grinning like a man who has just made love, and is pleased with himself. Capt. Travis tried to facilitate as many of those sorts of moments as he could. He was successful many times, but sometimes not. When the client had a big one on the line and lost it Capt. Travis would switch his manner from entertainer to consoler and companion. He'd say,

"Unlucky, unlucky, leave that behind." or "Fresh start, fresh start."

He would get Chief's attention upstairs and make a little circle motion with his finger- that was the move that meant 'Let's go.' As the engine fired, Capt. would take the client inside the cabin for a drink, and all trip long he made those kinds of concessions and gestures, negotiating the mood of the boat, and promising a pleasant adventure, a few high thrills, a few close calls.

The trips we took were a blend of bottom fishing and trolling, one kind after another. We bottom fished at a few known wrecks and trolled everywhere in between. When the catching was good, we filled coolers of fish from cobia to amberjack to drum, depending on the season. We were not far enough out for marlin, and some people who asked about it were disappointed we did not fish for them because there were pictures of marlin on the brochures we gave out.

At every leg of our charter, Capt. Travis would make peremptory remarks about the day, the fishing, the weather.

"When the catching's good, it's good. When it's not, it's not."

He said that almost everyday, as well as sayings like,

"There's more biting today than I've seen in a long time, let's rope em in."

Or, if there was a school of fish visible from the boat, he'd say,

"The herds are running, let's get on em."

If he was helping a client prepare to fish off the stern, he'd say,

"Sidle up here, partner." I could never tell if he said 'sidle' or 'saddle'

There were other token phrases he slung up and down the deck. I've since forgotten them but they all involved some reference to the west, to cattle, herding, roping. I don't know where he got them, because he did not talk to his crew that way, but nonetheless, they added to the dimensions of his personality, his turning cowboy on the big waves.

The sea was his stage, and he was a different person on shore, entirely; composed, business-like, civil, guarded- with a talent for staying well organized, keeping his crew busy, and at least from appearances, distinguishing us from our slip neighbors whose cluttered rigs, though operable, were noisome, filth-ridden, and downright ugly. Opposite our slip was one such vessel called "Ump", an offshore clamming boat that was a shanty unto itself. It was a boat that lived up to its name, a runt of a boat. Across its transom the name was chipping, the ropes that fastened it to cleats were brown and growing strands of algae, the rails and ledges were spattered with bird droppings, hardened over, and when it left each morning, the hull dragged a trail of translucent green seaweed underneath, like a shaggy beard. Ump was a wharf boat par excellence. Its captain was a fat man named Chippy, who we hardly saw, and when we did, he kept to himself. The one time he said anything to us was when we were cleaning our boat. He said,

"Looks like somebody's trying to win a beauty contest."

He had a brown coil of rope under his arm that he chucked to the floor of his boat. As far as I know, that was our one and only interaction.

Chippy's 'Ump' was one of many ships that had fallen into an irremediable state of disrepair. Not so for Capt. Travis. He had a repulsion for letting things fall apart under his eyes.

For a boat as new and full of potential as ours, he cared about appearances as much as he did about utility. Weekly we power washed the deck, hosed the hull and coolers, bleached the floor, polished rails and knobs, desalted reels with fresh water, vacuumed the cabin; all manner of tidying and spit shining. It was our home away from home after all.

45

At the end of a trip Travis often left us cleaning and went to make calls and book trips in the scant office, which was more of a 'post' or large closet. Over time we added a few things to it; a coffee pot, a pile of fishing trade journals, a desk calendar and a hanging calendar, and we left sweatshirts and hats. We booked clients by last name and scribbled them in, marking them 'half' or 'full' depending on how much fishing they wanted. I also began to bring order to our office. I installed air fresheners and vacuumed each week. I also made cubbies for each of us, where we could stow extra gear, shoes, hats. I had so little say over anything else on ship, that office was a small corner I cut out for myself.

The deck cleaning became a bond of fraternity between myself, Wills, and Chief. I say fraternity because it described the spirit of the work, the togetherness of our hands, each on a separate task, the continuity of labor broken occasionally by jokes, requests for help, bantering, anything that came to our heads that this work brought out. If there was ever a time in my life that I thought less about being a young woman on a ship with men, it was then, during that season. The boat and the sea and the filthy wharf had a way of diminishing whatever concern there was of equanimity between us. I cared simply that I would contribute fairly, equally, and respectfully. That much remained true as long as I stayed- any other concern was dubious and never amounted to anything. I can't speak for the others.

I may have been thought an outlier to one, or all, or none of them, but I certainly did not feel so or experience any moment of unwelcomeness or disclusion. From the moment I arrived there was never any catcalls or uncouthness. The three of us, the support staff, were each other's keepers as much as we were the boat's. We were there for one another, but that trust took time. Like the long settling of sediment after a storm, eventually the water clarified. We grew comfortable in each others presence. We began to see into each other's lives, to share histories, troubles, contentments. I mentioned my leaving school, my lost friendship with Bev, my brother's legs.

Wills, the most introverted of us, told us about his brother who lived in town but who he never saw because his brother suffered from a severe form of schizophrenia. And Wills said he worried for himself if he would have it too, because he shares the same blood. When he told us that, I initially thought it was dumb thing to say, that that's not how it works. But I let that comment be. And the older I've gotten the more I believe he may have said something profound and wise, that I was all too ready to pass over. About how our blood inclines us toward certain troubles.

Of the three of us, I felt for Chief the most. He was not much younger than Mr. Bruce, and in those first months we learned he was a recent divorcee who had lost his boat, spoke infrequently with his children, and had all but wandered his way to work here at the wharf, for a Captain who was much less experienced, and much different than he was, especially as it pertained to the running of the charter. All of this he told us after the fact. It was surprising because for many months he led us on to believe he was nothing but jovial. I remember one afternoon when the three of us were cleaning after a trip. Chief received a call and stepped off the boat to take it. When he came back he wasn't saying anything. I asked him if all was ok. I was moving bluefish from the cooler to the stern. Wills was hosing them off as I lined them up on the floor, one after the next, tail to tail, their eyes black and their mouths cracked, showing their jigsaw teeth. They were a good looking fish. Good fighting too.

Chief said nothing for a while. I looked up at him again as he leaned against the ladder going up, his arms crossed and the same sullen look in his eyes, a lack of expression- frozen almost, like one of the fish faces. Wills called up to him,

"Any word? How'd the call go?" That snapped him out of whatever thought he was in.

"I'm sorry?" Chief said.

"The call go ok?"

"No." he said. "Not ok. My mother in law passed yesterday."

His head fell and he leaned back with both hands against the back of the rail. We all stopped working. We stood silent in our spots. The gulls were sitting on the edge of the dock and atop the pilings, bouncing and waiting and peering at the row of fish. Wills sprayed them away with the hose.

"I'm sorry, Chief." Wills said.

"Me as well." I said. "Don't worry about staying here any longer, we'll do the rest."

"No." he said. "Appreciate it though. I need to do something with my hands, or I'll do something I'll regret. I'll clean too."

He went inside the cabin and brought out bleach from the cleaning closet to scour the floor bed with, after we finished loading the fish to the bins and taking them off the boat. All three of us took fish and filled the same bin. We stood around it dropping fish, adding ice.

Chief said, "Hell of a day. Oh hell."

I waited before I said anything, then I asked "You were close? To your mother in law?"

He looked at me and gave me a smile to intimate the nature of my suggestion. He put two more fish in and covered them with ice.

"Nothing farther from the truth, unfortunately. To be blunt; I hated her. She resented me our entire marriage. Even after we got married she never once called me by my first name, and she never acknowledged her daughter having my last name - she still addressed her by her maiden name, as if she would change it back eventually. For 32 two years." He stood up, his legs still spread from lifting, and looked at us.

"32 years. Can you imagine?" He wiped his nose with his elbow and went back down.

The bin was full. Wills hopped onto the pier and Chief, with only a bit of my help, lifted the bin to the rail, and Wills balanced it over to the catwalk pierling. Chief wiped his hands off on the back of his pants.

"I guess she got her way in the end."

He fetched the bleach from the corner where he had left it and scooped it by the jug ring. By the haphazard way he swung a hold of it, I knew his mind was elsewhere, seized by the thought of that woman. Wills returned, and I made enough eye contact with him to say 'Let's get the coolers.' one on each end. When Chief saw us he said,

"What am I doing?" He put the jug down and helped dump the dirty ice overboard.

"Sorry, you two, I'm in a haze."

"It's no problem, Chief, we can do it. Why don't you take some time off the boat? Rest up a little." Wills said. But the words seemed to have no effect; it was like they were passing through him. He lowered his head again and fixed his eyes on a blank spot on the floor. When he looked up, he appeared to have heard nothing again because he said,

"No, she never did like me. That's something I never got to the bottom of. I'm not lying either. She didn't care that I worked on boats, and she didn't care that I came from a divorced home. She never saw past that. When we had kids she softened some. But just toward them. Not to me. She would welcome them, and keep me at a distance. Even in her home I felt horribly uncomfortable- to sit down, to have a glass of water, to turn on the television. I stopped coming over. That was my own choice, and I'm not saying it was right. It was what happened though, and I regret it."

"When's the funeral?" I asked.

He sighed, acknowledged me with a side glance, and resumed his thoughtful posture. He nodded gravely.

"She just told me and I forgot already. Damn. I'll need to go to it though." he said. "Somethings you don't miss, no matter your hangup. She was my family." He nodded again. "She still is my family, in a hard way."

We took the last cooler and dumped it over the side. The bed of the boat was brown and bloodied from the fish and our own stepping through it. Wills stepped back with the hose. I pulled the two white coolers off to the side and opened their tops for spraying. Chief held the jug of bleach with his middle finger. He said,

"Listen, before we finish, I need to take back what I said earlier, just now, about me hating her."

Wills stopped the hose.

"She was hard for me, but no doubt I was hard for her too, and hard for my wife, and more people than I'd like to recall. My kids. It was never one way. We both walked the road." He sniffled hard and stood there in the corner with the bleach. He looked like a boy, the way his shoulders slumped forward and he kept putting his lips together and sniffled. When he spoke up again his voice was nasal and emotional.

"It's no way to remember someone, by their wrongs alone. Learn from me, that's all." He uncapped the jug and began emptying it across the deck. To this day the smell of bleach, that strong, sanative smell permeates my memory of the scene. Wills hosed everything simultaneously and the jet pressure sent the yellow jug cap skating across the floor bed.

I laid the coolers open to drain alongside the blood-brown runnels that ran off the back of the deck into the water. And after all was washed, scoured, and bleached, we stood there, the three of us, looking upon the fruit of our labor- the final strong, clean whiteness that was its own visible reward and achievement. And though we had performed the task so many times previous and so many after, that moment was unique, holy if you will, set apart. There was a look of ablution over the gleaming surface, not a trace of blood. It was an image that expressed all the words before it, and more.

46

After that episode Chief was more careful with what he revealed to us. Especially those parts of his life. Confessing in that manner, it was like he acquired also a new contempt for himself, a compunction for feeling he put too much on us. Months later he would still reference that moment and apologize for it to me and Wills. We said it was no issue and that we appreciated his honesty. But who knows if he accepted it truly.

In place of private travails he supplanted fishing tips, seafaring wisdom, and a bottomless provision of boating lore. Wills and I were his wards, and he took it upon himself to teach us what he knew. He taught us in small asides, never formally, and never compulsory. He was sensitive that it was not his boat, and not his place to commandeer the crew like they were his own. Over many months, close to a year, a friction arose between him and Capt. Travis. It was evident in their short, passing exchanges. So whatever teaching happened, happened under wraps, usually when we returned from a half day charter trip, and were cleaning and prepping for next day. Chief would show us how to rig mooring lines properly, how to unkedge an anchor, how to perform regular engine maintenance, when to bait alewives and when to bait herring, and how to bait them- through the snout, or eye socket, or through the back fin. The uses of snell hook, of a treble hook. He was a reservoir of practical wisdom; a reservoir that was constantly seeking some outlet.

He reminded me of Mr. Bruce and my father in that way; beneath their cool exteriors was a remarkable enthusiasm for the water and boating, for all the art and livelihood of fishing. At times that savviness was repressed, and other times it had nowhere else to hide, so it spread, and those in its path received a share in it, and in turn passed it along to others without trying.

There was more to our mentor-mentee relationship than common interest, or friendliness, or agreeableness, though it implied each of those qualities surely. It was commity, a keeping of each other beyond our natural duties, an eye for each other's good, that never so long as I participated became flattery or sweet talking. No; we were bound by our obligation to Capt. Travis. There was work to do. And there was firmness and difficulty in the work we did which made it hard to overspeak while doing it. You do not theorize about cleaning the bilge. You clean the bilge. You share the theory after, or you do not share it at all. We left when the work was done, not sooner. And when we left, we left together, on an unspoken principle.

The bond between us came slowly. It was not everyday that we worked in high spirits. There were those days- but they were as regular as the lonesome days, the irritating days, the belabored days. But we saw each other all the time, and that was key. Fealty was daily.

Of all the lessons Chief taught us, by far the most vivid was knots, the tying of knots. For skippers and boat crews, knots are an indispensable tool, and knowing how to tie them well is an indispensable skill. I came aboard knowing only three kinds of knots; two variations of shoe tying, and a figure eight cleat knot, which my father taught me. Every month Chief gave us one knot to practice. Wills was good already when we began but I was not. And as I came to see, the learning curve was not as basic as I first assumed. There were knots for everything: simple loop knots for life savers, universal fishing knots, square knots. They had many names; the granny knot, clove hitch knot, the anchor band, the rolling hitch, millers knot.

My favorite was the eyelet knot, used for making eyelets on a single strand of fishing line. It was used so that a hook might be attached higher up than the bottom weight without using a swivel or leadwire, which some fish are wary of. For the eyelet knot, I practiced on a regular rope before trying on monofilament. It was difficult; I could recreate it under Chief's close supervision, but not otherwise. I would get close, then fumble and it would fall apart. Over many, many attempts, I finally began to get it. It was an extra challenge graduating from the thick green sailing rope, to the fine, clear, fishing line, where the knot is formed principally with the fingertips, not the hands. With more and more practice though, I began to come around, and the satisfaction of having conquered a knot was no small thing. I made it for as many of our clients as were willing, I practiced on my own shoelaces when I was home. I used them above and under and sideways and indiscriminately. I dappled the boat with eyelets.

One day during the height of my accomplishment, Chief asked if I had mastered it yet and I said I had. He handed me a length of line and said "Now show me- but without looking." I took his challenge and went slowly tying it. A few times I missed the small hole the knot had to go through to be completed, but on the third or fourth try I felt it work; I pulled the tiny hoop agape a bit more so that it was the size of a finger ring in circumference, and then the most gratifying part- tugging both ends apart and cinching the knot firmly into place. The snugness, the bead of hardness. I opened my eyes and he was nodding his head in affirmation.

"Not bad, not bad at all. Next time- single handed."

I looked at the little knot I made blindly. It was, if I may say so, a wonderful little creation, a triumph of smallness.

"You can do anything with that." he said.

However he meant that comment, I understood the meaning of it. Before then, I never imagined that two ends of filament could bring so much satisfaction- not least the tactile sensation, or the systematic, slow way of braiding and twisting, pulling a chaotic shape into a useful form. But also the neatness of the knot, the nimbleness and patience required to make one, the attractiveness of watching it hold and endure through pulling, yanking, abuse, and sheer dead weight. These were triumphs.

47

As I mentioned, those days I lived alone in a studio apartment, fifty yards from the commuter rail. Many nights I would wake from windows rattling from the train passing, and my legs cramped from the day before. Not that the two were related, just that I remember them that way. Rattling and cramps. But I don't recall if I woke for the rattling or the cramping.

For many months at the beginning of the job my legs were jello beneath me. They couldn't stand the big swells, neither could my stomach. I was still conditioning to the sea. I tried to make myself inconspicuous by leaning against railings and edges while I was completing tasks, but it must have shown through. I remember each of my crew mates, at one point grabbing me by the elbow to give me balance. If they were aware of my handicap, they were at least good enough not to make a scene of it.

I called home about once a week, and went home once every two months. I talked to my mother mostly. She was the confidant. She had the update on everyone's life. Most times we talked she'd say,

"Nothing new around here." and I'd say "Same here." She'd

asked me what I was eating, and I'd name the same five things every week. A few days later I'd get a letter in the mail from her with a casserole recipe written on a 3x5 card, and the motherly encouragement,

"Constance, this one is easy. Share it with your team."

I got a kick out of her writing "team", and not "crew". Of all the people who comprehended what exactly I was doing out in Virginia Beach, I think she understood it the least. In spite of that, she was the one who supported me the most from afar. She called me and we talked mostly about nothing. Yet, for all the nothing we talked about, I appreciated those calls. I needed them. It was good to hear her voice. Sometimes she would put my brother on the line, and I would ask how he was. He was alright, he said. He was working as a receptionist at my father's office. They drove in together to Washington DC. I tried to imagine that. He said Adley was never home. Once when I was talking to him I heard my father in the background say hello, but that was all.

I thought of them a lot during my time away. No matter how I described what I was doing, I never felt like I was able to adequately capture the color and details of my whereabouts and daily living. I also didn't try that hard to. So that's how it was with the family. We were away but not separate. We were linked but not united. Reporting but not revealing.

There are chapters in every family's life when you taste the plainness of life and it satiates you with a kind of sadness. I'm thinking of those times of temperance and boredom when there are no great turns to be taken, or uncertainties, or imminent perils to intensify that bond of kinship, a necessity of belonging, when everyone is simply getting along. Such were those times.

. . .

Eighteen months passed like nothing. The Atlantic ocean was a majestic and monotonous place. Some days I was stung with such lust for its power and beauty- the same I had when I was young- to be abroad, capturing the whitecaps, sledding the infinite hills of deep dark blue, away, away from land, away from family, away from the steadiness and flatness of shore. Other days I grew sick of it, the same way museum guard must get sick of the marvelous paintings they see all day. For me it was the unchanging horizon, the high noon sun, the prosaic realities of getting along with a crew; we wore upon each other steadily, like any group stuck together for long stretches would. Capt. Travis gave me a few more assignments around the boat. I began booking trips in the office, and making weather reports for the week ahead. If the forecast was rain, interest in our charter dropped immediately, and many groups canceled when they heard the forecast.

Ironically, the best trips we ever led were in downpours. I remember one where we were drifting on the edge of a storm. Twenty miles away or so lighting was striking the sea, and even at our semi-safe distance, the sky and the ocean were the color of gunmetal, and sharp flashes of heavy rain pelted intermittently, pounding the deck. During downpours we rested inside the cabin and emerged when it cleared. The voltage in the air made the hair on my arm stick up. It made me think of the storms on Weems.

For three hours we caught nothing but red drum. The whole seascape was cloaked in that halfway dark of dusk and night which made it feel later than it was. The rain stopped for a while, and the air that came blowing in its place was fresh and cold. The sea had not calmed. It swelled on, and we rocked, and far off the lightning fell the same, and the clients kept pulling red drum. We were on break when Wills, looking out the back yelled "Fin! Fin!" He pulled me and pointed.

"See it?"

It was hard to make out what he saw in that light, because it essentially had the same color as everything else- but I saw it briefly skate across the surface, then dive below. The boat was rolling and the engine was gurgling in idle. We were prepared to move. Chief was mapping our next step. Capt. Travis was with the men who came fishing- two middle-aged brothers with bald spots on the back of their heads. One of them had a bow legged gait. They were inside the cabin. I slid the door to the cabin and said to Capt. Travis,

"Shark fin, if you're interested." He looked at the other two and raised his brows, then he said to me,

"Bull's out of the ring, let's go."

By the time they came out, Wills had rigged a rod with a hook the size of my hand and skewered a whole fish head on it, one of the freshly caught red drum. The head was the size of a loaf of bread. He hooked it through the eyes. On the same line he had attached a red, half blown balloon, the floater.

The bow legged brother, who was wearing a poncho, stepped forward and said,

"I'll take the first crack." He scanned the water and saw nothing. "Where'd you go? No need to hide."

"Get him. Show me some action. Get him now." his brother jeered.

He threw the rig overboard and we all watched the red balloon rise and fall on the dark sea. His brother came beside me and Capt. Travis too. Their hands were on the rail, their knuckles were wet, and all of them were scanning the water. Wills saw the fin again, and pointed,

"Fin! Right there, right where my finger is."

The bow legged brother took an extra hold on the rod and readied himself.

"It's close." Wills said.

Right then the balloon disappeared and there was a

thrash of tail on the water's surface followed by the zinging of the line as the shark dove. Zing. Zing. Zing.

Chief, who had been watching from above said,

"Looks like a hammer!"

When the bow legged brother heard that, it sent him heaving and struggling all the more. Cluck cluck cluck cluck cluck. He cranked as fast as he could, keeping the rod steady. He snorted as he breathed and put the end of the rod into his gut. While he reeled his brother wahooed and taunted him,

"Don't lose it now. You hand that rod over when you're tired out. There's two of us here."

The bow legged brother surrendered it finally. The other brother took it, heaving, shifting in his sneakers, snorting the same way. Then he was gassed. Then the other took over. Back and forth they passed it- increasingly out of necessity and willingly. Still the rain fell, constant and murmurous and cold, thickening the battle.

Twenty or thirty minutes they fought. At times in the battle they held what looked simply like dead weight on the other end of the line, a stalemate in the tug of rope, each side waiting for the other to bend. But the brothers were steady, and they urged each other on, saying,

"She's slowin, oh she's slowin down."

and the one holding the rod said,

"I sure hope thats her slowin and not me. Take this now!"

And his brother would relieve him and take up the fight, and when he was done and spurred on to his limit, back it would go.

Captain Travis, who for once was only an understudy in the scene, offered the big chair to be used, but one of the brothers, speaking for the two, said,

"No sir, we want to take this puppy on our own two legs."

Closer and closer they brought the fish to the surface.

While the brothers were still at it Chief called Capt. Travis to the ladder. Wills and I were close enough to listen in.

Chief said, "Let's get it to the surface to see what they caught, but I see no purpose bringing it aboard, not if it's a big hammerhead."

The Captain shook his head.

"Chief, you let me handle that. They've been fighting it for this long, they're going to want to bring it aboard, you understand."

"I understand what you're saying. What I'm asking is what we'll do with it once we bring it on."

Capt. Travis shook his head again and blew out his mouth in frustration.

"Will you let me be Captain?"

"I'm just saying-"

"Will you?"

He turned around.

"God." he said.

He turned to Wills and said "Get the club and gaffs."

Over the talking came the sound of a thud against the boat. Capt. Travis joined the brothers at the rail. I looked up at Chief who was already turned aside and wasn't watching anymore.

"Look at that bull!" Travis exclaimed. "Look at it. Roped her in!"

The brothers were laughing and giddy. They were wiping the sweat off their faces. The rain began again and now the sky was darker yet- the two exuberant faces were shaded and glistening, and I watched how the rain slickened the bald spot on their heads as they stared over the rail, and Capt. Travis helped them bring their catch along the side of the boat.

Wills, following his orders, clubbed the shark in the head until its jerking ceased, and all that remained pulsing through its grey body and fins and mouth and tail were the dregs of its strength.

It was a hammerhead like Chief said. Seven feet long, with pink and white scars on its skin. The brothers stood back and high fived, waiting for their prize to be pulled aboard. Until then I had only been watching, but I offered to hold the rod aright as Wills gaffed the shark in the corner of its mouth, and Capt. Travis gaffed it through the hilt of the tail.

When they had hooked it firm, they hoisted it over the side and onto the deck, lifting with all their strength. As it came over it nearly fell upon them, and Wills slipped on the deck.

"Now that's what we came for." the brother with the bow legs said.

"Lordy, lordy. It's much bigger than I thought. Holy hell." the other said.

For a moment no one said a thing. The fatigue and rain reduced us to silence. There was only looking at it and the movement of feet and the interminable rain. I was leaning against the opposite rail and saw that there was hesitation on the faces of the three men gathered in the middle. I remember the rain as it ran off their backs, and off the deck, and off the bloody creature with its grey eyes: how it patterred and drummed noisily on the tossing sea making everything appear squalid, sinister and cruel. When the shark was motionless a while, Wills took the end of the gaff which was still hooked inside the shark's mouth and turned it over so he could disgorge it. As he did so he inadvertently flipped the creature on its side where it lay exposed.

One of the brothers reared back and exclaimed,

"Look at that mouth." It had dozens of crooked, sharp teeth. Trails of blood ran from the mouth, down the chin, down the belly.

The other said,

"Look at that gut." From that flipped angle we saw what he meant. The shark's underside was ivory white, whiter than the boat itself, and its stomach was bulging. The brother with bow legs said,

"Goodness. Hell is that? Looks pregnant doesn't it?"

"It's either pregnant or it swallowed a soccer ball." the other said. He stepped forward and nudged the shark with his shoe. They both looked at the Captain.

Capt. Travis spoke up,

"We don't know for sure." he said, "We don't know."

The brother's faces were wary. They bit their lips. The brother with bow legs had his hands on his waist and he moved back and forth looking at the shark from different angles. The other brother nudged it again with his foot. They turned and looked up to Capt. Travis again.

"Should we have kept this?"

"We can't let it-"

"No." Travis said boldy, cutting in. "Not anymore. This one's over. She's dead. This one's dead."

They heard that correction at the end, and looked up at him.

"We couldn't have known." he continued. "That's the game we play out here. That's how it is."

The rain softened to a cold drizzle. Capt. Travis motioned to Chief who was seated in the dark of the canopy under a single console light. Chief started the boat, and it was too dark by daylight for the rest of us to see so he turned the back floodlights on. No one touched the shark. It did not move except for its gill slits, which puffed up and down weakly. After we removed the hook, we cleaned the area of blood and went inside the cabin to dry, and Chief steered us home.

Half an hour later there was a sound like a crack that

came from the stern and I went to see what it was. The rod that was used to catch the shark had been flung to the ground from the rail where it had been leaning. The shark's tail was arched and it was the closest thing that could have done it. Still, it was a heavy rod, and I presumed that the creature was long dead by then. I looked at the shark. The gills no longer moved, but even so it was the tail I believe that did it, like the creature was hoarding up a final retribution, a last pained swish of its tail.

Even before we were back the trip weighed heavy in my mind, and felt heavier the longer we were out and our catch remained lying on the bed of the boat. I looked to Chief for some mutual expression, a consolation to see how he was doing, but he was turned forward in his seat, stolid. To their benefit the brothers did not lose their good humor, even when we disembarked. It was their mood that allayed the dreadful tension that descended over our work thereafter.

"What is there to do with this shark?" they asked as they prepared to leave.

"Most of it can be used for chum." Capt. Travis said.

They thought about it then agreed,

"We'll take the head to taxiderm- the rest can go."

"Kind of a pity, but can't do anything about it now."

While we cleaned, Capt. Travis arranged for the shark to be taken away and cut to pieces. There was a neighboring boat at the wharf that made chum exclusively. Three of their workers came down the pier and took the shark out of the boat. Two of them dragged it by its tail to the large fish cleaning station on the wharf. The third guy, a black man with a thin mustache, produced a long lean knife and flayed off the fins and tail, and then the head, which was stubborn and difficult to dismember with the slender blade he brought.

I watched them for a while, then I lost interest and stopped. Wills was behind me on the deck and we resumed our regular chores. Chief, unlike Wills and I who stopped to watch the chummers worked straight through. It looked like he wanted to leave as soon as he could. Capt. Travis was back at the office checking the schedule, giving out fishing reports, everything as usual if I had to guess. There was more to be recollected and explained from that trip than was ever debriefed in the days following. I waited (foolishly I suppose) for a moment for Chief to speak his mind liberally to Wills and I about what was going on, but he never did. He retreated into himself, hoarding a private world of thoughts.

A few days later, I was relieved of thinking about that trip by something else going on at home. My father called and left an odd voicemail saying that Antonio, his brother from Texas and his family were visiting soon. It was Friday when he called, and he said they would be arriving later that night. He asked if I could come. Again, it was odd not only because it was about Antonio, but because of the timing. He ended by asking if I could come home. I called back and said that I could come. Besides, with all that was going on at the wharf, I needed some time off the water. I needed to be away.

48

That day I showered and neatened myself, and left early in the evening when the boat was tucked away. I thought of all that was happening at the wharf and at home now. I tried to recall the last time I heard anything about Antonio, much less his family. It was a long time. Ten years, maybe more. I did not know what to expect or how this trip came to be, or what would come of it. Did my father invite them? On the way, I called my mother and asked her about it. She said my uncle's wife, Maria, had a sick relative in Virginia that they were visiting, so they decided to make a longer trip of it and see us as well.

I arrived at home only twenty minutes before Antonio and his family arrived. I had hardly dropped my bags off and said hello to my own family before there was a knocking at our door. Three light raps. There was no preamble about manners or 'Be nice', or what kinds of topics to mention and what to avoid. There was no time for that. My mother opened the door, and warmly welcomed everyone, these people I had never met and did not recognize, but somehow knew.

It was Antonio, his wife Maria, and their two sons, David

and Feli, who were Adley and James's age respectively. As they entered, we shook hands- there were a few hugs, but mostly shaken hands. My mother and I greeted them first, followed by my father, then James and Adley- Adley who I hadn't seen in close to a year. She had dyed her hair blond since then.

When we were all inside I remember us all smiling at one another awkwardly, the big group of us gathered in the doorway, unsure where to go or what to say. My mother, leading the crowd, said,

"Here, this way." and showed us to the dining room, where the table was set, and a meal was prepared. The smaller table had been set beside it to accommodate more places. The two families stood one at each end of the table.

"Come, sit." my mother said, urging us on.

For dinner she made pasta and salad. The food went around the table, chairs were shifting and situating. It was unusual to be in that dining room, hosting that kind of meal.

Before we ate, my father cleared his throat, and looking round the tables at everyone who was there, said a blessing over the food, and made the sign of the cross, the first of many surprising gestures he made those two days. Soon enough the spell of quietness ended; the other Gonzalezes spoke good english and were quite outgoing. They talked about life in Houston, where they lived, and my two cousins talked about the local college in Houston they attended. Both of them were well mannered, and very American. They kept calling each other 'dude'.

Antonio, like my father, was watching the rest of the table as conversation developed around it. Mainly it was the wives questioning the other set of kids on things like school, interests, extracurriculars. My uncle had a thick, dark mustache which grew over his front lip, and gave him a humble, even distinguished look. A few times I heard him speak in a discreet voice to his sons, chiding them not to take so much food, but the one time he spoke aloud he addressed me, and asked what I was up to. He said,

"Constance, you are in school, no?"

"Not anymore." I said. "I used to go."

I could see my father move uncomfortably in his chair and look down. Before I could say more my father spoke up for me and said,

"She works for a yacht company in Virginia."

"Ohh." replied my uncle. "A yacht, so nice!"

He nodded his head affirmatively. It seemed he was impressed by that. 'Yacht company'. That was one way to spin it, but I dared not clarify. That was the extent of his questions, and after that he was happy to let others take over the table talk. During one of the pauses at table Maria asked me,

"You have boyfriend?"

"No." I said. "Not-"

The table got quiet and I lost what I was going to say. I quickly put something in my mouth to avoid having to say more, but I was troubled by the question. It was a perfectly fine question for someone like Maria to ask, but it caught me off guard and drew everyone's attention.

"Well, not yet." my mother said, covering for me. "Right, Constance?

"Right." I said.

From then the wives resumed their chatter, and the conversation carried on good naturedly for awhile, until everyone had finished dessert, and was ready for bed. My mother showed everyone where to go, and soon enough the lights were out and the whole house was sleeping.

The next day we had excellent weather, warm and sunny. After breakfast both families went outside and each strayed to different parts of the property. My mother and Maria sat in the adirondack chairs at the end of the pier. They got along well together. I was standing in the yard and I remember looking out and seeing them there, their ponytails falling over the backs of the chairs and bouncing as they laughed together; Maria's shiny black hair and my mother's blonde. Maria was a cheerful, humorous woman- voluble, passionate, a good storyteller, and someone who laughed often. If they had spent more time together, she and my mother would have been good friends.

My mother had no one like that in her life; no one whimsical or frivolous or romantic. Maria drew that out of her. I heard my mother chuckling throughout the day to something Maria had said. It was a rare sound, it was nice to hear. While they were sitting in the chairs the blue heron tried to land at the end of our pier, but my mother raised her leg while sitting and kicked at it to go away, and Maria copied her and said "Shoo-shoo". When the bird was confounded it flew off for another post and the two of them laughed some more.

The cousins took James on the boat. Antonio and my father had rolled the trailer from the shed and threw the oars and life vests into it. For a few hours the boys circled around Weems creek without nets, fishing rods, or crab pots- purely exploring. They were enjoying themselves as well. I could hear them across the creek, yelling and laughing, and I saw them moving restively about the boat as poor James sat still on the middle bench. I knew he enjoyed their company. The more I watched my cousins the more I saw how like their mother they were.

Adley came outside and stood close by, but it wasn't until she said something that I realized she was there.

"So," she began, "what have you been doing?"

Taken back somewhat, I said,

"Here, you mean?"

"No, in general."

"Oh, just working."

"At the yacht place? That was the last I heard. Or, wait- what do you do again?"

"I work for a charter fishing boat in Virginia Beach."

"Like a boat company?"

"Sort of. We take people out fishing. That's our business."

"I see. And you have to cut up the fish and all?"

"Every day." I said.

She nodded.

"And you?" I asked.

"Just school. Nothing else. I haven't been home at all, even though I hate Salisbury. I understand why you came back so often. I pretty much stay there though."

I felt the conversation stalling. For as long as I could remember our exchanges always stalled like that. Three statements and a hush. We were sisters, but we never spoke well with one another. This time, not wanting to let it die completely, I said,

"You changed your hair too."

"The blonde, you mean?" She ran her hand through it. "Oh yeah, I guess you haven't seen it since. I've had it for 8 months like this probably. That sounds long when I say it out loud."

She shrugged her shoulders, "I'm used to it by now. I'm also getting eaten up right now by mosquitos. I'm going in."

"Ok, I'll see you in there." I said.

And that was it. She left and I saw her no more that day, nor when I had to leave. Even so, for as spare and piecemeal as our conversation went, it was an improvement over many others. I could tell there was something changed about her too. It was subtle. She seemed less cynical, less in my face, or out to spoil. Maybe it was the fact that we carried on for the sake of carrying on, or that she started the conversation. Maybe that was a beginning. It was a small opening, but in that opening there was not a hint of sisterly animosity. There was no tally of old grievances or past remarks. It was plainly small talk. How nice that was, small talk. It was like we were acquaintances again, not strangers.

I wandered the yard after she left thinking about these things. Later I peeked into the old outbuilding, and then came inside to help make lunch with Maria and my mother. I had such difficulty understanding the ancient strife between the families. I did not get it. All those things my father said. Where did it come from? All I had were the stories I was told when I was young, but even those were wrapped in vagueness, and I forgot the details.

My father and Antonio spent the day together, walking the property and Teal St. side by side. They looked and acted so much alike; the way they made hand gestures, or puckered their lips when they were listening intently to one another. I never noticed that about my father until I saw Antonio doing it as well.

At lunch he told the story of how my father saved him from drowning by plucking him by three hairs from the pond behind their house. My uncle was a reserved, warm man, but when he was pressed into telling a story, especially at his wife's insistence, and his manner changed. It was like a quality that had to be summoned first, but then it overtook him and his face became red and beaming, his volume rose, his laughter shook him, like he was not fully in control of it. His laughter shook those around him too. The more that others reacted to his story, the more his personality grew, the tremors of his joviality rippling through the room, and it was a long time soothing him back to his reservedness. I watched my father's face as his brother told it, the reminiscence coming back. James said he had never heard that story before. Antonio's eyes widened. He spun to my father and said,

"You never told?"

It was funny to see my father exposed that way. It was the kind of cornering that only a sibling was capable of.

The day's affairs left me with a dilemma regarding these other Gonzalezes. I liked them. Should I have? Was I allowed to? It was so enjoyable. The stories and the company. The weather. In feeling so, I realized I had come home expecting something else, something morbid. I imagined stiffness and terseness; passive-aggression; the playing out of some overdue bad blood circumstance between brothers. Then the inevitable falling out and two groups eyeing each other suspiciously from behind their patriarchs.

But where was it? Where was that? And who were these good people? If there was something foul, I could not sniff it, not even from my father- and my father is not a subtle man. Throughout the afternoon I watched my uncle Antonio closely, remembering the letters my father received long ago that threw him into a fit when reading them, the letters that made him pace. I looked for a man indignant, obtuse, self-righteous, the very words my father pinned upon him- the man at enmity with my father- but I could not find him.

Here was another wrinkle, another complication in my conception of family history. When someone is a plain faced villain, and you have been warned so, it confirms the black and white judgements we apply to make quick sense of the world. It is easier to go through life sorting people that way, pegging them according to old stories and strong persuasions. Easier maybe, but not better. Therefore, all the things I had heard about these relatives before, I suspended that day. I met them as they were.

Before dinner I came in from outside to find both sets of parents in the living room. My father, my mother, and Maria were on the couch. Antonio was standing up before them trying on blazers. On the floor before him was a cardboard box I hadn't seen before, with the words 'jacket, suit' written in marker on the side. I sat down, followed by my cousins who came in right after me. We were sitting and watching this dress-up. My uncle folded the lapels down and reached his arms through the sleeves to check the length. Looking at me and his sons, he said,

"These were your grandfathers."

My father said,

"We had them since we moved. They were upstairs. I hadn't seen the box until I took him up to show the rooms up there."

James wheeled into the room and sat listening and watching with the rest of us from behind the couch.

"Fits pretty good." my mother said.

"Not bad, no?" my uncle said. He pointed to his sons and waved them up.

"You try on- come, try on." he said.

My cousins took a navy and a black blazer from the top, and I took one to hand to James, a grey wool jacket which smelled like the inside of an antique dresser.

What a scene it was- to have all those men trying on their ancestor's coats- joking and fidgeting, the cousins pushing each other as they went. Antonio was adjusting his sons, and I helped James get into his jacket. Antonio turned to us all and said,

"How do I look?" and Maria said,

"You look good."

"That good?" he said."I'll need a new job if I'm going to wear this coat!"

At that point my father was the only one who hadn't yet put one on.

"Edgar!" Antonio called, "For you-" he said, and tossed my father another navy jacket. My father joined the spirit of the moment and put it on. When they were all wearing something, Maria took a picture of them, the Gonzalez men together, standing side by side like department store misfits.

The jackets hung all which ways- some had extra wide shoulders, some had extra long sleeves, some had extra short sleeves. None of them fit the way they ought, and yet every ill fitting detail gave to the scene its final humor; here was something silly, and human, and wholesome. A shining metaphor. For what was family but bodies in lumpy heirlooms crowding together, smiling for the camera?

49

Home life, for all the serene benefits of shelter, is addled with sameness- its very security dulls it, its very repose shuts it in, contorts it, makes it lonely. Yet some moments stand out; when the windows are opened after a long shut, and the doors squeak with frequent passage, and guests have come from afar and made the place, the tired place, a new one entirely- the walls are stretched back, the roof lifts, moments like that stand out because they are few- when a home is effervescently itself, when there is felt among the inhabitants not an ultimate splendour or comfort, not perfection, but as much as heaven allows a foretaste of an everlasting bond, a deep embrace of persons, none apart from the dwelling itself, and the place- the ceiling and the floor, the light bulbs and the piano and the kitchen, the pines and the bank and the creek- all separate things joined again, and more; enjoyed.

Even as the night unfurled with this distant family, I was aware of the house undergoing a transformation. In the rooms where people sat came a kind of music, rare and mellow, when voices rose together; when someone laughed richly, and the confluence of each kind of conversation; idle chatter and storytelling, pauses and silences, came together from all corners, and the piano- I remember James playing the piano then. All of it singing through the night. And I stayed awake before I slept, missing this place, and missing my girlhood bed, wishing that our guests would not leave, nor I- that life and duty, would not take up their usual post come morning. But so they did; and as unexpectedly as I came, so I left- making for the wharf, and the crew, and another trip.

The morning I left was blue and dark. Fog hung over the far side of the creek, and dew sat on the grass, blanketing the firewood tarps, and the lime-tinted piling covers on the pier. Being the first to rise, I gave the place a long look before I left. Silence crept over the place and along the narrower necks of Weems as I drove down Teal St. The homes were dark, the water was still, and the air was quiet. The only sounds were the coo of a dove and the putter of the engine- my solitary vessel, tilling its way.

What was only a day and half felt far longer. During that reprieve I thought nothing of the charter, or Wills or Chief or Travis, not even when I was back on the road, well onto the highway. Brief though it was, I kept thinking of my time at home, and as soon as I left I began playing back the day through my mind, the faces of Antonio and his family, the look of my own, the sound of Maria's laughter, the box of blazers, the dinner table. I was homesick already, missing the place.

Certainly, spells of lonesomeness are broken and happiness revived among the right people. And maybe that's what home meant: the assembly of loved ones speaking face to face, the commitment to a shared life. *People* were home, weren't they? Or, home was not a place, was it?

I suppose so. But as I drove I found I could not separate the two so easily. To think of one was to think of the other. When I thought of the house I thought of the faces in that house and could not imagine them anywhere else. Belonging depended on memory, and memory on place. And our place was on Weems, where the ibis stalked among the eelgrass, and the marshweed blew, the dogwood bloomed on the banks.

Maybe I did not know what home was. But I knew this much: I did not miss anywhere, nor did I miss anyone. I missed somewhere, and someones.

As I drew closer to the open coast I felt there was a cord stretched invisibly behind me, a part of me lingering after the scraps of homelife, and also some indefinite foreboding, an uneasiness I could not part with, regarding my time on the charter. It was unclear, as yet, what it meant- it is enough to say that this feeling was as real and regular as a pulse, and that I watched it diligently like someone keeping a close eye on a symptom they cannot explain.

50

The very day I returned and the weeks thereafter were the most beautiful and exciting I spent on that boat to date. My legs were under me. We were catching like we had never caught before, and the money was good. It was late summer, a profuse and illustrious season at the wharf.

What merriment it was to get back to the streams of bright feet trafficking the pier, poring over the day's catch. The stir of curiosity was everywhere, even among the regulars and salty boat captains. How memorable were the young boys sitting atop their father's shoulders, the bawk of seagulls, the din of voices settling over the slips. It was fun for all of us. Our boat was in its groove. In we came and out again, catching without effort, fruitful and prodigious. We had only to lower our rigs below the surface of the water, and something was biting. Wherever we dithered and sailed, that generosity followed us; schools of fish appeared from nowhere, fins rent the waters. We emptied each day's bait supply in full. We were caught in an upwelling of luck- to the point I felt guilty for it, and almost anxious for its end. Those weeks we revelled in the sea, the primal sea, who was mother and vanguard of our successes. The days were long, hot, and free; there was not a sensible note of discord among us.

I must chasten the report a bit and state that it was not all a dream, though at times it felt like it. We still had to work. There remained the regularity of a hard trade, the cleaning, the repair jobs, the danger, the caprice of nature, and the foreknowledge that the catching would not go on like that forever.

Fishermen do not become poets when the catching's good. They do not muse about the gifts of the sea, because they know the sea too well. How it gives and how it takes. It may harden them, give them a bad mouth, but I also never saw a fisherman curse the ocean one week and not embrace it the next. It was so near to them, like a blood relation. Many of the watermen I've known become unintelligible the moment you ask them why they do this trade. They can tell you how they do what they do, but saying why is harder, and some are honest enough to say they don't quite know why, except that it's the right thing for them.

A distant observer can see that these yachtsmen possess appreciation, or more precisely, admiration, for the craft and its toils. But those words, right as they are, are only faint. They are tin words compared to the truth, that beneath all covers there is *amor*, love in bondange to the sea, an obedient and shrewd love. It's very demands are what keeps them; what kept me.

The precipitate luck ended as all spells do, in normalcy. After that, the regular amount of fish we pulled was like a shortcoming, and so far as the winning weeks had concealed any tensions among us, so did the recession reveal the previous fault lines, and new ones. I don't pretend to know all that happened on the boat and off. Despite working in such close quarters I remained unaware of many sins, many grievances.

Once, I came back to the boat after a day trip and Wills was on the dock at the fish cleaning station. From a distance I could see that he was not right. He was holding a fish, scaling it aggressively- with careless strokes, like he was shucking it rather than scaling it. I called his name twice, and he did not respond. A third time I called and he turned, looked at me with a straight face, and went back to his task. The exchange was small, but not small enough to go unnoticed. He was upset, I knew that much, and I doubted I would ever hear about it from him. Wills was the quiet one, the plodding, brooding type when the hurt concerned his own.

I asked Chief privately about it, and he said he didn't know, but he heard Capt. Travis reprimand Wills shortly before I arrived, and he heard Capt. Travis say to Wills,

"Are you crazy?" more than once, and that phrase set him off, and we knew why.

I was in my own head during that time too. Part of it was the work itself, which became second nature over time. Secondly, I was thinking of home more often. That feeling of return persisted. My aunt's question about a boyfriend came back too, and I found myself mulling over my situation, wondering about my state in life, my eligibility, my looks and my age.

I found a picture of the crew when we first started. Then I looked at myself in the mirror. I was so much rougher than before. I wore the same clothes many times a week. My boots smelled permanently of guts and I kept them outside the apartment but wore them everyday. My nails were grimy. I had gained weight too.

I talked to my mother one evening and she cut me off in the middle of what I was saying and said,

"Your voice sounds different."

"What do you mean?" I said.

"It's hoarse. Are you getting sick?"

I said, "No. It's because I yell all day over the wind, and over other people."

"I guess." she said.

There was a pause in the conversation. The next thing she said was,

"You'll come back from this, won't you?"

"The crew, you mean?"

"Whatever it is you're doing there."

"Eventually-" I said. "I don't know when."

"You don't know when?"

"Not now. I can't say. I don't know what I'd do back home anyway."

"Constance-" she said. She emphasized my name, then said it again. "Constance-"

"What?" I said.

"There's not always something to do. There's not- oh, what is it I'm trying to say. Life isn't always like that. Doing something, then doing something else. That's the way your father talks. Everything has to line up. No it doesn't. You can go back to school. You can work at the boatyard again. You can go back to the restaurant. You can just be with us. There are times when not much is going on that you can talk about, and that's ok. You can be here. I'm here-"

Her voice raised, and I couldn't tell if it was a laugh or a sob that I heard.

"James is here. It's me and him, you know. I'm saying you don't have to do something to be here, that's all. I'm not angry."

"Yes, I know." said. "I'm not either."

. . .

And I knew she wasn't. But she was pleading I know, as I was. We said goodbye after talking a bit longer, and when I hung up I stayed at the table in the apartment looking at the pile of mail that came earlier. Half of it was addressed to a previous tenant. The rest were car ads and grocery ads. I picked up the car ad and read it outloud to myself three times over. I tried to listen for the way my voice changed like she said, but I couldn't hear it.

51

It was fall when this was happening, when the ground was unsettling for our crew, each of us clutching some grievance or decision or discontent close to their chest, and giving it little to no public vent. I'm speaking of myself, Wills, and Chief. Captain Travis remained an enigma. He seemed to pass artificially from one season to the next, never visibly struggling, never apparently unsettled like the rest- not that he should have been, but that he appeared to us even over a long time as a man with no history, a man who told no stories except from trips on the water. He had mentioned he was a banker before he bought the boat, but that too, he glossed over. I was in the office once, and his wallet was out and his i.d. showing. Feeling curious I looked at it- it was a Connecticut license, and I realized that in two and a half years boating with him I never knew that. I figured he was a transplant from the south, with his phrases and accent, but that was another story.

There was something surreptitious about him, something discreet and disturbing about his evergreen contentment and the way he smiled without cause, and how rarely he took his sunglasses off. There was a perpetual glare about him from the reflection of the sun beaming off the lenses, which admitted nothing of the eyes behind them. My conversations with him had a dronelike cadence to them- and times when I tried to introduce a topic beside boating they died hard, so I stopped trying.

It was not for lack of words that he gained no trust among us; it was that we never knew him, for he never spoke of himself. His attention was always centered outward, toward the clientele, and even to some extent, to us. He would ask questions, he would prod and joke, and obtain for himself a share of intimate, selective stories and revelations. But he never let the pendulum swing back to him. In a way, he prized what he himself could not do. If that habit was puzzling to observe at the start of our endeavors, it was sad as time went on- the parlor charm had faded.

There was a poison in the air, noxious and life-killing. We were all scurrying from each other. I did not know what Wills and Chief harbored, but knew it was something, and I knew it was only a matter of time before one or all of us could not take it anymore, and that we would peel our separate ways.

Chief was the first to move- the first to reveal where he stood. We were finishing a boat clean. Capt. Travis, per usual, was gone and it was Chief and me and Wills on the boat. We were in silence and I decided on no uncertain terms to breach it.

"How is everything?", I said to Chief.

He laughed a bit and said,

"How does it seem?"

His laughter was dark and sarcastic, and he followed it with a straight face and more silence. I returned to cleaning.

Then he spoke up, this time addressing Wills as well as myself.

"You both know it, how this boat is run and managed." He turned, looking around, to make sure no one overheard him. "Or I should say, 'mismanaged'."

He was holding a rag in his hands that he flipped as he spoke.

"He jips us, and the boat." He thumbed backward, in the direction of the office. "He gives me 60 miles of freedom, that's all- And usually that means we go to the same spots we always go to."

He dropped the rag by accident and picked it up.

"With this much boat, what a waste. But he doesn't want to spend gas, he doesn't want to go out. He says we'll have to spike the cost. I say, yes, we'll have to raise them no doubt, but that's what you do to catch bigger fish, that's just what you do. It's what every boat running on this dock does, besides us. Every single one. That's why they come back later."

He shook his head.

"All that to say: I'm not sure how long I want to be up there fiddling around. When I signed on he told me otherwise. Said we'd be running week long charters. But he likes what he likes. I don't want to complain until I'm blue, but what I'm saying isn't unreasonable, is it? Can't you see it, either of you?

Wills was mopping, and he gave a nod to Chief. Chief looked at me.

"You?" he said.

I said, "Yeah, I see it."

"Right." he said. "We're a charter fleet." he said sarcastically, imitating Capt. Travis.

"I don't know where he gets 'fleet' from, since we're only one boat. Far as I know, we're a charter rig functioning like a party boat. If we don't catch, it don't matter. We just pour everybody beer and say it was God's luck, or whatever it is that phrase he uses. And then everybody has a good time, and forgets we were there to fish in the first place."

Chief had been twisting and twisting the rag, finally he let it loose. Exasperated by his own talking, he cut himself off and said,

"That's enough, I'm shutting up. That was just on my mind for a good while. And you asked." flicking the rag at me. Wills finished mopping and stood leaning against his pole. Each of us were reflecting on what he said.

"One last thing," he said. "Is that in three years, however long I've known him- I know barely more than you. It's been 'all good?' 'yep, all good' from the start, just variations of the same kind of exchange. I don't know a thing about him, which is plain weird."

He looked up, shook the rag out and stuffed it in his pocket.

"Anyway, I'm done now. Promise."

I never heard him speak like that, with so much consternation. Those words must have been bottled in Chief for a long time. I don't know how Wills felt, but I related entirely to Chief's appraisal of our crew and the boat and the whole experience. Before then I had not spoken of it.

Three weeks later I overheard Chief tell Capt. Travis that he was leaving and that he would finish out the month. I did not see or hear Capt. Travis's reaction, but I don't doubt he was greatly surprised at the news.

I did not know how to go about leaving as well. I wanted to leave, but I did not know exactly when and I was hesitant to offer unfounded reasons for doing so. Weeks before Chief's departure, I thought it through over and over; more than was good for me. My reasons, though they felt subtle, were nonetheless simple and true: I was tired of the boat and my time upon it. In a greater sense I was tired of that way of life, which as far as I could tell, bore no great promise at the end of it. It was about home too. I missed my family sorely. That was another reason. In the end, that was the reason I gave to Capt. Travis when my time came, which was not long after Chief's telling, and must have seemed like the two reports were related. Part of a double betrayal. Capt. Travis would have no crew for weeks, and we had left poor Wills on that lonely wharf; though to his discredit, he said nothing at all to either of us during that time. He had become shut-in, and remained so after we left.

On Chief's last day, Wills and I got a beer with him at Skuppers, one of the seafood restaurants bordering the wharf. Travis said he would come, but didn't.

At Skuppers Chief said to us "You can't please everyone, but I'm glad you two are here." He wished us well and shook our hands, and said that if we were ever in North Carolina, to give him a holler. After drinks that night I walked back to the office to pick up a pair of shoes I had left the trip before- the light was on, so I knocked, and I heard Travis say, "Come in."

He was sitting at the desk with a notebook of charter reservations opened before him and a pen laying across the middle crease of the book. He had put it down and was eating canned soup with a plastic spoon. I found my shoes and thought of leaving without a word, but as a gesture of friendliness I said,

"What's for dinner?"

He looked up and rotated the can so I could read it.

"How is it?" I said.

"Not bad." He took a bite, then leaned back in his chair and looked up at me.

"How was your thing?" he said.

"It was good. We missed you."

He nodded.

"Good, thanks." he said. It was a strange reply, a thoughtless, nervous response, that came almost instinctively to his mouth.

"I wanted to come," he said. "But I needed to spend time on this, because of all the - " he took another bite, "the transitions."

The way his voice rose after he said 'transitions, it was like there was something he still had to say, but he began to rub his eyes with the back of his spoon hand. He rubbed them hard and it was painful looking. When he stopped his eyes were red and bleary. He said,

"Sorry, my eyes hurt from looking at this too long."

"I'm heading out." I said. "Bye."

"Yep." he said.

He turned his face back on the page and ate his soup.

52

The sequence of events that led to my leaving the wharf at Virginia Beach was unmarked by sudden shifts or dramatic words. Looking back, it happened gradually, foot by foot. At the same time, the change was not merely a mind shift. The steps were real. I could point to real events, real signposts and signals that altered my course, which is an important distinction. It was the difference between turning from something and turning to something. If the same responsibilities had simply grown dull over time, that would have been a normal, but perhaps less convincing reason for leaving, than if something else was inexplicably calling me forth, and I found myself drawn to that thing.

It was both, I admit. I was seasick and homesick, but more homesick than seasick. The particular signposts: Antonio's visit, the hammerhead incident, Chief's outburst, my mother's comment about my voice, the can of soup, even to some extent the stretch of perfect weeks in late summer. Each played a part, and one moment was the final gust, the wind that turned afoul the rig and sent me sailing back for Weems.

. . .

It was during the gap of time when Capt. Travis was navigating since Chief was gone. It was just the three of us and a man who had driven from Delaware to fish. We were camped over a usual fishing spot; a wreck 40 feet down. The engine was low and then it ceased. It was the last stop at the end of a trip. The man had caught a few small fish; porgies, blues, nothing special. As he pulled his last line up, he waved and said,

"Lookee here."

Wills and I looked over the rail and saw, swimming across the surface of the deep, two blue crabs, one mounted above the other. The bigger one was atop and it had one claw extended and the other claw gripping the smaller crab beneath. The smaller crab had claws like bright red nails.

"I've never seen one out this far." the man said. I thought the same thing.

Wills said, "They've got some way to go."

"They do." the man said. He tapped me and said, "Bet that reminds you of Chesapeake, doesn't it?"

"More than anything." I said.

I kept my eyes on those crabs until I lost them on the waves. Then the engine stirred, and the boat turned around, and we were on our way. I had not seen or caught a crab in a long, long time, but that little sighting affected me a great deal because no single creature summoned a place so purely as the blue crab to my home waters. There is a devotion to the blue crab as strong as the names of the rivers and waterways and townships it thrives among; Potomac, Severn, Choptank, Nanticoke, Hogba.

The scientific name of the blue crab I remembered from grade school; Callinectes sapidus it's called. "Beautiful swimmer." A name never fit so well.

. . .

I left the wharf on a Tuesday, two and a half years after my first day. There were no trips booked that day and Capt. Travis and Wills were at the pier when I stopped over to say my goodbyes. Wills came down and gave me a hug. Capt. Travis said his farewell from the bow while he folded a hose on deck.

"Good luck." he said. "We'll be here."

And he went back to work. When I drove away, the last image I had of them was of their two backs hunched over in cleaning. I left the wharf and headed down route 16, past the big hotels and the open coast, toward Maryland.

53

When I arrived at home I pulled into the driveway with the same trepidation I had when I left school early and showed up with no plan- it was a kind of looming self consciousness. They knew I was coming back, but still, I knew I would have to explain myself, direct myself, and find my way again. For all the deep blue ocean I had ventured, I feared the unknown of home again, the long in-betweenness that happens to be so much of life.

My mother opened the door, and James sat by it, keeping it open from his chair. We lugged all the bags in and left them in the foyer and had a snack.

"We've missed you so much." they said.

"I've missed you too. It's good to be back."

My father arrived later from work. He stepped around the crowded entrance and joined us at the table. He looked worn from the day.

"You're back." he said. "And the bags are back."

"They are." I said.

He nodded, like he understood.

My homecoming made no big stir on the whole. In a way I was glad of it, simply to be grafted back in on such few terms and not scrutinized. Later that night, as I unpacked with my mother, it occurred to me that perhaps it was her who felt no need to involve my father in the situation and let time take its course normalizing things- and if that was true, I remain grateful.

There was nothing that I was anticipating before me. The act of being there, in a place, with no plans for a while was what I wanted. Home could be a rest then- a haven. And though I was still self consciousness, the feeling did not hound me as before. Being back put it off the scent.

My father was away during the daytime which left me, my mother, and James, to running errands and making meals, taking naps, and cooking. I missed that fellowship having been so long without it. I moved into my old room and put my clothes away in the dresser. The domesticity was good for me- it was productive but not overwhelming. My sea legs reacclimated to the steady shore. Besides, it was nearly winter when I came home- the outbuilding was locked up, the rest under tarps.

Three months passed in that pleasant course. Occasionally the hours became too solitary, and I would get that footless feeling of being inside too much, and doing too little to actively steer my course- but my mother had words for me at opportune moments. More than once, sensing my struggle, she said,

"Constance, Constance." until she had my attention. She would put her hands out in front of her in a slowing pacifying gesture.

"You'll get there." she said. "You will. Right now, we're not worried about what's next. Whatever's next in our path will be good. It will find you. I see it in your face. You're hasty. Don't be hasty."

When she spoke, I thought of how she blended the words

'we' and 'you' as if my searching and hers, my waiting and hers, were intertwined, not separate. "We're not worried..." "Our path..."

"It will find you." she said.

And I began to wonder what would find me, or who.

54

Glancing over my shoulder, those words possess a wideness to them that I could not see then, in that moment when they were first spoken to me. I don't know if my mother knew all that she implied, or if by some preponderance she knew the extent to which her words would spring like a trap upon me. But however she meant them, they've widened with every passing year. The years have heard her out, and then some.

Those unpolished months upon my return, when I was a help around the house and nothing more, I had time on my hands. I was able to alleviate the continuous caretaking my mother gave James. In a few years his legs had deteriorated terribly and were shriveled, anemic, and leaned to one side. His face and his arms lost their firmness. His disease took full hold of his life. Without assistance he was immobile, and the combination of his sedentariness, and the demands of his health requirements, appointments, and therapy overtook him.

He had the task of replenishing the fruit we bought from the grocery. He would park his wheelchair beside the kitchen counter and open the green produce bag in his lap and replace the fruit in the wicker basket one by one. There were other small chores like that that he did with great happiness and willingness. He enjoyed playing some productive role, albeit small, in the home. Most of his life was marked by prohibitions. These small assignments safeguarded a dignity of his. The time we spent together those months were the most we had spent together since childhood. I pushed him and he followed me, like it was before. I strolled him up and down Teal St.

He told me he wanted to go on a boat again. It had been a long time. Not since the cousins came. And that wasn't the same. I said I'll take you, James. When it's warm again.

My mother told me in private that since I came back it was the best she'd seen him in a while, that my presence lifted his mood.

On the tail end of winter I decided to go to the outbuilding to see how the equipment stood the cold, and to prep some items for spring. I brought James with me. I pushed him over the hard grass. He was wearing a thick jacket and a black winter hat, and basketball shorts, which is what he wore around the house if he wasn't going anywhere. I told him we wouldn't be long. I opened the door after a struggle and pushed in, wheeling him backward over the door ledge, and parked him inside. The lights were out, so it was dark inside, but there was enough daylight coming in that I could make my way around. One of the first things my foot hit was the tackle box. It was sitting by the door, not in it usual place. My cousins must have moved it during their visit. I opened it on the ground, then closed it and gave it to James to hold.

"We'll organize this later." I said.

I went back to the corner where the fishing poles and boat were resting. The rods were taken apart in twos, and I began instinctively to match the pieces and join them back together, and reel the separate lines tight. Then I climbed the ladder to the garret and saw the crab traps and the fishing nets, things that hadn't moved. I climbed down and was about to turn the boat over to check it when James called me.

"Constance."

His voice took me by surprise, for it was dark and he had been so quiet otherwise.

"I'm here." he said.

I looked at him, and the moment I turned, there was a single stripe of cold winter light, golden and crisp, falling across the walls, across his hands, across his lap. One of his hands was holding the handle of the tacklebox. The rest of him was dim.

"I'm sorry." I said. "I got caught up and left you here."

"It's alright." he said. "I was still here."

"I'm sorry."

"My legs are cold." he said.

He grinned when I freed the wheels and started out. I locked the doors to the outbuilding and we crossed the yard in a howl of wind. I put my head down and pushed, and we bumped our way across the cold, tufted grass to the sound of hooks, bottom rigs, lures, clattering in his lap.

55

For once in a long time my sense of home was reviving. More than a temporary shelter, now it was a place to remain. A place of my making, a place that relied and benefitted from my presence and contribution. I was learning how to be here, to stay. And I rebuilt some semblance of a quiet life.

In our spare time we each had hobbies. I organized the outbuilding and removed piles of whatever there was lying around or out of place. I just liked moving things around. Picking them up, turning them over. It didn't always have a purpose. My brother played piano. My mother crocheted. I had forgotten she did that. One evening I saw her on the couch with her head tilted in concentration.

"I didn't know you did that?" I said.

"You didn't?" she said.

"I forgot." I said.

"How could you forget? I'm surprised, you're not one to forget. I've been sewing since you were small. Not everyday, but you should remember."

I laughed. Later that evening I took her yarn and showed her the knots I learned at sea, and she was impressed by that. I showed her the eyelet knot, the one I knew best.

"Here, let me try this." I said, borrowing her yarn. But the thread was so soft I did not get the knot the first few times.

"Almost." I said.

"What are you trying to do?" she said. "What is it?"

"I haven't tied a knot with yarn before. Fishing line is different. It's surprisingly easier. It's a harder material, so you can feel what's going where. But this yarn..."

My eyes were fixed on my fingers gingerly pulling end through end. My mother was looking up at me from the couch.

"You can do it." she said. "You just have to be gentle."

Then I messed it up again. It came undone.

"Agh." I said.

As I began again I shook my head.

"Gentle Constance."

I looked down at her and rolled my eyes.

"Well," she said. "Gentler."

Between James on the keys and her with the needle and me meddling in the outbuilding, moving piles around, there was a metaphor for everything. Something to be noticed, though I couldn't say what. In life, moments of sharp grief and joy are embroidered beside moments like that; my mother on the couch, or James in the dark with the tackle box- pale patches of quotidian life, which in their paleness are no less lovely by being so, nor less remembered.

For so we are stitched; color to uncolor, sackcloth to silk, swath by swath, hemming the whole so long as the days allow. Yet even then we do not know in full what we have made, except that all our living is a quilt, woven by remembrance. And what we hold in our laps is but an unfinished corner that we start again and stop again, and while we work is already tattering.

. . .

I succoured where I was. My domain was small, but I enjoyed it that way. I knew its demands. By moving back I had shrugged an old illusory pressure to make something of myself. There was no one to watch me. Not even my father. Not as before. I would stay for good, as long as they would have me.

But just as soon as I had rebuilt my quiet life, it was about to end, to halt, and I did not know it. I would meet the high road of my life. That spring I was 28 years old and eager to be outdoors by the water, near the boats. I called the boatyard parts shop, asking for Mr. Bruce, but someone I didn't recognize answered and said that Mr. Bruce only worked one day a week now. He gave me his number, which I already had, and I called him.

On the phone he sounded tired, more than before, like there was a heaviness in his voice that was new to it. I had to repeat my name for him twice, for him to understand me, but even when he did recognize me, he said only,

"Oh, hi there."

I said I was back living in the area and was wondering if the shop needed help. He said that there was a new man running it and that his hours were cut.

"It's not the same, Constance." he said.

I asked what happened. He said the boatyard traded hands of owners again and was now owned by two young European yachtsmen, who were planning to make the boatyard into a state of the art racing hub, and that they were getting rid of all the junk boats and fixer uppers.

"Not all of them." he said, "But lots. Who knows if that shop will stay around anyway- these guys will have bigger plans for it too. I don't know what to tell you." he said.

"Don't worry about it." I said.

I thanked him for the update and said I'd be in touch.

56

My next move was to work at the restaurant where I had worked before. Despite the other changes around the yard, the restaurant was much unchanged from before. The longtime manager, Jim, was still in charge and surprisingly he remembered me, and was willing to give me a job as a daytime watier. Since the change in boatyard owners, business at the restaurant had picked up and "Clancy's" (that was the name) had earned a reputation in the local paper as having some of the best seafood on the Eastern Shore. When I interviewed again Jim remembered I had worked at the part shop,

"You worked there too, didn't you?"

And I said "Yes, when Mr. Bruce was in charge."

His face fell and he said,

"Before he had his stroke then. Maybe 8 or 9 months ago by now."

I was shocked. I said I talked to him recently and he did not mention it.

"No, no, he wouldn't- even if he was at half the capacity of what he was, he wouldn't. It's a deep source of shame. There's not much wind behind him these days."

"Is that all?" I asked.

"I couldn't tell you, but be in touch with him, I'm sure he'd appreciate that."

I felt horrible for weeks. I had no heart to call Mr. Bruce in that manner, to extend my sympathy without him having told me first. When I told my father I was working at the restaurant, he asked about Mr. Bruce, and I told him what I knew.

"You sure you want to work there?" he said. "You don't have to."

"It's more to be back down there by the boats, then the work itself. It's part time."

"They're changing it you know, the whole boatyard."

"I heard."

"We'll see how it goes. I didn't mind the last one, the last guy who owned it. What was his name? I forget. He stayed out of people's way. Now it's in new hands. These new owners are here to 'transform' it, as they say, from a humble, dusty, down creek boathouse, to a sleek, country club of marinas. We'll see how it goes."

Still, I decided to work for Jim, and it was during that time that I became unusually close with a coworker, a line cook named Sonny. He was new at the restaurant. I met him the first time outside, behind the restaurant in the employee parking lot, where he was emptying a cooking oil container into the dumpster. I was arriving for my shift. He looked at me and said,

"I see you moving around quick in there." He pointed inside and made a running motion with his fingers, and laughed.

"Yes, it gets busy." I said.

Again he laughed. His laugh was sort of a high chuckle, warm and energetic. He put out his hand.

"Sonny." he said.

"I'm Constance."

"Good to meet you, Constance. I never heard that name before."

"It's not common." I said.

He nodded again and smiled, and we walked in together. During my shift I saw him in the back preparing food. I was intrigued with him already, in one meeting. Each consecutive day I worked that week I saw him more, and I looked for him through the slit partition separating the kitchen from the dining room. I saw him pacing in his white smock, and I wanted to talk to him again, and I did. To this day I can't say why I liked him on such short terms, but I did, and I had not felt anything like that in a long time. It was a genuine crush.

Sonny had a large personality, a humorous one. He was slightly taller than myself and a little bit chubby. His face was round and his skin was dark, and going by his accent, some kind of Latino. We had more exchanges like the first. He smiled often and I liked when he smiled. I also liked watching him interact with others. Once I came to retrieve something from the kitchen, and I walked through the revolving doors into that hot space and he was there. He asked if I needed help with anything but I said no, and I found what I was looking for- an extra booster seat. They stored them back there for some reason. As I was leaving I turned to nod bye and he said to me,

"Do you want a tomato slice?"

"A what?" I said.

"A tomato slice." He held it up.

"No, thank you." I said. "I can't."

"Yes. Here, have it." he said. He laughed and brought to me. "For your good work."

And I took it with my free hand and ate it. I just ate the tomato slice. It was things like that which intrigued me.

There was a sweetness to him that drew people around him. The kitchen, which was co-run by other Latino cooks, revolved around him and his laugh. His laugh was higher than you would expect coming out of someone with his body- it was almost a giggle. I heard it in the back each day, and it was pleasing all the same to hear the group of them together making noise, the sing-songy banter, the sound of plates sliding quickly across the service counter, the scurried frock of white coats moving about- all of them enjoying themselves, and their busy work. And this colorful new cook at the center of it, Sonny.

It was his likeableness that developed my interest in him over time; an unaffected simplicity which had something to do with his heritage, something to do with his personality, and something to with the courtesy he showed everyone, from the kitchen staff to Jim the manager. He was Sonny. He fit his name. On busy shifts his face would glow with perspiration, and he would stick his tongue out like a tired dog and smile at me.

We spoke to each other on break, and when my break did not overlap with his I would loiter in the kitchen and talk with him and the other cooks.

Sometimes when I would come in, the other cooks would get quiet and look at the ground with smirks on their faces.

"Sonny." they'd call to get his attention. "Somebody here for you."

"Ay ay!" another would yell.

And I would blush because they knew something was up between us. One of the other cooks said to me once,

"The only time he works is when you come in here. This guy is lazy." pointing to Sonny, "Lay. Zee. But look, you come, and he is working harder than all of us. He could do it all!"

. . .

One day as I was leaving out the back I heard the door swing behind me and he was walking quickly toward me, gesturing for me to wait.

He said, "I forgot to ask earlier, but it you're around this weekend some friends and family are having a cookout- by the water. Some of the others will be there too, from the kitchen. You should come."

I had a huge smile on my face.

"I would love to!" I said.

"Perfect."

He told me when and where, and I asked if I could bring something, but he said "No, no, just come. We will have too much food already I'm sure."

The rest of the day and all of the next I looked forward to the gathering. I was giddy and nervous too. I kept thinking about him rushing out the back door to ask me. No one did that before. This guy likes me, I thought. Wow. It was a rare thought to indulge those days. That much I speculated.

I did not tell anyone at home about my plans except that I was going to a cookout for a friend. The day of, my mother stopped me before I left and said,

"That's a nice outfit you're wearing. I haven't seen you wear that dress in a long time. Who's your friend?"

"He's a coworker from Clancy's."

"It's a he?"

"Yes, a he."

She smiled and said "Have a good time. Tell me about it when you're back." And off I went.

. . .

The cookout was at a state park near the Nanticoke river. It was tucked back from the main thoroughfare, with access to the creeks. Sonny's family was set up under two picnic tables in a large shaded area under the oaks. It was windy that day; cups and plates were toppling off the tables and table cloths were falling off. Everyone there was Latino. The women were heavy and they spoke Spanish and laughed like Sonny. Sonny welcomed me and introduced me to a few members of his family, his grandmother, aunt, uncle. Some of our co workers from the kitchen were there as well. I asked about his parents and siblings, but he said they were not coming that day. I saw he was the same generous individual wherever he went. He made me a plate of food, and a group of us sat talking at one end of the table.

I looked around the park and recognized it from a long time ago. I had come there with my father. At the other end of the park from where we were was a public fishing pier that my father used to fish from sometimes. When we came we entered from another entrance down the road; there were yellow rule and regulation signs nailed to the trees as you drove up to the parking lot, and one sign in particular I remember because it was skewed and someone had scratched out the letter L in "Public Fishing Pier" so that it read "Pubic Fishing Pier". I thought that was funny. Who knows if my father noticed it. That sign was still there, just the same way as it had been years ago, although the graffiti had been smudged off. It is funny how one can perceive something slightly off; an off centeredness, an asymmetry, and be familiar with it after all that time.

I was slicing in and out of conversation in and out of listening, thinking about the park, then and now, and what had brought me that day. The wind was still whooshing through the trees and Sonny was there laughing and carrying on. The park at that time in late afternoon, under the daylong billowing influence of the wind, with the strewn blankets about, and the murmur of voices, and myself gathered among those friendly strangers, and the old memory it awoke in me; there was something melancholy to it. The wind kept sweeping over the table pushing the tablecloth off center, exposing the dirty planks beneath, and one of the women stayed by the cloth putting soda bottles down on the corners to keep it from lifting- this made the same melancholy feeling, of something scarce and impermanent, the sensation that time is short, and nothing stays.

So many years ago when I had come with my father, I pitied those picnic grounds, with their unused charcoal pits, and wondered who used them. The pits were never being used. But now I saw it was this family, this large Latino family with the heavy women who were smiling; women who draped the dollar store tablecloth over the table to give it dignity; to make it a meal.

After eating, the men went to the creek edge and fished and caught nothing with the frozen bait they brought. They put their paper plates and soda cans on the rocks and leaned back, talking and joking. I stayed by talking with Sonny. The men had an extra rod they lent me, which I hooked and baited myself. That took Sonny by surprise.

"You fish?" he said.

"I grew up fishing. I worked for a charter boat."

He laughed and turned to his friends and said something in Spanish which I could not understand, but which they found funny. He turned back, leaned close to me, and said,

"I said to them, She's going to catch more than all of us, because you have the skill."

"I doubt that." I said. "No."

And I was right, I had the same luck as everyone else.

At the end of the cookout I helped put food away and fold the table clothes and tie up trash bags. Everyone helped, but I think the women who were the aunts and cousins were somewhat embarrassed that I was helping since they did not know me and did not speak English.

Sonny relieved me and walked me to my car in the parking lot.

"Thank you for coming." he said. "You had a good time I hope?"

"Very good time." I said.

"Good, and we'll see each other soon."

"Yes." I said.

"Yes." he said. "Just you and me next time."

"That sounds good."

He peeked over his shoulder nervously, to see if anyone was around us. There was a pause, then he leaned forward and kissed me on the cheek, very briefly, almost inconsequently, but it was the first gesture he had made toward me like that. Then he went back, yelling toward his friends, and when he was turned around I looked back at him, and I thought of him the whole drive back.

You think this is a love story, but it is not. For a while, even after he kissed me, even after many more weeks of an offbeat, discontinuous courtship, little happened. I thought something would happen soon, I waited for it. But it was like a candle being lit, then extinguished, lit then extinguished. Whatever it was termed- our series of encounters- there was nothing solid that I could act intelligently on. There was pursual (what I thought was pursual)- but it was misread by both sides, and the longer it went that way, the less I put any equity in it or strove after it; not because I was guarded, but because I was unsure, filled with ignorance, and somewhat abrasive toward the idea of romance. Any inklings I had about it seemed stifled, or at least dilatory, like a set of instructions I never really learned and came to late.

But it did come eventually.

One night, many weeks after the barbecue, Sonny and me went on a walk to the end of one of the piers at the boatyard. It was late, after a shift. He still had his uniform on, so did I.

"You've been here?" he said.

"Yes. My father's boat is just over there."

"I must be careful then." he joked.

"Of what?"

"Oh, nothing."

"No, what?" I said.

He was moving slowly.

"What, come on." I said, waving him forward. "It's ok."

"We won't get in trouble?" he asked.

"No, no, come on."

I was holding a piece of carrot cake from the restaurant in a plastic to-go box. We were going to split it. There were no seats at the end of the pier, so we took our shoes off and rolled our pant legs and sat off the end. It was dark except for the track lights along the pier. I opened the box and took out the plastic forks I brought.

"No." he said. "Something better." He reached in the pouch of his coat and pulled out a bundle of silverware taken from the restaurant.

"You stole it." I said, smiling.

"Shhh. Don't tell."

I took the fork from the bundle and ate a bite of the cake.

"I didn't know you did things like that, Sonny." I said.

"Usually no." he laughed.

"You break rules now?"

"Maybe."

"Why's that?"

"Good reason." he said, raising his eyes.

I passed the cake to him and he took a bite with the spoon. We passed it back and forth until it we finished the cake.

"So..." I said.

"So..."

"What are you thinking?" I said.

"Same as you." he said.

"You think?"

"Yes."

"So, then, are we...together?" I smiled.

"I think we are."

"This was good." I said, pointing at the cake box.

"Very good."

Then he kissed me.

"But that is better."

I moved close to him and he held me for a long time, and we looked out over the dark, still water. When we stood to leave, he threw the metal knife far into the water, making a splash. I raised my eyebrows at him.

"I can steal more." he said, laughing. "Only for you."

He grabbed my arm as we walked back and said,

"You have to keep me safe."

"From what?" I said.

"I don't know. Spiders."

"Spiders!?"

"You never know."

And I felt his fingers run up the back of my shirt.

Romance, so long interred, came around. It grew out of dry earth, like a green vine reaching up, twining a gable. And I savored it. I savored the flowering and growing, the greenness and the reach, which was a revelation to me- to be the object of desire, the object of someone's attention. A shutter was opened: light came through. I remember it as a time when I was overcome with much laughter, with laughter and speaking to Sonny.

Camaraderie I had known at many times and in many forms. But there are times when one tires of camaraderie and desires intimacy- to be whispered with, touched. It seems silly to write, but it is true. Those times with Sonny were real to me then; and not in any way diminished by what became of them later. Even after many more months of a high and generous relationship where we would spend many hours together, and I came to know his friends and he came to know my family, I resisted him. That is the best word for what it felt like- to be followed by a quiet, constant inhibition, an unpeace. Sometimes when we were closest I felt it the most.

On the fourth of July I felt it so pronounced that I took my arm from under his and wrapped it around my knees. We were watching the fireworks over Annapolis, sitting on a popular hill next to dozens of others. Up the fireworks went; plumes, crackle, darkness, BOOM, the wisp of summer air- piquant and perfect. Yet there it was again- that unmistakable, inexplicable loneliness beside this man, this luminous man.

Throughout the show I watched the water below- the calm surface of the Severn River swaying softly, the reflection of the sky in it, velvet, dark and dotted with lights from boats.

Against this very calm backdrop I heard something. It came in the quiet of my heart, unsummoned, and clear as a bell and true as my mother's voice- a dialogue with myself. An exchange. The more I've tried to recall the exact words, the more they escape me, but what I knew from this exchange was that I would not be with Sonny any longer, and that I would (be ok as I was) not be anyone like that any longer. I would not marry.

. . .

A voice arousing fear may be discarded, ignored and forgotten. But what I've called the 'exchange' with myself, was none of that. I knew it was true the moment it was spoken- or awoken- for it felt that the words did not enter me from outside, but were roused from within. To put it in an unusual way: it was myself asking permission of myself to do what was truest for me. I needed my own permission. It was not a command or an imperative; they were a permission, a blessing- I know that if I had let the words go in good faith, they would not have pestered me again. They would have gone and never stirred a bitter thought again. For this self, this true self speaking within me, honored my will. It was utterly free.

Sonny, suspecting nothing that evening, brought me back home later, then left, for it was late by then. My parents were up still, sitting in the living room; they had watched the fireworks from the dock.

"How is Sonny?" my mother asked when I came in.

"Fine." I said. "The fireworks were beautiful. We sat on the hill by the Academy, we found parking this year."

She must have heard something more than I offered because she next said,

"There's something else?"

"What do you mean?"

"Anything, really.", she said, diminishing her suggestion. She shook her head. "It's late, I'm just talking. You know how I get."

Then she sighed and said "Why don't you go on up. You look tired."

"I am." I said, and I went up.

I went to sleep that night relieved of what had happened and what I felt. I did not feel afraid. I knew that my parents, like most parents, had a knowledge of me that was deeper and denser than my own estimation of their perception. That I was seen in spite of my privacy. The way my mother said, "Something else?", with such angledness, with such talent of discretion, to play it off as an aberration of her own fatigue- I can only marvel at, and wonder what other insights they had about me, that I would come to realize at a later time.

57

Soon after that night I told Sonny I didn't want to be together any longer. He was not outraged, or frantic to reconvert me, but I could see that his brightness was trimmed, and could not bring himself to smile. After I said what I said, one week passed and he came again and told me he had had a feeling something would happen. I asked how he knew. He said he began to feel it when I stopped coming into the kitchen as much.

He also said he kept something from me- a confession that he had not shared. We were at the boatyard, between shifts. He had removed his cook's hat and folded it in his side pocket. He pulled a wallet from his rear pocket and took a picture from it. The picture was folded and creased to the point of coming apart. He unfolded it and turned it upright to me and pointed to the woman in it.

"This is Linda." he said. "I'm engaged to her, but it's not what you think. Don't be mad, please." I didn't say anything, so he continued.

"She has two boys and no money at home, in El Salvador. I met her years ago because she knows my family. Our mothers know each other- we were engaged one year. Then she said she didn't know if we should marry, if we have no money. So we said we will not talk for now. That's when I came here, to earn money to send back. But I stayed here, you see. I didn't return, I didn't contact her. I still hear from them, through my family, through my mother and hers, since they are close. Her boys ask when I am coming."

He folded the picture and kept it in his hand.

"I said nothing to you, I'm sorry, I haven't known what to say. If I go back, I have nothing again. I don't know what to do."

"You miss them?" I said.

"Yes I miss them. Very much."

"Why did you not say anything."

"I'm sorry." he said. "I was afraid. I was, really. So afraid. I thought maybe I will leave all that behind. I will write them, and say I cannot come back. I have been going back and forth. I told myself they will find someone else. Linda will find a way. Her boys- they will move on, they will forget me. They will be ok. They will be good. It's too long anyway. Too long."

"No." I said. "I don't know what you should do. If you should go back, you go. But don't go because you feel bad for them. That will not help them. You go because you miss them and want to be with them."

"I do." he said.

"You won't be happy if you stay here. I know what that feeling is like." I said. "It will follow you."

I took the picture and looked at it one last time, then gave it back to him. I was filled with braveness speaking to him, a braveness I did not think I had.

"You are afraid now, but you will find something. You'll be happier if you go. That's your family, you know."

There was a melodrama to our conversation- like the

lines were scripted from a movie, that this wasn't the way real people talk, or that maybe the scene was not our scene, that we had intruded- that I had intruded.

His face was still sorrowful and pensive. He looked at me and said,

"If I *can* go back."

"Why couldn't you?"

He tossed his head. "I have no money to go."

"You would go if you had money?"

He paused, he shrugged.

"Would you?"

"I would go."

He looked at his watch, then at the restaurant.

"I have to go soon, I have a shift. I'm sorry." he said.

Before he left he put the picture away and gave me a hug. His face was still sorrowful. He turned and walked away, and I called his name,

"Sonny!"

"What?"

"Will you laugh for me?"

"Why?"

"Because I want you to laugh. Not to be so sad. So laugh."

"At what?"

"Oh, come on."

"I can't just laugh-" and as he spoke he began to laugh. "Ah, you trick me, Constance!"

"That's better." I said. "Now have a good shift. You're a good man."

"Yeah, yeah." he said. "I knew I liked you."

. . .

The next day I mailed him a check with a note that said "I will accept your apology if you accept this gift. Take care, Constance."

I did not hear anything back after that. I saw that the check was cashed, he turned in his notice and he was gone. I did not hear from him again.

58

However life unfolds, with whatever cadence and stride it ambles from one chapter to the next, the timing is never quite matched to our expectations. We step oddly together, us and time. The pages flip either too rapidly through our story, or too slowly. But rarely are we content with the hand that does the turning. Transitions jar us; waiting withers us. Days stretch on with great boredom. Then moments of sharp pain or joy assert us, wake us. I own that human instinct of wanting to either return to a place or scurry ahead to another. But lingering is the challenge. And one could trouble themselves to think their way out of the present, but it doesn't work that well.

So it was when Sonny left. Gradually I saw very clearly that he was not the high road of my life, but neither was he negligible to that part of my story. Because in retrospect he was preparing me, inclining me to the high road. And I believe and hope that I helped him find his own high road too.

Something I had not fully believed until my time with Sonny, including my time at home, was that I cared about people. And what was more- I cared *for* them. How unprofound you could say. But that was something I was never conscious of before. It was nothing anyone had told me about me. It emerged. It was something I was discovering about myself; that I had a nurturing side, or a nurturing desire- which is different from being helpful and running errands, though it includes that. I found myself wanting to give more of my time away. To assist someone even when it added nothing to my account, and even when it took some away. Speaking bravely to Sonn. And being with James. There were times that spring when I wanted to take the dory and fish alone, but I took James with me instead and rolled him down to our pier and set him a fishing pole. And I was happier for it, waiting with him.

That is nothing to brag about, and I don't intend to overblow the realization as an epiphany; like St. Paul being struck on his steed. It wasn't that- and I won't claim it. There are people in this world who have given themselves so completely and earnestly to others that I wouldn't dare compare myself. My mother being one of them. That's not the point. It's only to say that I wanted to be more like those people, and that I felt more myself when I imitated them. I suppose it could only have come at time of loneliness, too, a time when I could study the pattern of my consolation and try and learn from it.

Until my last conversation with Sonny, when I had the instinct to send him a check, I had never really thought overlong about what I wanted my life to become. More than what I wanted to *do*, but who I would *be*, the kind of person I would like to become. I was 29 years old, sitting on the cusp of 30. And I had no clue except that I cared about people and I loved the water, and that was it.

All that time I never estranged myself from the water- the Nanticoke, Weems, Chesapeake Bay- the shoals, the marsh, the lookout points- all of them leading out to the ocean. How was is that for all my forwardness- to move, to work, to be of use, I had been slowed by the water, made sad by the look of it, fled to its edge when a fight erupted in the house or the bunny died, or when Uncle Antonio's visit thrilled me- how was I still rapt by it? The look of the tide brushing against the pier. There is something there I have never gotten over. Maybe that is what a good metaphor is- the thing you don't get over till you're over. I don't know. But that is enough discursion.

Around that time I began to think about Adley again. Her absence, or rather, her long disappearance from this place continued to form in me an unfair impression of her that never smoothed itself out since our childhood. I caught snippets about her whereabouts from my mother, who said such things in so transitory a tone, in so careless a pitch that they lost some of their reality. They were mixed with comments as commonplace as

"Grab that door, it keeps coming open." "Your father's back from work." "James, when was your last appointment?", always stating, reminding, scheduling, but rarely offering a judgment. She rarely mentioned Adley. I could not tell if my mother spoke that way on purpose; if that was her way of saying "This is your sister- she's lost at the moment, but she'll be back.", or if there was some genuine relinquishing on her part, that she had given up Adley to her own way. Nonetheless, it was the fact that she heard from Adley at all that was enough. Hearing was something. Hearing was as close as we got at that time.

My mother had always been the peacemaker between us. The older we grew, the more dissimilar we became. Adley was the city girl who never quite got far enough away to the city. Not the big cities. She was a local beauty; elusive and cold, but always beautiful. She had a long slender neck and white skin, like my mother; I had more of my father's darkness.

Adley desired sophistication and lamented that for all our money, we never showed it; she took odds with that, I think. I had more or less quit any kind of search for sophistication long ago, but she held out. It included our embarrassment of our family too, which I have mentioned, and which in her absence I held against her. What was she afraid of? Why would she live so close but never come around? I thought she was embarrassed, and that stirred my anger.

Years ago she went out with Beverly's brother, Tate. They were very secretive in the beginning. Later on less so. But I knew about it from the start because my room overlooked the backyard and creek. I would see him arriving late at night, coming across the creek in his punt- a lightweight boat. I remember he carried a flashlight- he didn't have a stern light, or anything of the sort. But even that small light he traveled with gave him away. When he was close, the light would extinguish, the back sliding door would open, and the light would reappear two minutes later, pointed out bumbling toward the dark of the water, and I would watch them go, wherever they went, the dark, thin boat and the shape of their two figures tilling off the shallows.

I never told my parents. I stored it up against her but never told. As far as I knew, in my whole life she was never disciplined or scolded like James or I, and I'm not sure why that was, why she was able to escape reprimands. Part of it was her temper- she was very good at pleading hurt, of pretending to be mortified and stricken. She showcased her nerves. Harsh words, corrective words sent her into long drastic spells where she would not say anything, eat anything, or respond to anything until my mother worried for her. By then she had won; she wanted to be worried after and concerned for.

Often I questioned my mother's softness toward her, but there were times when the gavel of her love came down hard and left no doubt about what she thought of my sister's wiliness. When Adley was in high school there was another boy involved. It wasn't Tate. I don't know who it was. One day she came home with a wounded wrist. Her arm was swollen and purple. My mother asked what happened and my sister said she fell and hurt it.

"You fell?" my mother said.

"I fell, I just fell."

The wrist turned out to be fractured, and a cast was put over it, bright green. She had everyone sign it, including this boy. He would call the house and ask how she was, how her arm was doing, which was admittedly chivalrous for a high schooler, but my mother didn't like the situation. It bothered her from the start, because she smelled some dishonesty in the sequence. The simplistic injury and then suddenly the groveling suiter.

"Why is he so concerned?" she would ask. "Did he have something to do with it?"

"No." she said. "I told you already."

"Yes, we know- you fell- and the more times you remind us the more unbelievable it sounds."

Adley only needed the cast for a short time; it was only a bone line fracture the doctor said. However, for a month after her wrist was healed she wore it still and would not take it off. She said 'it did not feel right, it did not feel strong'; some avoidance like that, that my mother saw straight through. But she let it play its course.

Finally, one day my mother said,

"Enough is enough- that thing is filthy and your wrist won't get back to normal if you don't take it off. Tell me- why don't you take it off?"

I could see the despondence spreading over my sisters expression as my mother said it.

"No reason." she said. She turned to leave the room, but my mother, pressing her, said,

"Is it about that boy- the one who's been calling like crazy?"

"No." she said. "Who? I don't even know who that is?"

James and I were in the kitchen as this unfolded.

"Stop!" my mother said. Her voice was loud and commanding. "Stop right now. You know what you're doing. It's part of your game. Now stop it. The boy's responsible for what happened, he had something to do with this 'falling'. But now she keeps it on to keep him around. Is that it? Speak. Enough, speak. Take that silly thing off."

"No." she yelled back. She turned to face my mother but did so at a slant, with her casted arm in the shadow of her figure.

"Come here." my mother said. She stepped forward and took my sister by the good arm and led her over to the countertop. Adley began to writhe and moan, offering no physical resistance, but letting out her emotional and dramatic rebelliousness. My mother, deaf to all complaint, single minded and insistent, took the casted arm and laid it upon the countertop. While James and I, and Adley, watched in simultaneous horror as she grabbed a serrated knife from the block, and pinned my sister's wrist with her other hand.

"No!" Adley yelled, "No!" She took her other hand to repel my mother, to cover the cast.

"Take that off, right now."

"No."

"I'm taking it off, move your fingers."

"You'll cut my arm!"

"I won't, stop it."

My mother pushed the fingers off and quickly put the blade in their place. Adley hung her head back, stamped and yelled as my mother began sawing, the dirty green shavings falling on the counter. It was a spectacle. James and I said nothing, although I think our presence exacerbated Adley's reaction. When my mother cut through the cast, she took kitchen shears from the same block and began cutting around. Adley continued bemoaning. She was teary and angry.

"I don't even care about my wrist." she said

"You don't want it to heal?" my mother said.

"I don't care about healing."

When she said that, my mother dropped the shears on the counter and took her by the half cut cast and pulled her close and said,

"Ok, stop speaking so quick." She shook her to gain her attention. "You may not care about yourself, but I do."

Then she picked the shears up and finished the job, and the ugly green cast came off in two chunks. Shaking her head, my mother threw it into the trash, and my sister stood there looking at her wrist which was pale, limp, and stinking to high heaven.

To my discredit I thought little about that exchange after it happened, although it certainly changed the mood of the house that day. I thought little of my mother's prudence, and how she had cared for someone who did not want to be cared for. Growing up I perceived in moments like that something about the life of parenting that I could not understand- a sort of shallow and unavoidable abasement that parents gave in to; a supervisory, authoritative instinct-henpecking. I saw the strains without the pleasures. To parent was to carry shears.

59

Around the time when I was thinking about Adley, she called me out of the blue, twice, both times when I was at work, so I couldn't answer. She left no voicemail. The next day she called me a third time when I got home. I answered and immediately I said,

"Hi, sorry I missed your calls. What's up? Did you want to speak with Mom?"

"No, I need to talk to you, actually."

"What is it?" I said.

"Could you go to a private place to talk?" she said.

"Sure." I said.

I was nervous. I went to my room and shut the door.

"What is it?"

She took a moment. "It's about Beverly." she said. It was ominous the way she announced it in such spare words.

I got a wrenching knot in my stomach.

"What about?" I continued.

"She has something to tell you, or something to ask you. I don't know what it is exactly. She wouldn't say."

"What do you mean she wouldn't say? You spoke with her? What happened?" I said.

"She got a hold of me through Tate. She said she got a new phone and didn't have your number, so she tried me. But she wanted to speak to you weeks ago, like more than a month ago."

The knot tightened again. Beverly I thought. How long had it been? It was painful to count years between our last communication, that abrupt and unceremonious falling out.

"Take her number and call her." she said. "She doesn't sound good though."

"Like what?"

"Like she's in trouble. I didn't recognize her voice when I spoke to her until she said who it was, I was about to hang up. She wasn't speaking straight."

"Ok." I said. She read me her number and I wrote it on a small sheet of paper.

"I'll call." I said. "I don't know what I can do, but I'll call."

We hung up and the knot, the lump of uncertainty persisted through the day and night. I kept thinking about Beverley, wondering where she was, and why she had sought to contact me after so long. I thought she might have considered suicide, or needed money, or committed a crime. I don't know why I assumed those scenarios, but I did. Something about her sounding in trouble my sister mentioned. The more I rehearsed the possibilities, the more afraid I was to speak to her. But finally I called her.

Her voice was calm when she answered, unexpectedly so.

"Bev?" I said.

"Yes?"

"This is Constance."

As soon as she knew it was me her voice changed. It

changed to that tone my sister alluded to. Portentous, shaken.

"I'm glad you called." she said. "I've been trying to find you for a while. I lost your number, and- then I tried to reach your sister to tell you-"

I could hear her catching herself as she spoke, trying to steer the conversation away from its imminent point.

"My god," she went on, "It's been so long, hasn't it? How long has it been?

"Eight years, I think. Yeah, about eight since I left Salisbury."

"What have you been up to?"

I told her about what I'd done since then, then I asked her, "And what about you?"

Her voice became quiet.

"I don't know how much I want to say." she said. "Mine's a longer story- not a good one either, where it's led me." I heard her put the phone down and say something to someone, then pick it up again. She took small pauses between her words as if each were heavy to speak, laborious. But she went on.

"I joined the army after school, after Salisbury. I hated school all the way through. That won't surprise you. We had that in common. Well, for a time. I got off on the wrong foot. You know about that. I should have done what you did and gone back to my old place. But anyhow, I joined the Army- I was in ROTC my last two years at Salisbury, then I went overseas."

As she spoke the image of her wearing fatigues in some desert climate came across my mind.

"Then-" she continued, "Then I came back. I went back overseas, to the Middle East, and the second time I was there I got shot in the leg, which took me out of the field and made me depressed. I tried to harm myself a couple times because of how bad I felt- I really did. I remember laying there sweating in a cot, with my leg swollen and infected because I picked at the wound, and the whole room smelled like urine. Damn." she said, "I don't need to tell you all this, I'm sorry. But I know you remember how I get in bad stuff. Like the night you took me to the hospital."

"I remember."

She sighed into the mouthpiece. "I don't mean to ruin your day."

"You're not." I said.

"Anyway, Oh- let me tell you what's happened recently. After all that I was sent back to New York, where I was stationed. They gave me some admin duties in an office on base, while my leg got better and my mood improved. Tate came to visit. Same with my parents."

"That's good." I said.

"Well- yeah, it doesn't end there unfortunately."

"What happened?"

"I met someone here, during that time, the man whose office it was, he was the head of it. A colonel. Name's not important. What happened was we came on to each other and kept it up for a time, a couple months, real bad. He's married and everything, lives here on the base. And the thing kept going- the thing between him and I. It went until I told him one day, straight to his face 'This isn't good. I don't want to get in deep, you know-' He said 'There's nothing to worry about' He was all calm about it. And fool that I am I believed him, went on with it, took his word."

She coughed hard twice, away from the phone.

"Excuse me-" she said.

I was listening intently. I had gone from sitting on my bed to standing up, to sitting on the floor with my back against against the dresser.

"Constance-"

"Yes?" I asked.

"I could go on. There's more to it, but-"

"What is it?" I said.

"I could- I don't think I need to."

"What do you mean?"

"Nevermind."

There was a pause.

"Bev?" I said. "Beverly? What happened?"

"Nevermind, sorry."

"What is it?"

I heard her sniffs and I could tell she was crying quietly, trying not to make a loud sob of it.

"What?" I said. "Can you say?"

"I can say, but you can guess without."

"Guess what?"

"Why I called you."

Her tone carried all the meaning that it implied. The quieter she remained on the other end the more she coaxed me into saying what I imagined was the reason for her calling.

"You got pregnant." I said.

"Yeah. But also-"

"But also what?"

"I am pregnant. Still."

"When was this?"

"Two months ago I found out."

"What did you tell him, the colonel?"

"I told him. I told him to his face. In his office. He was in his chair. He nodded his head like he was getting a news brief. He didn't look at me. The next day he said one thing to me. He said 'I'm figuring it out.' A week goes by- business as usual. Next week, he calls me in, shuts the door. Pulls a chair close to the desk. I sit down. I'm terrified. He smiles and says 'You're not worried, right?' I said no, but I was- I was depressed all over. He reaches into his shirt pocket, then retracts a bit and says, 'I want you to know I don't condone doing anything egregious. Know that first, ok? This is not my doing. I told my wife I made a mistake. I told her about what's happened. She knows. She doesn't know you, but she knows about you. She gave me this-' and he pulls out of his shirt pocket a blue credit card, and says 'She's less lenient than I, my wife'. She says to me, you've got two options- get rid of *it*, or get rid of *her*, just choose one, then end the game. Make sure there's a charge on that card. And she hands me this, which I'm handing to you.' He says this, and then he offers me the card, pushes it across his desk. 'For what?' I said. He purses his lips and looks over the ground, then up at me. Why did you tell her? I said. You didn't have to tell her anything.' He shook his head. 'She would have found out.' 'How?' I said. I was getting louder and he kept trying to get me to quiet down. I didn't want to. Then he says, listen to this: 'My conscience was gnawing me.' When he said that I almost fell over in my chair and killed the baby that way. Can you believe that? 'My conscience is gnawing me?' Now it's gnawing, you fucking coward? And not before? Too late I said. I pushed the card away and said 'Get that away from me.' 'Be sensible.' he said 'For both our sakes, and this whole base.' I said 'No.' 'Why?' he kept asking, and I wouldn't respond."

She sighed again, coughed hard into the mouthpiece. All of her speaking was taking a toll on her, but she went on,

"I said to him, 'You would get rid of me?' and he said 'Don't say it like that- you would just be transferred somewhere else.' 'With this child? Your child!' I said. He said, 'You'll have to move somewhere else, regardless.' 'Why? What would happen?' He said 'If anyone found out, we would lose out posts instantly, not to mention the scandal and grief for my family.' Then, like any colonel needing his objective at last, he says 'What will you do?' He taps the card on the desk, and puts it out between his two fingers. I never saw something more offensive and hideous in my life as him holding out that card. 'Keep it.' I said. Then he sits up in his chair real tall, and turns his ear, 'Keep it? Keep what?' And I said, 'Keep the card. I'll find something to do with the child, but you should be ashamed. And don't ever speak about grief or scandal, and wave that thing before me again.' He said he would make provision, accommodations for care and a hospital, somewhere in the next county. I got transferred three weeks later. That's where I've been ever since, doing the same kind of work. The same day he told me all this, he asked me if I needed a ride home. I said nothing. I gave him eyes like I was going to kill him. Can you imagine that. What we just spoke of, and then for him to say 'Do you need a ride home?' I walked on my own. Usually I took the shuttle, but that day I walked all the way back. i called Tate but he didn't pick up. And you know how my leg is. It took a while."

When she had stopped speaking, I didn't know what to say.

"Bev, I-" I began, but she said something instead,

"Constance, that's when I tried to call you and couldn't. Then I gave up on it. But it kept coming to my mind to call you. When I would lay in bed before I slept- it would be hard to sleep, but I tried to think of better times, and I had to go back, way back. I thought of the farm. When you would take your brother and I out on the small boat, just around our creeks. Back at the house with the plot my dad gave us. All that stuff. That was so long ago. I missed that. I do miss that-" she laughed a bit.

"I remember." I said.

"Do you remember- a long time ago you said you would be there for me if I needed anything, anything at all. You remember that?"

"No," I said. "I don't remember."

"Well I do. You said it. And I've never forgotten it because I knew you meant it."

Then, like a wave of her hand, like nothing at all, she put before me the high road of my life.

"So. You wouldn't want it, would you?"

Her ask was so clear and simple, like a blade pruning away the chaff of language. It shook me and I could hardly register a coherent answer.

"What do you mean?" I said.

"The child. I'm giving it up for adoption. Would you want it? That's why I've called. All that to ask you."

"What about your family?" I said.

At the same time, she said, "You don't have to tell me now."

"My family? You think they know? the only one who knows anything is Tate, and not even he I've told the whole story to- he doesn't need to know the details. Constance?"

"Yes?" I said.

"Think about it is all. You can't do anything worse than what's been."

"What should I tell my family?"

"Not all I told you- just that I'm giving the child up for adoption. Let me know, ok?"

"I hope I'm not the only one you're ask-"

"Ok? she said. "I've got to go now, sorry. It was good to speak to you. I have to go. They're checking on me. Bye."

She hung up. My knees were balled up to my chest. I held my hand out in front of me and it shook. The knot inside me was knot of dread, a knot I couldn't wish or think or talk my way loose from.

My door was closed shut, but someone knocked as I was sitting there, and then came in.

"It's me." my mother said. She pushed in and came standing over me. I don't know what I looked like after that call- what expression was on my face, but I have no doubt the dread came across when she saw me. There had been no time elapsed to bury the story and tell it for another time. So I told her everything, including what I was not meant to tell.

"And she wants you? she asked, after I said everything.

"Yes, she's asking me. That's what she called about."

"How do you feel about it?"

"I feel sick right now."

"Queasy?"

"Queasy. Dread. More dread than anything."

"It's understandable."

In that moment of consolation I wanted her to say something decisive like "Forget about it, you don't need to worry about it, but she didn't. She said,

"It could be worse." She was sitting next to me. She patted my knee, then she said "Let's go eat. That's why I knocked the first time."

At dinner she steered conversations away from my end of the table and talked generally about plans and errands. She asked my father about his day, and dinner ended on that mild, reportorial note. Days afterward I heard nothing from Beverly and I tried desperately on my own to rid my mind of the trouble the scenario presented. The same surreal sensation of scriptedness I felt in my last meeting with Sonny returned. I worked extra shifts. Two of the mornings I ran the boat up the river and back, fast. I craved motion. I desired any sensational form of liberty to prove that I could unload the question and return to my simple way of life- the noisy thrill of the engine and the sleek snug turns of the vessel and the restaurant and caring for James and being home and not being pushed anywhere. I had not boated that fast for years. The long streaks I made skidding across the surface were some confirmation of that. I was free to chose, completely free.

Except that when the engine died so did the sensations I tried to prolong, the artificial carefreeness. Before and behind me and beside me lurked the other mandate that would not go- I was not free *not* to choose. Someday soon I would call an old friend who was in dire straits and say something that would drastically change her life, and mine, and a newborn's, and countless others. That thought beleaguered me.

I was fear stricken. A great deal of my fear was that I had no spouse to rear the child with. It would be me, and I was living at home. Would the child too? Would I keep working where I was? Would I not? I felt my circumstances were pitiful for being a good parent. However, I was also drawn to it. I felt that I would like a child to call my own, to care for personally, to raise. Both sides were genuine. I would have carried on like that forever if it were not for conversations and moments of insight that pushed me in one way or another

"You're still dreading it?" my mother said to me one day.

"All the time."

"I talked to you father." she said. "You haven't spoken with her, have you?"

"Not yet." I said.

"We went back and forth." she said. "He and I...and what it comes down to is that he doesn't think you should. He thinks you should let her continue with her plan of giving it up for adoption. As for me, I'm not sure you shouldn't."

"Shouldn't what?" I said.

"Shouldn't keep her child. I know how that must sound. But listen, and know that I don't know the right answer. You're almost 30, that's a reality. That's not to say you can't marry or that you won't, but all I mean is that there's not someone in the picture right now, and we can't plan for things that aren't in the picture. What's here is here. The other part is your friend and this child. She's offering this child- she's offering you her child. You may be thinking of this adoption as a favor you'd be doing her. But I would caution you from having the idea in the back of your mind that you would be doing something honorable and great for this troubled woman. Or thinking in anyway that you might save a life, or be the heroine by taking this on. It may be a good thing, a wonderful thing, you know- to offer yourself for this child and your friend- but don't let it be a favor you're paying anyone, because that instinct never goes away, the people-pleasing instinct, that ledger of our good deeds we keep. We're no good accountants, I've learned, and if you pursue that attitude, I tell you it will follow you well after you've raised the child- and you'll idolize what you did and didn't do, if it was appreciated or underappreciated- 'how much have I given? how much did I do? DId they notice the birthday cake? the clothes at Christmas? on and on. You learn pretty soon by raising one that your body and your time aren't yours. Not like they were before. Look at me." she waved her hand over herself. "I don't hide this anymore. I'm older, that's how we get. See? You'll give up a lot whether you say yes or no to this child. You say yes? well there goes your independence and your wallet and your plans and your free time. No? well there goes your opportunity to bring someone up, to teach them right from wrong, to show them what is beautiful, let alone to receive a child is this manner. It's a rare thing- you wouldn't be the same. No, of course not. I'm not the same because of you, Adley, James. But I also was never asked like you were. Your answer has to be wholly your own. And I don't have the right answer, like I told you already." She laughed a little there at the end, I don't know what from-

"However it goes," she said, regaining her point, "Know that you've received much, and that it's yours to give one day or not. Many people don't. Second, sort out what that dread is you keep mentioning. It's not the same as fear in my experience. I had dread with each one of you- especially your brother- I thought I couldn't do it. That I'd rather die instead, when it was at its worst. I have dread still- hearing your father pull into the driveway; ha! None of this is a rule, you know- I'm not trying to moralize, but this is a big decision and I want to speak as clearly as I can about it, for you. You'll have to see it for yourself. You said you hadn't talked to her yet?"

"Not since our call."

"That says something to me."

"What does?"

"That you haven't spoken yet. I'm telling you, if you were convinced you couldn't do this or didn't want it, you would have paid the call already, two weeks ago."

"I don't know." I said. "I don't know what's what?"

She said "When you took the boat out the other day, going real fast. I haven't seen you run the boat like you've done recently, in years. What was that about"

"I needed space."

"I understand."

"You never took James."

"I know."

"He asked about you."

I kept quiet.

Finally she said "We're here for you. You know that."

My mother was never one to pull me or my siblings aside for little talks, to share tidbits of motherly wisdom, pearls of knowledge. She exemplified what she believed. When I recall what she said to me during that moment of indecision, I recall how much the words affected me. The way that they were spoke out of a firm, visceral necessity. I could not stand any longer behind the plea of my uniqueness. All my life I harbored a pity for myself, for all the turns in my fate that followed no recognizable pattern- for my tomboyishness, for a lack of friends, for not finishing school, for being one female in a boatyard of men, for the night at Shane's island, the fallout with Sonny- the list went on. There was never a line that fell parallel to my own, but only crosswise. So I believed.

Some things were more petty than others but all of them endured, and what time had not diminished the importance of, it magnified. Together, the hundred pities amounted to something worse than pitifulness- pride. Never the yelling kind that makes much ado about nothing, but the low, simpering kind that lasts and lasts- but like all forms of pride cherishes memories of injury, preserves them- exalting in those differences. The very habit I witnessed in my sister and detested, her extreme sensitivity, I could not discover in myself, until my mother exposed it.

My mother was not a combative person; but she had an imperative- before I received that call from Beverly it was like my mother and I stood on opposing shores with the river between us moving parallel, but never needing to go across. And then one day when the decision must be made, needing to get to me, she speaks her word and her speaking parts the river like Moses and she walks dry shod down to the bottom. She calls me and I meet her there and we talk, in the dredged valley of the channel.

60

It was two and a half weeks since I spoke to Beverly. Time was heightened. Everything was heightened. I could not comprehend how I got here, neither could I think past it. I spoke to my father separately and he gave me his warning- his very practical warning. That a child without a father would be deprived, would grow up missing important parts of their formation. To emphasize his point he included the story of his mother and father, and why the family split long ago.

"It's because she, your grandmother, had a child with another man, and when my father found out, they split- so you see what can happen to a broken family? When the pieces aren't there to bring stability?"

I listened to him all the way through his high impassioned speech without saying anything about the faulty analogy he drew between the two situations, or the pervasive sense of fatalism that came through his warning. In short, I was discouraged by that conversation, but it did not move me the way my mother's words moved me.

The last to know were Adley and James. Surprisingly Adley came back for a visit, and when I had them together at the table I told them the decision I had to make. None of them reacted or said anything for awhile.

Adley said, "You gotta do what you gotta do, that's all I know." and shook her hands clean of the matter.

James said, "Constance, I agree with her. But also, I wouldn't mind being an uncle."

There was one final moment that was personal, that I told no one about it until I wrote it here. It involved me and the water and a pier and fishing and a little bit of superstition. It happened in the midst of these conversations. One day I drove to the public pier down the road to find asylum, and while I was there unloading my gear the idea came to me that maybe if I caught something that day it would be a sign. That tells how conflicted I was. I was looking for a sign from anywhere.

I thought of my father who bought our house because he swore the heron that alighted on the pier right as he prayed was a sign. This was my version of that. Besides, it's an old superstition that probably goes all the way back to the first fisherman, that catching a lot is good luck, and getting skunked is bad luck. True or no, those were terms I played with. Again there is the humor. If I catch a good amount the answer is yes. If I don't the answer is no. The funny thing is that I had never caught anything at that pier and I knew that going in. My father had once, but that was long ago.

The pier was crowded that day, more than I had seen before. I found a spot between two talkative black men, old timers who seemed to be impressed that I came alone and that I knew what I was doing. Until dusk the catching on the pier was skimp and scanty. All the way up and all the way down. The water was bland and calm and sometimes the people around me got so quiet waiting for a bite, I would turn around and forgot how crowded it was. Well, I told myself, I know what my answer is. At dusk, a few little perch were caught around the pier but nothing more. Nothing touched my line. People began to leave. I gave myself one more cast, then I would leave too. I folded my chair and rested it against the piling. One of the black men beside me yelled down the dock,

"Who's gonna catch something here? Enough is enough. Who's catching dinner?" His friend laughed, shook his head, and few of the others laughed lightly, but then the silence and the waiting and the draught resumed.

Then, as I was reeling in my line, I heard a commotion on the other end of the pier. The pier was T shaped. I was on the far right side- the noise came from the far left. On a day like that, when nothing's biting and then someone catches something big, there is bound to be a commotion. I heard a few whoops, an aluminum folding chair get knocked around, and the sound of scattered footsteps over the boards running in that direction- grown men and children who wanted to see what it was. We all wanted to see what it was. I craned my head, provoked as everybody else to see what he had.

There is a rivalrous phenomenon on public fishing piers that makes you want to both look and not look, especially when one man's got all the luck. But that day, we were all looking, all the necks from my end down- some people had left their lines in the water to crowd the man fighting the fish.

You can tell by the shape of a rod what someone's got- a small fish can put up a big fight and jig the rod down pretty hard, but a big fish doesn't nibble, and the rod doesn't jig, it doubles over and looks like it might snap. That's how this guy's looked. He was a middle-aged white man, jeans, tennis shoes. He arms were tensed with the fish. I got up with the others and followed this crowd and we formed a semicircle around him- old black guys, latinos, a few kids, a few wives, myself.

"What's he got?" someone said.

"Bet it's a skate- only a skate's going to put up that much resistance."

A skate is a river stingray. They're big, bottom dwelling loners that fisherman don't like to catch because they're impossibly hard to pull in. Their flat, muscular shape makes them notorious for breaking lines because they suction themselves to the bed of the river and lumber about the bottom snagging the line on rocks, branches and other hazards. Plus no one eats them. They're not table fare.

But there we were, the rest of us cheering this man on, hoping he pulled this creature, whatever it was from the mud river.

It was a long fight- long enough that people began to dwindle and one of the black men who had been standing beside me turned back and said,

"That skate's gonna snap his line, just watch- all that for nothing, just watch."

His friend said,

"Least he's got something on his line."

And the other guy said, "Hey, he can fight that all he wants."

There were not many of us standing around after a while. The man with the catch seemed to be at an impasse and even he glanced back and shrugged at us, not sure what to do, and I wondered if he would cut the line himself. It got close. Right as he pulled the swiss knife from his pocket, the line zagged, the fish moved, and the toil continued. I noticed beside him to his left there was a young asian family- a man, his wife, and a small boy. The wife was holding a white trash bag in her fist. The man held a knife in his. The boy was beside his father, at his leg. All three of them were watching the water closely.

Amazingly, after a long tousle the skate began to surface and the crowd that had waxed and waned now pressed in; those who had gone away returned with new curiosity and some with disbelief. The man with the catch had a neighbor who helped him the whole time, clearing room around his feet. As the skate got closer, the neighbor got to his knees and leaned over the pier edge, handling the line, guiding it slowly in until it surfaced all the way.

Skates are not thrashers- they're gliders, so there was no wild show atop the water. The heavy weight just emerged slowly. Someone from the crowd lent a gaff and the neighbor hooked the skate on the mouth and groaned as he brought it up and plopped it in the middle of the pier, this massive brown and black speckled skate. The tail was flaccid and wagging, the wings were going up and down, like it thought it was still sailing through the water. We all stepped back and watched this hideous thing, this creature that very few anglers ever pulled aboard, and even fewer *wanted* to pull aboard- as its mouth blubbered and it died slowly in the puddle it made.

The two black men were standing beside me again. There was a moment of hush as the man who caught it rested his rod on the deck and his friend plied the big silver hook out of the skate's mouth. A couple cheers from the crowd, nothing big. The skate made a huge dark wet circle on the pier. One of the old men beside me said,

"Look at that thing."

His friend said,

"I can't believe he brought that in."

"It's ugly, ain't it?" the one said. Then the other said,

"Yeah it's ugly, but best catch of the day, hands down. That's all ours skate the way I see it. He caught that for us all."

I went back to pack my things and reel my line in. On my

way out I stepped before the scene of commotion again, where everyone had left. The asian man I saw before was knelt over the big puddle, cutting off the wings of the skate-two big, mud brown slabs, and his wife held the trash bag open as he put them inside, and the boy watched. The man cut the tail and put that in too. I looked at him as I passed, and he looked up at me a moment and nodded and gave me a thumbs up. He had white rubber gloves on. And how happy he looked to be squatting on the ground, cutting this skate. The wife holding the bag smiled and we nodded to each other as I left.

61

I was changed fundamentally by that scene; not in some loud outward way, but subtly and swiftly, like the cold undercurrent sweeping around your ankles when you swim into deeper water. It got to me. Burrowed into my imagination. Of course, I could not help but think of it in reference to my decision. The black men scoffing. The man who caught the fish. The family who butchered it to morsels. What did it all mean? I thought back on the heron on our pier and my father's prayer. In the same way this event somehow rendered a word about what I should do next. I felt that my very frame of reference had been switched from under me- it was no longer I who was casting, but I who was cast. I was the fished line, the lure being retrieved irresistibly through the river to some starting place; pursued by answer as much as I pursued one.

I have come to know that the pier is not only a superstitious place, it is a sacred place. A place of mixed fortunes, where one heaves victoriously with the one man catching, and curses in the same vicarious way his catch. Fishing is not as simple as it lets on. If it were simpler; if our lines were but lines, transparent and slight, and our waiting simple, as weightless as cork- to catch much or little would make no difference. Yet our casting soars as far as we can throw it, and I have known the most unbeguiled fisherman to address the water as if addressing person, to summon her. It may be that the river bestows an oraclar gift to those that seek it.

Regardless, the memory of the skate cut a vivid image in my mind from the moment I left- the ensanguined pier, the naysaying onlookers, the silverness of the hook pulled from the mouth of the creature- all of those incisive particulars suggested to me then a mysterious telling- an ultimate meaning of fishing- an inseparable connection between hobby and fate. How we tie our hopes to peculiar things- how a strange moment, an obscene one may be as persuasive as the next.

And by the time I reached home I had come to a decision. I wanted the child and I was sure of it.

When I told my family what I was going to do, they stared at me dumb, neither mad nor exuberant, but watchful. It was my father, mother, and James. I don't know what was running through their heads- but the more I heard my own thoughts committing myself to it, the better I responded, the more confident I felt that I was doing what was right.

I told them straightforwardly,

"l doubt I'll ever have another chance to do something like this- to raise a child, to make them part of a family."

"What made you change?" my father asked.

"Lots of things made me change- lots of things made me open to it. I don't believe any of it's coincidence. I thought of myself 10 years from now and where I want to be. I'd like to be a mother I know that. As unprepared as I am."

. . .

Even as I was speaking, the words I used were surprising- not that they were untrue, but they were bold and unrehearsed, and I stood in their presence- as did these people who would be there for me- in awe of all of it.

For the first time nothing contemptuous came back to me. We had talked the matter into the ground by then. Now they waited for me to make the call.

I called Bev that evening from my room. I sat on the floor as I had before, bracing myself, nervous and nauseous. She picked up right away. Her voice was husky. I wasted no time and said,

"Bev, I want to adopt your child."

"You what?!" she said.

She could hardly believe it.

"I want to adopt the baby."

There was an immediate whimper, like she had covered her mouth with her hand.

"You do?" she said.

"Yes. So what do we do now?"

I heard someone at my door- the three of them were looking in, their eyes big and staring. When I finished talking with Bev my mother came and sat next to me on the floor and hugged me. I had no words. James was parked in the hallway. "I'm going to be an uncle?" he said. He sounded astonished. My father was standing in the doorframe looking in and deep in thought. He thumped his hand against the doorframe twice, not hard but like he needed something substantial to check reality against.

"Holy." he said. That was all he said.

PART III

62

There was more to do of course- much more. The adoption process was shortened beyond usual because of my connection to Bev, Bev's service in the military, and a special privilege the colonel acquired to accelerate the process when the plan was in place. Still, there was paperwork, background checks, finances, preparing the house, so much that aggravated our families busyness and our sense of duty and urgency. I was having a child; a child that would have our last name, who would live on Teal St., who would know Weems.

It would be naive and simplistic to suggest that peace came to me immediately after I put the decision into motion, and during those seven months following where we waited, where I waited, and everyone waited with me. We fought, we argued. The house came together. The house came apart. Moments of great expectation and excitement were checked by moments of terrible guilt- for having drawn my family so inextricably into my new responsibility.

Times like that I wanted to leave, and I nearly did. My father, sometimes with James's help, spent long hours prepping the house for a newborn; making a room, painting, uncluttering, cleaning. We all cleaned. When James helped, however, the task became more tedious since he was less maneuverable, and that long tedium broke now and then- in such regrettable scenes.

One afternoon they had finished some task and had come downstairs and were sitting in the living room, both of them angry and tired.

I heard my father say, almost in confidence,

"Whose child is it anyway- ours of hers? Whose helping prepare?"

James shot back,

"You're the one who needs help if you're asking that question."

My father was incensed by it. Senseless with indignation he rose and turned to his son, the anger mounting in his voice.

"What did you say? Nothing? So quick to speak aren't you?"

My father looked him up and down, a look of misery and mockery, and continued his game,

"What? You have more to say? No? And I'm the one who needs help."

The sound of his words were a goad, they fueled his resentments.

I stayed away, listening, hoping it would die off but he continued, heightening his trial,

"Whose sheltered you all this time? Who pays for your chair? For your therapy?"

"Shut up." James said firmly, without looking at him.

I knew it was bad after that. My mother came in after hearing the fight begin. But then my father said,

"Oh, you can stand without it?" He took the handles of the wheelchair from behind and threatened to shake my brother out. My mother and I yelled and protested and he pushed us away, then desisted, and left the room in a cloud of strife.

. . .

There were other times like that. And there were times that swung to the opposite extreme, when the days carried on with machine-like boredom and I looked forward to the birth of this child as a rescue from the patterns of smallness and unkindness that so often consumed us.

Perhaps it would rescue all of us in a way.

63

Of all the people in my family who were jarred by the waiting time, it was my father who was jarred the most. I used to think it would be my mother, but it was she who retained a productive home, a clean table, hot food. She kept her industry, and her industry kept her. She would not for the life of her, or for the sanity of the rest of us, allow the physical home to fall into disarray.

As much as she could direct my father to certain projects, she did- for she knew they were good for him, they established equilibrium. They soothed his mind. There were times when we were all home, when he would wander into our company and watch us preparing food, working with our hands, nearly in contempt of our work- and if he complained, my mother would ask if he could help finish whatever she was doing, and walk away, and then, chop by chop as he put himself to use, the complaints would end.

Sometimes to strengthen his attitude my mother would remind him,

"You'll be a grandfather, you know." and he received that like a shudder of reality.

. . .

For many years, the years when I was away, but even before, I saw that his wealth, with the security it provided him, and the justifying claims it made over so many of his decisions, was a deprivation that allowed him to fall into a lull of living. It allowed him to reign supremely over a set life. The battle of life was over for him. It was won already, and yet worse for winning.

The slow reduction of his ambition to immobility, the lack of challenge in his life, of having no great fight before him- zapped the fight from him. That his yacht could stay docked and paid for, for all eternity, by the same token meant that he would never need to take it out again- it was too obvious- it would wait there like a prized trophy, to be looked at, sat upon, enjoyed, but never tested, never proved.

Those months I visited Beverly a few times. I don't know what our encounters would have been like under other circumstances, but under these new conditions I felt a sweetness for her, a tenderness of being with an old friend, of having no pressure to divulge all that our previous years contained. And somehow we were journeying again down a simple way, the promise of companionship, and the mutual understanding that our lives would never fully part ways because of this child, who she bore, who I would raise.

She was weak all over I could tell- not full of jokes or spontaneity like she had long ago, but measured out, limited, worn by grief and deliberation, by thinking too much by herself, from some stoicism she had learned in the army, and simply by being too much alone. I was, I think, a welcome change. I told her about the preparations in the house and she gave me her medical updates, and both updates had a somberness to their delivery- she because she would part soon with this child, and me because the child was still very much hers, growing inside her, taking its heatbreat from hers. And I suffered that, not knowing what pregnancy is like, how a body accommodates another body, how it befits a mother.

Finally, the child was born. I asked not to know the sex until that day, October 10th, when I came to visit Bev in the hospital, and hold her hand. Tate was there and my mother too, and all three of us waited outside until she was ready. When I came in, the baby was in her arms. It was a boy. He had a small wrap around his head, light blue colored. Beverly was tranquil- her whole expression revealed it- there was an innocence about her holding something so small. Her feet were curled inward in a shy manner, that made me feel very dear to her at that moment, and made me not want to take the child from her. But she lifted him to me and said to him,
    "This is your momma. She's going to take good care of you."
    And poor thing, he began to shriek; as even one hour into this life he would know the difficulty of living, of leaving the place you know, of being held by someone you knew not.

I have tried to refrain from speaking too charmingly about that day- to memorialize it justly, without soaking it in excess sentiment and fervor. But that day was capped in wonder- all that was said, all that was unsaid- at the hospital, in the car ride, and at home, as we carried him through the door and he grew quiet and rested all his shrieking. All of it fell within this wonder of which I was a part. There's no such thing as false sentiment on a day like that. To look down on a fist curled in pristine newness, to feel the warmth and softness of the head, the shut of the infant eyes belonging to our world now; there was nothing so reverential as looking upon him, nothing so extraordinary than the thought that he would have a name you gave him and have it all his life.

64

Luis Avery Gonzalez.

Avery and Gonzalez were givens, but Luis was my choice. My father jumped when he heard it. I kept it secret the whole time, even when I did not know if it would be a boy. I had liked that name for a long time, and I liked that it had the ring of my grandmother- the grandmother I never knew- it was like somehow the name of this little boy linked us to her again. It chimed of remembrance.

Luis. We said it again and again that first week; rhyming it, yelling it, trying it over all our speech.
 "Where's Luis?"
 "There's Luis."
 "Hi Luis."
 "Come here, Luis."
 "Sleepy Luis."
 "Luis? Luis?"
He was extremely tiny, even for a baby. He wasn't

premature, just small, slight. Adley, who spent the better part of the week at home for the occasion, was hesitant, even resistant to holding him at first. The one outburst that week occured when he was being passed to each one of us, and a picture was taken. My mother was taking the pictures when Luis came to Adley from my father. She said, "That's ok. I don't need to hold him. Let James."

My mother dropped the camera and seared her with her eyes.

"Hold him! You will hold him. Hold your sister's child. Your nephew."

Luis began to cry.

"He's not going to like it." she said.

So Adley took him, and rocked him til he shushed, and something like a smile broke over her face- a smile that caught her off guard. My mother took a picture, and it is a good one. The best she took all day.

65

A birth splits a life in two. It splits many lives in two. It cleaves it into histories of before that person, and after. What else did I learn that first year, when my days, my attention, my way of speaking was riveted completely? I spoke so infrequently in the singular after that because he was with me. I worked twice a week at the restaurant. The other days I was at home, and as much as I could, I took him to the water. Just our yard- a look at Weems, a look at the trees. I would hold him as he looked out and name the things I could see, starting with the pine cones. And I would point. Watch a boat go by. I wouldn't say anything- he couldn't of course, either. Sometimes he would fall asleep and I would turn him around and let him sleep on my shoulder- but I would stay there, looking out, and the naming would continue in my mind - ash, dogwood, stunted pine, oak, pin oak, spartina, bulrush, a bright growing list of things- and I wondered with my head so close to his if he got any of that as he slept, if my thoughts carried. The minute I saw something, something I had seen a million time before, I would hear it announced inside me- not in the normal way I spoke to adults, but in the motherly way I spoke to him- soothing.

If he was awake I would say it out loud. When he was more than a year old he could imitate some sounds I made. He could not yet point steadily at an object, but his arms could bounce and by that gesture he reacted to certain words and not to others. Once in a while, the resident heron of our shore would alight on our pier and I would carry Luis closer. I would peek from behind him and watch his absorbed expression, his glossy brown eyes fixed on the bird, standing still.

"Heron, He- ron" I said.

His arms would bounce and he would make a deep sound, from his belly,

"Hoo, hoo."

"He- ron."

"Hoo."

"Yes, Luis. Good. Heron."

66

When me and my siblings were young, I remember our father taking us out to the Bay on a new boat that ran aground on the Tangier Sound on the way back. My father had to radio for help, and the family sat there grumpy, hot, and embarrassed, as a college-aged coast guard kid hitched our boat to the end of his little motorboat and eased us off the ground and back to buoyancy. As the kid unhitched us my father said to him,

"I appreciate it- it hasn't happened before." and the young man, pulling his lines in, said

"You don't know the Bay if you haven't run aground yet."

For our family, Luis was that small thing tugging us back to life, showing us, as it were, the Bay- wedging us out of our dormancy. There was another time at dinner I can think of. We were all there and Luis was in a high chair beside me. Across the table I saw my father pull a piece of hair from his food, a light strand of my mother's hair. My mother saw it too, and she put her utensils down to get him something else before he made a scene. But he didn't. To all our surprise, he didn't. He simply laid the strand aside and kept eating.

I can't say that Luis was to credit for the new discretions we took in our manners toward one another, but he was a major influence, and good reason to be- he imposed on us a new standard of behavior simply by being there, by being needy, by crying and smiling.

He lifted the spirit of the home as much as he demanded our attention and our help. Gradually I learned what proper care I owed him as his mother, and what I could expect from my parents and siblings, who he grew up around, and who were his first tribe of caretakers. Everyone was free to take him, win him, teach him, and that was my intent from the start- to give him a family, and not just be his one friend.

As he grew older and could distinguish between us, I began to draw certain lines of commitment around him and I, so that we formed a unique bond, and so that he understood that I was his mother- different than grandma, aunt, uncle, grandpa. We went on trips alone to the zoo and aquarium. I took him to the park and to the boatyard to look at boats. I took him boating when he was old enough. When he was three I took him and James in the little boat up and down the Nanticoke. He was three years old, with energy like Bev, squirmish, full of pluck and curiosity- with dark eyes and tiny round teeth. I sat him in James' lap and told my brother to hold onto him.

It was a tame ride, but lovely at every turn. We brought nothing but a crab net and life jackets. We went along the shoals near Black creek. It was warm that day, and the water felt good on the skin. I took some water from over the prow of the boat and rubbed it on Luis's small legs and he laughed.

. . .

The creek had changed in many years. It went back farther and was more winding. The water had pushed back the shore. Also the Siggins farm had come under new tenancy and the woods had thickened from planting years ago. I took one oar, and James, with Luis between him, took the other, and we pushed along the shallows; the mudflats and the marsh, while Luis looked up at his uncle, mesmerized by his face, or what he was doing.

The creek bent to the right between drooping, thick smelling saw and spartina grass, and made a thin alley straight through the marsh. Two feet of water and mud were below us. We were maneuverable though, and the oars helped us push off the spongy ground. After two yards of that oppressive grass and the heat that clung to it trapping the breeze, the lane ended- the grass parted and we drifted into a circle, a secret, shallow cove, perfectly calm. Splashing here and there with the motions of fish and little ghost shrimp and baby crabs. A small nursery of sorts. All fluttering.

It was a place carved out of the world. The water was copper brown- the color of good mulch, of reddened earth, a warm gentle color, marbled as we passed over it. This small world filled with silver streaks of perch and peanut bunker, and ibis standing off, and terns watching us in the low grass.

We took the lone net and swept it along the floor of the grass, shaking off the algae and sludge, and caught a small crab. We brought it to Luis's face. He was terrified and enamored. He turned to his uncle and put his arms up to be lifted when it came aboard. And as they watched the crab go clackety clack across the crannies of the hull, I pushed us off back through the mud lane to the place where we entered, where the spartina stood at low tide, wavering, but low, like wilted arms across the little way.

Our little way, a pool of wonder saved for us, for the child, that for all we knew never existed before that time.

67

There were times when he was young when I was struck dumb by the weight of his youth; the plenitude of his energy, the vigor of his play. Those times were as chastening to my sense of growing older as they were affirming of his own sense of limitedness. He would run and run- later he would row his uncle up and down our creeks and ride his bike across the yard. Anyone who saw him could see it. Gladness fills the kid. Like a skipped stone it flys a path of beauty, defies sinking. It ripples to us all.

The misfortunes rippled too. When Luis was 4 or so, our neighbor Corey died. Later in life he was senile and we never spoke to him, but I still remember that on the day I brought Luis back from the hospital he came to our door with a pie he had baked and patted the baby on the head. He said was happy to have another neighbor. He said it very droll and very kind. When he died it was the first story that came to my mind. It made me regret our family's long silence with him for so many years, because he was a sweet man; eccentric at times, but sweet nonetheless, and maybe we were not as kind to him as he was to us.

. . .

For a long time after he died no one touched his house. It became overgrown and the yard had a cold dampness to it from the trees that grew over there. In his absence, that overgrowth felt like the remainder of his presence in the world. I thought of the garden he kept and when he'd step into our yard with his bag of gardening tools and stoop in the dirt humming as he weeded the plot. His death I remember well because Luis asked,

"Where did Mr. Corey go?"

"He went away." I said.

"Where?"

"To another home." I told him.

And he said,

"But that is his home."

And I said,

"You're right, that is his home."

"He wanted to leave?"

"No." I said.

"He had to leave?"

"Yes."

"He won't come back?"

"No."

"But it's his home."

"I know."

68

Three times a year growing up, at Easter, Thanksgiving, and Christmas, we traveled to see my mother's side of the family. They were really the only family we kept in touch with for a long time. My uncles are still living, and have many children who live in Dallas. Grandma and Grandpa Pritchard died many years ago, a year apart from each other. Luis was only 4 years old. I remember my grandmother's funeral because it was presided by an Episcopalian priest, a woman named Dr. Comey, who did not look like a priest but a clinical psychologist. She wore none of the vestments; she wore slacks and button down, and spoke monotone, mild and uninflected, as you would imagine psychologists to speak.

At the reception I sat by Grandpa Pritchard with Luis next me. The reception was held in the banquet hall of the retirement home my grandparents lived in. The family had rented the reception space, which had green and gold, checkered carpet, two modest chandeliers, and a dozen tables with white tablecloths and padded metal chairs. There was a projection screen with pictures the family had sent in, that one of my uncles compiled the night before. The pictures cycled through, on repeat. My grandfather's head would move from the screen to his plastic saucer of cantaloupe and cheese, and back again, not saying anything. When he and Luis finished their plates I took them and got them more and looked back to see them slouching in their tiredness, their backs slumped the same way, their pant legs raised from sitting, revealing their dark dress socks, the empty seat between them.

The two are quiet, for their own reasons. Grandpa Pritchard was a quiet man; never silent, but he spoke in a way so that his words never got ahead of him. He was deliberate. When I had filled their plates I returned to see them sitting next to each other. Luis had changed seats and was sitting, listening. His nodded affirmatively to some question. I sat down beside, and gave them their plates, and grandpa Pritchard turned across and said,

"Constance, don't let me forget. I've got something at the house for your little boy."

His glasses were big, square frames with thick prescriptions. They magnified his eyes and pores. I turned to Luis.

"You hear that? You want to say thank you, Luis?"

Luis turned and said thank you. Grandpa looked at me again and forked a grape in his mouth and began chewing.

"I told him," he said as he started chewing, then he held one finger up to pause his thought and finish his bite. I watched his thin lips move. As he chewed, his jaw did not go up and down, but round. When he swallowed he said,

"I told him it's a surprise."

I looked at Luis and gave him a shake of the thigh.

"You like surprises don't you?"

He nodded again, and I looked up to grandpa, and said thank you on his behalf.

. . .

After the reception, the immediate family went back to my grandfather's house. Some people watched tv, some cleaned the sink and vacuumed, freshening the home as much as could be. Some sat at the kitchen table and talked.

Grandpa apparently had one thing on his mind, which was getting Luis his surprise. He went looking through storage closets filled with knick knacks, extra winter coats, and baskets which my grandmother collected. The longer he searched the more he grew frustrated with himself for not remembering where kept whatever it was he was looking for. I was sensitive. I did not want to impose my help. Throughout his rummaging I would hear the sliding of doors, and 'Agh.', a dispirited exclamation. I went in to check on him briefly. Perhaps he did not know I was present.

After digging through a closet, he would stand up, push his glasses back to the bridge of his nose, and bend again. He looked up and saw me there after taking a pause. "I'm having no luck. These aren't my things I'm going through. These are hers." I suggested he take a break, but he declined. "I'll find it, it's here, I'll check a couple more places. You can come."

He motioned for me to come with him to his bedroom, a room I had never before gone into, having no reason to. I had only seen into it. Now I stood a foot inside the doorframe, taking in the dim layout of the room, captured by the feeling and look of it. He turned on a bedside lamp. The room had a smell of bedriddenness; of unwashed sheets and uncapped ointments. I walked to the large, sliding glass door, which was covered by long white plastic lath blinds, the ones that hang to the ground, sliding back and forth, and shutter open and closed with a rod. I turned the handle slightly so that sunlight rustled in. My grandpa said,

"Oh no, honey, we keep that closed. We have lights in here."

I didn't argue the point.

"Ok," I said. Turning it back I saw the wood plank

inserted between the door and the wall to keep it from opening. I doubt it had ever been cleared. My grandpa turned on the one other meek bedside lamp that was no help searching the two dark closets with. Luis had come and was standing in the shadow of the doorframe looking in. Grandpa looked up.

"You can't come in. Grandpa's find you something." he said to the little boy.

Luis went back without asking, and as I watched his little footsteps go the other way I felt sorry for him to be left alone, but I stayed and tried my hand at helping.

I was pulling things out of the other closet in the room when it occurred to me that I did not know what we were looking for. I took my head out and said, "You'll have to come over here and check." After a minute more of his perusing the other closet he came over. I sat on the edge of the bed, watching him jostle and tug, his chunky velcro shoes deep in the carpet, and one of his back pockets pulled out somehow. Where he looked I could see the hanger bar jammed full of woman's clothes before him like a wall, and I smiled as he chose entry points, parting his fingers through gowns and dry-cleaned dresses, reaching and feeling behind them.

"Ah, I found it." he said. Extending his arm as far as it would go, he drew out a clear, crinkly plastic box with a short fishing pole in it. He looked it over with great satisfaction.

"He'll love that." I said.

"I knew it was here."

I called Luis and we stepped into the hallway and grandpa handed it to him. Luis took it with both hands, and could not stop looking at it. He looked up at me briefly, then at his pole, instantly devoted to it.

"Thank your grandpa." I told him.

"Thank you." he said.

Grandpa looked at me, pleased with the outcome, and tired from it too.

"I knew it was here." he said "We've got all kinds of stuff that needs to go eventually, but that one can be used. He'll use it alright."

I found scissors and cut the box open.

"Look, it even come with hooks and bobs." I said to Luis.

Grandpa's housing community had a small, artificial lake nearby that we decided to visit that afternoon. Grandpa wanted to come and he brought slices of white bread for bait. We parked on the street and walked down to the water. Luis ran ahead; I held grandpa by the arm, and we went down slow. We found a spot out of the sun. After I secured the hook and bobber, I helped Luis roll a few bread balls for bait. He attached it on his own. Then he capered to the water's edge, the line and rig dancing with his excitement. I came beside him for assistance. I took his hand in mine, and with both our thumbs we pressed down on the button reel. We took the rod back, and then SWING, we cast. The rig flew off with a zing, a lovely, light sound of line singing toward the water. Then plop. Into the calm, calm water, the red bob floating away.

I said 'Now we wait.' Luis waited right at the edge, leaning over almost, captivated by the game, by the anticipation; that bedrock feeling of eagerness, of naked waiting which is the substance of all good fishing. So on he waited in that high pitch of expectation. Grandpa was behind us on the slope. He was smiling, watching Luis. He hadn't said anything in awhile, and I couldn't help but believe he was the happiest of us all. How supremely ironic, to believe that then, on that day of all days- but I did. He was not sunk. He was many things, I know, but not sunk.

I have wondered to this day if was impertinent and

immature of me to have suggested the fishing on that day, to leave the rest of the family at the house to grieve without the widower- if it were not more fitting, at least more reverent, to remain with them and suffer what was sufferable. To be the company of bereavement. I haven't gotten over it. And still, the dilemma of a past choice is not wholly acquitted by our right feeling of it in that moment. I may have tainted the mood for some, but I know it was a relief for others.

We watched the boy fish for some time; watched the red bob as it drifted. There is nothing so hopeful as a bob, to track its bright shape ambling on the water's surface, and nothing so startlingly wonderful than to stand between great grandfather and great grandson, mediating four generations by line and floater.

We caught nothing that day, which was somehow not only acceptable, but amenable; right. That even the smallest among us be deferred excitement, should receive some share of grief on a day like that. There are some losses better than catching, and more important. The bread on the hook was goopy and untouched. When he reeled it in I doubted if anything but carp would have eaten it anyway, but there was no carp in that lake. I know that.

What remains a mystery is why grandpa thought of that rod when he did. Why he dug out every closet til he found it. Of all things his mind went to.

Eleven months later he died. His health steadily declined after our grandmother's death. He had been quite active before that, but her loss wrung the life out of him. I was in the boatyard when my mother called me those months later. The bait was icing, the hose was running. She spoke in a low voice, one I'd never heard her use, trying to keep her composure- but her sentences broke off in the middle, and I'd listen closer. I could hear as she pulled the phone away from her mouth, choked and overcome with sorrow. Trying to make sense with words.

When we hung up, all I remember was the sound of hose water falling over the side of the boat.

JM, my longtime dockmate, was there working, and he overheard me, and asked if everything was ok. He could tell by my response that it was not, because most likely the pallor showed in my face, and I mumbled something of what happened.

"You leave." he said "I'll clean up for you." He leapt out of his boat and boarded ours and embraced me. "You go," he said. "Go. I'll take care of this."

And I left, and he did as he said- he took care of things. We had people scheduled to fish that day and he told them an emergency came up and the trip was cancelled.

Grandpa Pritchard's death was so much like my grandma's that I had to remind myself that it was he, not she, that we were grieving. He was viewed in the same funeral home, eulogized in the same church, and remembered in the same banquet hall. Again, his immediate family returned to his home, and it was strange to be there without either of them for the first time. They were always there. Even if they were not saying much, you felt them. They would be sitting quietly beside you, not joining in the loud conversation, just listening. Watching the faces of those around them. Making small movements with their hands. Nod their head. Cough, or laugh some. A shy, almost childlike manner they had in their later days.

The bedroom was dark and unsettled as before. A tray of vitamins was on the nightstand, a weekly pill box, creams, compression socks; every last attempt at well being and preservation within arms reach. The pictures of the two of them had a spectral look to them now. One of my aunts attempted to make my grandmother's lasagna recipe, but something did not turn out right and it was apparent to all of us who sat around reminiscing at the dinner table that our family had become unanchored overnight, that a great loss was given us- so much we could taste it, we could put it to our mouths.

After dinner I took Luis to the lake again, just the two of us. He had remembered it from before, and I had remembered to bring his rod, the one he was given, that we kept at their house for when we visited. The lake was different now; young trees had been planted around the shore, mounds of dark soil heaped at the base of their thin, shiny trunks. Luis brushed the trunks as he went to the water. Like the year before we used floater and hook, and I balled bread for him, and he set it on the hook.

"Make this cast a good one." I said, "For grandpa."

I helped him. It was a poor cast, the first try, but the bobber drifted out slowly and assumed a decent spot, where we could watch it. When he retrieved the line the bait was gone. We rehooked bread and he cast again.

"You didn't feel anything that first time?" I asked.

"No." he said.

I believed him. I had been watching the bobber the moment it began to float.

"It can't be carp." I said. "There is no carp in this lake."

"It's something else." he said.

"Why do you say that?"

"I'm just guessing."

"Maybe you're right."

When he retrieved the hook the second time he did not rebait it. Instead he turned to me, holding the rod upright with the handle on the ground. His shoulders rolled forward and he sighed out loud. I knew that posture. It was the posture of a fisherman who was finished and ready to leave.

He looked at me soft-eyed and steady, like he was waiting

for something. A word, or anything I had to say in that moment. About fish, or bait, or grandpa.

Looking back, I'm not sure I said anything at all, or if I simply joined his motion to leave. In that moment I felt my dumbfoundedness as a mother; like there was some unavoidable limit to my knowing that precursed all the wisdom I could give to him. No word or explanation could do it. I could not tell him everything. I could not show him everything. Perhaps he saw me with great transparency then; imagining how little I knew about this world of ours. How puzzled I could be, or how few answers I could give. That my very best answers would always weigh with certain inconclusions.

"You done?" I said.

He nodded, handing me the rod.

Uphill we returned, him before me, wending through the trees again. He grabbed each by the trunk, sending the saplings shaking behind us.

69

Not long after, there was another piece of unexpected news that came my way. Mr. Bruce's wife called and said that her husband was in poor health, and that he had made a list of people he wanted to get in contact with. I said when could I come by? She said that the next two weeks were not good to visit because he was undergoing operations. I should see him afterwards. So I set up a time to come by three weeks later when he was back home.

The Bruce's lived in a house that looked like Mr. Corey's in a way, but less covered with shrub. A place with worn white paint and a gravel driveway, well shaded by trees. His wife was a tall, elderly woman. She welcomed me and showed me to his office. His shelves were filled with sailing books, and sailing trophies, and pictures of him sitting off the edge of yachts. The office was decorated with these belongings.

Mr. Bruce was sitting in a chair when I came in. He was wearing his hat and he looked mostly unchanged except there was cane looped on the armrest of his chair. He smiled, looking over.

"Constance." he said. "I heard you were coming over." His voice was quick and lively. It was different from before when he worked in the shop. There was a plush chair opposite his.

"You can sit here." he said. As he pointed he knocked his cane off his chair arm and I got it for him.

"Appreciate it-" he said, hooking it again. "Now. Here, all better." He looked up again.

"By now you've heard about my operations, I gather." he said.

"Just recently." I said, "How are you feeling?"

"I'm ok." He looked ahead. "Not great. Not terrible. But ok." He turned to me. "But how about you? Are you still working?"

"Some." I said. "Part time at the restaurant."

"Oh, you're back there. I see. What's that place called again? Clancy's?"

"Yes."

"Clancy's, that's right- it changed names a half dozen times as long as I've been there- and I haven't eaten there much either, as often as I've walked past it. Oh, that's good. And your family? They're still where they used to be?"

"They are." I said. "And there's a new member. You haven't met the youngest."

"And who's that?"

"His name is Luis. He's my son. I adopted him."

"Ho! That's some news. How old is the guy?"

"He's five already."

He frowned and leaned back.

"It's been that long since we've seen each other, hasn't it?"

"Longer than that." I said.

He narrowed his eyes and looked past me, then back.

"Adopted you said?"

"Yes."

"Good for you. Did you know my sister was adopted?"

"I didn't know."

"And she was my very best friend growing up. She's not with us anymore, but that's something else. I am happy to hear you've got a young sailor around. He likes boats?"

"He does. We've mostly toured around our local creeks and Nanticoke- not far. I haven't gone out as much since he's been here. I'd like to get back to it someday, you know, as he gets older. I miss it- being out there. We'd have to get something beside our little boat though."

"Oh!" he said, waving his hand "That's enough, you've got enough right there. You don't have to go far. Some of the best times I've had on the water were within five miles of this place. He waved his hand some more. "He'll get there." he said. "It grows on you, as you know."

He sat up in his chair and leaned forward.

"Listen though- you say you want to stay in it. Well, you know me, I get all sorts of calls. I was getting them when I was in the hospital. My wife wasn't so happy about that. But anyway, There's something I want you to take a look at- it's funny you should mention your son. But anyhow, I got a call from a guy up in Maine by the name of Joyce Briggs- Captain Joyce Briggs. You know the calls I get, Constance. I've known him a while. We've called each other back and forth the better half of thirty years, him for parts and me for nothing, I guess- he runs an old oyster boat. Excuse me, he *ran* an oyster rig out of Plymouth Maine. But he's giving it up- well, he *gave* it up. He's retired, and his boat, although it's taken a beating, is still running, but he wants to get rid of it. It's a hog, but it runs, and he called me just the other day to ask me if I knew where it could go beside the back alley of the boatyard, and I said I'd ask around. That was right before my operation- I actually thought of you. I hadn't thought of it since, not since you sat in that chair. I'm glad you came by though, because after my operation I've been forgetting things left and right. Things are falling through the cracks."

I said "That is something, isn't it?"

"It is."

"Not what I expected at all."

He laughed, "Life is often unexpected- but, do you have any thoughts about it?"

"I'm not sure. How much would it cost?"

He waved his hand again and shook his head.

"Now don't feel you have to say anything right now. I pulled that out of the air. I saw you, and that boat just popped into my head. I'm not saying it's a real thing. You might not even want it. Still-" he shrugged, "I don't think he's wanting to make a profit, I think he just wants it in better hands."

I said, "I haven't owned a boat like that, you know- I actually haven't owned my own boat at all. I'm not saying I'm not interested though. It's big?"

"27 ft, not so big. He's having the oyster rig sold to someone else who just wants the parts. You know, the oyster dredging rig, crank, pulley gearbox- unless you were interested in those too?"

"Those people don't want the boat too?" I asked.

"It's an older boat, that's why. But it gets around. I haven't seen it in person, but he's sent me pictures."

"What kinds of repairs would it need?" I said.

He shrugged.

"Oh, I'm not sure. Depends what you want it for, what you'd use it for. It's oysterted out, I know."

"But," he said. "For you and your sailor? Could you use it? Who knows."

He waved his hand, halting himself from trying to nudge it, "Don't you worry about this though. Your hands are full. This is just something that came across my path. Might be nothing. Might be something. All we're saying is if you wanted it, it's yours.

He tied me with that statement, and I said,

"I really don't know, but I'm intrigued. If it's manageable and usable, and not too ugly and won't cost me a fortune, then who knows." and he laughed at the way I put it. He said,

"What I'm going to do is find out more- that's all I'll do. Find out more,"

He held up his hand.

"And, just for the sake of it, I'll call the yard and see if there's a cheap spot on the south wall, next to the wood hulls where you could take your time brightening it up if you wanted to, before you get it in the water and start your own thing."

"My own thing?" I said.

"Whatever you want. You could charter. You could give tours. You could fish on your own- it's your choice, but I bet you'd enjoy having company on that boat- it's known a lot of company."

"We'll see what happens now," I said. "You can let him know I'm interested, but I need to think it over, and don't get me into something I can't handle."

I shook his hand and wished him well, and left bewildered by our conversation, what would come of it, and haggled by that familiar nagging feeling of possibility, of nerves, of some permanent alteration to things as they were.

The next week I thought about it a lot. I began imagining myself and Luis aboard our own boat. Whenever I drove past a boat I saw my son taking the wheel and me standing behind him, pointing toward the mouth of the river. And I felt desire lurching inside me. The more I thought like this, the more determined I was to take the rig, and I told myself I have nothing to lose. This time around, however, I decided not to say anything to anyone until there was actually a boat, under my name, with some purpose I had for it. I didn't even tell Luis, though I wanted to, because I could imagine the joy he would have hearing it, and how he would run his mouth and tell the world, which was not my intent.

. . .

I called Mr. Bruce called three weeks later and said,

"I'll take that boat if it's still around."

He laughed and said,

"I'm a step ahead of you."

"What do you mean?"

"It's all set up."

"What's all set up?"

"The boat, the slip, the transport."

"What!? How'd you figure?"

"I just figured that whether you took it not, it at least needed to be moved to a place where someone would take it. I was going to put a classified out next week.

"That's big news." I said. "Thank you. Do I owe anything?"

"Right now, nothing- just your word you'll take care of it- later we'll talk about the slip if you need longer to do repairs- the rest Capt. Joyce covered- he was happy to. He owed me anyway. I told him the boat would get in good hands one way or another, and that was a relief, a big relief. The boat's coming in next week, if you're around."

I was flummoxed, terrified, exuberant.

"I'm around." I said. "I'll need to shift my schedule, but I'm around."

I was still searching for the right words when he interposed,

"Constance, I'm absolutely happy with the way things turned out- I'm not sure when I need to hear from you next, but you know where to find me, and just promise me you'll take that young one sailing sometime. You'll do great- don't doubt your skills one bit."

. . .

The first time I told my father the news about the boat, I regretted it almost as soon as it came out of my mouth because he made a derogatory laugh and said,

"Just resell it."

"I could, but…"

"You could, then why don't you? You don't have time for it."

"That's not why I agreed to it." I said.

"Oh, I know it's not, but I would say just save yourself the trouble and sell it and buy something smaller and lighter. You can use mine also- it's got everything."

It was a response that took all the wind out of me. I didn't want to resell it, but now I wondered if I should. I regretted telling him anything, and it hurt because I felt if there were any virtue in taking on the project, he would see it. But he didn't, and he didn't think I was serious, and he ended his remarks with,

"You've got your hands full at the moment. You're not going to drag him into this, will you?"

I looked at him and saw he was speaking to me half attentively. He was flipping through spinsheets- the local boat classified. I began to walk away and I heard him put the paper down.

"Constance, what are you going to do? You can't take it. You know that."

"I am." I said stubbornly, with the anger he had aggravated, "I already said yes. I said I would and I am. If it takes long, then it does, so be it. A lot of things take long."

He took up his paper again and kept flipping.

The boat arrived on a cloudy day in fall. I canceled my shift at Clancy's and picked up Luis early from day school and brought him with me to watch the crane lift cradle our boat out of the water. We were a bit late and by the time we arrived the boat was already suspended and moving over the gravel. I looked at Luis. He was so excited. He pointed at it over and over,

"That's the boat, mom?"

"Yes, that's the one." I said.

We followed the crane as it transported the boat to its slip next to the wooden hull sailboats. When it was placed on its stilts above the chalky gravel we got the first good look at it. It was not what I expected, and my first impression fell. It was certainly a distressed ship, discolored and beaten like Mr. Bruce said; but worse than I envisioned. The marks were permanent from rigging line and apparatus swinging and banging - years of infliction from hard use, yawing, rolling, pitching on cold salt seas. All the trade uses of an oyster rig, including the abuse of time and the corrosion of salt exposure, which had stripped the boat of any luster. It was completely lusterless. I don't know what I expected, but I regretted it now that I saw it. The hull was grey and flaking paint. The stern and bow were yellowed and dulled a permanent eggshell color. Along the transom read,

"Elton Briggs - Plymouth, ME"

The letters were curly serif. They were the most intact outward aspect of the boat. Despite its blemishes and scars it had a fine shape- a high, v-shaped prow that widened smoothly at the cross section and remained that wide at the back.

We were given a ladder by the boatyard to help us climb aboard. The deck was spacious and clean, with preinstalled coolers, a small cabin, and a basic cockpit console on the right side.

"This is it." I said to my son. He was going around opening hatches and looking into the cabin. I don't know if he heard me. He came out.

"It smells bad in there." he said.

I went inside and he was right. It smelled like liquor and

burned rubber and musty lampshade. Standing there on that needy vessel, thinking of all that needed to be done- half of which I hadn't done before, and realizing that now this boat was *mine*, I became overwhelmed.

"We're going." I said. I went to the ladder, and Luis said to me, "Why are you mad?"

"I'm not mad." I said.

"You sound mad."

In a very short span- from a conversation that led to us inspecting our 'new boat', I lost faith. I wanted out. I was hungover in a swelter of discontent, made of troubled expectations, of a cloudy day, of my father who asked "How's the beauty?" when we returned. The words broke over me. I went upstairs for a long nap and Luis joined me.

I was better when I rose, and better a week after, when I returned to the slip by myself. I brought a square of sandpaper and a hose. I put my hands to it and began to hose the hull and sand it patiently. I began in one corner and worked incrementally over the whole bottom- foot by foot. It was toxic under the hull when I scraped the old paint off and applied the new, so I didn't bring Luis for that part, but for all the other chores above deck, he came, sometimes for an hour or two.

We were the oddest pair in the yard. I have no doubt about that - a mother and her young son, scrubbing an inherited oyster boat. If I thought too long about it, I may have stopped for good and given up. But much work defeats much thought. Some nights when we drove back from the yard, as he slept in the seat beside me, I was harangued by the conviction that it was all a mistake- that I had rushed into something headlong and heedless, that I had yanked him with me- this young child, who I wanted to have a good normal life, not buried in dust, and not returning to tell his grandparents that he spent the night with his mother under the fumes of mineral spirits, polishing chrome with a rag.

But we kept going, and shortly we were overcome with the project. That winter, which forced us to pause from working for many weeks, threw me into despair about what I should do. On top of that there were other abrasive experiences I kept to myself, that no one but me needed to hear about.

Some of the men in neighboring slips were scoundrels. The ones who owned the wood sloops. The more I came around the more they picked on me, asking things like 'When did my husband buy the boat?' or did I want to come aboard their own and 'fix things up nice and pretty'. Catcalls and carousing. These were not young fellows, mind you. These were the aged and infirm, and their degeneracy announced itself on numerous nights, when, following a shift at the restaurant, I walked under the fetid gaslights to row 'I', where the Elton Briggs and its companions were lined beside each other. These were vessels that were permanently grounded, having no voyage left in them; keels that once shadowed the waters as far south as the Florida keys now shadowed the ground, impotent slips with no launch date, having sailed themselves into a sad coma, and these nocturnal sailors who leered from their hideouts, stuffing themselves away in private berths, the clink of glasses spilling beyond their hatches and whoever it was (I never saw him) who would pass by my boat and knock on my ladder and leave remnants of clothes and underwear on the rungs. These figures I worked under. I never saw him nor any of them clearly but from the auspice of their balconies, in darkness, their faces indistinct, their voices crouped, the vessels under them like their owners: scant, rotted, drowsy, not going anywhere.

That poisonous nocturnal atmosphere compelled me to move on the project and not let it linger and die a slow death like the others. Come spring it was nearly there- the despair sloughed off and the more I worked the more I began to accept the boat and how it came to me. It was ours now. I stopped watching myself so closely and took the days as they came, one by one.

70

To see the end of any trial, any unwieldy demand is a great relief, and it stretches your previous conception of perseverance, granted you see it through, granted you persevere. The last thing to set right on our boat was the name and the port of call. What would we call it? Where would it be from? One day after school I asked Luis what he thought of the boat and he said what do you mean? I said I want to name the boat. I want to give it a name we both like. What do you think? Does it remind you of anything? He said it reminded him of an animal. "An animal? What kind?" I said. He said he didn't know.

"You must have had something in mind?" But he shook his head, he didn't. I was humored that that response came out of him instinctively, and I immediately began to see the boat that way too, if not as an animal, at least living, creaturely, animate. Suddenly something came to me.

"The hog. What about 'The Hog?'" Mr. Bruce had called it that in passing and the phase came back to me, and appealed.

"I like it." he said. "A hog like a pig."

"Yes, a wild pig." I added "They're harrier than a regular pig. But messy like a pig"

"Like a pig sty?" he said.

"That's right, like your room sometimes. They probably make a pig sty, or maybe it's called differently since they're a hog."

I thought about it,

"A hog sty?" he said.

"A hog sty. Maybe. I like that though. What about that for a name?"

"Me too."

"I don't know if that's a real thing, but I like it even better as a name. The Hogsty." I said.

And he shortened it to "Hogsty."

"Hogsty. Do you like it?" I asked.

"I like it."

"Is that the animal you imagined?"

"No, but I like it more."

So that's what we went with. Anyone who's ever rode with us, who's said they like the name and asked how it earned it, we tell we came up with it on the spot and it stuck. Most people, including my father, who was the first to see it when the new name was revealed, pronounce it, Hog-stee.

"Hogstee?"

"No, Hog-sty."

"There should be a dash, shouldn't there?"

"We're keeping it the way it is."

To me the name manifests all the bristle and spunk and unruliness of the boat itself- it's not a neat boat, it never was. The engines, we discovered, ran rough and squealy as soon as it was dropped in the water, and that too came as confirmation that the name was right. The name had found us. The port of call was more obvious. Skewesbury, MD. Most of the boats from nearby choose the bigger towns, but not Hogsty- a true Hogsty could only come from the marsh banks of that murky mud river settlement, Skewesbury.

There was no telling what we would do with it once it was in the water. For once I understood that dilemma of a project coming to an end and not knowing what's next, or what project would take its place. It's like a thousand piece puzzle- you get so used to little moves, piecemeal improvements, the thought of launching and boating and using it for its very purpose seems a foreign concept. But eventually it was there upon us.

On the very day the cradle lift took Hogsty off her stilts and placed her in the water, another boat took her place in that aisle of misfits. It was a sloop of unrivalled elegance and shapeliness- a shallow drafted, demasted bateau, made entirely of wood- one of the old obsolete crab catching sailcraft. The man beside it, her owner, I knew nothing about except that he was there, in the light of day, unlike the scoundrel bunch encamped beside him, who I never saw during the daytime, who came out only at night. As we got going, briefly I turned and saw him standing below his sloop with a large white canvas bag stowed with sails flung over his back like he were waiting to begin something, and I wondered what kind of boatsman he was and what would come of that bateau.

71

I had known that marina quite well without ever stopping to think just how well I knew it- how many boat names were etched into my memory by sight of contact: who had come, who had disembarked over the years. Now I stood with my son on the deck on the water, rocking for the first time on our Hogsty. He asked me,

"Where are we going?"

He must have meant that question to mean for that day, and I said,

"Out to Chesapeake Bay."

He nodded and looked off then back at me, like I had missed something in my response,

"What is it? I said.

"Nothing." he said. "Then we come back, that's all?"

"Yep, that's all. For now."

I lost my place in that immediate conversation and began to think of the other side of his question- the long view of "Where are we going?" For me it was a reference point, a bearing, ever since he started asking it. I cared where I was leading him, as all parents do. I was also deeply aware of the way he said 'that's all?' Probably he meant nothing by it, but I heard doubts in statements like that; doubts that were never driven away by tie or motherhood but that lingered as he matured, gained on me, caught up to me. The direction I provided him when he was a baby was only immediate and intensive. The caring was prompt, and in a good way, unreflective. My hands were full. He ate, he slept, he cried. As he grew, he asked questions and I answered them as best I could, but undoubtedly some, or many, hit the floor, and were left there to be picked up later.

"That's all?"

"For now that's all."

Looking back on Hogsty- those very first days of true ownership, as we stood on the deck and ventured out to Bay under my tentative piloting, we were together on a cusp, without knowing what cusp. Luis looked at me and I looked out; for landmarks, for buoys, for the edge of land- and I did not tell him because I did not know it then, that this grumbling boat would hold more fate than either of us knew, that we would be together on it quite a bit, charting our way.

It was almost as soon as we had taken the boat out fishing, and returned with a catch of rockfish and blues, that Hogsty gained a dockside and boatyard reputation for being a fishing vessel. Shipmates and visitors and prospective yacht owners would approach us and ask where we went, how we fared, and if we offered any sort of charter service. Admittedly, the boat did give off that look of a fishing operation, more than a recreational or cruising boat, but I did not want to encourage any idea of an operation early on. It was enough to be in the water, sojourning the rivers and coves and sounds as we saw fit. And so I turned people down often who asked. I had no qualms about it.

I was also under my parent's scrutiny again. They worried for me and they worried more about Luis, who was often by himself when I worked on the boat or at the restaurant. They told me that one afternoon a stray dog had wandered into the yard at home and Luis took it into the outbuilding and kept it there and brought it a bowl of cereal. Somehow the dog managed to escape his supervision, but my father saw Luis and brought the bowl inside and reprimanded him.

Later that week, when I heard about the incident I spoke to him and asked why he did it.

"I wanted to keep it here." he said.

"But you know that dog didn't belong to you, right?"

"I know."

"Then why did you put it in the outbuilding?"

"So I could play with it."

I was touched by his frankness, but also saddened by it- I could hear my own voice saying the same things when I was his age. Like one time, when I climbed into the pen with the skinny pony, 'Jitters', and opened the latch so the horse could 'roam' in our yard (I had been reading Misty of Chicoteague and was enamored with the idea of wild, free horses). Fortunately the scraggly pony had no desire to move. It stayed in the shade of the outbuilding nibbling on grass. And when my father came out I pretended I had opened the pen for myself.

In this case, I wasn't sure how to respond to Luis. So I said,

"Let's not do it again."

I took him fishing whenever something like that happened- whenever I heard that he was skulking, or quiet, or had tried to trap a stray dog; for I sought some saving grace in fishing, a satisfaction for his loneliness, a loneliness I thought I not only perfectly understood, but could amend with a little inspiration. I could divulge my affections. I could teach him how to rig the lines, and hook bait. How to set crab traps, and troll, how to tie all the knots I knew. I could point out the shoals and sandbars, how to read a tide chart, how to balance the draft line of a boat.

In short, I would give him the Bay. I would give him the instincts to spend a lifetime reaping its pleasures. I wanted him to befriend all that I had befriended; to succour at the sight of the sea, to receive from it the same fortification of spirit I had received, and the same means of escaping I had.

The trips we took were longer and farther away. One time we went as far as the Bay Bridge, anchored on the choppy waters, fished and ate our packed lunch. I noticed he wasn't fishing anymore, but was watching the cars overhead on the bridge go back and forth. I got upset with him and said,

"We didn't come all this way to watch cars. Keep your line in the water."

He didn't say anything. He put the line in but kept watching the cars. I saw his eyes float up then down to the water, then to me, then down to the water, dejected like.

"What's wrong I?" I exclaimed, frustrated at last.

"I don't want to fish." he said.

"Then why'd we come all this way then?"

"*You* wanted to come."

"No, Luis, this is for both of us"

"I don't feel good." he said.

"Then sit down." I told him.

To appease him I pointed to the bridge and said,

"Do you know where that leads to?

He shook his head.

"We're on this side, the eastern shore."

I pointed to the land on the right.

"And on that side, the other side is Annapolis and all that."

"What's there?" he said.

"Nothing special- just towns and cities and more people."

I regretted saying it with so much cynicism and disapproval, but that was my mood.

"You don't want to fish now?" I said in the same harsh tone.

"No."

"You still feel sick?"

"Yes."

"From fishing?"

"I don't know."

"Come on." I pleaded. "You don't want to have a good time? I'm having a good time."

He said nothing. His eyes were on the water now, they stopped floating up to the bridge at all.

"I bet other moms don't take their sons out fishing like we do."

He turned to me and said "Other moms don't fish."

"Excuse me. What did you say?"

"I said other moms don't fish."

I was hurt by those words more than anything he had said to me before. I brought all the rods in and turned the boat around and said nothing to him the rest of the way. When we got back I was in a fury still. It was the first time I was genuinely furious with him. In my anger I hastily made fast the stern of the boat to the cleat and the next day when I came to check on the boat by myself I found that the shoddy knot I made had come undone and the boat was knocking into the pierlings like an idiot.

When we got home that night from the Bay Bridge Luis went to bed without eating. My parents were awake and I was wide awake and rueful from what took place. James was watching television in his chair. When he saw me he lowered the volume and the four of us sat there not saying anything, but each of us thinking something. My mother got up and brought back a plate of small desserts from earlier. She put them down on the table and said,

"What's going on?"

I told her what happened. My father said,

"You went out that far? On your boat?"

I could tell my mother had something to say that she was holding back, so I looked at her and said, "What is it?"

She said, "Well, the first thing and most important thing is, you need to sleep. I can see it in your eyes. They need to shut. The second thing is that you need to rest- and you need to give him a rest. He's had a hard time of it lately, and I know that because he gets quiet, just like you did."

I interjected,

"That's why I've been trying to do things with him. To get him out a bit, to share-

"Yes, I understand." she said, "but it's too much. It's too much. I know where that desire comes from, but you won't be happy that way, pulling all the time- neither will he. Since you've gotten the boat you've gone on trip after trip like you're going to lose something if you don't. I've felt bad not to let him go with you, but there's been days where he shouldn't have gone, neither should you have, but you did. You're working also. It's a lot. You've got us here, but we don't always know how to help. You understand?"

I said, "I don't want to be a burden here. And I don't want him to be a burden here. When he comes with me he has something to do."

"But it's what *you* like to do, don't you see?"

I felt tears fill my eyes and my throat swell.

"This is not me telling you how to parent- you're already doing that, you're learning. We learn, and it's hard; that's that. What I'm saying is- slow- slower. You're wanting to give him the ocean all at once, and he can't take it, not yet he can't. He's 6, Constance. He can't appreciate all that you want to show him, and it makes sense why you want to do it because he's growing quickly. Childhood is gone before you know it."

Then she paused a moment and the room was still, waiting on her.

"But there is time. More than enough. Let him start smaller, let him go around our creek, like you used to. You did that when you were his age."

"I was older." I said.

"Not much." she said. "You did that because you enjoyed it. You don't have to write it all out."

I'm not sure if my father was listening anymore, but after my mother was finished speaking James said,

"You know, Constance- don't take this the wrong way, but he might like sailing instead."

All three of us laughed. I don't know why it was as funny as it was, but it hit home. It said something completely lighthearted, yet profound, as only James was capable. It disarmed me and struck me, especially coming from him because James never dominated a conversation in his life or wanted to weasel his opinion in anywhere. Whatever he added had an extra gentleness to it, a compassion that no else could offer.

And secondly, I had heard that recommendation before, and fairly recently.

"Are you hungry?" my mother ended with.

"I'm actually starving." I said. "I've had nothing but anger in my gut the past 5 hours."

"Let's start with that." she said.

She made me a plate of leftovers, and sat beside me as I ate. The other two went to bed, and we followed behind them when I was finished.

72

I don't know how long it went on- how many comments, interactions, questions, passages of time, moments of conviction developed my awareness of a fracture between Luis and me. I let off, then I let on, I was near, then I was far. I scolded, then I lavished. My temperament was more like my father's growing up than my mother's.

From the beginning, even before he was in my charge, there was a pain that sharpened over time when I envisioned his life. When it became my burden and also my responsibility, when I drew him close. It was me wanting to foretell the grief in him, the void that he will doubtless recognize as he grows older. If there was ever an attempt to shield him, it was that I was too motherly with him, I spoke with him too often. I asked him too many questions and left too many of his own questions unanswered, even as a young boy, hoping to distract him forever. One day he would ask me about his father and I would say,

"No, Luis, you don't have a father-"
"Why?"
"Because you don't. Not everyone does."
Where else would it go from there? Down and down.

Like a witness before a jury I played the conversation in my mind, making a trial of it, putting myself on trial. There was always that twinge of tragedy in the answer I would give, that bruskness. As if to say,

"Sorry it had to be this way, Luis. Sorry you've had to grow up in this place, sorry that there wasn't more that I could give you, or someone else to be with to take care of you."

Mind games like that are dangerous, and I played them willingly.

Around that time, in the thick of the quandary, when I was paralyzed in circumstance and unsure of how to be a proper mother to my son, and a daughter to my parents, a sister to my siblings, waitress to the restaurant, an owner of a fishing vessel, and somehow still raise my own sails in life- a good thing happened.

We received neighbors. Art and Sarah Reynolds, and their four boys: Mitch, Culver, William, and George moved into Mr. Corey's old house, filling all corners of the space, and spilling over. George was the youngest and we called him Georgie. Georgie was the same age as Luis and within two weeks the two of them were playing soccer in the yard and trading back and forth between our pier and theirs. Georgie and Luis, and later the older boys who came to play and roughhouse, were a natural bond between the families. They were our introductions to one another.

Art and Sarah were a younger couple than my parents by ten years, but their four boys, all of them loud and restless, bestowed on their parents a grace and maturity lacking in many couples the same age. They were firm, disciplined, weary, worn, exasperated, kind, and hospitable.

They had moved from Delaware so Art could be closer to his company. He was a salesman for a chemical fertilizer company, and as their family grew they needed space to stretch. Sarah had a pet phrase she used often 'room to run'. She said it more than she realized, but it was apparent what she meant- the boys needed open space, they needed shoreline, and acreage, and enough of both to contain their surplus of energy and voices.

It was really a month before we knew them, and many months before we knew them well, which for my family was unprecedented. In other neighborhoods, where the homes are close together and there is less privacy than there is here, maybe it is more common or easier to get to know the neighbors. But it was unusual for us. We had grown accustomed to the abandoned house beside us, which alienated us in a way. Before that we had known Mr. Corey as the only tenant, and he was not what you would call 'social' or 'hospitable'. We had other neighbors too, but they were farther down Teal St. and more nestled amongst the creeks and the woods- if they left we hardly knew it. We had hardly known them while they were there.

That's the way it was. All of Teal St. was content with anonymity, with an occasional wave or hi, or short conversation- but anything more was unusual, and usually avoided. Against this backdrop the Reynolds came. They came like a roll of thunder into a long settled glade. They prevented our place from being its own secluded peninsula facing the water. Art was a funny, practical, self-deprecating man. One of the first things he did when they moved in was take down a few of the trees separating our yards- an oak, an evergreen, and a holly. The cry of the chainsaw rattled through the neighborhood like an early warning- like a precedent of the noise they would bring thereon, and we (but my father foremost), like all curmudgeon neighbors- watched him with a wary eye.

"I don't know if he can do it." I remember my father saying, and my mother saying back,

"Let him be- those trees are his and he can do what he wants with them."

When Art was finished he walked through his pile of sawdust with two of his boys and came to our house to talk with my father. He told him what he was doing, told my father to take any firewood he needed, and to feel free to kick his boys off our property if they were on it.

"But Luis is welcome on ours anytime." he said. "He's no trouble compared to ours."

Art was a sincere man; a man made humble and kind-hearted by the demands of his family. He was a man that appeared to me both considerably bedraggled and considerably grateful- as if he was always storing some clemency for the very persons and tasks that he paid for most dearly with time, energy, and willpower. My father, I think, saw the same thing in him. He told Art he was welcome to stock his chopped wood with ours if he needed extra room, and if the boys ever wanted to take our little boat out, they were welcome to that too- we could show them how it's done. It was the first of many exchanges, of many uncounted favors and olive branches that passed from one yard to the next, from one household to the other, establishing more than a perfunctory neighborliness between our clans- but charity, pure and simple- a rooted care for these people. Their troubles were our troubles, and ours, we were surprised, were theirs.

The first year they lived here, both properties withstood a barrage of thunderstorms. They lost trees and we lost trees. They lost roof and we lost pier- but we each attended to the other's needs. Art would come over with his two oldest, who would hold tools for him, and help my father. And his two youngest would play with Luis. The grass between our yards died away from the footpath made between the houses. And their yard, which for so long was hidden behind heavy branches, was timberless soon, brighter than we'd ever seen it. The sun, sinking over the creek, stretched its light from our place to theirs. A clearing was made in the middle, a shining acre joining the homes.

73

Art, who was never a scrupulous or restrictive man, was yet someone with discretion. He cared for manners, for order, for a healthy kind of discipline in his family, and especially his boys. When the footpath between our properties became ugly and mud stamped, he took it upon himself to build a fence, a standard white fence around his property, and install a wide gate that swung open between our yard and theirs. The gate was never locked, but it announced a visitor with a squeak. As soon as it was installed the squeaking commenced. Squeak, click. Squeak, click. From inside our house you could hear the sound and you knew someone was coming.

More often than not it was a welcome sound- the sound of company, of playtime, of neighbors interacting. My mother almost always enjoyed the company. Sarah would often come over when her boys did. She came to supervise, but also to chat with my mother and get a break from her own household. The yards at any given moment contained an intermingling of belongings; a few of their possessions in our yard, a few of ours in theirs. If you lifted the tarp, you would find Art's fresh chopped orange hued wood stacked atop our pale dried pile.

In short, I could not overestimate the influence they had on our family. Nor could I overestimate the influence they had on me. One day Art came over by himself and asked to speak to me. He said,

"I know you've got a decent sized boat- and that you know the water pretty well. I wonder if you would consider taking me and the boys out one Saturday, if it's not too much to ask. We haven't been out much. I can pay for gas, tackle, whatever you need."

I didn't have to think twice about it. I said,

"I'd love to do that, and no need to pay for anything. This is our treat."

Two weekends later we went, a whole crew of us- not just him and his boys, but Luis, James, and my father too. We filled the boat. Whenever we anchored I stood in the bow making sure every person had a rod if they wanted. I took three blocks of frozen squid from the cooler and cut slivers of it, and the boys lined up, one by one, while I baited their hooks. When everyone was set I gave them a demonstration of how to release the bail, how to close it, how to set the hook, and told them to call if they needed any help.

Early on the little one George snagged his line, and he whined to his father for help, but his father was helping his other son, and he told George,

"If you have a problem, you ask the Captain, ok?"

So George called to me and I came over and unsnagged him, and after that he and the others started calling me Captain, which I got a real kick out of.

We fished off Solomons, we ambled into Annapolis. All day we went about. When the catching was good every person had a line in the water, the boat was rocking and there was a mesmerizing silence that came over the group; each of us, down to Georgie and Luis were dialed into our lines, focused, waiting, snagging, catching. We filled two coolers full of croaker and spot. On our way back, as the boys sat slumbering on the seats and coolers, Art came up to me at the helm and said,

"This has been one of the best fishing trips I've been on, for the boys too. You run a great operation, you know. Do you take others out? Do you offer trips?"

"I appreciate it." I said. "We've had as good a time as you. I haven't led any trips like this since we put the boat in the water. It was quite an ordeal even doing that."

"Oh, you should." he said. "There's not many out there in this area that run a good charter, a family charter at that. You've got Luis too. I've searched around because I said to my wife and the boys, if we're going to live on the water, we better find ways to spend time on it. Whether its fishing, tubing, sailing- we haven't done much of it either, but I've looked into the charters, and what you have is either commercial vessels, or deep sea charters, or old captains that cater to retirees, or private boats. What you've got is unique, and this is a great boat. A boat with spirit. You'd run a great operation, I know you would-"

74

So that's how I began to find my start in charter fishing, with those modest words at the end of that trip. In my experience, the most valuable encouragement is not the finely tuned words or speeches that stir the mood for a moment, but words spoken at an unaccounted time, offered with such candor and belief that they take you by surprise. Words like that *are* a surprise, and do not so much as lift you up like a balloon, as set your feet on solid earth, convince you of your own substance. They point to something unflinchingly and say 'Here- this is a boat made for fishing, and you, *you* are someone who should lead fishing trips. And you believe them.

From anyone else I may have doubted these words, but coming from Art Reynolds with four wiped boys and nothing to gain by them, they were writing on the wall for me- good writing too- they reminded me of the time when I was young, fishing with my father when he said,

"They're right under us-" and I could feel it.

Apparently Art believed in his words as much as I heeded them because shortly after our excursion I received two calls from two unknown numbers asking about fishing trips saying they were interested in booking something if it was available. I called them back and found out they were coworkers of Arts.

It put me in a position to act. I was nervous and unprepared, but also I was willing. I decided to take them out. Harder than saying yes to the trip was saying yes to getting paid for it. That's when things get serious. Your hobby becomes more than a hobby. You are a professional then, not just an amateur, and with that comes scrutiny, and reputation, and so on. To my benefit there was little time to overplan or over-rig the boat, so we went with what we had, and I followed the same tour I took with the Reynolds. I knew that way well. To my surprise again, both parties loved their trip. One trip was a father, mother, and daughter. The other was a college kid, his sister and his sister's boyfriend. Luis came on that trip and helped where he could.

As the saying goes, after that the ball was rolling. In my case, maybe the ball was only a rock that I kicked farther down the road, but it was going nonetheless, and at every stop it went a little farther, a little quicker, picking up speed. I could recount so many details of those early trips because of how nervous I was. I wanted the trips to be enjoyable and worthwhile, and up until the moment we returned, made fast to deck, and I saw their happiness and received their thanks, I really doubted it. Afterwards I doubted it too. But consistency is harder to doubt, and that is what I tried to build a reputation from, some consistency. Piece by piece I built an operation that was finding its way from a little corner of the Bay. I was finding the limits of it too, of my boat, of my knowledge of the land and water, taking it all in some sort of a stride.

I was energized by all this, and Luis was too. There was more work to do, but the work was rewarded by the time we spent on the water. It was not just Luis and me anymore. There were people now, and people gave the boat its purpose. Like Beverly, Luis loved the crowd. He wove in and out of the commotion, and was happiest when the deck was full of voices.

To make things more official, Luis and me salvaged a wooden board from the outbuilding, to paint a sign that said,

Fishing Charters and Tours aboard Hogsty:
Call for availability.

I took pride in that sign. There were times when I would look at it for no particular reason except that I liked it, that in its downright simplicity, it was becoming to me. It reminded me of Luis- that this boat was not just my boat, but ours.

Luis painted the words after I told him what I wanted. He is by no means a calligrapher, but he did his best. In the shade of the big doors of the outbuilding, I laid the wooden board down in the grass under a sheet of painters cloth. I wiped the dust off with a rag, then I opened an old can of white paint and stirred it with a screwdriver and set it next to the board. Then I handed Luis the brush. He looked at me uncertainly, and I said,

"We'll do the first word together. Go on-"

He stepped forward, then backed off and said to me,

"I don't want to mess it up."

"Don't worry, you won't. There's plenty of boards in there if we need. Just draw one line- the rest will come."

Very cautiously he dipped the brush in the paint, then dabbed it on the board, and instantly I saw the confidence fill his eyes, and he smiled.

"Yep, like that. Big," I said, "Big letters. Look at all this board. Here, let me show."

I took his hand and we drew the 'F' and 'i' together. I

heard the gate squeak behind us and turned and saw George coming over to watch. He began talking to Luis as Luis was painting and I said,

"George, Luis is trying to concentrate on something right now."

As Luis painted slowly, his friend stood behind him sounding out the letters in real time,

"F - i - s"

"Bigger." I said to Luis, and soon George started saying it too, "Bigger, Luis."

Luis looked back at us and shook his head. His legs were spread wide and the fresh paint was under him. I laughed,

"You see, Luis, you have to listen to your friend too."

"Bigger Luis." George said.

"I know George, stop!" Luis said.

"Hey be nice." I said. "And turn around, you're starting to drip."

It took him an hour, but he finished. There is a shakiness to the letters which endears me to their purpose and to the hand that wrote them. Capt. Travis and his state of the art yacht had a sign that was as tall as me, printed professionally, brimming with words, half of which were names of fish we had never caught.

I couldn't have gotten away with that. There were stretches, months at a time when I took no one out at all that first year. Like some skeptical reflex I would weigh my doubts- wonder if I could neaten something on the boat, add a word to the sign, have it repainted to look that much more enticing, but each time I let it be, and the next week someone would call.

75

A lot has happened since then. A mild amount of success has brought its share of dissenters and mockers. It was true back then, and remains so, an unequivocal curiosity to some people that I am a grown woman running a charter boat.

You know the kind of people when they walk by or when they call, expecting to hear the gruff voice of a sailor, and hear mine instead, not that mine is sweet.

"Is the Captain around?"

"This is she-"

All the initial interest peels away, and they begin speaking in the purely inquisitive, uncommitted language that reveals their mistrust.

"Oh, I was just calling to see what you offer, what's biting- just to see. I'm calling around..."

If I gave the most detailed, accurate, insightful fishing report they ever heard, it would not change their impression; but those are the restraints I work within. I have come to know them, accept them, and even learn from them. You earn your stripes by fishing well, by taking care of the people who come with you, by taking care of your boat, your lines, your engines. But you fish well, firstly, if that's what you're advertising. I've ended heckling, sarcasm, and downright stupidity from some of the boat owners nearby simply by laying down on the deck the fish we caught, a trick I learned from Capt. Travis and the Virginia Beach wharf.

One of the longtime snide remarkers was a Navy vet named Ed Gleeson, a few boats down from me. We never formally met, and I don't think he ever wanted to, because he would walk by but never stop. He would look in, and say something like,

"You got a scenic tour planned?" or "You taking someone out for a joyride?"

That's what I mean; to some I was a joyride. I took the fishing seriously to defray those comments, and it paid off. One of my first clients won a tuna fishing competition out of Ocean City, Maryland, and when they interviewed him, he mentioned my charter and gave me credit for showing him how to troll effectively. I don't remember ever telling him anything like that, but something stuck, and they reprinted his interview in the boating catalogue that made its rounds at every boatyard part shop. After that the dissenters went quiet for a time, and more calls came in, and I enjoyed a very brief and very local kind of fame, but I saved that catalogue, and brought some for my family and the Reynolds, and we toasted to it.

"To the woman who taught the prize winner everything he knew." Sarah said.

"It's far from true, but I'll raise mine to his success." I said.

With the attention we got I could have given our poor sign an upgrade- but it stayed the same, and it's better the fame went away with the tide and never reappeared. Things leveled out and became what they are today.

There are two other headboats beside Hogsty at the marina: one named 'Push-Come-Shove', captained by Mark

Dahlgreer, and one named 'Lady June' captained by Stew Sodstrom. We have a longstanding rivalry with both boats because we all fish the same portion of the Bay, and we're all eager to take clients. We don't have the liberty the ocean-side charters have. They have their off-season too, but it's more consistent year round, and they can go deep sea without restraint. The number of recreational boaters on the Bay has seen no drop- they're numerous, and they have the same equipment as us, maybe better. From June to Labor Day we fish for bluefish, striped bass, sea trout, black drum, rockfish, and the smaller stuff including spot and croakers and cobia.

Fisherman are competitive by trade and I've lost many a good night sleep over another boat's catch. Capt. Mark and I have a more antagonistic relationship than myself and Stew. Stew is an old timer. He was the first charter in this boatyard. Mark and I came around the same time and we're close to the same age. He's cocky and a swindler. A while back he was infamous for giving false fishing reports to get people to fish with him. The rumor is true. I've had Luis call him from a foreign number to ask for a report and he'd making something up- pure bogus,

'The blues are hitting.' he'd say. The truth is the blues haven't hit for 3 weeks. I've accused him of dishonesty to his face before, but he said 'You fish on your terms, let me fish on mine.' He refers to my operation as the 'the lady with the big boat' and he describes the boat itself as 'heavy set' and 'hard to miss'.

It is unfortunate to admit that he had to tow me from a sandbar a few years ago, and ever since then he has used the incident as a mark of jest, and maybe more- some proof of my being a second rate captain. I remember the grin he had on his face when he arrived that afternoon. I'd been trying to shove us off the sand with a gaff pole to no success.

He said 'Ms. Captain, the fish are out here I believe.'

He laughed and came aboard and tied us up, the

smugness written all over his expression, and I was obliged afterward to thank him for roping us to safety. That was the painful part. Luis doesn't have the same bitterness toward him that I do, and that's good for him. I imagine if my son ever continued this operation after I'm done, he'd have a new opinion of the man, but that's a long way off.

Like myself, Mark never married. I saw him get close once. And I saw him fritter it away over many arguments- many I heard at night in the marina when he and this woman would sit in the stern and their voices would rise and she would leave at some point in a tantrum. The woman stomped off and her shoe heel caved between the pier boards and snapped, and she fell with a rolled ankle. I was in my boat and heard it. She called for his help, but he did not budge. That was the pit of his ruthlessness. I cringed to hear it.

"You're not going to help?" she said. "Really? I can barely move." I kept listening for his response, but it never came. He was dreadfully silent. Finally I heard him say

"You can help yourself, can't you? You don't want to be here with me anyway."

It was not my conversation, but I got out of the boat and walked in that direction. Luis was with me. I whispered to him 'Go and see if that woman needs help.' He went sheepishly- this scrawny kid going up to a grown woman in heels who is collapsed on the pier, asking 'Can I help?' But he did.

She took his arm and stood and he walked beside her as she limped on. They didn't exchange a single word. She saw me standing off to the side and I believe she knew I was his mother, that I had heard the whole encounter, and sent him to help. But what did that matter? We were passed the point of discretion. We were all shamed.

Luis helped her to her car, then he returned as sheepishly

as he went out. There was a doleful look in his eyes. He looked down at the ground, embarrassed.

"Forget about it." I said.

But I myself did not forget about it. I thought of it the whole night and long after, every time I saw Mark. I thought of the menacing cruelty of words spoken in so tranquil a place.

Over the years our relationship has simmered. The same boat he used to tow mine hit an unlit buoy at night, and sank in little over two hours. Even I was dismayed to hear it. A disaster like that touches a concern and conviction we all share. The bond between fisherman and boat. Boat is home, livelihood, source of pride. He was much quieter after that. He relented from his onslaught of sarcasm and turned to complaining instead, which is not objectively better, but I think closer to how he really felt about things.

76

Between my heavyset Hogsty and Mark's 'Push-Come-Shove', there floats Stew Sodstrom's faithful craft, the 'Lady Jane', docked where it has always been docked as long as I have been here. Stew used to be a crab and oysterman before he devoted all his resources to fishing. His boat is a convert with all the old rigging, minus the pots and line, still fitted to the mainframe including a mechanical pulley that used to haul hundreds of pounds of crabs every week. I have been on his boat before; it's a boat whose performance betrays its looks. It's been bitten away by rust and hard use but it's no drag. Like Stew himself, the outside is rough but the inside is lean and strong, and lends no sign of letting up.

The pile of crab traps he once owned has dwindled. Now he has a handful only. He keeps one at the dock, tied next to his boat, and everyday during the summer, early in the morning, he lifts it out of the water and sets it crashing on the deck, drenching the whereabouts. It's not a light thing either. Even with all its holes, it's still a metal contraption that pulls a lot of water with it. His boat is far enough from mine that I don't always see him unless I've gone down deliberately to say hello, which I do. He's one of the friendliest men I know, and certainly the friendliest at the marina. He loves showing people the crab trap- for him it's a stride back in time when he pulls it up; there is a youthful excitement in his eyes to see what he has caught, to see what will come snapping out of the dark water. Only once have I seen him pull it up with nothing except the frozen chicken legs he put in for bait.

"I pulled it too soon." he said, shaking his head.

He has white hair shaved close to his head and loose turkey skin under his neck. His dry legs - "leather legs" as he calls them, he covers with high beige socks, and you can tell he was tall once but now he stoops standing and hunches when he walks. Despite his age, what is most surprising are the remains of his vigor. His strength has not waned as long as I've known him. He works long and owns the same forearms he had in pictures decades earlier- brawny from a lifetime of hauling traps and dredge nets.

The water and his work have shaped his appearance unmistakably. His eyes are molded into an almost persistent squint. Bright hazel if opened wide enough, but usually they're only half opened, the ocular disposition of someone who has fended sea glare all their life. He wears some combination of green and grey most days, and funnily his clothes are bleached by the sun and nearly match the color of the water, making him some extension of it. If anyone is an extension of the water it's him. Stew is living ballast to this place. I have seen no one that belongs more to Bay country than he does. It is his home- the habitat where he is completely himself. Fortunate for us, he treats me like a daughter and Luis like a grandson. With some lamenting he says how he wishes we had seen the Bay as it was when he was young.

"You wouldn't believe it if I told you- come here," and he takes me by the shoulder to the end of the boatyard, aways from his slip. There are twenty yards of dock between where we stand and the first lamppost stands above the water.

"This right here is the newest portion of pier we have." He points along the row of pilings in front. "Them pilings aren't old in the slightest, they're still white as they were when they put them in." He shakes his hand across the scene. "This used to be empty; just grass and sand; real shallow too. They dredged it out of course. But back when I first docked here doing crabs, I would use that ramp over there and come back on nights when there weren't no lamps like there are now. All I had was a lantern. I would wade over here, right where you're looking, anchor the skiff, tie the lantern to the back right over the water, and get out with net and wait. In twenty minutes, I kid you not, I'd come back and a bushel of blue crabs would be here, a swarm of em', bubbling away like they were starved." He holds an imaginary bushel up to his chest.

"It was the light they came for, like moths come to light. And all I'd do is go in with my net, and go woop-woop-woop," his arms swishing like he's using a broom, "take as many as I could. They couldn't swim away either, they were stunned by the light. It made them sleepy. It was the only thing around. I tell you, it was absolutely mad."

I look up at him and see that he has told the story with so much enthusiasm his lips are chapped.

"How many?" I ask.

He shakes his head. "Couldn't say, couldn't say. I had to pull them up with the rim of the net, the metallic rim. They would've broken the handle. Actually, once they did! It wasn't til I had packed them in crates on shore that I saw that my handle was cracked. Can you imagine? I would have lost em' all. But these waters- right where we are," he points again, this time with his pointer and middle finger, "used to be abundant, you didn't need bait, or if you did, very little. Not just crabs I'm talkin, fish too. A striper would hit bread on a hook, any shiny thing you threw at it. Nowadays I'm happy to catch three on a half day!"

"Oh," he says, bending over to scratch his shin, "it's not like that anymore. Every year these rivers lose a little. I'm not as lucky as I was. That's my own doing I'm sure. Who's to say it won't be better later on? I hope so. You've got a young one who fishes as much as I did when I was his age. I mean for him."

Then he stops speaking. He doesn't like to overspeak, and the older he's become the worse he's gotten. He shelves away a hundred facts or stories that he'll use another time. We look out. There is a courtesy in his silence as there is a courtesy in his speaking. An indebtedness to this place that refrains him from talking too angrily or dogmatically, especially about its shortcomings, or laying blame on others.

He has pulled me aside like that a dozen times. 'Any shiny thing.' is one of his phrases. Whatever he's talking about, that phrase will surface. Where he got it I have no idea. He has a wife too, but sometimes I forget he's married given how much I see him here and how little I've seen her. He's here most days- a living historian of this boatyard and these waters.

When he's done with me, he goes off and works. He boards his solitary slip. The solitude enriches his mind the way it unnerves others. He could boat by himself all day and not be lonely. There are not many people like that.

Once I asked for his help on my engine. He came aboard, took off his shoes and knelt over the engine block beside me for an hour, not saying a word. I held a flashlight for him. I pointed it where he looked. The two of us traded tools and a handful of words, that's all. When it was done he stood up, slipped his shoes on, and pointed for me try the ignition. It roared right away and I said,

"Wow, what'd you do?"

He shrugged. "Fiddled with it."

"I can't thank you enough." I said.

"Don't mention it."

"How'd you know what you were looking for?

"I didn't." he said.

"Then how'd you fix it?"

"I felt my way around."

"I owe you." I said.

"Don't owe me." he laughed. "Just catch more fish."

77

I've pulled my share of long shifts at the yard. I nearly missed my mother's birthday once because I stayed late to clean the boat. She called and said they're waiting, the cake's on the table. I said I'll come later, save me some. Well, she put Luis on the phone and made me explain to him why I was going to stay and clean a boat instead of coming home. The result was, I got off the phone and drove home and left my cleaning supplies where they were. The closer I got, the voice inside me kept saying 'This world does not need your clean boat. It does not need your clean boat.'

I wish I could say that I was never unhealthily attached to Hogsty- that it was never more than a boat to me, and that I saw my role upon it with unbeguiled clarity, with sincerity of purpose- that I was the pilot of it, and not the other way around. But that would be false all the same.

Another time I had a similar feeling during a fishing trip with a client. Luis was not with me that trip, and the man who was pressed for time said,

"Could we get back sooner?"

"Sure." I said. "Is there anything wrong?"

We were scheduled for a few more hours.

He said "No, it's been a good trip. The best I've had in awhile. But I'd like to be getting back to my family now."

I powered both engines and we started back as fast as the boat could go. Obviously too fast, because there was a small boom in the bow, and the boat shuddered, followed by smoke rising. I shut it down and checked. One engine failed and the boat toiled along by the power of one. It was a single engine boat for weeks before it was repaired. This was recent, only 6 months ago. I turned away many interested parties for fear that just as quick, with too much overuse, I wouldn't have a boat at all.

Every major repair is a setback, and a setback is good if it sets you back on the right road, not if you keep making the same mistakes. I had been running the engines too hard, the repairman said. An engine with that many miles under its belt should never, unless it was an emergency, run at full throttle. When I told Luis about what happened on the trip with the man who wanted to come home early, it was like I was talking about myself. A one engine boat- does that sound like anything familiar? The metaphor is perhaps too close for comfort.

All too often, but especially when business was well and chipper, the boat mirrored me. It showed me the reflection of my love of water, my love of fishing. I would run the engines full blast, I would bring groceries and camp in the cabin and take naps there. I felt totally comfortable. But it was not all good. I often swung between extreme carefulness and extreme carelessness. Like my own body, there times when I would care a lot about how things looked, and other times when I let myself go. I would spend hours by myself power washing the deck, but then I would tell passengers to forget about wearing their life jackets. One day I would work hard scraping barnacles off the hull, the next day I would be too lazy to wipe scum off the railing.

The boat was an image of my concessions; the wayward steps and the forward steps, going all the way back to when I was young, when the dory was a capsule to explore with, but also flee with, to be lost in, to hide from shore. In it I saw what I most wanted to see, but also what I feared.

78

I stay late again at the yard prepping for the next trip. My longtime friend and dockmate, JM- Jim Mcauley, arrives per usual in his suit and tie after a day at work trading stocks. He is an older man, 70 years, but active still. Night after night he brings a dinner in a plastic bag and a change of comfortable clothes, shedding his tie and jacket for jeans and sweater. He has been here 5 years with his 25 foot motorboat, 'Cynthia' which is 7 slips down from mine. The first time he arrived I judged him to be one of those wealthy white men who throw their life savings at expensive hobbies because they have nothing better to do. He was surprised to see me when I introduced myself and he acted a bit embarrassed when I asked him about his boat.

For months we waved. He has a long face and big white teeth. The first year he was here he had a marvelous, overcompensating smile on his face every time I saw him - a smile that said 'I want to be liked here. I don't know anything about boats, but I want to.' I wondered how serious he would become.

For a while he cleaned the boat, but not more. It was very new to him and I believe he was unsure of himself, what he had bitten off buying a boat, and what he planned to use it for. But he has come a long way in five years.

He has been welding in his boat the past week. The engine cover is off and he is bent over the hole in the middle, standing in the open cavity with that welder's mask on, and four or five work lamps clipped on pipe and wire and rail so he can see what he's doing. From my boat I cannot see his head, which is lower than the arm rail, so far down he is. But I see the light from the lamps and hear the tinkering. He is like a miner picking away into a single alcove. I credit him, that's hard work. Intermittently a stream of sparks weep over the side of the boat into the water- the welding makes a soft, sparky sound, sort of a 'tff, tff, tff'- constant and running, almost water like. I wonder if the fish below gather when they see the surface lit up like that, fire falling toward them gently.

79

JM has taken a break the past few days from welding. Last night Luis, who knows JM quite well, asked him what he was working on as we were leaving; JM said he was mending a crack near the propeller shaft, which is ambitious work, which I think he is self conscious of because he suddenly asked how we were doing. We wished him well and left. I forgot my phone in the boat so we drove back and JM was there, still dressed in his button down and slacks, his hands clasped over his belly, his legs outstretched and his eyes closed.

A late night troller came through and sent a mild wake through the docks, the motion stirring the still water through the slips. Our tired friend slept on: a grown man in a crib, rocking softly.

80

Here is something else- as soon as our first engine was repaired, the second failed. This was only months ago. I had a repairman come, a different one than before. The engines are inboard, under the deck. I helped the man lift the cover off and he descended like a mole into the muck and I watched him as he bent his neck around, peering into the oily dark with his flashlight. Then he looks up at me, frowns, shakes his head, and mounts out of the hole and sits on the ledge with his feet dangling over. He clicks off the light.

"Not good." he says.

"How bad?" I say.

"You need a new engine, that's how bad. Look here-" and he clicks his light on and points it into the hole at a jagged metal crack.

"What from?" I ask.

He smiles. He says, "People always ask me that, thinking it's something they did without knowing it, or if it could've been prevented. By the looks of yours- it's just aged and beat. That's what happens to things, even engines as faithful as this one- they all turn eventually."

I swallow the bad news, then he says,

"And if I'm being straight with you, you had better rebuild the other one too."

I said "I just had it repaired. I just replaced the fuel pump."

"And that's fine," he said, "But that engine block is in the very same condition as the other. See how it's warping here, already?" He clicks on his light again for me to see.

"I see it."

"That's going to widen and turn out like this other one soon enough. How often do you go out? Everyday I assume?"

"A few times a week." I said. "I've got a charter business."

He makes the same all knowing frown again.

"Yeah, you've got a tough one on your hands. Best bet is take them both out, bite the bullet- rebuild them. Might cost you more than a new boat- so it depends how attached you are to this one, and I can't answer that."

He jumped out and helped me put the cover back, and I thanked him for his consult. He was young, and he had that frown the whole time I was with him. I'm sure it was his usual face in his line of work. He's the kind of repairman who goes around staring into dark holes and giving bad news- that line of work is unkind to both sides, and I felt sorry for the two of us as he walked away pulling up his pants and holding his toolbox.

81

It has been a mild winter and we are approaching the tail of it; the start of March. We've had none of the deep blanketing snow of winters past, but the same frigidness and some snow here and there. I had been sitting on the engine dilemma for a month while the boat remained in it's slip. The marina is a shanty town in winter except for the restaurant. There is a ghostly feeling that comes when the snow falls and everyone disappears. Snow that falls on the pier deck sifts through the gaps in the boards and floats to the shadowblack water when you walk across it. There's no more than one set of footmarks on the deck those days, maybe two, and you know who came because the marks go right up to their pierling.

Everything is at rest and everything is either white or very dark, the tinted kind of dark that allows the narrowest amount of see through. An eeriness settles over the entirely white and dark and quiet and peopleless place. The bags of salt slump midway on the deck, and the shovels freeze to the post they lean against. They have to be broken free. The eeriness settles on the gulls and tern that walking about not flying nor crying or acting in the way you usually see them act the rest of the year, hyped and lifted, but this time of year they are grounded and mute, like lost travelers waiting for something. And the eeriness settles on the sailboats with their silver sparkling spires, and their arrowed wind vanes atop, swiveling, flitting, pointing, and the port holes that are the same vacant tint color as the water and the woods, and you see eeriness in the gossamer dusting of snow that accumulates on the wire cable rails. Eeriest of all is this: chained between our slip and the next is a standalone propeller, suspended half-dead beneath the tint dark water, idly churning to prevent the water around the boat from freezing to ice completely. From the middle of the spun water rises a warble, a sluggish eddy that goes on and on, cold and creeping, like an artificial organ holding the boat on life support.

I took the contraption out, then I had the boatyard take Hogsty out of the water and put back on crutches, though not in the same despondent aisle of boats as before. It is as somber to see the boat pulled from the water as it is exhilarating to see it put in the water, but that is how it goes. Every move costs money. I took our wood sign and locked it in the cabin.

The man fixing the bateau is still there, day after day, working on his beauty. He is one of the few men consistently working in this cold. Others come when it's warm and tolerable and there's ample daylight. This man works with the light he has. He is past repairing the hull and is working on something in the cabin. He has found a mast for it too. It is leaning against the side of the boat slanting above the rail like a jousting pole at rest. I am amazed. I have watched him out of the side of my vision all this time. I remember the first day he arrived, the sound of his sandpaper rubbing against the grain of the wood- thinking to myself 'you have got a long way to go.' And look, he has stayed with it.

Luis has not come with me the past few weeks while all this was going on. I have told him about our boat, I have shared my disappointments. He quickly loses interest if I go on too long about it. He's just a boy. But this man and his bateau- I want to crystallize them. The image of the two of them in the winter marina. I want to bring Luis and say 'Look at this man and this boat he has persevered with. You see?' The dream and ambition of the man is tremendous. I would like Luis to know something about this man who I don't know anything about except what I see, who has taken into his care the life of a weathered bateau; a boat that may return nothing to him but trouble and more trouble. I would like him to watch closely this man and others like him who file away at hulls patiently, taking a long view of things and seem somehow for all the inconvenience, for all the ingrainedness, and noncompliance of the act, to cherish restoration. There is perseverance in these men who work out their acre of destiny by the inch, who keep the foresight of a stern breaking water, the brown Bay beneath, glistening, ever before them. And not just for Luis must I recall him. I have needed to see him working there, austerely, for my own sake. I want to pay him some sincere honor- a word of encouragement. I can't comprehend all that I mean though.

82

I was home more as the boat awaited its fate. Hogsty, no longer the subject of my private obsession was released to the opinions of my family. They encouraged me to sit on it, not to act hastily, but the beginning of spring was breathing down the creek, calls coming about the charter, the general tempo of life increasing. One day I was sitting at home thinking about all of this when my father asked,

"Do you know where Luis is?"

I looked up; the question caught me by surprise, and I said,

"No, where was he last?"

"He was with me an hour ago, putting the bird feeder up."

"You don't know where he is now?" I said.

"I do know. I was asking you. You've been living in your head since the boat was taken out. I don't mean to sound dismissive, but it's a boat, just a boat. You've put a lot of work into it, I know you're concerned about it- but at the end of the day it will be there. It's ubiquitous. There will always be boats that need repairing. There will not always be these opportunities to be with us, to be with your son."

I said "Where is he?"

"He's on the creek with his friend from next door."

I left and went down to the dock and waited for the two of them to return. They were rowing back slowly, these two brown-haired boys seated beside each other, who looked like fraternal brothers. I helped them pull the boat in, and asked where they went. 'Milk creek.' they said.

"I've never heard of Milk creek before- is it close?"

"Down that way." they both pointed where they came from.

"How did you find it?"

"We just went there."

"And it's called Milk creek?"

"That's what we call it." Georgie said.

Reeling and releasing. The tightened line. The naming of things. What is it to make sacred but to call something your own? To give it a name; to give even the scarcest creek a name is to make a monument of it, to make it part of your place in the world. Days later the two boys are at it again. This time they stay close to our shore. Luis steers, Georgie fishes. There's a tall blue heron on the end of our pier, the resident heron who lingers from pier to neighboring pier. The bird with its long face composed of both fiery interest yet disdain reminds me of one of the onlookers from the pier, the pier where the skate was caught- like it will fly away as soon as the boys catch something.

I was back from the boatyard that day where I happened to meet the man with the wooden bateau coming out of the parts shop. Ned is his name. He had a manner like Mr. Bruce. Relaxed, succinct. He knew Mr. Bruce too. I told him I admire the work he's done. He said thank you, and asked about my own ship. I told him it was out of commission for the time being. Out of the blue I asked him if he gave rides, if he took people sailing. He said not usually, but for who? My son and me, I said. We've never sailed before. I'd like to take him at least once. Ned said 'At the moment I can't'. He said to come by in a few weeks and we'll check on things. Maybe that meant he'd think about taking us out, but it was nothing definitive. I stored that in my mind to take him up on that.

Back to the boys- they caught a fish, a small crappie, and brought it to shore. Luis unhooked it, pinched it by the gills and threw it in front of the heron who was sitting like a stoic on his usual post. The bird flew down to the fish, impaled it and swallowed it whole in three seconds.

Luis says to Georgie,
"Now Jasper's full."
I overhear them.
"Who's Jasper?" I say.
"Jasper's the bird." Georgie says.
"Who named it?"
Georgie points to Luis.
"He did."

Then the way the two young friends turn and look at each other and smile is like they are wise men withholding a great secret from me. And they are.

When I was not much older than them I would take the same boat out alone. Sometimes when I would return home having spent the day wending the minor creeks, fishing for pike and blue catfish, and return empty, having tasted no luck on the line, but still having savoured the trip- the unremitting good fortune of being boatweary, ensconced in brown river marsh, having napped on the boat tethered to a free branch drooping over the bank I'd fished along- I'd find my father at dusk in the great room, sitting by himself under the lone lit reading lamp, the one in front of the bay windows, situated snugly in his beige cushioned chair, the one with the chipped back leg which tilted its sitter- his thick lens glasses sliding toward the end of his nose, his grey hair oily from combing it with his fingers, and the movement of his eyes reading whatever was in his lap. One of his hands propped his chin and cheek, the other flipped the page. From a distance, he had a look of absorption in the material he was reading, but the closer I came I saw it was never a book but the last pages of a magazine, or boat ads. How long he would have it there in from of him, perhaps never really reading it, but grazing over it with his eyes, having that auspice of feigned interest, of one who has been caught in lassitude, whose eyes will rake over anything you put before it.

It was no coincidence that the sun sank over the creek that time of day and streamed through the windows in silky citrus colors that were blanched and blocked by the reading lamp. I'd come in hungry from my trip.

"Have you eaten?" I'd ask.

He would lean his head back, then I would ask again. He'd say,

"I made something earlier. You can finish it. It's in there."

In the fridge was a cold cast iron skillet covered by aluminum foil. I'd peel it back- inside was a chunk of boned fish, white rice, and a soft wilted ring of yellow onion. The smell of garlic. It was the kind of spartan meal that was nothing but sustenance. It reminded me how helpless he was without my mother. But I was hungry and not picky; I heated it on a plate and ate it at the table alone. Then I went back outside, took the rods from the boat and leaned them on the back porch, scraping dried bait off the hooks. The back door opened and he'd join me, yawn, stretch his arms to the sky. The day was blue and shadowy and still warm.

"What were you up to today?" he'd ask.

"I went fishing along the creeks.

"How far?"

"Up to the great marsh."

"Catch anything?"

"Not much. Some catfish, but threw them back. One big one that snapped my line."

"Oh, really."

"Yeah."

Here, the great secret I mentioned between Luis and his friend (that I was not privy to), would come between me and my father like a partition. I could not confer on him the balm I'd felt on the water that day, a peace that was invisible and thin, that was shy and also strong, like the best fishing line. And I'd have no way of transferring it by words or manner of speech. Somehow it would feel ostentatious, and I'd reserve myself for fear that peace proffered freely and unabashadley might increase his melancholia. For some reason I would not ask him what he did that day, imagining it would turn him inward and he would return to his chair more lethargic than before.

He'd go back in, turn off the reading light and go upstairs to bed. It was not yet 10 o'clock. I'd go inside and wipe the skillet clean and decide to sit in his chair. The seat would be still warm from sitting. I'd turn on the reading light and hold the boat ad in front. Soon I'd be as lost as he, tilted toward fatigue. Beyond the bay windows would be a starless dark, expect for the lights of houses across the way, across Weems. Where the Siggins used to farm. Under my hand would rest the crinkly pages, penned circles around yacht prices, the going rate of a new anchor.

83

There is another lucid memory from the time when Hogsty's engines were down. After two weeks sitting on the issue I decided to have the engines rebuilt. It was costly, but it would give the boat a new lease, another dozen years or more of faithful chugging. It was my plan that day to go to the boatyard and begin prepping the engines to be removed. The man who was scheduled to pick them up called earlier and said he had to reschedule- he didn't say why, so I stayed home.

It was a day in early April; a brilliant, unexpectedly warm day. Outside the ground smelled of wetness and mud and marsh. The water was calm; it had an olive green hue and a soft reflective shimmer. On the calmness came the sound of tail slaps pelting the surface of Weems, near and far- flecks and thumps that left ripples traceable to the very spot where something leaped, something was chased.

In the afternoon the Reynolds boys came over, and later Art and Sarah came to pick them up. The older boys were outside. I was inside with my mother and we could hear their deep teenage voices laughing, carrying on. They asked to take the boat out, and my father went down to help them push off. Adley was home too; she was outside with James and the two of them were talking. My mother opened the windows in the house and the smell of wetness and warmth and brine wandered in. So did the pairs of conversation going on. I cut fruit and made tuna salad with my mother.

As we were preparing snacks we heard something unusual; the side door was unhooked and swung open. We looked up and saw Luis and Georgie chasing through the house and out another door. The thing about that door is that we never used it, not since we were young. It was latched shut by nail and hole, with a brown rusted spring at the bottom that croaked when opened, and a knob that clunked when turned. It had an uncanny register to it from being so long locked. My mother and me kept turning to see what it was that made the sound. But that afternoon it swung back and forth, soughing blithely, as feet came through and feet ran out.

Behind the house I found Adley sitting, talking to James. She was sitting on one of the two apple tree stumps which had been worn to good stools over the years. I sat on the other one and we talked.

"I met someone." she said, "You may know him actually, Constance. He has a boat at your boatyard." She said his name, but I didn't recognize it. "You'll meet him soon, I hope. Tell me if you do."

She asked about Luis, about the boat, the charter- questions I didn't expect from her. And her voice was clear, less inflected. We watched the boys take turns on the dory- the older ones yielding to the younger ones.

"What is it they're yelling?" James said.

The boys were out of sight, but their voices, high, songlike, carried down current.

"I can't hear." I said,

"Neither can I." said Adley. "Why?"

He turned to us. He said, "What was that song we made

up a long time ago, when Constance took us out? What did we call it?

Adley and I in unison, said, "Brown rivah!" and laughed together.

"Brown rivah, that's right!" he said. He leaned back in his chair and smiled.

I said, "What made you think of that?"

He said, "When I heard them yelling back and forth I thought I heard them say it, I wondered if one of you taught them."

Adley said "I'm sure they have their own version they made up."

"I'm sure they do." I said.

We stayed there sitting on the stumps looking out, listening and talking for some time. It was funny to be in that spot together, where the apple trees once stood. You could hardly tell they were ever there. For a long time after they fell the yard looked stricken by their absence, but over time clover grew between the stumps and covered the base. It was as good a place to watch the water as any. Off to the side, the little tree stood in its old place. The bark has darkened some, and the apples are smaller than they were back then, but it blooms white every year without fail.

When I returned inside there was a sprig of uprooted mint laying in a paper towel on the counter. I could smell it when I came in. I broke off a tiny leaf and chewed it. I asked my mother what it was doing here.

She said, "Your father's giving some to Art to plant on their side."

"I didn't know we had any." I said.

"We didn't either. It grows like wildfire on the side of the house."

"How'd you find that?"

"Art found it when he was helping your father repaint part of the house. The Admiral must have planted it."

"Or his wife-" I said.

"Ever since he found it your father's wanted to plant other things out there with it, herbs and such. The mint has inspired him. It's the first time he's wanted to do anything like it. It all started with that mint bush."

"And Art-"

"Yes, he wouldn't have found it without Art."

There were other moments that day, proceeding from the last, that together brought me to an acute appreciation of our place, an affection for it; each conversation, each sound, the unhooked door, the laughter of boys and neighbors, the pelting of fish, the fresh bitter taste of mint, all these sharp details accountable to my senses. Other details, less sensational were still more elusive; my sister's kindness, the remembrance of Brown rivah, the prospect of my father growing herbs in the shade of the house, of lending those herbs to a neighbor- equal triumphs of meekness. I could not account for them the same. The more I tried to analyze their meaning, to find a reason for them or justify a motive, the more they hid, the more they dissembled, mystifying my memory, becoming fainter. The difficult thing was to accept them on their own terms. To add nothing. To admit also that all remembrances, the very fondest, are braided to inconclusions. If later, a coldness returned to Adley's voice, or our creek song went unsung, or the garden plans derailed, would it diminish the first grace of those moments, those plain epiphanies? No. They remain intact. They scintillate before me.

84

Benevolence is more startling than meanness and more impertinent. Benevolence is Jasper, the blue heron stalking the end of the dock. It hushes explanation. Not all memories need explaining. It is easier to offer reasons for the sake of explanation than to believe that there is something much simpler and much more valuable at play: an unpleading goodness at the heart of life, even the heart of Teal St.

That is the reach. That is the way a child names a river.

Returning to that day, as sunlight withdrew, weariness came over us like a spell. The Reynolds went home. Luis and I brought the boat ashore, dislodged the oars, and flipped the boat over on the ground, covering the gear and dumping out the hot creek water that had seeped to the bottom of the planks. The sky darkened and the air thickened. A storm was upon us. Inside, every seat, surface, and cushion held the lingering warmth of the day, To sit, to stand, to touch anything induced a soporific quality. It was not late, but it felt late, and the sky with its imminent darkness suggested the same. All of us were hungry. All of us were waiting for my mother (who was taking a nap) to come back, to start something on the stove.

In the hungry malaise of the evening we waited, listening to the storm amble like a faraway train, processing, building. James sat at the piano and played scales, then I heard the key cover come down. He was done.

"Are we eating?" he said aloud.

"We're waiting for your mother." my father said. "She's napping." He himself was half asleep.

As the wind ripened and blew cool currents through the room, fluttering the curtains, my father rose from his slumberous state and walked the perimeter of the room pulling down windows, leaving a crack for freshness. It occured to me that no one bothered turning the lights on while we sat there, so we sat in the dark. We sat waiting in that strange storm light, slipping headlong into the brew of the storm. I recall that detail because Luis was reading the book I had given him to read, Misty of Chincoteague, on the floor nearby me, and I remember thinking he shouldn't read in that light, since it wasn't good for his eyes. But I didn't say anything. He was much too absorbed and much too content. I let him read on. When the rain began I took a seat by the big bay windows and watched the rainfall build all at once behind the house, jogging its way steadily from the distant river, to the creek, to our shore. The wind whooshed through the pitch pines and the leaves flapped. My father, who had taken his seat again, began to snore lightly. Luis, finally unable to read anymore because of the dark put his book page down on the floor like a tent and came to join me, sitting on the footrest in front of me.

The surface of Weems was plum-black. The grass, the dock, the trees, had the same color, and when it rained at first, the sound was imperceptible. Then it grew swiftly until it was a downpour. Lightning flashed across the creek in a profusion of hazy, mist-white light, as I have always known it to. No thunderheads. No booms this time. Just heavy rain and flashes of light. The wind blew toward the house pebbling raindrops on the sill. Exhausted, Luis leaned his head back and I stroked his hair as he got sleepier, nodding further and further back. I could see the little boat from where I sat. The dory. It was dark under the rain, steadfast as a rock. Beneath it the oars were covered and dry. *Benevolence*.

The storm passed as quickly as it came. Storms in spring were like that- turbulent and angry, then suddenly gone. Gone. Whisked away, leaving the creek in a pristine mess; the rain turned up loose branches in the water and swept the shoals until each bank was mucked with foamy brownwater. Days afterward, countless jellyfish would emerge on the surface like gauzy film, one every two feet. But there is no whine of motors after a storm, and what you hear is the close dripping, trickling- now and again bird call, now and then the dash of snook on the surface of the water. But otherwise everything- the wet sills- marked with passing storm.

When my mother came downstairs she turned the lights on and found us tranquilized, utterly unconscious of the time, and past the complaint of hunger. She went to the kitchen. I asked if she needed any help. She said no. She asked how hungry is everyone. I said we're all hungry. Starving really. She said I don't have much. I said anything's fine at this point. In a few moments I heard the stove, the crackle of oil, then shortly after she called us to the kitchen.

"There's some food, whoever wants some."

Luis and I came to the table first, then the others. Adley came down from upstairs where she was napping too. My mother put a plate of fried plantains before us. The dark yellow slices were caramelized on the edges and sat on a paper towel soaking excess oil. How good it tasted, even one bite. Starchy and sweet, hot and fatty. The food of fatigue. The food of passing storms. *Benevolence*.

She brought a wooden bowl filled with white sugar and we took turns blowing off our slices, dipping them in the bowl. A few slices were all we needed to be satisfied. My father and James ate after us and my mother ate last. When everyone was filled Luis cleaned the plates and put them away. For all his youth there is an old soul in him. A dutifulness, an intuition of gratefulness that I take no credit for, but I hope remains and grows as he does. Since Luis came into this home, I began to notice one thing about this family that was so commonplace before that I should miss it altogether: for every violence, there was a counter violence; for every outburst, a reservation, for every famishment, a sweet plantain- a selfless act that beautified the whole.

Before I slept that night I hooked the side door and ear marked the place in Luis's book where he stopped reading, my eyes browsing over the pages he just read. A passage about wild horses crossing a dangerous strait. A pencil illustration on the next page showed the manes keeping above the thrashing water. I shut the book and went up to my room. I fell fast asleep.

85

There was another treat in store for us too. Days after the storm passed, Ned, the man with the wooden sloop, called me. First he apologized for our previous interaction,

"I'm sorry if I sounded short the last time we spoke." he said. "You had caught me at the worst time. Boat work is always slower than you budget, and I had just found out my launch date was going to be later than expected. I'm over it now. I'm sorry."

I said "No need to apologize, I understand."

"The other thing is, I didn't know you knew Bruce so well." he said.

"I do."

"Yeah, I talked to him earlier this week- he gave me your scoop. He's a friend of mine. Anyways, if you're game to go out, the boat's almost ready. I can take five of you, but that's about all. She's an old bird."

"I would love to, and I may have some interest from others. I'll round a group together."

"That'll work great."

So we set a date for a week later and he finished by saying,

"I'm sorry again- I hope this trip will make up some of it."

The following days I recruited and gathered our crew. Myself, Luis, James, Georgie, and Culver, the second youngest Reynolds boy, since my father could not make it. I felt unsure about James, not knowing if his handicap would be a difficulty for the trip, but I called Ned and explained the situation, and he said,

"Not a problem. The boat's old, but stable, and we'll find a good place for him. Bring him on. Yes, bring him!"

It was early Saturday when we left from the yard. Ned had gotten there early and prepped the boat. The boys were yawning when we arrived at the dock. The sky was a slab of ash-grey with a long sliver of pink painted on the horizon. Ned was accommodating and friendly, and he seemed particularly chuffed at the prospect of the young crewmates I brought with me. He shook their hands as they stepped aboard his boat, 'The Annabelle'. I boarded last with James. Ned and Culver helped my brother come aboard. Ned had already made a spot for him in the bow, by the tiller.

More than I surmised from our first interaction or our phone calls, Ned was a man of great humor and volubility. He was playful as the boys ambled around the boatdeck as we boarded. The group of us were stirring with enthusiasm for the outing. For most of us it was the novelty of being aboard a sailboat, and not just any kind of sailboat- a bateau. The Annabelle was slender and slim, with beautiful curvature from end to end. It reminded me of the wing of a plane. It was one thing to appreciate the craft from shore, the look of an antique yacht. It was another thing altogether to step aboard its laths, to feel under your tailbone the creaky construction of the boat, and trust it.

Ned was in high spirits as well, which seemed to come more from the nature of this special occasion than from the boat itself. He stood the sage among us, a wise courtier of Chesapeake Bay, the Hogba, Nanticoke, Magothy. He knew the marshes, the sounds, the intertidal waters by heart. And yet, for all his experience, for all his faring, our trip was probably an unlikely one. After unfastening a few lines and pushing off, he leaned to my ear and said,

"I sure hope they enjoy themselves. I hope they don't get too bored."

Then he stepped over me and loosed more lines from the bow, descended to the berth and started the engine, which made a pleasant ticking sound, like a bicycle chain beginning to revolve. He pointed me to the front and told me to help guide the stern away from the front pilings, should it get close. The boys sat together in the front facing forward and watched as we pulled out. Ned steered an initial direction out to the main river, then asked James to hold the tiller steady as then he went about prepping more lines, attaching the mainsail and jib, transporting things in and out of the berth. From inside the cabin he would peek his head over the top of the stairs and direct James additionally.

"Get me a few more degrees starboard."

When we were well on our way, and the nose of the bateau was poking precisely toward the pink horizon, Ned's original chattiness subsided and he acquired a new manner; a gravity that spread over his vessel and crew. I could hear Culver yawning ahead, and the mush of the water, and the wind beginning to fripper the Maryland flag hoisted high off the transom.

From the mouth of the Nanticoke we fared out main Bay into the open. On a generous field of water, Ned jumped below, cut the engine and prepared us to sail for the first time. He called us to the bow to watch him and told us where to sit if the boat listed on its side, or 'heeled', when it took wind. James was his tillman who he directed as he secured the standing rigging- the shrouds, the forestays and backstays. He cranked the winches and the sails rose, immaculate, tall tongues of white.

Almost as soon as the sails raised the wind took us, swept us and we sailed.

We sailed, we sallied, we sprung, we split. I laughed out loud. The boys did too, even with a hint of fearfulness. We felt that first mythic sense of levitation as the force of wind collected onto our course and sent us; that powerful, elated, precariousness with which the bateau made leeway.

Giddyup, loft and riding; the bateau, glassblown, enlarged by the wind yet small to it, exposed, obedient, heedful, capturing, trivial, trivially beautiful. Ned at helm, his hand over James's. The boat effusing lightness, not of frailness or hollowness, but of something shedding its heft and quickening as it goes.

The caprice of the wind sent the canvas loosing, luffing. I see it now as it happened. Ned grasped the tiller and directed us to keep our heads from the spars, the mast and boom, but especially the boom, the solid horizontal wooden arm extending the mainsail, that comes swinging across the stern of the boat when the boat tacks, when it moves in and out of the current of wind. A fast, violent swing it makes across. The pinch of lines. The canvas catching again. Then catching some more. Ned's hands and legs pulling and tightening, winching, looking afoul, looking astern. A bull wind rearing us up. The weightless sensation again, the way it feels to be taken off your feet by a ski lift, but more involved, more encompassing. Swifter. This time the boat tacks, zigging and zagging upwind, into the crisp sun. I wonder if we are doing enough. I can't see Ned, and I wonder if the boat in his control, or if he is standing out of its way letting it run by its own intelligence. Again I feel our lightness, our being borne in motion. We are as light as balsa. A toy ship. A toy ship, tacking.

The boat itself, the skate path of the hull below, is *weatherly* as sailors say. It 'points well'. And the course we sail, discursive and slicing, is a revelation to me and to the boys who are watching this Captain with fast wonder. He returns to helm, and at times along our route the beating wind thrums the sail so forcefully that it tempts the boat dangerously aside, which is called luffing. In the commotion we keep our heads safe from accidental jibes, when the boom swings recklessly to the other side. Ned embraces it; his fearful crew mount the alternate side, making natural ballast, the boys linking their arms to each other and to me. Ned's hands alternate between the different chocks and stanchions. Now it's on the winch. James, the least maneuverable of us holds his position.

Ned raises his voice above the wind,

"Now we're running."

"Now we're running." he repeats, pleased to say it again.

He looks over at us.

"Don't worry, if you think this is tacking all the way, we could go more, but not today. Today is a taste, to get you back out here again. You're safe. I've got a good keel on this Annabelle. She won't turn on you." The keel is the counterweight at the bottom of the hull, the reason the ship doesn't capsize.

He begins to winch the sails and the boom slides center and we slow.

"You see where we are?" he says to us.

He points back and makes a hook shape motion with his finger.

"Now we're coming the other way." He points to an opening on the Bay.

"This is Fishing Bay. Good for what it's called, obviously.

The water's high from the storm past. It drops usually. There's big banks of mud along the shores, by the marshes. Years ago I came here with a friend who worked for an agency that monitors fisheries in this area. He and I were fishing in there. We're coming along the shore and we see an osprey stuck in the mud."

He turns from telling me and James to getting the boys' attention.

"You boys see those big nests? Way out there, above the water?"

They nod.

"Those are osprey roosts. You've seen them before, haven't you?"

Again they nod, obedient and timid. Ned turns back and continues his story,

"Well this bird was stuck and the tide was coming in. So my friend and I came close to it. And we need to do something or else the tide would have come and it would've drowned. So my friend throws a towel over the bird to keep it from panicking. I steer- it's real real shallow where we were- but he brings this muddy creature aboard with the beach towel wrapped over it, then we drive over to the roost it fell from, and somehow manage to get this thing up into it. He says to me 'Get ready to go', afraid the bird is going to dive on us when he takes the towel off, but it doesn't. As soon as he takes it off, the wings on the bird just plop." He drops his arms at his side. "Just plop, he had no strength left. He used all his strength trying to get out of the mud. But look, we got him up there. Close call, for us and the osprey."

Ned goes on like that while we cruise. He names places, lookouts, necks, points, creeks, marshes, inland townships, launch spots, people he's met there, people he doesn't like there, what used to be, what is. Like Stew and Bruce, his knowledge of these local waters and surrounding areas is keen but not showy. It is a living knowledge.

He could go on, but doesn't. "Stay put." he says.

He descends the cabin and returns with a six pack of coke on plastic rings. He thumbs back to the cabin,

"Can't let you down there yet. I'm embarrassed, it's a mess still- But here, I brought these along."

He hands them to me and I pass them around. As we sit together sipping cokes on this bateau, I look at Luis and Georgie.

"Are you having fun?" I ask, and they reply in their boyish, reticent way, with a nod and smile. I check on Culver and James. James looks happy as can be. He has not said much during the trip, but he has laid one of his legs out straight across his seat, and the sun has stretched across it, and all can think is, what a lovely, lovely sight to behold. I don't know how long it's been since I've seen him rest his legs like that, but it moves me tremendously.

The longer we sail, the more I'm aware how the Annabelle is an icon of her owner, like Hogsty is to me. There are certain obvious similarities, such as the white sails and the glow of the teak wood, which reminds me of his skin color. The skin of a sailor. But it is the clandestine features that I'm most fascinated by- the port windows covered from the inside with blue cotton curtains, the messy berth he doesn't allow access to, the way the boat floats low in the water- reminds me of the way I saw him whenever he was at work at the boatyard, covered to the eyes with a dust filter mask over his face.

I ask him how long he's had the boat,

"Two or three years." he says, "Most of that time spent on repairs."

No bitterness comes through his voice, but some exasperation does. It is a response that acknowledges and admits the kind of task he's been at.

"You bought it?" I ask?
"No, it was free. It was a salvage."
Then he looks at me and smiles,
"That doesn't mean it was cheap."

I tell him about Hogsty and the repairs of late. He says firstly, that's a good name, an unusual name, and secondly,

"That's the way boats are. Boats are boats. They take their spills like everything else, they're just more expensive when they do. I always thought my first serious boat would be my last- if I only took care of it the right way, maintained it."

He laughs, starts counting on his hand.

"How many has that been now, since Annabelle? Five? Six? See, you just don't know. But with yours, hey, maybe it will serve you like that, then your son can take it."

After we talked some, he stood and said to the boys,

"Ok, now that you're relaxed, how about we have one more run, before we head back?"

His commanding presence renewed and he gave the boys roles in the makeup of the sails. It was a fortunate sternness he showed us; fortunate because the boat, if improperly handled, can be a greater hazard than the water. He said he had seen crew members cleared straight off the boat by the boom. So we watched that boom with awe and terror, knowing it could take a man out clean, knowing it was also essential to our speed and prowess over the waves. Ned directed tack and jib. He complemented his words and commands with gestures- pointing, calling, miming the actions he was looking for- manual articulations.

When we were all at our posts, the captain's quiet achieved among us. I felt the witchcraft of sailing then; different than our first run, different than anything I had experienced before- the loft again, but also the moan of wood the boat made. How it made the river feel at home yet someplace foreign, and made boating feel like something I'd done all my life, but never tried before.

Unlike pure motoring, sailing is a heedful art, the art of catching and letting go, of waiting to be taken. It is an act of dependency, of waiting (sometimes painfully) in the absence of the wind. I say to him,

"If I'd have known sailing was like this."

"Many days are not like this." he says "I can tell you, many. That's why people give it up."

The boat tacks along, running clean across the brown waves. The boys are getting the hang of it too, and it's translating into swift maneuvers the boat makes through the water. I can't help but look down at this neat craft, watch the water sluiced and cloven off the gunwales. Salvage, I think. Salvage. *Benevolence*.

Our vessel sashes, climbing along its leeward route, the wind afoul. The way it sounds, it sings, moaning from the wood. The boom, the mast, each spar extended to its widest and tallest breadth and none inflexible. Today they are light, a ballerina's arm, lithe things.

The wind eventually ceases. The hinges holding the boom rasp back to center, the lines relax, trimmed. We are close to port. Ned turns the little engine on and sets about unclipping the sails, steering. At the mouth of our river there is a nest like the one we saw in Fishing Bay, and he says aloud,

"Now what kind of roost is that? Who was listening? Who remembers?"

My son says "Osprey."

"Good memory." he says.

When we left that day, Ned shook our hands as we stepped off, and said to me, in confidence,

"I hope they had a good time. I hope it wasn't too boring for the young fellas."

He returned to his Annabelle to bag the canvas and stow it below.

The car ride back was quiet. James sat up front, his eyes shut, his thin legs leaning together. Culver and his brother rested their heads on one another, and Luis, perhaps as tired as the rest, stayed awake. His window was down and he rode his hand outside into the wind. He looked tired, but alive. His face was sweet with the light of day; a gift boys bestow when they have spent their energies abroad.

"Not too much air on the other two." I said. I tapped his leg behind me to get his attention. He brought his hand in and moved the window up. It was just past two in the afternoon. Boredom? I humored to myself. No, not that day. Not boring.

86

So it has been over many years of living on Weems; leaving, returning, sailing for the first time recently, that I've remembered a good deal of what's happened and how it's happened. More than I knew when I set out. I've tried to be alive to it, to remember it and honor it. Sailors keep their ships aglow each year with polish and conditioner and call it brightwork. So remembrance has performed a kind of brightwork over my own life and continues to.

When the engines were finished being built, two mechanics came from the shop and delivered them to the boatyard to be reinstalled, which took two days. The engines were painted bright orange and arrived plastic wrapped on wheel carts. One of the mechanics, rising out of the hull during the installation, said to me,

"She's practically a new boat after this- a whole new boat."

The day after they finished, the crane came to lift Hogsty back to where it belonged. Luis was with me and we stood aside as the crane operator fit the large loopy straps under the hull. As the crane lifted Hogsty off the eight stands holding it up, half of them fell over like abandoned crutches to the ground. The laboring crane crushed a slow, heavy path to the ramp and water. When the boat was in the water I climbed aboard and threw Luis lines from the bow for him to help guide from the pier.

Then the moment of truth; I tried the engines. One turn and the ignition clicked, the engines roared alive, shaking the whole frame. Luis yelled to me,

"Sounds good." and I gave him a thumbs up.

There was a roughness to the boat as the engines warmed and lubricated- the exhaust belched black smog, making a god-awful burning rubber smell. Then it slowly soothed, pacified, tapering down to a steady, satisfying rumble. That's when we moved it back to its slip. I threw Luis a rope and he walked it along the catwalk pier like it was a horse he was bringing to stall. I thought of his book too, the book I gave him to read. Luis took our charter sign from the cabin and placed it by our slip as it was before, then he called and asked for my help- a knot had come undone. I stopped the engines and got out. I kneeled at the loose line and he stooped beside me as I remade it, demonstrating slowly so he could see.

"Ah," he said. "I go under too early when I do mine."

"Yes, once more around, that's the key. That's what keeps it."

While it was fresh in his mind he checked the others, kneeling and retying where he saw fit. And when he had finished we left for good, confident that the boat would be there when we returned. In the car he took his book to read. We motored off on a road that crisscrosses Weems at various points, and beyond it through woods, shines a length of Nanticoke purling and dark. At every bridge Luis put the book under his chin and looked out. Not a word between us. I dreamed the way back, but not of the future nor of the past.

I dreamt of the sovereignty of ropes and knots, of twin engines running, how our lives are tributaries of greater things. When I looked aside he was sleeping. Of all that I've seen, a boat keeping float is a perfect thing, and a boy dreaming of horses is too.

A NOTE FROM THE AUTHOR

Dear reader,

Thank you for reading. It's a joy to tell stories and share them with you. I look forward to sharing more soon.

If you've enjoyed this book, I'd love to read your thoughts in a review.

For updates about new releases and special giveaways, sign up for the newsletter on my website: mattballeza.com

Much appreciated!

Matthew's books on Amazon:
https://www.amazon.com/author/matthewballeza

ABOUT THE AUTHOR

Matthew Balleza grew up along the waterways of Annapolis, MD. He now lives with his wife and children in Nashville, TN. He writes stories for adults and young readers alike. His go-to dad line is, *'I'm just a thorn among roses.'* (which is true). In his free time he loves playing tennis, fishing, and concocting specialty cocktails.

website: https://mattballeza.com/
instagram: https://www.instagram.com/mattballezabooks
newsletter: https://www.buttondown.email/mattballezabooks/

Made in United States
Troutdale, OR
09/20/2023